THE CARIBBEAN

SAINTE DOMINGUE

TORTUGA

Basse Terre
Cap Haitien
Port de Paix
Gonaïves

SAINTE
DOMINGUE

GONAVE

Cul de Sac
(Port au Prince)
Léogâne
Petit Goave
Aux Cayes
ILE DES VACHES

0   100   200   300   400   500

Scale of Miles

N
W   E
S

TY OF PERU

THE Golden Hawk

FRANK YERBY

THE
Golden
Hawk

THE DIAL PRESS · 1948 · NEW YORK

TO Flora

1

THERE WAS NO WIND in all that sweep of sky. Now and again one of the black-gray mountains of cloud, too heavily laden, sank almost to the surface of the Caribbean; but that was where the wind was, and the towering domes and pinnacles of mist were rent into shreds and sent scudding to leeward to be lost in the white boil of spray where the waves crashed in thunderous fury over the rocks of the Isle des Vaches—Cow Island.

Kit Gerado sat very still on the coil of tarred hempen line. In actuality, his lean body was in constant motion as he swayed in counter to the *Seaflower*'s frenzied pitching; but so deftly did he manage the matter of balance against the trim brigantine's devil dance with wind and storm that he seemed not to move at all.

He was so still that Bernardo Díaz, moving aft with great difficulty against the hissing, wind-driven spray, stopped to gaze at him. But for the great mane of tawny gold that whipped in the gale like a cavalry standard in full charge, Kit might have been a wonderfully lifelike figure from a Velásquez canvas; his slim body, lithe even in repose, was etched all the more vividly against the white wall of hammering water by the somber blackness of his doublet and full Spanish pantaloons. He seemed quite the young hidalgo of the Hapsburg courts, except that upon coming closer Bernardo could see that the doublet was open from throat almost to navel, and the broad expanse of Kit's chest, glistening with storm spray, was bronzed from long exposure to a tropic sun.

About his lean belly, board-flat and ribbed and corded with muscle, Kit wore a broad sash of cloth of gold, contrasting vividly with the soberness of his other garments; and even as Bernardo watched, Kit's lean fingers toyed briefly with the knot that held it in place. The knot gave after a moment, and Kit drew the sash off, holding it across his wide-spread knees with both his hands.

Bernardo, who had seen this gesture many times, sighed deeply, for he knew what it meant. From where he stood, he could not see the device of the Black Heron on a field of gold that ornamented the banner Cristóbal Gerado now wore as a sash; but he knew it was there, for he had been with Kit when they had first seen it. No, he could not see the sign of the Black Heron, but he could see Kit's face, see his mouth drawing into a hard line, his blue eyes becoming glacier ice, and the knuckles of his hands tightening until they showed white from the strain.

On that earlier day, Bernardo recalled sadly, the Heron Banner, which as much as anything else on this dreary earth was responsible for their being aboard this hell ship, had fluttered gaily in the afternoon sunlight from the pikestaff of a helmeted and cuirassed horseman. The man had sat boldly on his dancing Andalusian steed, leading a procession of riders through a narrow street in Cádiz.

Cádiz—ah, Cádiz!—rising white-walled and dreamlike, a city of pearl above a sea of indigo, a cluster of low, flat-roofed houses and a tangle of streets. Was there indeed such a place, or was it too false, a trick of the disordered imagination, as empty of reality as the name Kit bore, as difficult to comprehend as the swift flow of liquid Castilian from the lips of a lad whose eyes were as blue as a Norwegian fjord, and whose hair, falling in great curling masses about his broad shoulders, was like Iberian sunlight, heavy with gold?

Shaking his head, Bernardo bent forward against the wind and plodded toward where the young first officer sat. An odd sight indeed was Bernardo Díaz, converted Jew. His shoulders were twice as broad as those of the average man, and his arms were great coils of muscle. His chest was huge, but his legs were pipestems and less, thin and crooked beyond belief. Twelve years in the galleys of His Most Christian Majesty, Philip IV of Spain, and four in those of the Caliph of Barbary, do that to

2

a man. Now, at thirty-nine, Bernardo looked fifty. "Arab or Christian," he would say dryly, "their whips bite deep."

He looked at the bare masts of the *Seaflower,* held to the wind by one flying jib and the small spritsail, then back at the young first officer.

"I have news, Kit," he said. "Bad news. The men are growing ugly."

Kit shrugged. "I know. When are they not half a point from mutiny?"

"Today they are less than that. We're in for a blow, and they know it. At sea that would be bad enough, but to lie here two miles outside the best harbor in two hundred leagues and be beaten to pieces is—well, they don't understand it."

"They know why." Kit's voice dropped even lower, but there was a fine, bright edge to his tone. "Would they take on a fleet of two dozen well-armed vessels?"

"Have the French so many craft in there?" Bernardo asked incredulously.

"Yes. And to them the *Seaflower* is an English vessel. I grant you there are not ten Englishmen aboard, but so long as Lazarus commands her, she is English. And if they granted us consideration of the fact that we do not fly the flag, do you think they'd let this leper bark into their harbor?"

"Lazarus!" Bernardo spat, his voice cold with loathing. "There's the root of the whole matter! True, there are no longer any lazarettos in Europe where he could hide his rotting hideousness, but here in the colonies there are many places where . . ."

Kit's lean, tanned hand reached up and caught at the white-gold spike of a beard that bisected his firm chin. He gave it a gentle tug, and his eyes rested speculatively on Bernardo's lean, Semitic face. Bernardo, who was not wanting in perceptiveness, caught the unspoken reproach at once; but he considered the matter too grave for nicety of sentiments.

"Look, Kit," he went on doggedly, "I am not without sympathy for the dreadful scourge that devours him. But what right has he to expose you to contagion? You and I and every man aboard this pest ship? Who are we that we should implement his

3

vengeance against a world that cast him off in most understandable horror?" Bernardo bent closer, persuasion moving urgently through his tones. "He is an old man. Now, if you were captain of the *Seaflower* . . ."

Kit turned away and stared toward the shadowy harbor. "Were I captain," he said slowly, so that his words came out measured and spaced, ice-hard, and as free of warmth, "I would sail this sea witch into the harbor of Cartagena to the citadel above which the Heron Banner flies, and blast my way house by house to Don Luis's door. Under Lazarus at least they live. Under my command, they'd die like the dogs they are!"

Bernardo looked down at the wings of the Black Heron, spread wide on the cloth of gold.

"You cannot forget him," he murmured, "can you?"

"Forget him!" Kit breathed. "Forget Luis del Toro? Not until my hands have torn his heart from his breast!" He leaned forward, his eyes intent and hard, a little flame of madness leaping in their depths.

Nor am I likely to forget him either, Bernardo thought bitterly. Don Luis is a monster of wickedness—a true son of evil, in whom Satan, his father, will never find cause for shame. He lifts a finger and I am bereft of lands and goods just because I am born a Jew; he gestures and a woman dies of torture, a coward takes his own life, and we, Kit and I, are hurled across half a world into a leper bark from which all men flee in shrieking horror. . . . He bent forward again, shrugging his great shoulders. Del Toro was of no importance at the moment. The matter of the leper captain crowded all else out of his mind.

"Listen to reason, Kit," he said. "You know how it is with us. What happens when we go ashore? Every woman up to the age of sixty flees shrieking at the top of her lungs. We are cheated of our treasure. There is no man who will bargain with us fairly; we are not even permitted the freedom of their rum shops. We are not lepers, but we might as well be for all the chance we have of taking our ease or indulging our manly appetites. Good God, Kit! The men will mutiny before long, and you and I will die along with Lazarus's stinking hideousness. Now, if you were in command . . ."

4

Kit's eyes rested coolly on the face of his friend.

"If you were in command," Bernardo persisted, "we could sail into Basse-Terre or even Port de Paix and be welcomed. Since De Cussy was killed at Cap Français last year, Saint-Domingue has a new governor. The Sieur Ducasse understands the ways of freebooters, having been one himself. Why, Laurens de Graff, and even Daviot, the worst butcher since L'Ollonais, sail in and out of the harbor of Port de Paix with impunity."

"So?" Kit said.

"Why shouldn't Christophe Giradeaux, Frenchman, do the same thing?"

Kit smiled. "I am but half French, as you well know. What of Cristóbal Gerado, bastard of a Spanish grandee? Or Kit Gerado, the English sea dog the whole Caribbean believes me to be?"

Bernardo grinned at him. "I think that Kit of the golden mane comes of all nations. The choice is up to him."

Kit's smooth forehead furrowed with thinking. He remembered the day when Lazarus had first removed in his presence the mask that hid the face of living death from all mankind. The fingers that fumbled at the strings were terribly swollen and dead-white; moreover, they stopped short at the second joint without a trace of nails. Kit had leaned against the door frame, waiting curiously. Then the mask had fallen away from Lazarus's face, and Kit had peered into what seemed to be the countenance of an ancient lion: the nose was huge, rimmed about by heavy nodules, the brow ridged and furrowed with wrinkles, the cheeks flabby, with spots of ghastly whiteness on them, and the ears huge, thickened and elongated beyond belief.

The blue eyes looking out from under the great shelf of the brows had been for a moment infinitely sad, then rage had flared in them.

"I am to be obeyed, lad," Lazarus had roared, "not stared at!"

That had been the beginning. Now Kit realized Lazarus's loneliness, and the terror that haunted him. He had learned, too, that but for his horrible disease, Lazarus might have been a kindly and greathearted man. He looked up at Bernardo.

"No," he said gently. "I will not sanction the murder of an

5

old and broken man who in his own way has been good to me."

"Who said anything about murder?" Bernardo demanded. "There are thousands of islands in this sea where a man could live out his days in the sun, with fruit and shellfish for food, and fowls too, dropped by a fowling piece. Why, we might even buy him a Negress or a Caribbee maid, young and hot of blood, to warm his old bones. It would be a blessing for him."

Kit frowned. "It's odd how bright a glow a man's oily tongue can rub on villainy," he growled. "No, Bernardo—no more of this." He turned away.

The wind was coming from the east, blowing straight across Hispaniola, so that all the palms bowed together before it. Now and again a long fringe of palm would tear loose from its trunk and be hurled out to sea. The great waves swelled, rising with deceptive, heavy slowness, as though the sea were made of a thick sirup; then they would crash down to batter the *Seaflower*'s stern with tons of white water. The brigantine ran baremasted, except for the jib and spritsail that held her due west, so that only her narrow stern took the smashing impact of the waves. She slid down a long, oily gray trough of sea, only her two masts visible, then rose sickeningly, her bowsprit angling skyward, hanging there for long minutes before a caprice of wind and water dropped her downward again.

It was then that the little knot of men pushed their way out of the forecastle and headed unsteadily toward Lazarus's cabin. As if by instinct, Kit glanced up and, in one motion, was on his feet and striding toward the leper captain's door, aware that the long-threatened mutiny was about to flare up. Inside the fetid gloom of Lazarus's cabin, the captain looked at him sadly.

"What is the urgency, Kit?" he asked.

"The men . . ." Kit began, anxiety in his voice.

"Mutiny?" Lazarus growled. "I've been expecting that. Well, Kit, shall we put it down?"

Kit looked at him in astonishment. " 'Shall we put it down?' " he echoed. "Is there any question of that?"

"Yes, Kit," Lazarus said slowly. "There is a question. If I die, you will become captain. Should I deny you that for the

6

dubious pleasure of a few more years of this—this existence? What is my life, Kit, that I should cling to it?"

Kit looked at the leper captain, his blue eyes very clear.

"I would not have it at that price, sir," he said quietly.

"You're a good lad, Kit. I would have liked a son like you. But no matter. You've made my last years good ones." He stood up slowly. "I'll dicker with the swine, though the outcome matters little to me."

"Then let me face them!" Kit barked. "It's time they learned to come to heel for good and all!"

"Time enough for that when you're captain, Kit," Lazarus said, his hideously deformed fingers fumbling at his mask.

"Do you think that will ever be? In any mutiny I'll go over the side one splash behind you. I've led these dogs over the rails of twelve galleons, but what use has it been? They still resent my advancement. They're overdue for a lesson from me now."

"Then they shall have it," Lazarus said mildly. "You are armed?"

"Yes," Kit growled, touching the silver butts of his great pistols.

"We will not kill any unless we must," Lazarus said. "It will be better to cow them. These, I think, will serve." He took down a duck-foot pistol for himself. Kit stared at the curious weapon. It had four barrels spread out fanwise, so that it could cover the entire deck of a vessel with its fire. It had only one flintlock hammer, all four barrels firing at once from a single pull of the trigger. Kit watched Lazarus load it, cramming an unusually large charge of powder into each barrel, as well as half a dozen small shot on top of each charge. One blast from this multiple hand cannon and the whole deck might be swept clean.

"George of England made it," Lazarus said, "for the express purpose of putting down mobs. Now if you'll take down that blunderbuss dag up there, you'll be as well armed as I. Don't be afraid to touch it, Kit. It has been cleaned many times since I put it there."

Kit took down the tremendously heavy little gun, which,

7

though it was as short as a pistol, had a rifle stock. The great bell-shaped barrel had been polished until it shone.

"Load it with scrap iron," Lazarus said, "above a triple weight of powder. It will kick like a Spanish mule, but if we have to fire, there will be none left to oppose us."

Kit loaded the weapon, all the time glancing toward the door. Lazarus shook his head. "They won't rush us here. They would have to come one at a time through that door, and we could pick them off at leisure. Never fear—they'll await our pleasure."

Kit stood up, the short, ugly weapon draped over the crook of his arm.

"One thing more, Kit," Lazarus said. "When this thing is over, we sail for Port Royal."

Kit's brows rose. "Jamaica? Why?"

"To put me ashore on English soil. I'll give myself up to the authorities while you slip away. Wait, lad, hear me out! Though England and Spain are united in this damned mésalliance against France, the worst that can happen to me is to be exiled to some deserted island. This truce with the dons can't last. I have sunk more Spanish galleons than any Englishman since Drake. Alliance or not, my countrymen feel as I do. Besides," and he grinned wryly, "where will they find a hangman who would dare touch my skin to loop the rope about my neck?"

Kit frowned. "Is that your wish?" he growled.

"It is, Kit. I'm weary of the sea and fighting. And youth must be served. Come now."

They weaved their way, bracing themselves against the pitching of the vessel, to the deck. The men were drawn up in a semicircle facing the cabin, their faces black with scowls. Only Bernardo stood apart from them, his great pistol belt crisscrossing his shoulders. As Kit and Lazarus strode on deck, Bernardo came over quietly and stood beside them. Kit smiled mockingly.

"Have I ever deserted you yet?" Bernardo asked huskily.

"Never," Kit answered. "I should have known you would be on our side."

8

"You are likely to die with him now, Jew," Lazarus said. Then, to the men, "Speak your piece, lads, and have done with it!"

A man stepped forward. It was Tim Waters, a wizened little Englishman with the scar of a cutlass swipe ridging his face from brow to lip, one eye gone, and the top lip drawn upward by the wound so that his ugly yellow fangs showed forever in a macabre grin.

"Well, Cap'n," he began, "we've been thinkin', me an' the lads . . ."

"Deviltry, no doubt," Lazarus growled. "Go on."

"Lookee, Cap'n, we're in for one hell of a blow, as ye kin see. And here be the best harbor in the Windward Isles, not four leagues off our starboard."

"Correct. And in it are some twenty French vessels ranging from frigates to sloops of war. What do you think of that, Timothy!"

Waters scraped one bare, horny foot against the deck. "Them Frenchies," he said slyly, "is awful easy wit' freebooters. 'Specially wit' them as kin parlay frog. Now, if the *Seaflower* was to beat in wit' a fleur-de-lis streamin' from the masthead . . ."

"And with Captain Lazarus, who has sunk over thirty Frenchmen, in command? You have an answer to that one too, Timothy?"

Waters hesitated, twisting his hideously scarred face to glance at his comrades.

"Me an' the lads," he got out at last, "was thinkin' that ye'd agree to step down. Now, with Dupré here in command"—he nodded to a squat, thickset Gascon—"them frogeaters would welcome us like brothers. We could hide ye in the hold, an' put ye ashore later. Then ye could beat it for the hills. Live like a king up there, wit' twenty black wenches to wait on ye hand an' foot."

"I see," Lazarus said quietly. "And if the French came aboard and searched the vessel, you'd deliver me to them—in irons—wouldn't you?"

Waters glanced uneasily at the others. A mutter rose and

ran from man to man. Emboldened, Waters turned back, a wicked grin on his face.

"Well, if ye want to put it that way, Cap'n," he said, "looks like we better git it over right now!"

Kit could see the men gathering for a rush. He stepped forward, the blunderbuss leveled. "I think," he said evenly and clearly, "that it would please me greatly to blow half of you to hell."

"And I the other half," Lazarus snarled, leveling the fan-shaped, four-barreled pistol.

"And if you leave even one," Bernardo added, laughing, "I'll shoot him through his gutless belly!"

The men stopped as though they had run against a wall. Kit could see their eyes, opened in fear, jerking from the enormous bell-shaped muzzle of the blunderbuss to the four black owl's eyes of the duck-foot pistol, and again to the slim dueling pistol that Bernardo held in his hand.

"Now, lookee, Cap'n . . ." Waters quavered.

"You witless, yellow-bellied curs," Lazarus said slowly, "do you think you're a match for Lazarus?"

"No, Cap'n," Waters whined. "We didn't mean to do ye harm. Why, me an' the boys was merely going to tie ye up a bit, so's ye wouldn't git hurt."

Lazarus's pale-blue eyes rested on Waters's face. They were glacial in their coldness. Then a little pinpoint of fire shone in them suddenly.

"Yes, Tim, you're very considerate. I must admit that. Kind as a brother—a blood brother." He thrust one deformed hand sidewise toward Kit. "Your dagger, lad," he whispered. Kit passed it over.

"The Caribbees have a ceremony," Lazarus said quietly, "by which they confer blood kinship upon those they love and trust. . . . Keep them covered, Kit." He took the dagger and drew the edge of it across his own wrist. It went across cleanly, and after a moment the bright blood oozed through. "Now, Tim," he said gently, "put out your hand. I would honor a brave and faithful comrade."

Waters stood there, his face graying, his voice gurgling like liquid in his throat, unable to shape a single recognizable sound, his one good eye bulging from its socket as he looked at that sickening, corpse-white hand, those abbreviated nubs of nailless, diseased fingers, over which the thick blood oozed. He sank to his knees.

"Cap'n," he got out, "Cap'n, for the love of God!"

But Lazarus advanced upon him slowly. When he was close, Waters collapsed in a quivering heap, slobbering like an animal in terror. The leper captain bent down and lifted Waters's left hand. Waters struggled feebly, trying to jerk it away, but those shortened fingers had a grip of iron. The captain slashed Waters's scrawny wrist until the blood came, and then, slowly, impassively, he pressed his own self-inflicted wound against it, so that their blood mingled. Then he stepped back, smiling peacefully.

"Throw down your arms, men," he said. "There'll be no mutiny here."

The pistols and cutlasses clattered to the deck. Kit stared at the men, his own stomach a little sick.

"Back to your quarters!" Lazarus barked. The men slunk back, whipped.

Then, after a moment, Waters raised himself from the deck and staggered after them. They whirled on him, daggers glittering in every hand. "Keep away!" they roared. "Leper!"

Waters faced them, the tears from his one eye penciling his scarred face. "Lads," he quavered, "lads, for the love o' God, I fought wit' ye . . . I broke bread wit' ye . . ."

A bearded man growled: "You did, but never again! Go to your brother. Go to Cap'n Lazarus!"

"Yes, Tim," Lazarus said gently, "come to me. Come and see how it feels to be rotting while you're still alive. Come watch your hands shrink, joint by joint, until they're animal's paws. It's not too bad. You feel no pain. You can put your hands into a candle flame and watch the flesh burn, and laugh. But it grows lonely, Tim. It's hard to have the whole world against you, praying for your death. Will it not please you to go ashore to find that the foulest strolling wench in Basse-Terre, half-blind of the French sickness, will run away from you shrieking? Yes, Tim, come. Come, brother leper!"

Waters's cavernous mouth came open, and a long, high animal howl of pure madness shrilled from his throat. He raised his hands, curved like talons, against the lowering sky, and started for his comrades.

"Whoresons!" he bleated. "You dirty bastards! Bas . . ."

He never finished the word. Kit saw the bearded man's leather jerkin tear open, saw the horny fingers close around the butt of a hidden, unsurrendered pistol. Waters was so close to the man that his tunic caught fire from the blast; then he crumpled all over at once, becoming suddenly boneless, sprawling grotesquely in death.

Lazarus shook his great head mournfully. "Now, who," he asked quietly, "is going to heave him over the side?"

The men stared at the corpse in breath-gone fascination. Not one of them, Kit knew, would dare lay a finger on it.

"Let him lay," the blackbeard growled at last.

"Yes," Lazarus said, "let him. Let him lie there until he rots, and the winds sweep the stink from his bloated belly into your nostrils. I think, lads, I shall not be lonely any longer." He turned then, and went down into his cabin. Kit followed him.

"Take the helm, Kit," Lazarus said, "and head for Port Royal. They've had their lesson."

"But Tim . . ." Kit protested.

"Tonight I'll heave him over myself. But leave him there all day. It will throw a scare into them they'll never forget."

Kit went aft and took his place at the whipstaff, holding the *Seaflower*'s prow due west. On the foredeck, the men stood as though frozen and stared at the body of Tim Waters. All day they rode before the wind, the trim vessel breasting the mountainous waves like a playful dolphin, but when night came they reefed even the flying jib, using only the spritsail to maintain steerageway. Yet such was the force of the gale that when morning broke, the fair coast of Jamaica lay before them.

The crew, finding that Tim's body had disappeared during the night, fell to work willingly. The *Seaflower* scudded toward the harbor of Port Royal. But as they nosed into the bay, Ber-

12

nardo, who had climbed up the foremast, roared down: "Hard aport! Hard aport, for the love of God!"

Without a second thought, Kit swung the whipstaff all the way over. The *Seaflower* responded at once, swinging about on the first arc of the circle. It was her handiness that saved their lives. A slower, less responsive vessel would have been only half-way around when the tidal wave hit. As it was, the mountain of water struck her three-quarters aft and hurled her ahead like a chip. The whole world for Kit was a white wall of water, blotting out the sky, pounding his eardrums senseless with a torrential deluge of sound. Standing on the little platform between decks, protected only by the low, arched cover, he was hit by a tag end of the wave that had all the weight and apparent solidity of so much stone. If the impact of the water had not been broken by the high sweep of the poop and the arch over his head, so that its force was largely spent, it would have smashed every bone in his body. As it was, it struck him with sufficient force to knock him unconscious.

Minutes later his eyes flickered open. The unmanned whip-staff stood up before him, straight and level, as though the *Seaflower* were drifting in a dead calm. Kit staggered to his feet, shaking his head. He remembered the wave, but now . . . He looked aft. Half the crew was gathered on the poop, staring toward Port Royal. Kit called to one of the men and gave over the whipstaff. He made his way aft.

Behind the *Seaflower* the water was calm, with only a little swell, and the wind that blew in from the sea was gentle. But on the shore a great plume of smoke stood up above what had been the town of Port Royal—an immense plume, a column of white so broad at its base that it covered the entire city. It rose straight up so high that its domed head seemed to touch the very floor of heaven. From where he stood, Kit could see that it was fed by the red tongues of many flames. Then near the shore another wave started, much smaller and weaker than the first. As it raced toward them, Kit saw the few remaining houses on the shore swing back and forth crazily and come crashing down. Off to the left of the city, a hill lifted its head. Now, as they watched, the hill split in half, and the great rocks rumbled

13

downward, directly upon the city. Kit could see the inch-high figures of the people of Port Royal running wildly about while the earth writhed under their feet, and now and again yawning chasms opened up and swallowed them. From the firm decks of the *Seaflower*, it was all curiously remote and unreal—an extraordinarily vivid nightmare; but before his eyes a city was dying.

Bernardo came and stood beside him. Together they watched the mad scramble as the people put out to sea in anything that floated; but near the shore the earthquake tremors raised mountains of surf, and red lava from the yawning chasms turned the shoal water into live steam. Not one of the small boats got through.

Kit turned and saw Captain Lazarus coming out of his cabin. "What is it, Kit?" he asked.

"I think, sir," Kit said quietly, "that very likely there are no authorities for you to surrender yourself to. Look!"

Lazarus's gaze followed Kit's pointing finger. "Merciful God!" he whispered. "What is it?"

"Earthquake, sir," Bernardo told him. "I saw one once in Italy. But nothing like this!"

Kit stiffened suddenly. From one of the coves near the city a tall Spanish galleon was beating out to sea. That a Spanish vessel should be in the harbor of compatriots of Drake, Hawkins, and Henry Morgan was only another irony of seventeenth-century power politics, which sometimes made allies of hereditary enemies. The growing power of Louis XIV had forced all Europe into an alliance against France, while the rotting hulk that was Spain, for all the vastness of her possessions, was no longer to be feared under such a king as Charles the Bewitched. Straightening, Kit turned to the renegade Spaniard he himself had made third officer.

"Shorten sail, Pat," he said softly.

Patricio Velasco relayed the command to the men. The *Seaflower* lost headway rapidly.

"Gunners at stations," Kit said. The filthy, half-naked buccaneers leaped to their guns, the tarred matches flaring in their hands.

14

Kit watched the tall Spaniard beating through the boiling surf. She came on, overtaking the *Seaflower* with majestic deliberation. Kit's hands whitened, gripping the rail. Beside him, Patricio and Bernardo stood, scarcely daring to breathe. The Spaniard would have to come much closer before the *Seaflower's* guns would have much effect on her massive timbers. On she came, moving with maddening slowness, a mighty ocean monarch overtaking a dwarf. Kit wondered why she had not opened fire. There was something contemptuous in the way she ignored the *Seaflower's* existence. Kit's mouth hardened beneath the white-gold mustache.

Suddenly he felt Bernardo's great hand tightening on his arm with a bone-crushing grip. Startled, Kit half-turned. But Bernardo was staring past him, pointing wordlessly at the pennant that fluttered from the masthead, just beneath the flag of Spain. It was a simple device: a Black Heron on a field of gold! Kit leaned forward, unbelieving, a tumult of fierce joy hammering through his veins—at the sight of the banner of Don Luis del Toro.

"His ship!" he whispered, his voice hoarse with exultation. "*His* ship! By the saints, Bernardo, I will crust his filthy bones with salt before nightfall!"

Bernardo's dark eyes narrowed, watching the galleon with the Heron Banner as it drew abreast. "Better put her over, Kit," he growled. "She's not truly a galleon, despite her lines. I'd say a ship of the line, mounting a hundred guns."

"Damn her guns!" Kit snorted. "Damn her and her guns! I'm going in! Hard aport!" he roared at the helmsman.

The *Seaflower* veered, angling in the direction of the great ship. The lines of their tracks converged.

"Three points to sta'board!" Kit called. The *Seaflower* veered again, coming about on a track parallel to that of the great Spanish vessel.

"Stand by for a broadside!" Kit commanded. The gunners bent over their pieces, their faces ashen with fear.

Bernardo said nothing. He knew that one blast from those huge cannon aboard the Spaniard would lift them from the water. But he knew also that there was no stopping Kit.

Kit lifted his hand in the signal for firing. But he held it there, suddenly arrested by a commotion on the Spaniard's upper deck. She lay a pistol shot off the *Seaflower*'s port side, and the men on the deck were plainly visible. Down the wind the hoarse hallooing of their laughter beat faintly on Kit's ears. Then his hand came down, inch by slow inch, without giving the signal to fire.

For on the deck of the Spaniard there swayed the willow-slender figure of a woman. Kit hung over the rail, his eyes filled with the dazzling whiteness of her flesh amid the tattered rags that were all the Spaniards had left of her clothing. Even as he watched, rough hands seized her again, the brown fingers digging into the golden blaze of her hair, forcing her head backward until the white blob of her face was blotted out by the hooked beak and black mustache of a Spanish seaman.

"Dogs and sons of dogs!" Kit howled. "Bring me a musket!"

A seaman leaped aft and returned with the heavy, clumsy weapon. Kit settled it across the lee rail, taking careful aim. But before he could fire, the woman tore loose from the Spaniard's grasp. Her hand shot skyward, and bright in it glittered the sheen of the Spanish seaman's dagger. It crashed downward, disappearing to the hilt through the snowy globe of one bare breast. Kit saw her crumpling slowly to the deck, and the rage in his throat was as bitter as wormwood. His finger tightened on the trigger; the musket numbed his shoulder with its recoil as the Spaniard went over sideways, one half of his face entirely gone.

Instantly the Spaniards began to scramble toward their guns. Kit lifted his hand and let it drop all in one motion. All the *Seaflower*'s guns opened the sky and the sea with one stupendous bellow, kicking back on their wheeled carriages to the limits of the hempen breeching rope that anchored them to the sides, the brigantine rolling with the recoil, and the clouds of smoke washing out the horizon. But when the smoke had cleared, though there was a pile of dead seamen on her decks, the giant Spaniard seemed scarcely to have been touched. Instantly, from her high deck came a storm of fire from her murthering pieces: swivels, rabinets, falconets, falcons, and minions.

16

The small shot shrieked through the *Seaflower*'s rigging, inflicting small damage. In another minute though, Kit knew, she would be able to bring to bear her immense full cannon, hurling sixty-four-pound shot. That two or three hits from those great guns would be enough to sink the *Seaflower* he knew even better. He raced toward the helmsman, shouting commands. Those crew members detailed to the task shivered the fighting sails, throwing the *Seaflower* rapidly back so that she dropped astern of the Spaniard almost at once. Then the sleek brigantine veered sharply to port, bringing her prow dead astern of the Spaniard, so that that great vessel could bring only her light chase guns to bear.

It was at this point that Lazarus mounted the deck.

"You handled it well, Kit," he said, "but as you can neither board nor sink her, it is only sense to run away."

"Never!" Kit spat.

Lazarus smiled. "Be reasonable, Kit," he said. "What chance has a brigantine against a ship of the line?"

"That ship," Kit got out, "sails under the colors of a man I am sworn to kill."

"You'll have to wait," Lazarus said calmly. "It's quite impossible now."

Kit opened his mouth to protest further, but a shout from the men on the forecastle stopped him. He ran forward, followed by Bernardo and Lazarus. A group of seamen were clustered near the bowsprit, pointing up at the Spaniard's towering stern. Kit gazed upward, his jaw dropping open.

"Mother of God!" he whispered. "Have they all the women of Port Royal aboard?"

High on the poop deck of the Spaniard, another slender figure struggled in the arms of a broad-shouldered hidalgo. From the short distance separating the two vessels, Kit could see that she was very much like the first, except that her wildly disheveled hair was not golden, but as red as a sunset. So intently did Kit watch her that it was long seconds before something in the hidalgo's appearance struck him as being familiar; then his breath left his lungs in a huge gasp, for the Spaniard who held the slender girl to him was Don Luis del Toro. Kit whirled, his hands searching for a musket, but when one had been put into them he stood there transfixed, unable to fire. There was not one chance in a thousand of hitting Don Luis without also wounding the girl. Then something very like a smile played about the corners of his mouth.

Slowly, carefully, he lifted the musket. It roared, and splinters from the lateen yard showered down on Don Luis's bare head. The grandee whirled, releasing the girl. As Kit reached for another musket, he saw her poised above the carved and gilded gingerbread work just under the stern lantern, then she arched downward, cutting the sea as cleanly as any knife. Kit lifted the second musket, but Don Luis flattened himself behind the lateen mast and called to his own musketeers.

The girl's bright head, the color of a scarlet hibiscus against the blue water, broke surface. Instantly five Spanish musketeers leaped to the poop, their weapons pointed downward. For them to miss at such a distance was an impossibility. But before they could take aim, the *Seaflower*'s chase gun fired. When its lionlike roar had ceased echoing, ten yards of the Spaniard's stern castle had been carried away, and with it the musketeers. In two swift glances, Kit saw Don Luis scrambling downward toward safety and the girl stretching up her arms for help. There was time for only one of the two actions called for. Kit let the musket clatter to the deck and threw a line to the girl.

A dozen hands leaped to grasp the other end, and the slight figure of the girl was hauled swiftly over the side. Kit released the rope and caught her at the armpits, dragging her aboard. He stood her on her feet and stepped back, gazing at her. The long red-gold hair streamed wetly over her shoulders, haloing a slim face with high cheekbones that gave her eyes the illusory appearance of having an odd, Mongolian slant. Now, resting on Kit's face, her eyes widened until they were enormous, making her small face even smaller by comparison. They were a deep green, curiously light-filled; they matched exactly the emerald that Kit wore in his left ear.

Kit's blue eyes sought the crimson curve of her mouth, held tightly against pain and terror, then his gaze fixed on the white

column of her neck and her slim figure, only partially concealed
by a single shift rent in half a dozen places and clinging with
drenched fidelity to every singing line of her young body. Behind
him now, a low snarling mutter ran through the ranks of the
crew. Kit whirled to face them. Woman-starved, pent-up far past
the bursting point with years of unsatisfied desire, how long
could he or anyone restrain them? Them—or himself?

But at that moment Lazarus stepped forward and touched
the girl's arm with the slender stick he carried.

"Come," he said gently. Silently the girl turned and accompanied him into his cabin. Then the door was closed behind
them.

Kit stood there with the rest of the crew, staring at that door,
hearing the echo of their muted rage rumbling in his own throat.
What can he do with her? he wondered bitterly. Old as he is
and rotten with disease? The thought checked him, bringing
him up short against an icy wall of terror. That fair skin, white
as the snows of the Spanish mountains with the dawn light on
them, would it know the touch of those fingers of living death?
Would that matchless, marvelous brush-fire hair whiten and
fall out, and the skin, stretched taut above those fine-cut cheekbones, deaden into gray-white ringed with purple?

There was need now for cessation of thinking. Turning, Kit
barked commands at the crew. They scrambled among the
rigging, cracking on all sail until the *Seaflower*'s two masts
groaned under the burden of canvas. The helmsman put her
over hard to port, and she veered away from the great castled
Spaniard with which she had fought so indecisive a battle. Kit
headed her toward Hispaniola and stood on the forecastle, his
mind black with unbidden thoughts.

After nightfall, he turned and moved aft, step by step, toward
Lazarus's cabin. A few of the crew members still ringed it,
staring hungrily at the closed door.

"Away!" Kit roared at them. "Get your arses to work, or
I'll see how a touch of the cat can speed you! Step along now,
right hearty!"

The buccaneers slunk away like sullen hounds, their greedy

glances fixed backward on the door. Kit stood there silently for a long moment, then the door crashed open and the huge silhouette of Lazarus was framed in the lantern glow, reeling there and bellowing Kit's name.

"Aye, aye, sir?" Kit answered.

"Come," Lazarus whispered. "Come and take the girl away. I was a fool, but I have been lonely so long . . . and her skin was so fair . . . Before I died, just this once, it seemed that fate owed me some recompense for all my suffering. But no. Come, Kit, and take her to your quarters."

"What happened?" Kit growled.

"She asked me—to remove—my mask."

"Oh!" Kit whispered.

"She did not faint. I could have stood that. No, Kit, she looked into my face—and vomited from sheer disgust. Come and take her, Kit."

Kit entered the dim, foul-smelling interior of Lazarus's cabin. On a chair, the girl was bent over, half-swooning, her shoulders shaking. Kit put out his hand and touched her gently. She whirled, her eyes green blobs of naked terror; then the fear in them subsided a little.

"I have come to take you away," Kit said in the stiff, accented English he had learned from Lazarus. "Have no fear. I will not harm you."

Silently the girl rose and came to him. Kit led her up the ladder and across the deck, one hand resting on the butt of his pistol. Behind him he could hear Lazarus muttering: "She looked into my face—my old, dying beast's face—and she . . ."

Kit opened the door to his quarters and pointed to his hammock. "Lie down and rest," he said. "You are hungry, perhaps? I will get you food."

"Food?" the girl echoed, the word shuddering up from her throat in tones of near-nausea. "I shall never eat again!"

Kit stared at her blankly.

"Where will you sleep?" she asked.

"Outside," Kit said. "Just outside, so that no one may enter."

"And you—you'll not come in?"

Kit shook his head. "No," he said simply. "I shall not trouble you."

The girl turned on him angrily, her emerald eyes firelit in their depths.

"Do you think that I believe that? You're a man, for all your handsomeness, and all men are beasts!"

Kit studied her, his blue eyes somber. "I'm sorry you believe that," he began.

"Believe? I know. Didn't Don Luis put into Port Royal to save us from the earthquake? And you saw how he helped us! Beth, my sweet sister, dead by her own hand on the deck, after those swine had finished with her. While I—I was more highly honored. Don Luis reserved me for himself. And here on this vessel—this English vessel—that horrible, disgusting old man . . ."

Kit's hand stole inside his sash and came out with the great pistol. "Here," he said, "take this. If any man enters—even I—use it!"

The girl looked up at him, her green eyes widening. "Thank you," she whispered.

Something in her eyes sent a glacial chill stealing through Kit's veins. "Not on yourself!" he growled.

"Why not? What have I left to live for? Would a decent man—if there is any such thing—have me now? Could I go back to Jamaica to Reginald and say, 'Here, take me, used, befouled thing that I am'? I could scrub my skin until it reddens and peels and never remove the stain. It's inside upon my soul."

"Give me back the pistol, then," Kit said.

"No," the girl said softly. "I shall not harm myself. If I had the courage, I would have done it before now. No, I will live —and many a man shall suffer for this day!"

Kit looked at her, and his blue eyes were very clear. He left the cabin, closing the door softly behind him. But even as he lifted his hand from the knob he heard the crash of a pistol shot. It came from aft. He started toward the sound, but before he had covered half the length of the deck Bernardo met him.

"Kit," he said, "Kit . . ."

"Lazarus?" Kit growled.

"Yes. Through the mouth."

Kit pushed past him and entered the cabin. The great bulk of Captain Lazarus was sprawled on the floor, a pistol gripped in his hand. Kit covered that huge, shattered head with a blanket and knelt beside him, muttering swift Castilian prayers. Then he took down the captain's hammock and rolled Lazarus's inert bulk onto it.

He called four members of the crew. They lifted the hammock by the guy ropes and walked slowly to the side. They paused there while Kit lifted his head and said in English: "Forgive him, O God of the heretics, for though his sins were many, he was greatly put upon. Amen." Then the body of Captain Lazarus slid over the side to make a muffled splash in the darkened sea.

Kit could see the men scurrying off to wash themselves. He followed them more slowly. When he was clean and had eaten, he went back to the door of his cabin. Wearily he sank down. As he sat there, the creak of his hammock swinging gently against the swell sounded in his ears. It went on all night, a slow, maddening sound. His mind formed the image of the girl, lithe, soft-curving, nestling there amid the bright blaze of her long hair.

Finally, as the first flush of morning was graying in and the ragged outlines of Cow Island were visible on the horizon, Kit got up stiffly. He pushed open the door and entered the cabin. Inside, it was yet dark, but he could hear the girl's regular breathing.

He lit the lantern and stared down. She lay in the hammock, relaxed in sleep, her mouth soft and a little parted, dew-petaled, inviting. Kit stood there staring at her until some of the desire in him slipped away to be replaced by a great and aching tenderness. Then, kneeling beside the hammock, he kissed her mouth. She came awake at once, her green eyes terror-filled and flaring.

"You!" she whispered, her voice hoarse, chest-deep, filled with loathing. "You too!" Then, before Kit could move, she swung the long pistol over and fired at point-blank range. Kit saw the wall of fire exploding before his eyes, felt the white-hot stab of pain, then clouds of darkness closed in upon him from all sides at once. But as he lay there on the floor, slipping out on the tide of roaring blackness, he imagined he felt the soft, fragrant weight of her body pressing upon his in the gloom, and his hand moved briefly, caressing her bright hair. Then night crashed down, complete and utter, with no ray of light and no sound at all.

2

Early in the morning, the Black Heron extricated itself from the folds of the golden banner that had held it so long imprisoned and flew across the tiny space of Kit's cabin. It furled its ominous wings and sat on the foot of Kit's bunk. Kit watched it a long time, staring into the bird's strange eyes, which were lidless, golden, unalive. Then, with a low croak, the heron moved forward and stood on his chest. And try as he would, Kit could not move it.

There seemed to be something the matter with his arms. He could not raise them. He made the effort, the beads of perspiration standing out on his forehead, but his arms lay at his side like so much mutton, lifeless and inert. The heron sitting on his chest was much heavier now, pressing down with such weight that all his breath seemed to be leaving his lungs. And suddenly, inexplicably, there was a shifting in time and space and the heron was no longer there. The weight was still there, however, somewhat lighter than the heron; but instead of being confined to his chest, it lay on his entire body, warm, fragrant, soft-fleshed, moving. It seemed to be weeping, and the great tears dropped like warm rain into his face. There was a sweeping motion, and a lock of hair, damp and smelling of salt water, brushed across his face. He knew, without being able to see it, that it was like hibiscus petals, like poinsettia, like flame.

He put up his fingers to stroke it, and this time they moved, seemingly without effort. And the pale face above him blurred momentarily into focus, the mouth flame-scarlet and trembling uncontrollably, bending down to find his in the darkness. The warm lips moved closer, parting as they caught his, pressing

24

until all his breath stopped, the body pressing too, making of itself one long caress, breast and trunk and thigh moving upon his, the little snow cones, shell-rose-tipped, soft-stabbing his bare chest like widely separated fire points. And all his life was caught up in one wild surge of flame that roared out into the dark. . . ..

The next time he came back, it was to vivid brightness, and the Black Heron fluttered once more on its golden banner from a pikestaff being borne through a street in Cádiz. . . . Kit saw himself, the boy Kit, standing on the roof of his foster father's house with his mother, a lovely creature all pink and white and golden whose tongue still spoke with the accents of Normandy, and with Bernardo Díaz.

Below them, lolling in their saddles in contemptuous arrogance, a party of grandees were riding. Kit could see them now, like figures from a bright tapestry strangely come to life, their faces vague and indistinct above the rich black-velvet tunics, blurred into curious anonymity except for one face.

Remembering that face, a sound tore at Kit's throat—a muted syllable, voluptuous with rage, that started as an animal growl, low and bestial, and rose to a groan that was half a sob, brimming with raw and quivering pain. He half-rose on his bunk, and someone who watched beside him pressed him back. For a moment, the actuality of Bernardo's troubled face came clear before Kit's sight. He opened his mouth to comfort his friend, to say . . .

But the words remained forever unspoken, for before he could utter them, Kit was back again on a rooftop in Cádiz. Below him, once more the Heron Banner danced in the sunlight, and the grandees rode through the crowds that scurried fearfully away at their approach. Kit watched the spectacle idly until a low, explosive gasp from his mother's lips reached him. He could hear her breath strangling in her throat. Then, to his vast amazement, she turned and ran, as fleet as a girl, down the stairs. Bernardo was two steps behind her and Kit followed hard on his heels. But neither of them was swift enough to catch her. She plunged out into the street, and while Kit stood in the doorway as if turned to stone, she threw up her hands and caught at the bridle of one of the horsemen.

25

"Luis!" she shrieked. "Luis!"

Kit saw the man's whip go up, arching against the sky. Then it sang downward and the lash hissed across his mother's face like a serpent, cutting it to the bone.

Kit saw her sitting in the roadway, holding her face in her hands, the bright blood oozing out between her fingers. Then he was off, the rage roaring in his throat, stretching out his hands for the grandee's neck. He got a vivid impression of the man's face, swart as a Moor's, with a bold, jutting nose and a chin marred by a tuft of inky beard. Then one of the lancers who accompanied the grandee let down his lance so that the shaft came heavily across the boy's bright head. As Kit lay there in the street, with the rooftops reeling in circles above him, he heard the hoarse laughter of the hidalgos. . . .

That sound now was curiously mingled with the soft wash of the seas outside his cabin, and with the noises inside his head. He lay listening to it until he could no longer distinguish which was laughter and which was sea wash, and sank at last gratefully into slumber.

When he awoke again it was morning once more, and for almost an hour he knew where he was. He could discern the oak beams of the bulkheads, see his own garments hanging from a peg, and the weary form of Bernardo slumped over in a chair in a sleep of pure exhaustion.

"Poor Bernardo," he mused, "to what a pass have I brought him!" He raised himself halfway up on the bunk, but the action set the hammers to swinging inside his skull so that he fell back, and darkness crashed down once more. It was a confused darkness, filled with dreams that hurled themselves with lightning-like profusion before his eyes, without regard to time or space. . . .

He saw himself a child in the house of Jeanne Giradeaux and Pierre Labat, wigmaker to the grandees of Spain, come like many another Frenchman of his time to Spain for reasons he guarded jealously. Kit heard once more the whispers: "Don Luis . . . Luis del Toro . . . Del Toro . . ." whispers that ceased abruptly whenever he entered a room, only to linger on like an undefined menace always hovering above his bright head. . . .

26

He stood, at one and the same time with no sense of transition in time or space, and pumped the heavy pistol balls pointblank at Del Toro, seeing them flatten against the gleaming breastplate the grandee wore, the mighty figure reeling under the impact and clattering ignominiously to the cobblestones, entirely unhurt save in spirit. Afterward, he and Bernardo were fleeing, endlessly fleeing, breath-gone and lost, with thunderous hoofbeats pounding after them through the streets of Cádiz.

Kit saw himself stop and fire, saw Bernardo do likewise, and when finally they had reached the shelter of the ancient tombs the Phoenicians had dug centuries ago above Cádiz, Kit found that he had the Heron Banner in his hands. . . .

This time he sat fully upright in his bunk, and his voice rang out: "Stop it, you beasts! Oh, most foul, murderous, torturing dogs!"

Bernardo sprang at once from his chair and tried to push him down; but in his delirium Kit had the strength of ten. His eyes flamed with pure madness; the anguish on his face under the great swath of bandages was almost greater than Bernardo could bear. Then the vision that passed before Kit's sightless eyes was one that he had never seen in reality, but in the curious, disordered dream world of delirium it was far more clear than any of the others. Kit groaned terribly, pushing his knuckles into his blue eyes and grinding them cruelly in the attempt to shut out the pictures that persisted in coming with such hideous clarity:

He could see, as though he stood there, the subterranean chamber beneath a stone castle and the brawny figure of the executioner, glistening all over with sweat, in the ruddy glow from the brazier in which the irons were heating. He could see the man's face hidden in its cap of leather that fitted over the shaven bullet head and came down to the mouth line, to form a mask through whose slits the small beady eyes shifted; and before him the lovely white figure of Kit's mother stretched hand and foot around the outer circumference of the wheel that creaked as the man tightened the cords. By such an implement, the arms were dislocated at the shoulders, at the elbows, at the wrists, the legs at hip, knee, and ankle, until at last the bones

27

themselves gave. Then the small, willowy rods of iron stroked lightly, just hard enough to break the soft ribs of a woman's chest, until her body was a thing of rubber, utterly wanting in skeletal support. And beside the great glistening brute, the robed and saintly figure of the Inquisitor asking delicately:

"Where is your son Cristóbal? Where is he? Where? Where? Where?"

Kit could see his mother's fine head thrashing about on the slim column of her throat as she moaned:

"I do not know! Truly I do not! By the Virgin! By Saint Anthony! By the Blessed Infant Jesus, I do not know!"

He saw her faint. They loosened the rack and revived her. Then they began again, questioning, insisting, probing through the long hours while the irons that had been heated for application to her white skin, and the other ugly implements, waited. The knout. The boot. The thumbscrews. The Iron Maiden, that form-fitting coffin studded with five-inch iron spikes. In the field of inhuman bestiality, at least, there was no end to Spanish inventiveness.

Kit sat there on his bunk, half-supported by Bernardo, his bandaged head swaying with the slow weaving roll and pitch of the brigantine, and his words came out hoarse-voiced and agony-laden: "How long did it take, Bernardo? How long for a small and lovely woman to die?" Then, bending down his bright head, he gave way to the convulsive racking of great sobs. Gently Bernardo pressed him back upon the bunk, and this time Kit made no resistance.

Throughout that day and the next, Bernardo was able to follow quite clearly what was happening in Kit's fevered mind. He saw Kit relive their escape from Cádiz Harbor, diving from the Torre del Vigía into the sea and swimming to an outward-bound Netherlander. He saw Kit's face light up with fierce joy as they were told that the Zeeroover's destination was the Indies, for they had already learned that Don Luis del Toro had left Spain for Cartagena the night before the civil authorities tortured Jeanne Giradeaux to death. He saw the battle in which their vessel was overtaken and pulled down by the pirate brigantine Seaflower, and the calm air with which Kit accepted service

28

aboard a vessel commanded by a man whose very touch was death.

And finally, joyously, Bernardo saw the young man whom he loved like the son he had never had slip into normal, dreamless sleep, cool of skin, breathing calmly.

So it was that on the fifth day after receiving the wound, Kit looked up from his hammock into the face of Bernardo Díaz. It was a very solid, perceptible face, without any intervening haze of darkness shifting between it and his eyes.

"Thank God!" Bernardo whispered, his voice rich and vibrant with emotion.

A weak ghost of a smile wavered about the corners of Kit's colorless mouth. "I have yet sins to commit," he whispered, "before I gain admission into hell."

"It's a narrow squeak you've had, Kit," Bernardo said. "The ball creased your skull, cracking the bone a little, I think. Anyhow, you're mending now."

Kit's hand stole upward and touched the great wad of bandages swathing his head. "The ball?" he echoed. "Yes! She shot me. Where is she, Bernardo? She is not harmed? You did not permit the crew . . ."

"Youth," Bernardo sighed, shaking his head. "Oh, to be twenty-one again! . . . The wench comes within a hair of sending him into the next world and he inquires about her health!"

Kit struggled to sit up. "Answer me, Bernardo! She is not hurt?"

"That I do not know. The lady is—no longer with us."

"What!"

"She went over the side as we passed Cow Island. I saw her gain the shore. The red-haired one is a wonderfully expert swimmer."

Kit was sitting fully upright now, swaying in the hammock, supporting his head between his hands.

"But Cow Island, Bernardo!" he got out. "Every French freebooter in the Antilles holes up there!"

"Yes," Bernardo said grimly. "No doubt she received a warm welcome. Do not waste your sympathy on her, Kit. After all, it is not her fault that you are still alive."

29

Kit sat very still, staring at the bulkhead. "Nor hers that she used that pistol," he whispered. "She was so young, Bernardo—so young and so fair. And she had been foully abused."

"That I know. But there are other fish in the sea, Kit. Now that Lazarus is gone, there will be wenches aplenty to stroke those fair cheeks of yours. What a blessing that she aimed high! Your hair will cover the scar."

"I shall never get her out of my mind," Kit said.

"Never is a long time. In twenty years you will find how easily the faces of a dozen maids run together indistinguishably in the mind's flux. . . . But there are other matters more pressing than this of the lass."

"So?" Kit growled.

"The crew. This tongue of mine, whose oiliness you've seen fit to complain about in the past, alone has maintained your captaincy."

"My captaincy!" Kit said. "Mother of God! I'd forgotten that!"

"Time you remembered it," Bernardo said dryly. "I think you'd better put in your appearance on deck. Can you stand?"

He put out his arm and Kit grasped it. But when Kit's feet had reached the floor, the cabin oscillated dizzily before his eyes and Bernardo had to catch him to keep him from falling.

"Tomorrow, then," Bernardo said. "I'll bring you some hot broth. In the meantime, I'll keep these dogs off."

On the morrow, Kit woke with a head that ached only a little and eyes that were entirely clear. Long before Bernardo entered his cabin he was up, swaying lightly on his feet. Another bowl of the steaming broth, and yet another, sent the strength curling steadily through his limbs. Bernardo helped him dress, and together they went up to the quarter-deck.

Bernardo cupped his big hands and roared to the crew: "Attention! Line up, and hear Captain Gerado!"

The men shuffled into position, their faces blank and hostile.

"Look you, lads," Kit began steadily, "life aboard the *Seaflower* has not been a pleasant one. That I know well." The buccaneers growled assent. "We've piled up treasure only to have it stolen from us because the people of Basse-Terre believe us befouled with leprosy. That must be changed."

"Aye," the black-bearded ruffian growled, "but how?"

"We will heave to near the coast of Cuba," Kit told them, "and clean the ship. All of Lazarus's possession must be sent over the side, and sulphur burned in his cabin. Then the vessel will be swabbed from hold to crosstrees. After that you men will scrub your filthy hides, trim your hair and beards, and dress yourselves as honorable seamen. When this is done, we will put into Basse-Terre."

"*Sacrebleu!*" Dupré grunted. "What difference will it make? Still we ride the *Seaflower*—pest ship of the Antilles!"

"I will change that," Kit said evenly. "If I should fail in this, I will step down and allow you to choose another man as captain. But," he added, his voice dropping even lower, his words coming out slow and spare and deadly clear, "I will stand for no grumbling until the matter is put to the test. If I fail to fill your coffers with gold and make it possible for you to take what pleasure you will ashore, I will step aside. Till then, look alive and step nimbly! To your stations now!"

Watching the men keenly, Bernardo could see that the look of sullen hostility on their faces had lessened considerably. They went about their tasks with energy. All day the *Seaflower* tacked through the Windward Passage until she came to a sheltered cove and nosed into the quiet haven. Minutes after she had dropped anchor she was alive with activity, which ceased only after night had fallen. Her decks were swabbed until the oak planking gleamed dully. Fresh gilt was applied to her ornamentation, the black pitch paint was applied to her hull until it took on the look of newness. Kit ran her in so close to shore that by low tide she was almost entirely out of water, and the hammers rang against the chisels as the barnacles were pried loose from her hull. The stifling fumes of sulphur poured out of her ports, and all shot-torn and gale-rent sails were discarded for new canvas, and fresh, newly tarred hemp replaced the worn guy ropes, clew lines, and stays of her rigging. Three days later, the *Seaflower* was as trim a vessel as ever cleaved the sea of the Caribbees.

She put out to sea, heading across the passage between Cuba and Hispaniola. As the low hump of Tortuga came in sight, the crew lined up for Kit's inspection. They were dressed, every man of them, in nondescript finery taken from the holds of vessels they had scuttled. That the colors they had selected were ill-matched, so that they looked like a garish lot of tropical birds, made little difference; the men of the *Seaflower* were a brave sight. Kit passed along the line of the crew until he came to the black-bearded ruffian, Smithers, a fugitive from the gibbets of half the North American colonies and a veritable prince of scoundrels. Smithers was a young man towering by an inch over Kit's own six feet of height, but his face was so buried in the great dark swirls of his beard that it was almost impossible to determine how he looked.

Kit gazed at him, a mocking light dancing in his clear blue eyes.

"Scissors!" he barked. At once one of the ship's boys ran to fetch them. Kit took the gleaming shears in his hand and advanced upon Smithers. Something very like terror leaped in the buccaneer's eyes as Kit growled: "Time we saw what lies behind that vermin's nest. Hold him, men!"

The men flung themselves on Smithers with howls of delight. Kit's hand flashed, and black clouds of whiskers drifted to the deck. Kit did not cut them all off; instead he left the howling, swearing scoundrel a neatly pointed Vandyke, and an upswept flourish of mustachios. Then he stood back, surveying his handiwork. Shorn of his beard, Smithers was an extraordinarily handsome devil. Kit's hand went inside his coat and came out with a small silver mirror. He thrust it out before Smithers' face.

"Here," he said grinning, "see for yourself."

Abruptly Smithers stopped struggling. His mouth dropped open. He stared at himself in unconcealed awe.

"Mother of God," he whispered, "I'm right pretty!" The crew roared.

The rest of the voyage went on with uncommon smoothness. Smithers, who had been root and branch of much of the trouble aboard, stood more than half the time by the mizzen staring at his own image in a flat piece of brass he had polished into a mirror. Now and again he would pat a stray hair back into place in his black spike of beard; his mustachios were smartly waxed and both his hair and his Vandyke were oiled and drenched with perfume.

"Vanity," Kit remarked to Bernardo as they passed him on their rounds, "has its uses!"

When they came into the harbor of Basse-Terre, Kit did not, as Lazarus had done, anchor the *Seaflower* far out and apart from the other vessels. Instead, he slid her in among the other pirate craft, manned by men of a score of nations, that lay tied up in the bay of the city that lived on stolen goods.

Bernardo looked at Kit, who was dressed after a fashion that would have delighted a lord of the court of Versailles, then back to the city.

"To think," he said with a chuckle, "that as a boy I used to dream of digging up pirates' treasure!"

Kit's cool blue eyes lighted with amusement. "Before you knew Basse-Terre, eh? If there is any buried gold in the Antilles, it was by the hands of whores and rum-sellers that it was hidden. God knows they get it all!"

"Though not in the past from the *Seaflower*," Bernardo mused. "Yet if the daughters of joy do not this night receive their share of our spoils, another foot will tread the quarter-deck tomorrow."

Kit frowned, his eyes catching the pinpoints of fire from the dancing waves. "I do not care for the honor," he said quietly, "if there be any honor in captaining this crew of cutthroats. But there are two matters I must attend to."

"Two?" Bernardo growled. "Del Toro, and . . . ?"

"And she of the flaming hair and the ready trigger finger," Kit answered simply.

"I'll wager that your methods in these pressing matters will vary widely," said Bernardo.

"I'll not deny that," Kit said. "But come, we'd best be putting ashore. It seems that the citizenry of Basse-Terre are preparing their usual hearty welcome."

At Kit's command, a plank was run out from the *Seaflower* to the wharf. He and Bernardo marched down it, followed by the heavily laden crew. As they filed down the wharf, Kit saw a manservant of one of the merchants busily engaged in drawing a line across the sand of the beach.

33

Kit moved toward him slowly, his eyes light-filled and dancing. As he came closer, the women in the crowd, who had set up their usual screeching at the sight of the *Seaflower*'s crew, fell silent suddenly. Those of them who had started to run away, looking back over their shoulders all the time, slowed to a walk, then to a full halt. Kit walked on with grave deliberation toward the man who was busily drawing his line in the sand. The sunlight broke through the crests of the wine palms and fell full on his great curly mane. Beneath the broad brim of his maroon felt hat and the proud silver of the ostrich plume it gleamed like gold in the morning light. Kit's slim hands, ablaze with great diamonds, rested carelessly on the silver hilt of his Spanish sword, and his mustache and spike beard were white-gold.

He reached the manservant amid a silence that could almost be felt, broken only by the faint echo of the surf offshore. He paused a moment, looking at the man's broad back, before he dealt him a kick that sent him face forward into the soft sand with such force that his chin plowed up a furrow.

The silence exploded into laughter, and high above the hoarse masculine guffaws rang the clear soprano peals of the women. The manservant got up, bellowing. Kit put the tip of his beribboned cane against the man's chest and held him off despite his enraged struggles.

"I do not fight with lackeys," he said. "Tell your master there will be no more lines—ever."

The manservant lunged forward, still bellowing. Kit jerked the point of the cane away so suddenly that the man almost fell. Then the stick whistled through the air, biting into the servant's back and shoulders. For a long moment the heavy-muscled fellow took the savage beating, then he turned and fled howling up the beach.

Kit pirouetted on one high red-leather heel and faced the merchants. Their countenances were beet-red, their fat jowls quivering.

"From this day forth," Kit told them blandly, "you will deal with the *Seaflower* as with any other vessel that puts into Basse-Terre. No lines, fair exchange for our goods. Do I make myself clear?"

34

A low, rumbling mutter started among the merchants and ran from man to man. Kit caught the words "Lazarus" and "leprosy." He threw back his head so that the heavy mass of golden curls shifted about his shoulders.

"Lazarus is dead," he said flatly, "and buried at sea these many months. His gear has been heaved over the side, and the vessel fumigated. There is no leprosy among us."

The merchants broke into small groups. Kit could hear their voices rise in debate.

"One moment, gentlemen," he said, his voice bland and patient. "I fear that you mistake me still. We do not come as supplicants, bending a knee for your favor. It is our intention to be dealt with fairly and honestly, as all other seamen are. No lines, fair trading—and the freedom of the town. This bickering is bootless. Here are our goods. Come, make your offers!"

One of the merchants stepped forward, his cheeks purple. "And if we refuse?" he growled.

Kit shrugged his shoulders, an eloquently Gallic gesture, and turned back to his crew. "The gentleman speaks of refusing!" he said, his voice light and filled with mockery.

In two strides Smithers and Dupré were flanking the merchant, long knives gleaming in their hands.

"Shall we open his fat belly, sir?" Smithers inquired gravely. "Or just cut his throat?"

"Nay, lads, I think an ear will do for a starter," Kit said, shaking his fair head.

Instantly Smithers' knife rested on top of the merchant's ear. The man squealed like a stuck pig.

"Captain!" he wept. "Good Captain, have mercy!"

"Mercy?" Kit drawled. "A strange word, isn't it?"

Smithers' knife pressed down gently, and a tiny trickle of red stole down the merchant's fat face.

"I agree!" the merchant shrieked. "We agree. Gentlemen, tell him! Speak, for the love of God!"

The others broke out in a confused babble of assent, their faces pale as death.

35

"That's better," Kit growled. "Leave him his ear, Smithers. He will need it."

Timidly the merchants stepped forward and appraised the goods the *Seaflower* had brought. Then, with trembling voices, they offered higher prices than the *Seaflower*'s crew had ever heard from them. The men bent forward eagerly, ready to pass over the silks, leathers, perfumes, laces, and mounds of plate and bullion. But Kit stopped them with a curt gesture.

"No," he said. "It is too little. Make me another bid."

The merchants fell back, shrieking louder than they had for fear of their brother's ear.

"That's the way, Kit," Bernardo whispered exultingly. "Stick 'em where it hurts—in their miserly purses!"

Kit drove the price upward three times more before he consented to the sale. And he took his own share in golden crowns and louis d'ors. Bernardo did likewise. But the crew, with no thought beyond the present, were content with rum, a handful of écus, sols, piasters, and pieces of eight—and assignations with the women of the town.

By nightfall, Basse-Terre was loud with revelry. After years of semi-imprisonment aboard the *Seaflower*, her crew found their new freedom sweet. But Kit walked alone on the moon-silvered beach and watched the indigo water break white over the rocks. It was there that Bernardo found him.

"Kit," he said, "it is bad to absent yourself like this. The crew are asking for you. They cheer your name to the echo."

"So?" Kit growled.

"Join them in a glass, Kit. They will think all the better of you for it. And you will have need of the goodwill of your crew."

"Yes," and he sighed, "that I will. Very well, Bernardo." He glanced down at the canvas sack Bernardo carried. "What have you there?" he asked.

"Medicines," Bernardo answered, grinning. "I have here lignum sanctum, called by some guaiacum. It's said to be a specific against the French sickness. Also China root, the tuber of smilax, like our sarsaparilla, which is supposed to cleanse the blood of the great pox. When the lads have finished their pursuit of Venus, we shall have need of both."

36

"Are all the women diseased?" Kit demanded.

"No, not all. But how is a man to tell?"

"I do not care," Kit said morosely, "since there are none among them with hair like fire and eyes like an emerald sea."

"So!" Bernardo laughed. "The wind still blows to that quarter, eh? Come with me and we shall see how long this moonsickness of yours can withstand the hot caress of reality."

"Always!" Kit growled.

"Always is a long time," Bernardo said. "Come!"

They marched along the streets of Basse-Terre until they came to the largest of the taverns. Through the doorway there sounded the bellow of sea chanteys, the boom of deep male laughter, and the high breathless titter of female voices. Bernardo stood back while Kit put his head inside. Instantly there went up a great bull-like roar of welcome.

Still Kit hesitated. But not for long. While he stood there, a group of young girls, ranging in years from sixteen to not above twenty, hurled themselves on him. They tangled their slim fingers in his golden hair, they caught at his arms, dragging him into the tavern. Grinning, Bernardo entered the tavern in his turn and closed the door behind him.

Early in the morning, when the sun broke through the row of prickle palms that fringed the eastern border of Basse-Terre, Kit sought out Bernardo. This in itself proved to be more difficult than he had anticipated. Kit found it necessary to search through more than a dozen houses and all the rooms above the taverns before he found his second in command.

When at last a wizened, toothless harpy had cackled a "Yes, of a certainty, he is here, M'sieur le Capitaine!" and indicated a rickety stairway leading to the loft of her palm-thatched house, Kit hesitated a moment before mounting the stairs. Then he started up them.

He poked his head up through a trapdoor and looked around. Almost at once he saw Bernardo. There, on a pile of hay, his friend slumbered, his peaceful snores rising from his half-opened mouth. Kit stood very still, his blue eyes widening, for in the crooks of Bernardo's great arms nestled two of the youngest and fairest daughters of Basse-Terre.

Kit's firm mouth spread into a slow grin under his golden mustache. Noiselessly he tiptoed across the rush-strewn floor until he stood over the sleeping trio. Then he brought the open palm of his hand down across the ivory curve of two fair bottoms so smartly that it made a sound like two small pistol shots. The girls leaped to their feet, shrieking. Then, seeing Kit, they contorted their supple young bodies into ludicrous positions, in a futile effort to cover the most salient points of their nakedness.

Bernardo cocked open one weary eye. He looked at Kit and closed it again, groaning.

"Up with you, shameless one!" Kit roared in mock wrath.

Again Bernardo opened an eye. Then a slow, wicked grin stole across his dark face. Wearily he lifted a hand and pointed to the place where the reddening imprint of Kit's palm and five wide-spread fingers showed on a girl's fair skin.

"It was bad enough to wake me that way," he said, "but did you also have to brand them?"

"Get up, Bernardo!" Kit was grinning. "Time we were off. Otherwise that hooked beak of yours will be imprinted on the countenances of half the next generation of Tortuga."

Bernardo considered this remark gravely. "They could do worse," he said, chuckling. "What of that jutting Hapsburg chin of yours? I suppose you spent the night in prayerful meditation?"

Kit's face reddened under its tan. "'The sheep's business is none of the goat's concern,'" he quoted. Bernardo sat up, pillowing his head in his hands.

"Off with you, lasses," he growled. "The Captain and I have matters to discuss."

The two girls ran squealing down the ladder. Bernardo turned his head cautiously on the column of his neck.

"It's not unhinged," he muttered. "I would have sworn . . ."

"Enough of that nonsense," Kit growled. "Come, get dressed. I need you."

Bernardo's great hand groped for his pantaloons. He found them, and stood up. Then, poised on one leg like a gigantic crane, he eyed Kit speculatively.

38

"The last I saw of you," he began, "you were the subject of a tug of war between the tall brunette and that plump, rosy Bretonne. Tell me, which of them won?"

"Enough!" Kit roared. "We have work to do. We must round up the crew. I want to make Cow Island tomorrow. If we wait too long . . ."

"Damn that red-haired witch!" Bernardo said. "She's not half so fair as some of the maids here in Basse-Terre. I tell you, Kit . . ."

"Get up!" Kit blazed.

"Look you, lad," he said quietly as he drew on his doublet, "the crew will be ill-disposed to leave Tortuga so soon. It has been years since any of them has tasted of the fleshpots. The course of wisdom is to let them enjoy the fruits of victory under your command for some time before setting a course that might cause mutiny."

Kit's fair brows crowded together over the bridge of his nose. "You're right about that," he mused. "Still, there are coasting hoys that ply between the ports of Saint-Domingue daily. Come, Bernardo."

"Mother of God!" Bernardo groaned. "Such impatience! I will not stir a step until I have coffee to clear my head of last night's fumes. If the red-haired one made either Cow Island or Aux Cayes, she is beyond the need of haste. Still less if she didn't make them."

"You said she gained the shore," Kit growled.

"Did I? Perhaps I did. It's not important. By now she is dead of either abuse or drowning. What does it matter now?"

Kit's hand moved out and caught the front of Bernardo's leather jerkin. "If you don't hurry," he said, "nothing in this life will matter to you."

Quietly Bernardo freed himself of Kit's grasp and sat down to draw on his jackboots, cursing all the while in a sibilant mixture of French, Spanish, and English. A moment later he stood up.

"I'm ready," he said. "Let's get this over. For till they lay the wench's bones before you in proof, there will be no living with you. Come."

39

They made the wharves in a few minutes, and woke a fat Frenchman who slumbered beneath the single mast of a round-bellied boat hollowed out of a cypress log. A moment's conversation and the musical clink of gold pieces were enough to rouse him into astonishing activity. He kicked the Negro slave who slept under the long arm of the tiller, and started clumsily to unfurl the single sail. Kit aided him, and five minutes later the fat-hulled hoy was butting its way out of the harbor of Basse-Terre toward the southern part of Haiti, and Aux Cayes.

Kit stood in the bow, gazing at the shore line of Aux Cayes that grew more distinct with a slowness that was pure torture. Before the hoy had pushed its prow into the sand, he was over the side, wading through the surf. Bernardo followed him from a distance, seeing him racing up the beach toward a group of French freebooters who lay in languid conversation under the shadow of the palms.

They looked up at Kit in some astonishment. It was some moments before the tangled jumble of his words became clear. Then broad grins split their leather countenances.

"The little red one?" one of them said. "But certainly! She came ashore over there—on the Isle des Vaches. We've heard she stabbed five men before she was subdued."

"Subdued? Pah!" one of his companions spat. "That red-haired sea witch was never subdued! She came wading through the surf naked as a newborn, with a knife in her teeth, and . . ."

"Damn your eyes to deep-blue hell!" a third put in. "These creatures of a most incredible imbecility have not yet the right of it, Monsieur le Capitaine! The little Rouge came ashore, and those stupid beasts on Cow Island . . ."

Kit looked from one to another of them. "Do any of you really know what happened?" he demanded. "Were you there?"

"That, no," the filibusters said reluctantly, "but we have the intelligence straight from . . ."

"Damn their intelligence," Bernardo growled. He had come up during the Gallic uproar and had heard most of the dispute. "Let's cross over to Cow Island and get the truth."

"Aye," Kit growled. They retraced their steps to the hoy and silenced the protest of the weary captain with another louis d'or. An hour later they hove to in a sheltered cove off Cow Island. Then they inched their way quietly ashore between the throngs of French vessels that always tied up there.

Kit's queries made him at once the center of a voluble crowd. Of the many who attempted to tell the tale, there were three who spoke with authority.

"But yes," an old Gascon said, "we were there. This child with the red hair swam ashore on the seaward side where a corvette lay at anchor. She hadn't a stitch on her back and her skin was like the milk of eyes, like pearl, like . . ."

"That I know," Kit growled. "Go on."

"She was exhausted, the poor little one. But for the blind stupidity of those insane ones, she would have had no time to rest. Instead of lining up and taking their turn like men of discretion, they began to fight over her. Seven men were killed in the fight. I do believe that this little Rouge enjoyed it. When at last most of them were wounded, she got hold of two pistols that had fallen to the sand and pointed them at the men. She forced a little Parisian to remove his doublet and trousers and dressed herself in them. This done, she made them bring her water and food."

"They did not rush her?" Bernardo demanded. "All of them together could have . . ."

"They were too bemused by her beauty—and her courage. No, the knaves swore on the nonexistent honor of the strolling street wenches who bore them that they would not molest her further, and asked her to choose a husband from among them."

"And did she?" Kit growled.

"No. She laughed at them. The next night, since the captain of the corvette had fallen in the battle over her, the crew of that vessel set about electing a new leader. In the midst of the dispute, the little Rouge strode among them and declared that since she had more wit and courage than any twenty of them, she would be their captain, and that the election was at an end."

"Mother of God!" Kit breathed.

"All seamen," Bernardo declared, "fear the presence of a woman aboard ship worse than the plague."

41

"But yes," the old Gascon agreed. "Still, they looked at the milky curves of her legs under those tattered trousers, and her young breasts pushing their way half out of her shirt, and decided perhaps that once at sea . . ."

"Where is she now?" Kit demanded.

The old Gascon swept his arm out over the great blue curve of the ocean. "Out there," he said. "And I will wager my life, what there is left of it, Monsieur le Capitaine, that wherever she is, she commands that vessel still."

"Why do you believe that?" Kit said quietly.

"Because in her there is a hatred that is absolutely bottomless, a cruelty that burns bright as the flame of her hair. She has declared war on the whole race of men. That war she cannot win. But many a brave matelot will die in his blood before they swing her from a yardarm."

"That," Kit said slowly, "they will never do. Not while I have life. Come, Bernardo."

"What now?" Bernardo said as they tramped through the sand toward the waiting hoy.

"Back to Basse-Terre. Back to the *Seaflower*. Then, Bernardo, we will comb the sea of the Caribbees. Till I find her again, this little Rouge, there will be no rest for me, nor any joy in my heart."

"*Diablo!*" Bernardo muttered under his breath. "Would God they had cut her throat!"

Kit glanced at him over his shoulder. "What did you say, Bernardo?" he asked quietly.

"Nothing," Bernardo growled. "I need my feeble breath. Let us be off."

But Kit was already gone, running hard toward the place where the hoy danced in the freshening surf.

3

DURING ALL THE TIME that Lazarus had commanded her, the *Seaflower* had been forced to sail shorthanded, but now at last Kit found it possible to take his pick of seamen to man her. Of these, the greater part were Frenchmen from the provinces of Brittany, Normandy, and Gascony; but the remainder included Welsh, Irish, Scots, and Englishmen who had fled to the French Antilles to escape punishment for crimes committed in their homelands. There were boys, too, who shipped as powder monkeys and cabin boys, and one or two runaway Negro slaves. Kit had appointed Bernardo his master's mate, and the two of them stood by while Smithers and Dupré read the sailing articles, the former in English, and the latter in French.

"Each man to bring his own powder and shot," Smithers bellowed, and Dupré repeated the announcement in French. "No prey, no pay!"

The circle of men nodded grimly. They were quite accustomed to such arrangements.

"Our good captain, Christopher Gerado, receives one thousand écus in pay. Our master's mate, seven hundred. Our second mate—myself, lads—five hundred. The carpenter and shipwright, three hundred. The surgeon, two hundred and fifty, including medicines. All others one hundred, except the boys, who get fifty. Recompense to the wounded is as follows: Six hundred écus or six slaves for the loss of a limb; three hundred écus or three slaves for loss of a thumb, an index finger of the right hand, or an eye."

"But matey," a Welshman protested, "I be left-handed!"

"Them as favors the use of the left gets the same as others

do for the right," Smithers ruled at once. "One hundred écus for the loss of any other finger. Each man to select a partner or matelot to fight at his side, to nurse him when hurt or sick, and to inherit all his goods if he be killed and has no woman." Smithers paused for breath.

"Now for divvying up the loot," he continued. "After the pay and the recompense to the wounded is taken out, we share in this fashion: Six portions to the cap'n. Two to the master's mate. One and three-quarters to the second mate; one and one-half to the shipwright; one and one-quarter to the surgeon. All others one share, except the boys, who get one half-share. Fair enough?"

"Fair enough," the throng of grimy men agreed.

"Then aboard with you!" Smithers bellowed. "Look alive and pull right hearty!"

Kit watched them as they came aboard, then turned to Smithers. "You may up-anchor now, Mr. Smithers," he said quietly. The courtesy was deliberate. Lazarus had taken care to instill into Kit all the niceties of seamanship, even to the courtesies usual among officers of Their Majesties' Royal Navy. That this formal turn of speech was somewhat out of place aboard a freebooter apparently never had entered the old leper captain's head. As for Kit, he followed what he had been taught without question.

The winch clanked and the thick coils of tarred hemp tightened. Slowly the ring of heavy, hand-hammered wrought iron broke water. At Kit's side, Bernardo Díaz cleared his throat.

"What is it, Bernardo?" Kit asked.

"This—quest of yours for Rouge," Bernardo said in a tone inaudible to Smithers, who stood not two yards away. "You do not intend to tell the men?"

Kit's firm mouth widened into a slow smile beneath the white-gold mustache. "No, I do not," he said. "Always long of head aren't you, Bernardo?"

"I've reached nigh on to forty winters by taking thought," Bernardo said dryly. "See that you do as well. You have a responsibility to the men, Kit. You cannot sacrifice them to your desire to take vengeance on Del Toro or your quest for Rouge. Unless they find enough loot to make the voyage worth while. . . ."

44

"They'll mutiny," Kit finished for him. "That I know right well. But consider this, Bernardo: If Rouge is herself seeking treasure, will she not ply the same sea lanes frequented by the Spanish plate ships? Can't we kill two birds with one stone?"

"Yes—if you don't consider it a waste of time to board a Spanish vessel instead of continuing your search!"

Kit gazed upward where the men were swarming amid the rigging, bending the *Seaflower*'s broad sails to the wind. When he turned back to Bernardo, his eyes were smiling.

"When I die," he said, "it will be in the great bed of a manor, soft with linen sheets. I have no desire to be hanged, Bernardo. Besides, such limbs as hers should be caressed by silks. What vessels cross our paths, we take. Rest quietly on that score."

"Good!" Bernardo grunted, and cocked his weather eye aloft. "We'll make good speed," he added. "The wind is almost dead astern."

The *Seaflower* slid quietly out of the harbor of Basse-Terre and headed westward, along the long arm of the upper peninsula. Bernardo looked down at her knife-sharp prow. Already it was breasted with foam.

"The wind will hold," he observed. It was the season for the trade winds. They could cross the entire Caribbean with a wind that varied no more than three points off dead astern. On the other hand, the Spanish vessels coming from Mexico and Peru would have to tack into the wind. The advantage in speed would be all in their own favor.

As he retired to his scrubbed and polished cabin, Kit had the feeling that luck was with them. The *Seaflower* seemed a thing alive, rolling gently with the rising swells, and running before the winds like a great white-winged bird. True, most of the Spanish vessels would lie at anchor in the roadbeds of the Mexican and Peruvian harbors, waiting for the winds to shift. But some of them would start to inch homeward toward Spain. The insatiable maws of the homeland would brook no waiting. Spain was too near disaster to wait long for the treasure that she was tearing from her colonies.

The *Seaflower*'s luck held, and in four months she had captured and sunk seven Spanish vessels. The booty was excessive,

45

the Spanish ships having been loaded with the treasure that was now so urgently needed in Spain. Kit was firmly entrenched with the crew, for in addition to their rich spoils, the losses aboard the *Seaflower* had been light. But during all this time there had been no sign of Rouge or of a ship sailing under the banner of the Black Heron.

Late one day they espied a dainty caravel, convoyed by a fleet of four Spanish ships of the line. The *Seaflower*, with her tremendous advantage of speed, bided her time during the late afternoon and early evening, then under cover of night swooped in among the cumbersome ships of the line and cut the caravel out of the miniature armada. When Kit and his men boarded her it was early morning, and she was already listing dangerously. By the time the *Seaflower's* crew had combed her for booty and taken the captives aboard, she was heeling for her last plunge into the deep, night-black waters of the Caribbean.

Among the captives were two women, whom Bernardo half led, half dragged before Kit, who was standing at the rail.

Kit turned to the women. The elder, a lean and formidable matron of some fifty winters, spread her arms as though to shield her charge from his impious glance. Kit put out an arm and set the duenna gently aside. He stood there a long moment, staring at the younger, a mere slip of a girl no more than eighteen or nineteen.

Bernardo Díaz watched his face keenly. Now, the Jew exulted, now the red-haired witch will be forgotten. If blood flows in his veins, he will forget her for this one! . . .

Kit's blue eyes, cool and grave, studied the girl before him. She was as slender as a willow sapling and as graceful. Her hair hung loose about her shoulders, as black as a vulture's wing against the spring snow of her face. Under her slim brows her eyes smoldered blacker even than her hair, and firelit in their depths. Kit watched the corners of her mouth, blood-rose red, tender-soft. Her lips were moving, shaping words, but it was long before their sense came over to him.

"I have no English, Señor Captain," she whispered. "But if you do not know Spanish, I will try French, although poorly."

46

Kit's mouth spread into a smile under the white-gold mustache. "Your Spanish will serve, señorita," he said in flawless Castilian. "Go on."

The girl drew herself up proudly. "I would like to know the meaning of this!" she said. "What manner of man are you, to wage war upon women? Why did you sink our ship?"

Kit took a step toward her, looking down on her small face from his great height. "I ask the questions here," he said quietly. "What is your name?"

"And if I do not choose to answer?"

"The señorita will not be so unwise. I should regret having to employ harsh measures."

The girl's black eyes flashed somber fire. "You would not dare!" she spat.

"Would I not?" Kit asked softly. Then, turning to Bernardo, he said, "Bring me the whip!"

Bernardo hesitated, searching Kit's face. But the blue eyes were impassive. Shrugging, Bernardo went forward, and returned after a moment with the weighted lash. Kit slipped the loop over his wrist and played the nine-foot lash out along the deck. The girl hung there, her face ghost-white, staring at it in breathless fascination.

"Your name, señorita?" he said quietly.

Mutely the girl shook her head. Kit drew his hand far back, and held it there; but it was the duenna who broke.

"It is Valdiva!" she screeched. "Do not strike her, you murderer! You'll pay for this, just you wait! The house of Del Valdiva is mighty."

"And so is your tongue," Kit said wearily, and brought down the whip so that its loaded tip cut through three of the duenna's many petticoats. The duenna leaped skyward, shrieking.

"Tie her up," Kit commanded. "And gag her. I'm tired of her noise." He turned back to the girl. Putting out his hand, he lifted her chin and gazed into her small oval face.

"No," he said, shaking his head, "I'll not whip you. Your skin is much too lovely to be striped." The girl jerked her head away angrily. "What is your name?" Kit asked again. "The rest of it, I mean?"

The girl stared up into his face, seeing it pale bronze, the mustache and Vandyke white-gold, the hair gold too, like a great mane about his shoulders, and the plume white above the maroon of his broad-brimmed hat.

"It is Bianca," she whispered.

"Bianca," he muttered, "the fair one—it fits."

Bianca del Valdiva stood looking up at him, her black eyes endlessly dark, searching his lean face.

"Señor Captain," she said, "I am innocent. If you plan to be dishonorable toward me, I ask that you take my life instead."

Kit looked at her and slowly, deliberately, began to laugh. "Dishonor you?" he chuckled. "Señorita, you flatter yourself."

The girl stiffened as though she had been struck, her warm mouth tightening into a thin line.

"Then set me ashore," she snapped. "I am betrothed to a good and generous man, who will reward you for your kindness. By your speech you are from Spain, though your hair and eyes belie it. Surely you must have heard the name of Don Luis del Toro."

Kit stared at her. Then, slowly, his head came back and laughter crashed from his throat. It was a hard, bitter sound, entirely without mirth. Hearing it, the girl drew back in terror. Her eyes widened.

"You—you know him?" she stammered.

"Know him?" Kit echoed. "His stars and mine have been entangled since my youth—so much so that I cannot pluck a mermaid from the bosom of the sea upon whose hand he has not set his seal. But I have sampled that grandee's vaunted kindness many times in the past. God save you from such a marriage!"

Bianca's hands flew up like two white birds and covered her ears. Kit stood there a long time, studying her face before he turned away.

"Very well, señorita," he said, "have it your own way." Then to Bernardo, "Take her to my quarters until I decide what to do with her."

The duenna struggled furiously at her bonds, her lean face livid above the gag that stopped her mouth. The girl looked at him imploringly, her own small face white with terror.

48

"She may have her woman with her," Kit added. Then he turned on his heel and strode aft.

Bianca del Valdiva stood there staring after him, her black brows knit and puzzled. Then as the old shrew joined her Bernardo heard her whisper: "Why does he hate Don Luis so?"

Bernardo took the women to their quarters and left them there. Then he sought Kit. He found him on the poop staring aft, his face grave and serene. Bernardo came up to him, his own dark face twisted with forebodings.

"Why, Kit," he demanded, "have you taken prisoners of no conceivable use to us—or of any value. More, they are an actual hindrance and a danger. Is it your intention to revenge yourself on Don Luis by molesting her?"

Kit turned to his friend, a slow smile lighting his eyes.

"Truly, my own duenna matches and exceeds hers. Still your long and worried tongue a bit and listen. Can't you understand what a stroke of luck this is? That girl in her own small and dainty person represents half the wealth of Cartagena."

"How so?" Bernardo growled. "You're devious, Kit. Explain."

"The girl is dear to Don Luis. Dear enough to bring a ransom of say a hundred thousand crowns. Did you note the emerald on her finger—those green stones for which the district about Cartagena is so justly famed? Were we to dispatch it to him with a note, might it not occasion some concern within his heart? Followed later by one of her small fingers to speed him?"

"That you would never do!" Bernardo spat.

"Of course not, you know me too well," Kit sighed. "I would not harm her. In some strange way she reminds me of the other, though God knows there is no similarity between them."

"Except that they are both beautiful," Bernardo said.

Kit looked up, his blue eyes questioning. "Is she?" he said. "I had not noticed it."

"Your masculinity!" Bernardo swore. "This one is as beautiful as the angel of dawn moving under the wing of night! Have you eyes? Or has that red-haired witch enchanted even them?"

"Yes," Kit said, "she has. And while she lives, I can see no other woman."

Bernardo frowned thoughtfully, peering out to sea. "This

49

ransom plan sounds good," he said. "But how would you manage it?"

"I would leave her under guard at Basse-Terre," Kit began.

"That would be noticed," Bernardo growled. "And no don would be foolhardy enough to put into Basse-Terre for any reason whatsoever. And neither could we enter the Boca Chica in order to deliver her ashore at Cartagena if Don Luis should pay us the ransom. Between the twin fortresses of San Luis and San José we'd be caught like rats in a trap. And the Boca Grande is too shallow to even think of putting in there."

"Therefore," Kit said, "we must select another cove into which Don Luis might come. What do you think of Cul-de-Sac?"

"Excellent! He could land in Cuba, then beat straight across the Windward Passage with little danger of being intercepted. Cul-de-Sac is of no importance. The French keep no garrison there."

"All of which Don Luis knows well. What troubles me is that if I give Don Luis a safe-conduct to retrieve his bride, upon what pretext can I then cut his evil throat?"

"He will give you excuse enough, once he arrives. But there are other considerations. Under whose guard would you leave the maid?"

"Yours, of course, Bernardo."

"No, Kit, I know my own desires. The maid is too fair—I have a weakness for such. And that ancient she goat, could I restrain myself even from her?"

"You refuse me, then?"

"I must."

"But there is nobody else. Look, Bernardo, these satyrs of mine would ravish the girl, and perhaps even the duenna, by the time we were out of sight of land."

"Then you must stay yourself."

"I?"

"Yes. I can put the *Seaflower* across the Caribbean and heave to off the Boca Grande channel while the message is dispatched by dinghy. Meanwhile, you can learn something of the ways of women—a lesson that you sorely need."

Kit looked at Bernardo, frowning. "But what about Rouge?" he growled.

Bernardo grinned. "I strongly suspect that by the time we return Rouge will be of scant concern to you. If I am wrong, there will be time and to spare to search for her. Meanwhile, we gain a fortune, and maybe your vengeance too."

"Yes," Kit sighed, "it is a pleasant thought."

At this moment Bianca put her head through the cabin door. A shaft of sunlight fell across her face, lighting her eyes. Above her snowy skin her hair was blue-midnight jet, startling in its contrast to her fairness. Bernardo leaned close to Kit's ear.

"It will not be too hard to stay, will it, Kit?" he whispered.

"No," Kit growled, "it will not."

So it was that the helmsman put the whipstaff of the *Seaflower* all the way over so that she came about in a wide circle, heading back toward Hispaniola. After that, the great boom of the fore-and-aft sail on the rear mast swung back and forth constantly as the trim vessel tacked into the teeth of the wind. Her progress was necessarily much slower than it had been before, but she still made good speed.

They slid by the towns of Léogane and Petit Goave in the night, seeing the lights dim-flaring and yellow beneath the palms. When they had rounded the point of the lower peninsula, the sea was quiet and the dreadful pitching that had kept both the girl and her duenna confined to the quarters that Kit—much to the astonishment of his crew—had vacated for them ceased. The waters that lay in that blue crescent between the upper and lower peninsulas were well sheltered from the trade winds. The *Seaflower* beat eastward through a sapphire sea broken only by the long iridescent swirls of sargasso weed, and now and again by the rainbow flash of a flying fish.

The women appeared again on the deck, followed by the eyes of the entire crew. Only Kit ignored them with an almost studied unconcern. Bianca's dark eyes strayed frequently toward his tall figure.

Standing there against the deep blue of the southern sky, with the great masses of tawny gold hair spilling down over his broad shoulders in leonine curls and the trim spike beard and pointed mustache gleaming white-gold in the sunlight, Kit was totally unaware of the confusion he was causing. Bianca's glances were no longer furtive; she was gazing at him openly now, a tiny frown marring the smooth expanse of her forehead.

Doña Elena, the duenna, leaned close. "Have a care, my girl!" she said. "You're making a spectacle of yourself!"

"Oh bother!" Bianca said. "I don't care a fig what these ruffians think."

"Nor what *he* thinks?" Doña Elena said, jerking her head in Kit's direction.

"Of course not!" Bianca snapped. "Why should I?"

"That I cannot tell. But it is strange that you made me spend two hours piling up your hair today. Don Luis is a great grandee, a man of parts and property, while this curled and beribboned jackanapes . . ."

"Hold your tongue!" Bianca ordered. "I dress as I please—and for my own amusement!"

"That may be," Doña Elena said gloomily. "All I know is that I left Spain with a pure and innocent maid in my charge, and I wonder what I shall deliver to Don Luis."

Bianca whirled, the tears sparkling in her black eyes. "You wicked old woman!" she cried. She might have said more, but Kit's step sounded lightly above the soft wash of the seas, and a moment later he stood before them.

He swept off his hat and made them a bow compounded equally of mockery and courtesy. "I trust that the ladies are enjoying their voyage," he said smoothly.

Bianca's black eyes widened in her pale face. "Enjoying?" she got out. "We are expected to enjoy a voyage to God knows where, with only heaven above knowing what fate awaits us?"

Kit's face was grave and unsmiling. "This is the second time you have mentioned the hideousness of your fate—perhaps not in quite the same words," he said slowly. "On that point I cannot reassure you, not knowing precisely what fate you consider hideous. But if you will permit me, señorita, I might state that you are completely safe from any fate that requires my active personal participation, as I am relatively fastidious in such matters."

52

Thereupon he bowed again and was gone, leaving the girl standing white-faced and close to tears.

The *Seaflower* moved quietly into the harbor of Cul-de-Sac. On the shore the palms had taken on a brownish hue, for it was long since it had rained. The waves ran slowly up the white beach between the long seaward-pointing fingers of the mountains, and all the brush was burned and reddish from the heat. The *Seaflower*'s sails flapped listlessly in a ghost of a breeze, and the midday sun stood just above the mast, fixed in a yellowish-white sky from which every trace of blue was gone, blasted out by the heat.

Bianca waited at the rail, gazing at the rows of tumble-down palm-thatched cabins that looked fitter for occupancy by swine than by human beings. She heard the groan of the winch and the splash as the anchor went over the bow into the water. Turning, she faced Kit, one hand nestling at the base of her throat.

"We—we go ashore—here?" she faltered.

"Yes, señorita," Kit said calmly, "here."

Kit assisted Bianca and Doña Elena into the dinghy, then took his own place. They were rowed in by the old left-handed Welshman who would serve them as servant. Kit had selected him because whatever the man's intentions, his advanced state of senility made their accomplishment impossible. Bianca sat in the bow of the small boat while the old scoundrel grunted and strained, winking his one good eye at her whenever she glanced his way.

The instant the prow of the dinghy had pushed its way into the slushy sand, the entire population of Cul-de-Sac turned out to greet them. This consisted for the most part of blacks, with a thin scattering of mulattoes and here and there a white man. The whites were usually old men, buccaneers who had quit the sea or criminals wanted in the larger towns of Hispaniola, come to this God-forsaken hole to die. They were, Kit surmised, no doubt responsible for the mulattoes; but there were more pressing matters to occupy his attention at the moment.

Addressing the populace in French, he made his wants known. In a few moments every able-bodied man was busy in the

53

erection of two new huts, on a site some distance down the beach from the rest of the town. When they were finished, Bianca noted that they smelled fresh and clean, which was more than could be said for the other huts of Cul-de-Sac. She noticed, too, that Kit and the Welshman had taken up quarters together in one hut. She and Doña Elena, then, were to be granted privacy, at least. She opened her lips to sigh with relief, but the sigh did not come. A little puzzled frown hovered above her eyes. She was safe. Apparently, this outlandish pirate captain meant merely to hold her for ransom—this outlandish young captain whose hair was spun gold, and whose eyes were sea water. Her person and her honor were both safe, but she was not relieved. More, she was rather piqued at his indifference; through her small, intensely feminine mind ran the ghost of a scheme to bring him to heel.

Then later on I shall spurn him, she thought. I shall turn aside from him and leave him in the dust like the fool he is. . . . She stopped short, her black eyes widening into a night beyond her ken. At the moment she saw Kit coming up the beach toward her, and as she ran into the hut, she was not sure whether it was from Kit she fled or from herself.

4

Bianca stood on the beach a little distance away from Kit and watched the *Seaflower* putting out to sea. God grant her a safe voyage, she prayed silently, and a speedy return—so that I may go home to the good man who is to be my husband before . . . But she stopped her mind before it reached the final thought, and went back into the little hut she was to share with Doña Elena.

Sleep, she soon found, was an utter impossibility. Not only was there little abatement of the heat, but the very air sang with swarms of mosquitoes. Her eyelids were soon swollen shut, her lips, her nostrils—every exposed portion of her body was a stinging torment of itching, burning welts. Across from her in the darkness, she could hear Doña Elena groaning in her sleep, but the older woman's age-toughened skin fared better than her own.

She sat up on the edge of her hammock, great tears running down her red and swollen cheeks, her ears ringing with the sound and the impact of her own slaps. Her hands were bloody with the crushed corpses of half a hundred mosquitoes, but among the multitude of their fellows their demises went unnoticed. So busy was she that the man was entirely inside the hut before she noticed him.

She stood up with the long swirls of the gown which Kit had presented to her, along with a complete wardrobe—snatched, no doubt, from some poor unfortunate's back—sweeping behind her. There was time for the long rasping intake of breath before the rough hands seized her, then she threw back her head and screamed.

As the man bore her out on the beach, she heard the swift thud of running feet behind her. Then the heavy bark of a pistol sounded and the ball whined overhead. At once the man dropped her unceremoniously to the sand and sped away in the darkness. Kit strode past her, and took aim again.

She got to her feet and stumbled after him. When she reached his side, she said, "You—you would kill him!" Her voice was rich, and freighted with horror.

"Of course," Kit said calmly. "What would you have had me do—kiss him?"

"I know, but to try to shoot him like a dog . . ."

"When men behave like dogs, they should expect a dog's fate," Kit said. "But a thousand pardons, señorita. When another such—suitor comes, I shall not interfere with your—pleasures. Adiós."

He bowed then, and started back up the beach toward his hut. Bianca gazed after him, rage and fear contending for mastery within her. Finally fear won.

"Kit!" she cried. "Kit!"

He halted at once. She came running up to him, her young face pale silver in the moonlight under the blue-jet cascade of her hair.

"I—I'm afraid!" she confessed. "He—he tried to . . . Oh, Kit, it was awful, and there might be others."

Kit took her arm. "I shall not sleep," he said gently. . . . "But, Mother of God, what happened to your face?"

"The mosquitoes," Bianca said. "They're eating me alive."

"I might be able to help you. Wait a bit."

He disappeared into the doorway of his hut, and reappeared almost at once with a round earthen pot called an olla. In his hand was a thick pile of dried leaves.

He crossed to her hut and entered, paying no attention to the hysterical sobs of Doña Elena, who thought he was the would-be ravisher come back again. Kneeling on the floor, he packed the pot with the leaves and ignited them with flint and steel. At once a rich, fragrant smoke curled skyward.

"Tobacco leaves," Kit explained. "And here are more to replenish the olla when these are burned through. That should

56

keep the little beasts at bay." Then he bowed and went out. Bianca found the smell of the smoke pleasant; moreover, it was completely successful in driving the swarms of mosquitoes from the hut. So it was that, worn-out by terror and discomfort, she fell at last into a deep, dreamless sleep.

When she woke, the sun was driving a shaft of white heat directly into the window. She got up and dressed hurriedly. Then, followed by the groaning Doña Elena, she sought Kit. She found him surrounded by a council of the town fathers. She heard his voice ring out:

"Any other man who dares touch her will not get off so easily."

The men, Bianca saw to her vast astonishment, were nodding their heads in assent. She came up to Kit and took his arm, then dropped it abruptly, her face covered with blushes and confusion. Such a gesture, she realized, had been well enough last night under the cover of darkness and the stress of circumstances, but today, in the sunlight, before the eyes of half a hundred men . . . True, they did not know she was betrothed, and to another man. Strange how remote Don Luis had become; she was having difficulty in recalling his face.

Kit looked down at her, smiling. "I trust you slept well?" he inquired.

"Very—thanks to you." Her tone was much warmer than she had meant it to be, so she hastened to correct it. "Of course, if it were not for you I should have been neither in discomfort nor in danger."

"Alas," Kit sighed, "that's all too true. But it will be ended soon. Are you hungry? By now Jim should have our breakfast ready."

On an open fire before the huts, Jim was boiling palm cabbage in an olla. In another, plantains steamed, while on a flat rock thin cakes made of the sawdustlike flour of the cassava or manioc root were baking. Jim saw them coming, and a wide grin split his toothless countenance.

"Come and eat," he called. " 'Tain't much, but 'twill serve!"

Bianca sank down before the fire on the sand, and after a moment Doña Elena joined them. The older woman was much the worse for the heat, but Bianca noticed that it did not affect her appetite. Bianca tasted the strange fare gingerly at first, then, finding it surprisingly good, ate well. After they had finished, Jim brought them gourds of a pale liquor that tasted like beer. Bianca raised her eyes questioningly.

"*Veycou*," Kit explained. "They make it from fermented cassava meal. It aids digestion in this heat."

That might well be, Bianca thought, but after having downed half a gourd, she realized that it also aided the mind to giddiness and the heart to levity. For the life of her, she was unable to keep her lips from smiling as she gazed at Kit. This was a very sorry state of affairs. She forced the corners of her mouth down, but they persisted in crawling up again. Kit's frown deepened. Why in the name of heaven, Bianca thought desperately, can't I stop smiling?

It was at that moment that she felt something very like a white-hot needle entering her arm. She shrieked softly, and Kit bent over, his face filled with concern. With his thumb and forefinger he pulled out the little red insect that was burrowing into her skin.

"What—what is it?" Bianca quavered.

"*Bête rouge*," Kit growled. "It's a very serious matter. They lay their eggs under the skin and make ulcers. Jim, bring some fat."

Jim disappeared into the hut and returned with a gourd full of thick, vile-smelling hog fat.

"Smear it on your face and arms," Kit commanded. "It will keep them away during daylight and the mosquitoes at night."

Bianca sat there staring blankly at the evil-smelling mess.

"Do as I say," Kit growled. "I don't want you to get sick on my hands."

Timidly Bianca stretched forth a hand and took a handful of the grease. It was cool and soothing to the skin, despite its smell. Doña Elena did likewise, and afterward Jim and Kit.

So began the long days of waiting. This, the chief island of the Antilles, Bianca found, was far from the jeweled isle of romance that the tellers of tales have made of the green chain that dots the Caribbean Sea. In addition to the five thousand varieties of insects, all of which stung or bit, there were the

58

wild hogs that came rooting through the streets and which charged at the swish of her broad skirts; there were the wild dogs that howled all night, the hideous-voiced parrots and crows; there were the pigeons that made it unsafe to sit under the trees, and whose flesh was so tough and bitter that it was impossible to eat it. There were the horses and cows of the townsmen that poked their heads through the windows and frightened her half out of her wits; and there were the little chickens, the *pintadas,* which were always underfoot.

In the swamps the frogs boomed and the alligators bellowed. The great blue herons split the night open with their ugly asslike braying. Moreover, the white skin that all her life she had protected from the hot sun of her native Spain had here no protection from this much hotter sun. She burned bronze, blistered and peeled and burned all over again. Doña Elena kept to her hammock most of the time and this was an additional burden, for in her loneliness Bianca was forced more and more to seek Kit's company. His cool courtesy, his almost maddening indifference, were fast becoming a goad she could not resist.

If she could have bathed in the sea, it might have been better, but even this method of cooling body and nerves was denied her, because the great dorsal fins of the tiger sharks cut the water in plain sight of land. As she sat now in the partial shade of a wine palm, she could see Kit's blue eyes gazing at her, and her breath caught deep in her throat. I wonder what he's thinking, she mused. I'd give half a lifetime to know. . . .

Kit's thoughts at that moment were black and troubled. The *Seaflower* should be back by now, he thought. It must come back! She is so fair, this little one, so soft and so tender. And she is his—*his!* What concern is that of mine? There is still Rouge. Hold on to that. Never forget her, never. With her sea-green eyes that slant upward in the corners, her hair like hibiscus petals, and her skin like ewe's milk. No, never forget her who lay close to me when she thought me dying of her shot and wept out her despair; do not forget her for Bianca, who belongs to my enemy, who cannot be mine—for all her unstarred midnight wave of hair and her mouth, soft, tender, secret-smiling. . . . He got up abruptly and started down the beach.

Bianca stood up and took a step or two behind him, then her small shoulders sagged and she turned away. Behind her the jungle lay thick-tangled, cool and inviting. She started walking, slowly at first, then with gathering speed and deliberation, toward the matted brush. Inside, it was cool and dark, and a few yards from the now invisible beach a little stream ran placidly inland. I'll follow it, she decided. I can always find my way back. . . .

So thinking, she moved along the stream until she came to a place where it widened and deepened into a shaded pool beneath a bamboo thicket. The water was slow-moving, clear, and inviting, and the heat lay like a blanket about her head. Without thinking she kicked off her shoes—her stockings having long since fallen prey to the sand and rocks on the beach— and holding her skirts high, waded into the water.

Bianca could not swim. Such an accomplishment would have been unthinkable in a Spanish noblewoman. So she contented herself with wading back and forth in the cool green water, ·moving so smoothly and quietly that she did not disturb the giant bull alligator that lay like a gnarled log on the dark bottom. She might have kept up her wading indefinitely had she not moved farther out and inadvertently stepped into a hole. She splashed downward, the water coming up to her waist, drenching her garments.

"Holy Mother!" she cried. Then, as the coolness reached her skin, her temper vanished, and she laughed aloud. I'll take them off, she decided, and really bathe. She started shoreward, held back by the weight of her waterlogged clothing.

But the splashing and the laughter had disturbed the ancient cayman. Slowly he moved upward, his rusty snout sliding easily along the surface. Bianca neither saw nor heard him; she had reached the far end of the pool and put one slim white foot ashore when he reared, bellowing. The girl whirled and hung there a moment frozen as the great jaws, lined with hideous teeth, came open. Then she started to scramble up the bank, and as she gained it, her lips tore open and she screamed.

At the moment that the sound of her cry came to him, Kit was standing on the beach a few yards away, peering out to sea with profound relief in his heart, for there on the horizon was the white blob of the *Seaflower*'s sails. At the cry, he whirled and plunged into the brush. He saw Bianca floundering toward him amid the snarl of the underbrush, held back by the drenched weight of her clothing. She hurled herself upon him, and through all the layers of her clothes he could feel the pounding of her heart. He heard the crashing noise in the brush, and freed himself of her grasp. Then, as the great, clumsy beast came through, he fired one of his pistols, the shot going straight into the gaping mouth.

The alligator thrashed about in a frenzy, flattening the brush for yards around; then at last it lay still and hideous in death. Kit turned back to Bianca and saw that she was swaying, even her lips drained of color. Putting out his arms, he drew her to him.

She nestled against his chest, her shoulders shaking with sobbing. At long last, she quieted and raised her small oval face. Suddenly, without premeditation or conscious thought, he put down his head and kissed her. It was a gentle kiss, light and tender, entirely lacking in desire. She stood very still with her dark eyes closed, her mouth warm against his. Then very slowly she moved away from him, her eyes coming open, studying his face.

"Why did you do that?" she whispered.

"Why? Truly, I do not know, Bianca."

"Can't you say it, Kit?" she murmured. "Can't you say what I want most in all the world to hear?"

Slowly he shook his head. "Forgive me," he said at last. "That was much against my will. . . . Come, the *Seaflower* is in sight." He put out his hand and she took it, her face still averted, the tears rising like jewels over her lashes and spilling down her cheeks.

"Do not weep," Kit said. "It is all over now."

She whirled suddenly and faced him, turning her back toward where the white sails of the brigantine were growing on the horizon. She put up both her hands and let them rest lightly on his broad shoulders.

"I am betrothed," she said slowly, "to a good and honorable man. You should not have done that, Kit. You should not have kissed me. For now you force me to acknowledge what my heart has known all along: I love you and none other—now and forever and always, till the day I die!"

Kit looked down at her, bleak pain in his blue eyes. "You must not say that," he said. "You must not even think it."

"Why not?" Her eyes sought and held his gaze. "There is another," she breathed. There was no questioning in her tone. Her words were a statement, flat and controlled and dreadfully calm.

"There is Don Luis," Kit growled.

Bianca shook her small head slowly. "No, not Don Luis," she said. "What is she like, Kit, this woman? What manner of creature is she?"

Kit looked out past her to where the *Seaflower* danced on the horizon. "Like an angel," he said, "like a witch—I cannot decide. Her eyes are sea emeralds, her hair Greek fire. She kissed me once as I lay dying and brought me back to life. Her beauty is a wound in my heart that will bleed until I find her again."

Bianca gazed up at him, her eyes diamond-bright. "God speed you in your quest," she whispered. "I would not have you unhappy for all the world!" Then, rising on tiptoe, she kissed him, her mouth moving upon his, lingering, soft-parted, until his hands, gone beyond his will, tightened on her waist. Her face was twisted with pain, but she did not resist. At last, slowly, she swung back against his arm, so that he could see the streaks of her tears. He released her almost at once, and stood looking after her as she walked away, her head bent, her slim shoulders shaking. Then he turned back toward the *Seaflower*, feeling with a curious sense of finality that never again in life would he know either happiness or certainty or peace.

5

KIT STOOD on the beach of Cul-de-Sac with Bianca and Bernardo Díaz and watched the great ship *Garza* of Don Luis del Toro inching her way over the horizon.

"He's on schedule," Bernardo growled.

Kit said nothing. Instead he turned his head in a half-circle and gazed wonderingly at this sun-stricken, heat-killed land. It was the same, nothing had changed. And yet, magically, everything had changed. The long blue fingers of the mountains that ran down into the sea on both sides of the bay were an even paler, more pastel shade, until they seemed suspended in time and space like the sea haze that marked their base. Behind the tiny hamlet, the tangled fringe of marsh and jungle, which ran back for a few score yards until it too was halted by the omnipresent mountains of Haiti, seemed greener than he had remembered any jungle to be: a dreamscape out of neverland.

The *Garza* beat in across the Windward Passage with majestic deliberation. Of all the multicolored confusions about him, she was the only certainty. Kit glanced down at Bianca, seeing the girl's face pale and set, her mouth held in a hard line, her black eyes unwavering. Bianca looked up at him and put out her small hand.

"Good-by, Señor Cristóbal," she said brightly. "And many thanks for saving me from the ennui of a most tedious voyage. But for you I would have known nothing of piracy, mosquitoes, alligators, and other interesting matters."

Kit took her hand and held it. His lips broke into a slow smile. "Is this all you have to say to me?" he asked.

"Yes—what I would like to say, I dare not. It would only

pain you to listen to it, and shame me to say it. This way is better, isn't it? That we pretend that there was no yesterday. For when you find your Rouge I would not have you troubled by any fleeting memory, by one disloyal word."

"And Don Luis? What of him?"

"I do my duty," Bianca answered simply.

"I see," Kit said.

Bianca looked up at him, her night-dark eyes soft with tenderness.

"I think the world will someday learn great things of you," she whispered. "I think that you will become a prince—how else could you have been born so princely? And I shall make my final voyage to Cartagena of the Indies—out of your life, my Kit. And there I shall be a good and dutiful wife to a great grandee. I shall spend all my days forgetting you. And there will come an hour when I shall succeed in the attempt. Do you know when that will be, Kit?"

"No," Kit said. "When will it be, Bianca?"

"The day I die," she whispered.

Kit put out a sinewy arm and drew her to him. "You have bemused yourself with loneliness," he said. "I am not the man you think me. Remember what I am—a sea rover, brutal, poorly lettered, my soul besmirched into hell with the blood of the innocent, a murderer and a thief, unfit to touch your finger tips. Remember only those things, and forget the wretch who caused you so much pain."

Bianca straightened. "That, never!" she said fiercely.

Bernardo touched Kit's arm. "He's coming in now," he said. "Better get the girl and her woman up into the hills until this business is finished."

"Yes," Kit said. "Jim will take them there. I'll meet this murderous hidalgo face to face."

Bianca turned and joined Doña Elena, and the two of them followed the wizened little Welshman across the beach to where the thick brush nestled at the foot of the mountains. Kit looked after them for a moment, then turned back to where the *Garza*'s boat beat through the white wall of the surf toward the pale-gold sand.

He and his company, which consisted of Bernardo, Patricio, Smithers, and Dupré, walked down to the water's edge. Without hesitation Don Luis del Toro stepped out into the water, not troubling himself to remove either his black kidskin shoes or his fine silk stockings. He was clad altogether in black, after the fashion of the Spanish nobility, and Kit knew at once that here was an opponent to respect.

Don Luis del Toro, though not so tall as Kit, was well above middle height, a compactly built man whose body, even in repose, suggested enormous strength. Beneath the sleeves of his black-velvet doublet, his arms were as big as Bernardo's, and his shoulders were broader than Kit's own. His nose jutted boldly from his brown-granite face and his chin, whose deep cleft was hidden by an inky short beard, was heavy after the Hapsburg fashion. His eyes, brown, and deep-set under his heavy brows, rested quietly on Kit's face.

"Where is she?" he demanded in English.

"First let me see the color of your gold," Kit said in limpid Castilian.

Don Luis leaned forward, peering intently into Kit's face. "I have seen you before," he growled. "But where?"

"Many times," Kit told him, "over the barrel of a gun. In Cádiz, when you whipped my mother with your lash. In the harbor of Cádiz, after your people had taken her life. Off Port Royal, when you made pretended rescue an excuse for ravishment. And you shall see me again, when I am not bound by a safe-conduct to spare you. But enough of this. Where is the money?"

Don Luis nodded to one of the helmeted and cuirassed soldiers who attended him. The man stepped forward, grunting under the weight of an oak chest. When it had been opened, the dull gleam of the roughhewn pieces of eight gleamed dully in the sunlight. Kit picked up a few of the heavy coins, minted at Lima in Peru from a single heavy bar of gold, and all of them so roughly cut that there was not one of them that was truly octagonal, or bore all the letters of the inscription. He felt the sharp edge where the chisel of the mint worker had hacked the single coins away from their fellows, and hefted them for their weight. They were up to standard or even heavier, weighing as much as a hundred and eighteen grams rather than the hundred and thirteen specified by law.

"Fetch the girl," he said to Bernardo.

All this time Don Luis's gaze had never left his face. On the grandee's countenance was an expression less of anger than of regret—a look of baffled pride oddly commingled with admiration.

"You are as I should have expected you," he said, "knowing whence you sprang. But, Cristóbal, I did not order your mother's execution. Indeed, I pleaded for clemency. But the authorities of the town were overzealous. In this I crave your indulgence, and ask that I be not blamed."

"You lie in your teeth!" Kit spat.

Don Luis shrugged resignedly. "That the cub roars and has fangs I should have known," and he sighed, half to himself. Then his brown eyes lighted, for Bianca was coming down the beach, her face pale and colorless, her lips unsmiling.

Kit watched Don Luis sweep her into his great arms. This is nothing to me, he told himself; but a slow, deep feeling of sickness curled at the pit of his stomach. He noted with some satisfaction that Bianca turned her head slightly aside so that the grandee's kiss just missed her mouth.

"He has not harmed you?" Don Luis growled.

"And if I had?" Kit spat.

"You would die," Don Luis said simply. His tone was quite empty of emphasis or of any quality of threat. It was as though he were discussing the weather—a statement of fact so calmly, so confidently self-evident that Bianca's heart turned over within her.

"No, Luis," she said quickly, "he has not harmed me. Save for the abduction, he has been the soul of courtesy."

Don Luis studied Kit's face, as though to inscribe it on his memory. "You have your gold. Have we your leave to depart?"

"Yes," Kit said. "Depart and be damned!"

A slow smile played across Don Luis's dark face. "We shall see upon whose head the damnation will fall," he said quietly. "Come, Bianca." He turned, still holding the girl loosely in the

66

circle of his embrace. But at the last moment she whirled, freeing herself with one swift motion, and ran back to where Kit stood.

She swayed before him on tiptoe, the light in her dark eyes shifting behind the bright film of her tears.

"Good-by, Kit," she whispered. "God speed you, and guide you, and bring you every happiness." Then she was gone, running back toward where Don Luis waited, his face as black as a thundercloud.

Kit said no word. Instead he turned back to his company and said very softly: "To the *Seaflower*. There is work to be done."

The *Garza* was still big on the horizon when the winches of the *Seaflower* drew her anchor free of the blue water. The white sails unfurled beneath the yardarms, dropping downward until the light breeze bellied them out and the great fore-and-aft sail on the mainmast filled, the boom swung far over. Effortlessly, the sleek brigantine began to move out of the harbor of Cul-de-Sac, leaving it drifted in pale light-filled, rainbow-hued mists.

"You've done well," Bernardo said. "By this one coup you've gained us more than on all our last voyage."

Kit did not answer; he was peering at the *Garza*, drifting almost motionlessly on the sun-filled sea. Then he knitted his brows.

"Yes," he said softly, "but we have not yet brought home our treasure. Look, Bernardo."

Bernardo squinted against the light, following Kit's pointing finger with his gaze. "Fiends and whoresons!" he got out. "I knew that dog of a grandee was not to be trusted."

Kit looked out frowning toward the end of the harbor, where the twin lines of war vessels were converging, each of them coming from opposite directions, from behind the long blue fingers of the mountains. From one side four ships of the line came, from the other, three. Quietly he called Smithers to his side.

"Crack on all sail," he ordered. "Gunners to their stations. Stand by to repel boarders."

67

"If we could gain the open sea," Bernardo groaned, "we might have a chance. But bottled up here, we are doomed! Of what avail is the *Seaflower*'s speed in this deathtrap of a harbor?"

"If we can force them to break that line . . ." Kit mused.

"They are not fools," Bernardo snapped. "The trap was well baited and better sprung!"

Smithers came up on the forecastle and faced Kit. "Begging the Captain's pardon," he began, "I have an idee."

"Then speak, man!" Kit roared.

"Them dons draw twice and three times the water as us. Now if we was to put back into the harbor, they'd have to come in after us. Inside, they'd run aground as sure as all hell—leastwise enough of 'em to let us out."

Kit shook his head. "Ships of the line, Smithers," he said. "They mount basilisks and long culverins aplenty—with chaces of sixteen and twenty feet. They could stand out so far that only our one basilisk could hit them—and what good would an occasional hit with a fifteen-pound roundshot do us?"

"From that distance they couldn't throw heavier!" Smithers argued.

"Yes, but how many could they hurl to our one? Even fifteen-pound shot will smash the *Seaflower* to pieces if she's hit with one every ten seconds."

"Yet if we go out," Bernardo mused gloomily, "they'll lay on a broadside with sixty-four-pounders—full cannon, Kit. Four such shots as they throw can sink us. Suppose we were to lie low and wait for night. In the darkness, perhaps . . ."

"It's our only chance," Kit growled. "But pray God there is no moon!"

At Smithers' shouted order the helmsman came about on the whipstaff, and the *Seaflower* paralleled the line of Spanish vessels. Then she put all the way about and headed back into the harbor. As she neared the shallow water, every man aboard her held his breath. The helmsman put her about again, and she started a slow glide across the harbor, again parallel to the Spaniards, but in water so shallow that they could not follow her.

Now was the time for action, Kit knew. If the Spaniards

68

were seamen, they would kill the *Seaflower* in a matter of hours. All they needed to do was to close in until their immensely long and slim basilisks and long culverins were in range and they could pound her to pieces, entirely without risk to themselves. These long guns threw a very small shot, but they hurled it by such an immense weight of powder through such long barrels that they could outrange guns throwing shot of almost six times greater weight. The *Seaflower* had only one such gun aboard, mounted in her bow as a chase gun; but the seven Spaniards could muster among them more than fifty. If the Spaniards came in before night, the brigantine was doomed.

But to Kit's immense relief, they did not break their line. They continued to patrol the entrance to the harbor with majestic deliberation, crossing and recrossing the open mouth of the cuplike declivity between the Haitian hills.

Smithers ordered a ration of rum to give the men courage, but neither Kit nor Bernardo touched it. The day dragged on. The sun burned red as blood on the western horizon. Imperceptibly, it dropped to the water's edge, laying a track of orange and scarlet across which the Spanish ships crawled like black water spiders. The pastel-blue of the mountains became pale violet, then royal purple, then they lay night-black against the bloody blaze in the western sky. Kit could see the black-crowned silhouettes of the palms leaning over against the deepening blue of the night, then the sky darkened until they were drowned in night, blackness upon blackness, and the great stars rode the bosom of the sea.

He had turned to Smithers to relay an order when he heard Bernardo's groan. Above the reappearing edge of the mighty hills, the great pale-yellow disk of the moon was rising. It grew brighter. The palms stood up again, crowned in silver, the sky silvered into grayness, the water was like the vats of the Peruvian mints, a hard white blaze so bright that on the *Seaflower*'s decks one could have read the finest print without difficulty.

Kit looked around him, seeing the twin fingers of the mountains running darkly down into the sea, the black-trunked, black-silver-crowned palms bending seaward before the trade winds, the night soft and slumberous with spring, the breeze perfume-laden with all the flowers of Hispaniola, singing down across the bay toward where the dark outlines of the vessels of death passed and repassed in the moon-silvered night.

What a night on which to die, he thought. Turning to Smithers, he said quietly: "You may crack on all sail, Mr. Smithers."

Bernardo came up to Kit and put out his hand. "You're a fighter," he growled proudly. "I have seen many who bowed to odds—and died in the torture chambers and under the lash. There is no shame in death on the high seas when a man goes down with all guns blazing. I am proud to go that way, and with you."

Without a word, Kit took the great hand. Then he went into his cabin. A moment later he returned, bearing the *Seaflower's* pennant—a great golden hawk on a field of blue. He gave it to Bernardo.

"Bernardo," he said, "nail our colors to the mast, so that no man among us may strike them!"

The *Seaflower* stood out from the harbor with the wind quartering off her stern. And out there in the silver blaze of the moon track the Spanish vessels waited.

"Hold your fire," Kit commanded, "until we are too close to miss. We will take one at least of them with us this night."

Cannily, the helmsman held the brigantine in the lee shadow of the mountains, sailing her dangerously inshore, so that before the Spaniards saw her, she was among them. She slid into line so close to one of the great vessels that a stone could have been hurled by hand to the Spaniard's decks without great effort. Kit's hand came down, and all of the *Seaflower's* port guns spoke at once, making bass thunder, every shot going home.

Kit saw the Spaniard's masts crashing down, bringing with them a wild tangle of sailcloth and cording, and something like hope awoke in his heart. On the impact of the recoil the guns leaped back to the limits of the breeching rope.

"Point-blank range!" Kit roared, and the gunners lifted their hammers, knocking the elevating quoins from beneath the trucks of the guns. As the wedge-shaped pieces of hardwood fell

70

free, the muzzles of the guns dropped until they were pointing at the water line of the reeling Spaniard. The other vessels stood by, unable to fire their guns for fear of hitting the great ship, for the *Seaflower* lay so close to the ship of the line that such nicety of aim by the Spaniards was practically impossible.

Again Kit gave the signal to fire, and the broadside boomed out, shaking the ocean. Plainly, through the echoes after the fire, Kit could hear the crash of the Spaniard's timbers and the screams of her dying crew. Then, to his amazement, a glow of fire showed amidships of the Spanish vessel. Hungrily, it ran upward into the broken rigging; in three minutes the whole vessel was ablaze. This, Kit saw at once, was a stroke of ill luck, for what illumination the moon had so far failed to give was now provided by the blazing Spaniard. The *Seaflower* lay in the middle of the Spanish fleet, etched starkly against the dancing flames.

At once the Spaniards opened up with their great cannon, splitting the night asunder. Kit could see the yellow tongues of fire probing the dark for the range, then afterward sea and sky opened with the slow, rolling bellow, the echoes reverberating endlessly among the encircling hills. White geysers stood up like momentary columns all about the *Seaflower* while she fought back, giving them shell for shell. Such was the accuracy of her fire that in a few minutes not one of the Spanish vessels remained unhurt. But the Spaniards were getting the range now. A blinding explosion of fire, water, and oak splinters filled the air not ten yards from where Kit stood. He saw four of his gunners crumple like broken dolls beside their pieces, the pale scrubbed surface of the planking running thick and red with their blood. Beside them one of the demicannon had overturned on its carriage, lying grotesquely on its side with the wooden wheels still spinning.

Another ship veered into a parallel track, and swept the *Seaflower*'s deck with a hail of small shot. When she had passed, less than half of the brigantine's crew were on their feet. Kit saw Dupré sitting on the deck, his linstock flaring beside him, trying desperately to push the pink sausage rolls of his guts back into the gaping wound in his belly. He sat there a long time, pushing desperately with both hands, not uttering a sound, until at last his hands were too slippery with his own blood to be any longer effective. Then he let his intestines spill out, and sat staring at them glumly, with an expression of acute disgust on his round, swarthy face that did not change even after he died. It was only when a forty-eight-pounder hit the *Seaflower* squarely, causing her to roll and sending him over limply on the deck, that Kit knew he was dead.

"Mother of God," Kit muttered, "why don't they sink us and get it over with?"

But the Spaniards continued to slash at the brigantine with small shot, killing her crew one by one until less than two dozen men remained on their feet, and of these not one was un-wounded. Kit and Bernardo were but slightly hurt, only cut in five or six places by flying splinters. The helmsman was dead, hanging over the whipstaff, so that the trim vessel veered aim-lessly, losing steerage, wallowing helplessly in a trough of the sea while the Spanish men-of-war went by her one by one in a beautiful line and raked her decks.

Kit heard at last that most hideous of all sounds to a seaman, the splintering crash of a broken mast; then almost at once another, so that the *Seaflower* lay naked on the bosom of the sea, denuded of her white wings, unable to gain headway. He looked around at Bernardo, blackened like himself from head to foot with gun soot. Only the flesh about their eyes showed white, streaked here and there with the rivulets of their own blood. Kit put out his hand and Bernardo took it. He stood there with the young captain whom he had followed and counseled and guided across half a world, waiting for the death that both of them knew was imminent. And looking into Bernardo's eyes, Kit saw no fear.

It was a long moment before either of them realized that the Spaniards had ceased firing. They turned as one man, peering through the deafening silence to where the gigantic bulk of the *Garza* bore down upon them. The huge ship of the line rose in close and the grappling hooks dropped into place. Kit saw Don Luis, splendid in a coat of mail, climb down to the *Seaflower*'s decks, followed by a score of soldiers. Of Kit's men, there was not one left with either the strength or the will to oppose them.

Stiffly Kit and Bernardo advanced to meet the grandee. The moonlight glinted blue-silver on the armor, and white on the great plumes above the helmets. The Spaniards were a brave sight. Kit glanced from them to the broken bodies of his dead and tired, sooty, wounded living; the rage and humiliation in his breast was like white fire and poison.

Don Luis's even white teeth showed brilliant in his dark face. His big hand came up and gave his short beard a contemplative tug.

"You fought well, Cristóbal," Don Luis said. "Few captains I know could have stood us off so long."

"Words!" Kit spat. "Do with us what you will, and have done with it!"

"Be not overhasty," Don Luis said calmly. "I require of you only the ransom money. Where is it?"

Kit's blue eyes widened in his soot-blackened face. He nodded to Bernardo. The Jew started off and returned after a few moments with the chest.

"Open it," Don Luis commanded.

Kit's tired, stiffened fingers worked clumsily with the lock. When at last it was opened, the gold pieces glinted dully in the light of the moon.

"Take it up," Don Luis said to one of the soldiers. The man bent and grunted under the weight of the chest. Don Luis raised his sword to the visor of his helmet and saluted Kit.

"Adiós," he said softly. "And when you remember your mother, remember also that I spared her son." Then he turned on his heel and went back up the ratlines to the *Garza*, leaving Kit and Bernardo standing there caught in a vast stupor of astonishment.

"Mother of God!" Kit whispered. "Why in the name of everything holy did he spare us?"

"We shall know someday," Bernardo muttered. "But come now, we must bind up the wounded and bury the dead."

Nevertheless, Kit remained motionless, watching the long line of men-of-war beating out to sea, moving slowly, silently past the place where their fellow blazed, bloodying the sea and the sky with the ruddy glow of the flames. Then at last he went down the splintered, slippery deck, moving stiffly, automatically, his eyes blank and unseeing.

6

KIT SAT on the beach before Cul-de-Sac with his elbows resting
on his knees and his two hands toying with the soiled and
bloodstained folds of the Heron Banner. He was almost completely motionless, his blue eyes staring blankly out to sea, while
behind him people of the village were digging a huge pit into
which the *Seaflower's* dead would be tossed. Bernardo Díaz
looked at him, seeing his whole body freighted with abject
dejection. He crossed quietly to where Kit sat and laid a kindly
hand on his shoulder. Kit looked up quickly into Bernardo's
dark face.

"Bernardo," he said, "I've been a fool!"

"That's the beginning of wisdom," Bernardo remarked. "But
then, what man is not?"

"But none so complete, so colossal a fool as I. I am the crown
prince of asses."

"And I," Bernardo grinned, "am your prime minister!"

Some of the moroseness left Kit's face at Bernardo's remark.

"He has bested us again," he said slowly. "Whenever we
meet, he is always the victor. Why is it so, Bernardo?"

"Because he is older and wiser. You must fight him with his
own weapons, Kit. When your tongue has become as forked
as his, when you are as full of guile, then . . ."

Kit stared at Bernardo, his blue eyes narrowing in his tanned
face. "In my hands," he said, "I had the instrument of his
destruction. I could have made a cuckold of him before his
vows were said, delivered to him a used baggage, deflowered,
dishonored, damned! Whenever he looked at her, whenever his
hands touched her flesh, he would have been faced with the

75

thought that here were my leavings. **Only,** Bernardo, she was so fair—so gentle and so fair."

"All the better," Bernardo growled. "A forced maid freezes up her loins to pleasure, but one as willing as she so plainly was redoubles your joy with the fury of her passion. If it had been I, I would have set my mark upon her flesh so that he could never forget it!"

Kit studied Bernardo gravely. "He has wronged you too," he mused, "as grievously, almost, as myself."

"It behoved him to forget," Bernardo remarked dryly, "that the records of my conversion, my baptismal papers, are recorded in the cathedral. Only by forgetting could he appropriate for his own purposes my houses and lands and my ships. And on what pretext? That I am a Jew, a fact I can help as little as he can help being the Spanish grandee he is. But enough of this. What now, Cristóbal?"

Kit stood up suddenly. "First," he said, "we must cut a mast and erect a jury rig to take us back to Tortuga. Then we will commence anew." He looked at Bernardo, his forehead creased with frowning. "I shall put to sea again," he said slowly, "and skirt the coast until I devise some method of luring Del Toro from behind those walls of Cartagena which now so effectively protect him. During this time of waiting, I must take ships, many ships, and pile up a mountain of gold. For when I find Rouge again, I will build her a manor befitting her beauty."

"So you would still find your Rouge? I had thought that perhaps this other had . . ."

"Shaken me in my purpose?" Kit frowned. "No, Bernardo, in this I remain unshaken, though someday I shall perhaps discover why the thought of Bianca as the wife of that swart beast makes a taste like rotten mangoes in my mouth. But come, time enough later for thinking."

The task of making the *Seaflower* seaworthy was not an easy one. Before a day was gone, Kit was forced to give up the idea of duplicating her original rig. His crew was sullen and bad-tempered, held back by their wounds, but held back even more by their renewed conviction that the *Seaflower* was indeed a hell ship, cursed with misfortune at her launching. Fortunately

76

for Kit, they had neither the strength nor the will for open mutiny, so that finally the *Seaflower* limped back into the harbor at Basse-Terre, her green unseasoned mast bending before every stiff breeze, her ragged sloop rig pushing her along at a rate of speed so unbelievably slow that often Kit was in doubt as to whether or not she moved at all. Were it not for the singing perfection of the lines that her French builders had so lovingly shaped, the *Seaflower* would have been unmanageable. As it was, she barely maintained steerageway.

Night and noon and morning Kit and Bernardo had scanned the horizon, fearing the appearance of a line squall, or even mildly heavy seas, or most of all the chance passing of an English or Spanish vessel. But the gods of mischance had had their fill. The low, humpbacked form of Tortuga rose over the rim of the ocean, and grew with a slowness that crawled along Kit's taut nerves.

But when the entrance to the harbor of Basse-Terre was in sight, Bernardo sought Kit out, a most impious grin stretching his swarthy countenance.

"Kit," he said, "do you know what will happen when these rascals of ours go ashore?"

"Yes." Kit nodded. "They will spread abroad the tale of our misfortunes and we will not be able to obtain a crew of blind men, boys, and women, let alone seamen."

"That must be prevented," Bernardo said cheerfully.

Kit let his gaze rest on Bernardo's face, wrath gathering in his blue eyes. "And how would you do that, my good Bernardo? Put them in irons, so that they can't go ashore? Or perhaps we should heave them overboard at this point?"

"That," Bernardo grinned, "is a pleasing thought, considering their actual worth. But I have a milder suggestion. Think a moment, Kit. Why do these he goats go to sea?"

"To obtain gold," Kit said.

"Yes—but do they love gold for itself, or for what it can buy?"

Kit's frown relaxed, recognition lighting his eyes. "I follow your drift," he said. "If they go ashore hurt, beaten, penniless, with nothing to buy the dreams of drunkenness or the favors of women, that is one thing, but . . ."

"Shall I summon them?" Bernardo inquired quietly.

"Yes! Call them up. You are always long of head, Bernardo!"

In a few minutes the survivors of the battle stood sullenly before Kit. Most of them were clad in rags, and all of them displayed filthy, blood-caked bandages. They stood in a wavering line, their eyes filled with cold hostility.

"Men," Kit began, the ghost of a smile hovering about his mouth, "our luck has been bad, fiendishly bad. But that you know right well."

The crew stood there silently, the hostility in their eyes unwavering.

"Our misfortune, however, was not due to any fault of yours. You fought well and bravely. We were outnumbered and beaten. That is no disgrace. Because it was no fault of yours, because you did your part and more, I cannot permit you to go ashore empty-handed. Out of my own coffers you will receive your pay. Moreover, tonight at the Hôtel des Boucaniers we will celebrate our late defeat, and our coming victories—at my expense. Of course, if any of you are not disposed to accept . . ."

The crew turned incredulous faces toward one another, their lean, bearded jaws dropping open. Then the look of amazement was replaced by slow-dawning joy. Smithers stepped out of line.

"Cheers for our Cap'n!" he bellowed. "The best what ever sailed the seas!"

The men responded, roaring out their cheers in half a dozen tongues. Kit smiled quietly.

"When we go ashore," he added, "say nothing to the people. Within the hour you shall have your pay. Back to your places now!"

The men leaped to their stations. The *Seaflower* crawled into the harbor.

"In this expense," Bernardo declared, "I shall share, since it was I who suggested it."

Kit shook his head.

"No, Bernardo," he began, "I must take the responsibilities, since I am captain."

Bernardo grinned at him. "We will need new masts, new sails, new cording. There is ten days of work here for a shipwright

78

and ten sea carpenters. You haven't enough for the twin necessities of these repairs and conciliating the crew. Whether you like it or not, you must accept my help."

Kit looked toward the quays of Basse-Terre, growing slowly before the *Seaflower*'s slim prow. "You are a good friend, Bernardo," he said quietly.

The rest of the day passed quickly. Kit went out to the small monastery where the good Fathers kept his gold. For this service, they received a handsome yearly offering that served the wants of many of Basse-Terre's sick, poor, and aged. To those who censured them for receiving money gained in so barbaric a fashion, the friars said frankly that the good they so selflessly did with the gold at least balanced the evil incurred in its gaining.

Before nightfall, the carpenters and the shipwright were swarming over the hull of the *Seaflower,* healing her hurts with sound, seasoned timber. On the morrow they would begin to erect her tall new masts.

As for the crew, they were already half-drunk, noising abroad in the streets and the alleys the news of Kit's generosity. And many a stout fellow was already turning over in his mind the advantages of shipping aboard her once she was ready to sail.

That night at the Hôtel des Boucaniers the noise of revelry beat deafeningly on Kit's ears. He sat a little apart, cool amusement lighting his eyes. A slim, dark creature who had spent her childhood cutting purses in the streets of Marseille lay beside him, her head pillowed in his lap. On his right, the blonde Bretonne sat quietly, one arm encircling his broad shoulders. That neither of them had so far gained the advantage was the only thing that kept them relatively at peace. A tall beaker of cane rum rested almost untasted in his hand. That this revel was costing him his last écu he knew well, but there was something fitting in the knowledge. Gold gained from the bosom of the sea had a quality like quicksilver, running in bright drops through the open hand.

As for Bernardo Díaz, he joined gleefully in the riot. The gold he had gained at the risk of his life was now gone to the last sou, yet that seemed exquisitely comic to his richly ironic mind.

He laughed as loud as any of them, and pinched bottoms and took kisses, his broad, clean-shaven chin red with the rum of the Antilles. He had already chosen a woman to ensure that he would not spend the balance of the night in thinking or in vain regrets.

The revel lasted late. When it was over at last, Kit walked on the moon-silvered beach under the slim-trunked palms—alone. Now, as always, he took out the tattered, bloodstained pennant about whose somber symbol so much of his life had revolved. The moonlight fell on the wings of the Black Heron, so that the bird of evil seemed almost alive and poised for flight. And all that had been clear before was unclear now, murky and confused.

He could imagine Don Luis sitting now in his house in Cartagena, bastion of the Indies, a city whose walled strength could not be matched anywhere on earth either in the Old World or in the New. At one time that had meant little to Kit; he would have climbed over the walls and laid down his life gladly for the privilege of first flinging the hated grandee into hell. His hatred of Del Toro had in no degree diminished, but he was checkmated by his own new-found desire to live. And for that, Rouge was responsible.

"Rouge." Saying the name alone was enough to start kettledrums in his blood. Like white fire in his mind was the image of her swaying before him on the *Seaflower's* deck, the few tattered rags the Spaniards had left her clinging to her figure: sea-foam whiteness of hip and thigh, and breasts so proud that they flaunted their conical perfection like a challenge. Her mouth, wine-scented, poppy-petaled, a trifle full and petulant, self-willed, spirited; the shell-pink lobes of her nostrils flaring, and above them the oddly Mongolian slant of her emerald eyes beneath the flame of her soft-curling hair.

Before Rouge he had fed his soul on hatred, and battened on dreams of vengeance. Now, because of her, whole new vistas were opened up to him: he heard the ring of hammers and the rasp of saws and in his mind saw the vast edifice that would be her domain erected in fair and pleasant fields; his eye piled up vague, half-imagined furnishings of unbelievable richness—silks

80

soft enough to caress her skin, velvets, satins, jewels whose glitter paled the noonday sun. These he would tear from the holds of the Spanish plate ships, and lay in mounds at her feet. This would he do—after Luis del Toro was dead by his hand, his house in ashes about him, his Bianca widowed.

Kit stopped short, his face heavy with frowning. His imagination conjured up Bianca as he had seen her last, standing there on tiptoe before him, her dark eyes tear-bright, filled with haunting sweetness, with poignant, almost insufferable longing; he could see the clean, innocent outlines of her ethereal young face framed in the soft night cushion of her hair.

Bianca was an angel out of heaven, too beautiful to touch or believe; Rouge was born to sear a man's mind into fevered disorder—and he, Kit, was after all mere flesh and blood.

Of this he must not think too much. That way lay madness. "Rouge," he whispered to the night wind, "come back to me—for I am no fit consort for a saint. But you and I could make such joy on earth that angels looking down would desert their starry thrones. We could spin sunlight into garments, and wear the blue water like sapphires."

His mood changed suddenly and he groaned. This *was* madness. Rouge was far beyond his reach, or indeed she might even be dead. He was stunned by the thought as he listened to the muffled booming of the sea. It was a far, sad sound, not unlike the music of a dirge. Above his head the palm trees caught the sea wind and talked in dark voices. Somewhere inland, a parrot screeched hideously, making a sound like demented laughter.

Slowly, Kit walked up the beach, his high red heels kicking up little spurts of sand that caught the moonlight like silver as he moved. His head bent and troubled, he returned to the town, which lay buried deep in quiet and in slumber.

7

THE *Seaflower* swung southward down the chain of the Antilles, speeding like a great white-winged bird past islands strung like emeralds on a string looping in a great curve toward South America. To Kit's ears, even their names were like jewels: Hispaniola, Puerto Rico, Guadeloupe, Martinique, Granada, Santa Lucia, Trinidad. . . . And the sea that they encircled—cupped by them between the green poignard that is Florida and the long, rugged arm of the Isthmus, the blue crescent of the Gulf of Mexico and the towering peaks and mighty rivers of the mainland—was like sapphire, topaz, lapis lazuli.

Wherever she went, into whatever waters she pushed her prow, the *Seaflower* left a trail of broken ships bloodying the blue waters with the ruddy glow of fires as they flamed downward to destruction. From as far north as the mouth of the Mississippi to as far south as Rancherías, where the Rio de la Plata sweeps downward through the pampas of the Argentine into the sea, the black-hulled brigantine pulled down her prey.

True, she confined her attention to the galleons of Spain, but this discrimination was but little dictated by gallantry. Kit hoped one day to settle in France or in one of the French colonies, and hence wanted no black mark on his record. He spared the English, in part because they were fellow countrymen of Lazarus and Rouge, but more because they were almost without exception privateers embarked on the same errand as his own. The Dutch with their cargoes of hides, tallow, rum, and slaves interested him not at all; but the Spaniards bore bullion of gold and tons of silver plate, and he hated them with all his heart.

By mid-March of 1694, his name was known and feared

82

throughout the Caribbean wherever the Spanish tongue was spoken. He flew the banner of the Golden Hawk, like his golden, lionlike mane. Men spoke of the fury of his attack, of his cold and smiling ferocity. But the ones who could speak with any authority were few indeed, for they owed their lives to occasional lapses on the part of Kit's crew, who, being men and thus liable to error, sometimes failed to make sure that the Spaniards they left on the decks of the plate ships were all dead. It was not a thing that happened often.

Kit stood on the deck, his fingers moving softly over the cloth-of-gold sash that encircled his waist. The wings of the Black Heron on it spread fanwise over the bulge made by the barrels of his pistols. His blue eyes were cloudy with dreaming, for his thoughts were far away.

He was thinking, at the moment, of his mother. After the usual surge of pain at the memory of the cruelty of her death, older questions rose to plague him. How had she come to Cádiz, this gentle, lovely woman, as blonde and fair as her Norse ancestors who had settled centuries ago on the northern shores of France? Why, in the name of God and the Virgin, had she ever come to be married to that posturing peasant, Pierre Labat? That Pierre did not deserve his distaste Kit knew well, for with all his unmanly fussiness, he had treated Kit most kindly. He had adored the lovely aristocratic woman who had become his wife, and had provided for both Jeanne and Kit well, having made money as hairdresser and wigmaker to the grandees of southern Spain. They had come to him from as far away as Valencia and Barcelona to have their great blue-black manes fashionably curled; and those afflicted with baldness paid him princely sums for the magnificent wigs with which he so cunningly concealed their defects. In his small way, Pierre Labat had been an artist, but he had never wholly recovered from his awe at finding himself married to a gentlewoman of Normandy. If he had remained in his native France, that would have been beyond his wildest dreams.

Kit suspected that he himself was the cause of that particular mystery, for it was more than certain that Pierre Labat had never sired him. His own lean and towering height had never sprung

83

from that fat little dwarf Labat; nor did the fine, chiseled purity of line of his features bear any resemblance to the pudgy countenance of his foster father. There had been about Cristóbal Gerado from his earliest youth an arrogance and a swagger that bespoke proud Spanish blood.

Bernardo, Kit was certain, knew in part or entirely the answers to these riddles, for he had been a fast friend of Jeanne Giradeaux from that long-past day when she had first set foot on the shores of Spain. It was characteristic of Jeanne that she had never wavered in her regard for the greathearted Bernardo, though to maintain a friendship with a "new Christian," as the converted Jews were called, could be done only at considerable risk to herself. In the Spain of 1689, there were no others. Masses were being said in the former synagogues, and thousands of these brave and faithful people lay in indistinguishable heaps in common graves outside half the cities of Castile and Aragon. Pierre Labat had almost fainted in pure terror each time Bernardo had approached his door, but both Kit and Jeanne had stoutly championed his right to enter as a friend.

The father-and-son relationship had existed between Kit and Bernardo for as long as he could remember. Kit had lavished on that stout, battle-scarred old campaigner the devotion he instinctively withheld from the effeminate Labat. Yet even this was not enough to make Bernardo divulge any secrets. "Some things," he growled, when asked, "are better left unknown." And neither threats nor persuasion could move him from his stand.

Kit had half-turned toward Bernardo, but now he turned away, sighing heavily. His thoughts fled, unaccountably, to Bianca. Why was it that the idea of Bianca as the wife of Del Toro was so distasteful to him? What precisely was the emotion that he still felt toward that soft and lovely creature? Was it love? How was it possible for a man to love two quite dissimilar women at one and the same time? He could see them both as vivid as life before his eyes, both with their sea-foam whiteness of skin and matchless loveliness. But where Rouge's snowy body was complemented by the hibiscus fire of her head, the vulture-feathered blackness of Bianca's hair made her fairness doubly startling by contrast. Bianca was a song in the darkness, solace to a man's wounded spirit; Rouge was brush fire and volcanoes beneath spring snow. And he, God help him, loved them both!

In that moment a confusion that had long been troubling him was suddenly made clear. Why had he not, after so long a time, made good his vengeance on Del Toro? He realized that to try to take Don Luis in Cartagena was worse than foolhardy, rimmed as that grim gray city was with mountainous walls of stone; but subconsciously he had been troubled by Bianca, and the declaration of devotion she had made to him. If he killed his enemy, would he not of necessity be forced to assume the responsibility of Bianca? And however delightful that prospect might seem, what, then, of Rouge? Rouge was in his blood. The mention of her name was a kind of autointoxication. If only I had been born a Mussulman, he thought bitterly, I could have them both! . . .

He was, he was beginning to realize, driven by fierce surges of emotion that often ran quite counter one to the other, for besides the fact that he loved two women, and hated Don Luis with a hatred as bottomless as the pit, yet another current surged within him, no less strong than the others: a powerful, mounting tide of ambition. His boyhood had been spent under a cloud of mystery, in humble circumstances, but always he had had a hunger for greatness. Wealth? He had that. No, it was more than wealth that he desired. It was a name that men would reckon with, holdings spreading out from horizon to horizon, and tall sons of his loins to carry on his name.

Those sons—would they wear manes of scarlet on their heads, or would their scalps be crowned with night-black curls? That thought again! Angrily, he put it from his mind, and turned to planning the details of his manor, picturing it lovingly in his mind, furnishing it room by room with all the luxuries he had ever seen or heard of. The furniture would be hand-carved and brightly gilded, and on the back of each chair would be carved his crest. That thought brought him up short; a low, mocking laugh escaped his lips. His crest! What heraldic device could he employ? The bar sinister across an empty shield? Nameless,

85

fatherless bastard that he was, what escutcheon had he upon which to charge his nonexistent armorial bearings—the Golden Hawk, emblem of the plunderer bird?

He threw back his head to laugh aloud, but at that moment the unmistakable slow-rolling boom of gunfire came to him. He turned to Bernardo, but there was no need to ask. Bernardo was bending forward, his nostrils quivering, his whole body at attention.

"Crack on all sail," Kit ordered.

It was still daylight when they came on the scene. A low, black-hulled corvette stood in the midst of three huge plate ships and hammered at the gigantic vessels as though her crew were possessed of the fiends. Kit had no need to give the order, his men were already at their stations. One plate ship was a windfall that a man dreamed about for years, but three! Into these great ships the Spaniards crowded the plate and bullion that had once made up the cargo of a fleet of galleons, on the theory that one ship was more likely to escape detection than a fleet. This theory was quite correct—it was hellishly difficult to sight any one vessel on the great blue curve of the ocean. These ships, no doubt, were loaded to the gunwales with silver from Peru, which was explanation enough of the fury with which the corvette fought.

But without aid the little vessel did not have a chance. True, the plate ships were not handy fighters—the small buccaneer was escaping their fire with mocking ease—but neither could the light guns of the corvette dent their heavy timbers. After a while she would be forced to give up. The *Seaflower* swept down on the battle like a white-winged bird. When she was within range, Kit concentrated her fire on the plate ships' rigging. In four broadsides, the *Seaflower* demasted two of the great Spaniards. Seeing this, the third struck her colors.

At once the *Seaflower*'s crew swarmed over the sides and began the labor of bringing the heavy pigs and plates of silver topside. While they were thus gleefully engaged, the corvette slid to the opposite side of the Spaniard, and her crew too swarmed up the ratlines. In a moment, cutlasses and pistols were drawn as the *Seaflower*'s crew prepared to defend their spoils.

86

Seeing the approaching trouble, Kit swung down to the Spaniard's deck.

"Hold!" he cried. "There is enough for us all. We will share it with you."

"Who said anything about sharing?" a voice answered him. "These prizes are ours!"

Something in the tone arrested Kit. The voice was a clear soprano, like that of a cathedral choirboy. He whirled, his eyes widening in his bronzed face, seeing as though through a faint haze the mouth as red as a blood rose, the emerald-green of the eyes, and the long sweep of the hibiscus-red hair.

"You." His mouth shaped the word, but no sound came out, no sound at all. Rouge walked toward him, her bare legs white under the boy's trousers that reached but halfway between hip and knee. He could see the black lash of the Spanish whip that was coiled over one shoulder, diagonally across so that it lay between the young, upthrusting breasts which pushed their way half out of her tattered shirt. A sash of scarlet, exactly matching her hair, encircled the almost unbelievable slimness of her waist, and into it a brace of pistols was thrust. She approached him slowly, swaying lightly on her feet like a young willow in a spring breeze, and as she neared her green eyes widened in recognition.

"Kit," she whispered. "Kit of the golden mane! And I thought that I had killed you!"

"No," Kit exulted, "your aim was bad. I have searched the seas these many years in order to find you!"

He put out his arms and swept her toward him. At once her hands came up, dagger-taloned, reaching for his eyes. He caught them in midair and held them there, slow amusement curving the corners of his mouth.

"Have you forgotten?" she spat. "No man embraces me—not even you!"

"For five whole days," Kit said quietly, "I lay between life and death because of your shot. For that I shall exact payment—and now!"

But Rouge swung backward, wrenching herself from his grasp. She put up her slim white hand, which all the sun in the

Caribbean had been able only to freckle a bit, and grasped the butt of the Spanish whip. Then she slipped down and out of its evil coil, playing it along the deck.

"Come no closer, Kit," she warned.

Kit looked at her, seeing her young figure, lithe, soft-curving, revealed in all provocative purity of line by the abbreviated costume she wore, seeing her hair flaming about her shoulders, her eyes making green fire, her mouth scarlet, all the more inviting because of its fury. And, laughing aloud, he stepped toward her.

Her crew lolled against the rail, grinning. This indeed was going to be a show. Kit took another step. The lash whistled through the air and curled about his bare arm; when she drew it away, the slow, thick ooze of blood followed it. Kit did not even glance down. He took another step and another, until Rouge was forced to retreat, the whistling crack of the whip sounding all the time, and the stripes on his arms and shoulders growing until they crisscrossed; his fine linen shirt was a thing of bloody rags, and still he advanced upon her. Finally, in desperation, she swung the whip so that the lash curled across his face, leaving a bloody stripe from cheek to mouth. Kit raised a hand to his face. It came away wet with his own blood. Then, his blue eyes cold with fury, he sprang forward and caught her to him.

His hand came up and caught her chin, forcing her face upward until he found her mouth. She struggled furiously in his embrace for a long moment, then her struggles lessened, ceased, her hands hung limply at her side so that the loop of the Spanish whip slid down her slim hand and the evil weapon thudded on the deck. Kit kissed her slowly, lingeringly, moving his mouth upon hers, pressing her backward until her lips broke against her teeth. When at last he released her she swung back against his arm, her eyes star emeralds behind the shifting haze of her tears.

"You should not have done that!" she cried. "You should not have shamed me so!" Then, whirling, she ran to the rail and swung down the lines to the deck of her own vessel. Kit watched her go, a crooked grin on his bronzed, bleeding face. Bernardo came up to him and touched his arm.

"Those stripes," he growled. "They want attention. Come, Kit."

Quietly Kit followed him. But before he quitted the Spanish vessel, he called one of Rouge's crew to him.

"Tell your Captain," he said, "that I will discuss the terms of the division of the spoils with her—later." Then he turned and walked toward where Bernardo waited, his dark face heavy with disapproval.

"I suppose," Bernardo growled, "that this ends our voyage."

"No, Bernardo," Kit answered, laughing. "It means only that we do not go alone."

Bernardo paused in his sponging of Kit's stripes and looked at his Captain gravely. "I know well," he began, "that you will listen to nothing against her. But, Kit, she is not for you. When a man marries he should seek out a young maid, innocent and sweet of mind and body, pure in thought and deed, whom he can lead and instruct in the duties of wife and mother."

"And Rouge, of course," Kit said dryly, "does not fit this description."

"Judge for yourself. Aside from the fact that she goes half-naked, and has probably consorted with whatever member of her crew or . . ."

"Enough!" Kit snarled. "I will not hear this even from you!"

"She has the temper of a fiend, the will of a shrew, and the morals of a she goat."

"Enough, I said!" Kit roared. "Did you not hear me?"

Bernardo shrugged his enormous shoulders and fell silent, his deft fingers moving gently over Kit's bruised and broken flesh.

Through the heavy silence, broken only by the creaking of cording and tackle and the soft wash of the seas, came the noise of a new uproar. Kit could hear the high, clear tones of Rouge's voice, but her words were muffled by the distance. No distance, however, could hide the pistol-shot sounds of her whipcracks. Kit bounded to his feet and raced toward the deck, with Bernardo at his heels.

89

The two of them swung up to the lofty deck of the captured Spaniard, and running across it, peered down the other side, where the corvette lay. Rouge was walking on the foredeck, moving forward one step at the time, swinging the heavy Spanish whip while her crew slunk backward in a semicircle like a pack of cowed jackals.

"Dogs and sons of dogs!" she shrieked. "Knaves and whoresons, born of filth and abominations! Have I not told you that I am not to be touched? Must you be whipped to rags before you learn who is master here?"

Kit turned toward Bernardo, a slow smile lighting his blue eyes.

"You spoke of her morals," he said quietly.

"In that perhaps I was mistaken," Bernardo conceded. "But not in her temper. I would sooner mate with a fiend out of hell!"

"The matter of mating does not concern you at all," Kit said with a grin. "Come, let us go to her assistance."

Groaning, Bernardo passed Kit a heavy pistol, and the two of them slid down a line to the low deck of the corvette.

"Perhaps," Kit said mockingly, "perhaps we can be of assistance?"

Rouge whirled, her eyes a hard, emerald blaze. "Go back!" she spat. "Haven't you done me enough harm?"

"I?" Kit said. "I harmed you? In what way?"

"I have taught these dogs," Rouge said, "with good and sufficient example, that no man lays a finger on me. Then you come and spoil it all with your pawing and mouthing! Now they would like to follow your example, and I must whip them all, every man jack of them!"

"I see," Kit said gravely, but with cool amusement crinkling the corners of his eye. "Perhaps I should allow you to shoot me again to convince them you do not lie?"

Rouge glared at him, her small face hot with rage. "Don't tempt me!" she said.

"Nor shall I," Kit said lightly. "I do not like being shot—or whipped. But enough of these incivilities. I came merely to extend an invitation to my fellow captain to dine with me on my vessel this evening."

90

A little of the anger left Rouge's green eyes. "No," she said shortly.

"Why not? Surely you are not afraid. I shall not harm you."

"You cannot harm me," Rouge said contemptuously. "But I can think of no good reason for dining with you—or with any other man."

"The division of spoils," Kit said softly, "will give you excuse enough to offer your crew. As for yourself, I do not think you need any further excuse. Shall we say at eight, then?"

"At eight," Rouge said. "Yes—at eight hours after you arrive in hell! Off with you, Señor Cristóbal."

Kit made her a mocking bow and turned away; but as he placed his hands on the line, he turned once more toward the girl.

"Before you come," he said cheerfully, "do me the honor of bathing. I do not like my women to smell of gun soot, tobacco smoke, or sweat—it ruins their charm. Adiós, Rouge."

He saw her hand reach down for her dagger, and despite his agility, the broad blade of the knife hissed past him so close that it sheared off a lock of his tawny mane. He bent down and picked up the lock. Then he crossed to where the dagger still quivered in an oak beam. Before her astonished eyes, he quietly wrapped the bright gold of the hair around the hilt of the dagger. Then he hurled the dagger back so that it stood in the mast above her head.

"Keep it," he said, "as a tender remembrance of me—to be pressed to your bosom of nights!" Then he went up the line hand over hand, leaving her trembling with fury.

"She'll not come," Bernardo said.

"No? On that score I'll wager you a hundred écus."

"Done!" Bernardo growled.

Kit went to his cabin and bathed and dressed. When he had finished, he was as fine as any prince, ablaze with jewels, bedecked with yards of snowy lace and fine embroidery. Bernardo held up the mirror of polished silver before him, remarking as he did so: "Of three things there is no end: the cawing of the raven, the braying of the ass, and the vanity of a man in love."

By the end of the seventeenth century, masculine foppery

had reached an extent that was never again to be equaled in Western history. Five years later the reaction against its extremes had set in, but in April 1694 it still took Kit two and a half hours to dress himself adequately. So it was that when he again mounted the *Seaflower*'s deck he had a scant half-hour's wait before the time he had set for the dinner. Actually, his wait was shorter. Fifteen minutes later he felt Bernardo tapping his arm and, looking up, saw the leather bag of coins dangling from that worthy's hand.

"You have a way with women," Bernardo groaned. "Here, take your loot!"

Grinning, Kit pocketed the wager and walked eagerly toward the rail, over which Rouge's crew was laying a plank. He saw them help her up, then the significance of all this ceremony came to him. Rouge was clad in a gown of exquisite Córdoba lace like a mist of midnight, cut in extreme décolleté, its somber hue chosen deliberately to accentuate her natural fairness, so that above its black filigree work made in the pattern of strange, unearthly flowers the whiteness of her neck and shoulders and bosom was like a cry in the darkness of a man's heart.

The dress was caught about her waist and clung like the clasp of a lover; at one and the same time it shielded and flaunted the proud upflare of her full, young breasts; from her waist it arched down like the inverted bell of a black orchid plucked in a dream garden in a season of fevers and delirium.

On her head the great masses of her hair were piled so high that Kit had the impulse to stretch out his fingers and warm them at that living flame.

He put up his hand and helped her down. Then he stood a moment, looking into her face. He took a stride toward her, swift and purposeful, but he halted abruptly without taking another. It was her eyes that had stopped him. They were as clear as sea water, but a light of pure mockery danced in their depths with a glee that was almost diabolical. Do what you will, they challenged him, I can match and top every move you make.

"I changed my attire," Rouge said tartly, "not to please you, but so that we would waste no time in banter. I can masquerade as a woman still, though the woman I was died long ago."

92

Kit took her arm and guided her toward his cabin. "I doubt that," he said, "for if you are not alive, nothing on earth is."

"I live for one thing only," Rouge said, her voice flat, calm, curiously controlled, "and that is to see Luis del Toro, grandee of Spain, dead in his blood at my feet."

Kit poured out two goblets of wine from a stone flagon that had been cooling since morning. "I share that feeling," he growled, "perhaps with better excuse than you." He lifted the knife and carved slices off the breast of a smoked fowl.

"Perhaps it was only a small deed," Rouge said slowly, "as men count deeds. Only a bit of sport. . . . And what difference does it make if it cost my sister her life? Or that I was to be married in another month? I—who now must remain forever unwed."

"I don't agree," Kit growled. "Was your suitor so poor a man as to reject you for a fault in no way your own?"

"No, but I too have my pride. I could not come to him dishonored." She looked at Kit and her green eyes were very clear. "To him," she added, "or to any other man."

"I see," Kit said quietly.

Rouge lifted the goblet of ruby-colored wine. The dying sunlight came through it and touched her long, graceful fingers with deep rose.

"You said," she mused, "that you share my feeling about Del Toro. Why so, Kit?"

"My mother," he said, his voice husky, "died of torture—at his command."

Rouge drew in her breath sharply, her eyes widening until they dominated her entire face with their emerald blaze. When she spoke, her voice had dropped to a whisper.

"I'm glad I did not kill you," she said.

"And I too," Kit said, smiling. "Dead, I could do nothing for you. Alive, perhaps I can lead you back to happiness."

"I shall never be happy again," Rouge said flatly.

"That may be doubted," Kit said. "On the sea, surrounded on every side by rude men who know how to sink a vessel, cut a throat, and force a maid, but nothing else—perhaps not. But in a home of your own with a man who loves you as your husband . . ."

"You?" Rouge snapped.

"Yes," Kit said softly, "I."

Rouge stared at him a moment, her green eyes filled with soft lights that moved in unbroken progression as her gaze followed the clean, sculptured outlines of his face.

"You love me, I suppose?" she mocked. "How can you? You're a man, and men know nothing of love. Lust, yes—the satisfying of their grosser desires, but love . . ." She threw back her head and her laughter came out hard and mirthless. "Marry you? And when I have grown old and fat have you looking in the village for some younger maid?" She leaned forward. "Tell me, Kit," she said, "would you be so anxious to take me as a wife if I insisted on separate rooms and no intimacies between us? Would you marry me for the pleasure of my company merely, for the music of my sweet voice? Would you?"

Kit's gaze dropped and his whole face was a picture of woe.

Rouge's laughter rang merrily through the tiny cabin. Then abruptly she halted. She leaned forward across the table, and her finger tips traced lightly the lash stripe on Kit's face.

"I have hurt you," she said, "in more ways than one. And I am sorry, for in some ways you seem different from the rest."

She stood up, as if to go. Kit got swiftly to his feet and came around the table. He stood looking at her for a long moment, then, very gently, he drew her into his arms. As light as his touch was, he could feel her body stiffening, and with a swift motion she turned her head aside from his kiss. He released her at once and, bringing both his hands up, cradled the soft oval of her face between them, looking quietly into her eyes.

"You cannot go on forever evading life," he said, "or including me among those who have no other thought beyond their own gratification. You were made for me, Rouge—not for a day only, but as the partner of my soul. I must break through the wall you have built around your heart, so that you live again—warmly, as a woman should."

He bent down then and found her mouth. It was warm and sweet, but with nothing of response there—nothing at all. There

94

was something maddening in her coolness. His hands swept downward and encircled her waist, drawing her to him in a grip that was likely to crush her wholly, and his lips flamed upon hers, moving, searching, until slowly, softly, he felt the trembling start. Start and increase and move upward in wild, surf-pounding surges, her face slanting itself now across his at a sharper angle, so that her mouth fitted more and more closely into the contours of his own, her hands creeping up, moving slowly, caressing the surface of his sleeves until at last they met and locked behind his head, her fingers working through the heavy masses of his hair.

He could feel her lips slackening and parting. Then they were suddenly scalding, fiercely demanding, upon his own. Without freeing himself from her embrace, he dropped one arm to the level of her knees and, lifting her off her feet, laid her gently on the bunk.

"No," she whispered, her voice low and intense. "You must not!"

But he sank down beside her and stopped her protests with his mouth until she lay trembling in his embrace, her lips, soft-sighing, brushing against the hollow of his throat. He straightened after a time, and she lay there staring up at him, her eyes as green as emeralds, as deep as tropic seas. When she spoke, her voice was so low that he had to bend down to hear the words. "Loose me," she whispered, and turned over face downward, so that all the buttons and laces of her back lay under his trembling hands. . . .

Afterward, when time came blurring once more into focus, she lay very still beside him in the darkness, and a single ray of moonlight stole in through the porthole and fell across her face. He looked down at her, seeing the big teardrops filtering through her dark lashes, more jeweled than any diamonds in the world. And suddenly he felt curiously ashamed and unclean, as though his act differed not even in degree from the brutality of Del Toro.

"Forgive me," he whispered. "I never intended that you should be hurt because of this. Between us two there can be no thought of sins and sinning, for always it was meant to be thus." There was only silence from beside him except for a half-stifled sob. "Say that you forgive me," he pleaded. "Say that you will sail with me to Saint-Domingue, and there we will be married."

Rouge sat up slowly, the tears streaking her face, then she swung the long singing curves of her legs outward and down, and gathering up her clothing, began to dress, still without uttering a word.

Kit got up too and drew on his own clothing. When he had made some semblance of order among all his ribbons and laces, he turned once more to Rouge and drew her into his arms. She made no move to resist, but came quite woodenly, like one half-alive. He bent down and kissed her once more, his lips as light as a breath upon hers, as reverent as a prayer. She lay back against the circle of his embrace, her green eyes deep and somber, a little puzzled light moving in their depths.

"I must have time," she whispered. "Much time—in which to think."

Kit frowned. He had no way of knowing that the fear which moved in her eyes and shook her voice was of herself, of her tremendous capacity for response to him, who, of all men on earth, had broken completely through her defenses. All her ideas were in need of revision. Passion, in spite of the Spaniards' brutality toward her and her dead sister, existed in her after all. Her own blood, then, was as hot and eager as that of any panting animal of a man. . . . Yes, she must think; she must have much time for thinking.

"One year from today," Kit said gravely, "I shall put into the harbor of Petit Goave. If you have changed your mind by then, join me there. Is that time enough?"

"Yes," she whispered, "quite."

"Will you come?" he whispered.

She looked at him, a long, slow, searching look.

"Who knows?" she said. "Wait—and see."

8

THE SEÑORA BIANCA DEL TORO sat alone in her room. She was as still as a statue of marble, and almost as pale. But for the green fire of the emeralds from Muzo and Chiquinquirá, she seemed a masterwork by some priestly artist designed ultimately for the nave of a great cathedral. Only the occasional flutter of her snowy hands and the faint flare of her nostrils showed that she lived.

But her young mind, alert to the point of rebelliousness, was far from inactive. Behind the dark screen of her eyes moved thoughts so daring that they frightened her. Just four years before, the Sister Juana Inés de la Cruz, sitting amid the shadows of the cloister into which masculine disapproval of her brilliance had forced her, had penned her immortal answer to the Bishop of Puebla, Fernández de Santa Cruz, quietly defending a woman's right to have thoughts, and to express them, to cultivate the intellect that God had given her. And here and there throughout tropical New Spain an occasional woman had spoken out against the brazen, multitudinous infidelities that the swaggering grandees took as their inalienable right. But Bianca, lacking the knowledge that she was not alone in her secret revolt, prayed to the Virgin to be delivered from the dark tumult of her thinking.

If, she mused, I were not alone so much. If Luis would lessen his desire to devour the entire earth and take from it all its treasure, I might in time become accustomed to him. I might someday learn to care for him a little, for he is a man of great parts and even a little kindness. What more power can he want? He is president of the Audencia, commander of His Majesty's

97

fleet in the western Caribbean. He owns three haciendas—why, in Spain his holdings would constitute an actual latifundium; there are princes on the continent of Europe who possess less land. He owns mines at Cali, Muzo, and Zipaquirá, and his petition before the King for the title of Count will surely be honored. He has indigo, bananas, and cane, three thousand Negro slaves whose lives are at the mercy of his lightest whim; an *encomendero* over the services of another thousand Indians. What else is there in this world to gain? . . .

Her face darkened perceptibly as the answer to her question came unbidden to her mind. There *is* one thing more, which only you can give him—a son and heir.

But he has sons, Bianca recalled. I've heard him say . . . Mulattoes and mestizos, her reluctant mind taunted. Any Negress can give him a son, but only you can give him the noble Spanish son of his loins, the heir for whom he has built his empire. You alone can mother the straight-limbed, fair-skinned lad he dreams of, you alone can bring him the assurance that the proud name of Del Toro will not vanish . . .

She remembered well the day she had first entered Cartagena with Don Luis. As they had driven down the cobblestoned streets of the city toward the Del Toro mansion, a painted woman, clad in a saya cut so low that her breasts were in danger of complete exposure, came to a halt. Bianca had stared at her. Never before had she seen a woman so shamelessly dressed in public. The woman had moved toward the carriage, calling to Don Luis with obvious familiarity.

"Luis darling, what have you got now? *Diablo*, but she's a beauty! Oh, but you'll tire of her—the pale, pretty thing. Then you'll come back to me. I'll be waiting."

Bianca had turned a frozen face toward her betrothed. Don Luis nodded grimly to a hidalgo who rode alongside. The man spurred his mount forward, uncoiling a loaded whip as he rode.

"Luis!" the woman had squealed. "Stop him! Stop him, for the love of God!"

Bianca had seen the whip rising against the sky. Then it sang downward, wrapping itself halfway around the woman's body. When the rider drew it away, the cloth of the saya had been cut through as cleanly as with a knife, and through the break showed the bright stripe of the woman's blood. Her scream had been a dreadful thing, high and thin and edged with terror. Again Don Luis had nodded. The hidalgo brought down the whip again, the loaded lash whistling through the air. Quietly, Don Luis put his head out of the window and addressed the coachman.

"Drive on," he had said.

Now, recalling the incident, Bianca shuddered again. How can I give myself unconditionally to him? she whispered to herself. His lightest touch freezes my blood, and his caresses bring only fear and trembling. I think that if a woman's heart and mind are not opened to a man, her body will reject his seed. No, he must seek elsewhere for this son of his bosom. . . .

And you? Will you also seek elsewhere for fulfillment—even across the Caribbees, to where he with the star-sapphire eyes and a mane of tawny gold roams? Are you not really glad of your husband's absence?

"Yes!" Bianca said aloud, with a fierce kind of joy. "Yes, I am glad, and I will think no more of this!" She stood up suddenly and looked about her as though she were seeing the details of her room for the first time. Her eyes wandered over the great beams of quebracho wood—wood so heavy and strong that it sinks when tossed into the sea, so hard that it blunts the edge and shatters the handle of any ax used against it—down over the carved furniture with its gilt and brightly colored leatherwork to the cool red tiles of the floor. Great vases of Indian pottery stood in the corners, silk tapestry ornamented the walls, and everywhere there shone the moonlight gleam of silver mirrors. Through the open arch, Bianca could see the silver dishes glowing softly on the immense table of red lapacho wood, which was as hard as quebracho and as lasting. The dishes caught the flickering light of the candles that gutted and flared in silver sconces.

Beside her now the girl Quita entered the room as silently as a shadow and began brewing the yerba-de-maté tea over a silver brazier, the ruddy fire of the charcoal lending a slow, smoldering glow to the somewhat barbaric beauty of her face.

99

Bianca looked past the mestiza toward the fine swirling lines of the iron grillwork that barred her windows.

And these, of all the handsomely wrought details of her surroundings, registered upon her consciousness. In spite of all the delicate artistry of swirling vine tendril and leaf shape into which the iron had been tortured, they were still—bars. Such bars, she told herself, were necessary for protection against thieves and other intruders. But, her mind mocked, it is against the "other intruders" that they are chiefly designed. Since our fathers insist upon giving us in marriage to men about whom we know nothing, and since our husbands insist upon their right to sire bastards upon every Negress or Chibcha maid who crosses their path, they must pay for these privileges with the endless fear that we may retaliate in their absence, and we must pay in our turn for that fear by being kept prisoner in these splendid cages that they call homes. . . .

She stopped short, once more appalled at her own thoughts. There was something unfeminine in such thinking. It is only, she told herself again, that I am alone so much. . . . And there is nothing, the dark whisper in her mind mocked, of which you are more glad. And this of the bars—if Kit were to appear tonight at an unbarred window, would you not help him up and clasp him to you?

Bianca halted her thoughts at last, her convent-trained mind aghast at the dark, unruly tumult in her blood. Don Luis never woke such wild confusion within her. With him, she was the gentle, submissive wife who knew her duty and did it, repugnant though it might be. Perhaps her repugnance was the reason why, after all this time, there was no child. She would have been glad to present him with the son he so ardently desired; perhaps then there would have been peace between them. She sighed and turned to Quita. The mestiza stood there silently, the fragrant tea steaming in the silver bowl she held in her hands.

"No, not here, Quita," Bianca said. "Outside in the patio."

She got up and walked through the dining room to the enclosed square garden floored with tile, where a multitude of tropical flowers perfumed the night. She took the tea from

Quita's hand and sat sipping it slowly, her eyes dark and brooding.

"Señora," Quita whispered.

"Yes?" Bianca said without turning her head.

"Why are you unhappy?" Quita said slowly, shaping the unaccustomed Spanish words clumsily. "You are so lovely—with a beauty like the moon and the stars and the night. Why do you sigh? Why do I sometimes hear you weeping in your chamber?"

Bianca looked at the half-breed girl. "It—it grieves you, Quita?"

"Much."

"Why, Quita? Why are you concerned for me?"

"Because you give me things, and never speak harshly to me, and are kind and gentle and never have me beaten. So my heart is a stone within me at the sight of your grief. But why is it, señora? You, who have so much . . ."

"I, who have everything," Bianca whispered, half to herself, "save that without which all else is nothing."

Quita leaned close, her black eyes warm with sympathy. "There is perhaps a man?" she murmured. "A cacique greater than the Señor Capitan Don Luis?"

Bianca jerked upright, the red wings of anger beating in her fair cheeks.

"You are impertinent!" she flared, but the anger died as quickly as it had come. The smooth, kindly face of the mestiza was soft with pity; and, too, realism was replacing the early mysticism of her religious training in Bianca's mind. It posed a baffling question: In what way am I different from this slave girl? I have wealth, which cannot buy the happiness she has. She is enslaved, but am I free? When she finds love, she will go to her man and love him with all her body's passion, and it will be a clean thing, a fine thing, a thing far better than this—this bondage in which fate and custom hold me bound. . . .

Gently she put out her hand and laid it on Quita's arm. "I was hasty," she said. "I have no lover, Quita. But there is a cacique, greater than all the caciques of earth, whom I love. And but for the fact that he did not want me, I would not be here now."

"Then he is a fool!" Quita said fiercely.

"Or a man of honor," Bianca said wryly, "which is, perhaps, only another way of saying the same thing."

"Yet he will come back to you," Quita said firmly. "I will see to it!"

Bianca looked at the mestiza curiously, a pitying smile hovering about the corners of her mouth. "And how," she demanded, "do you propose to work this miracle?"

Quita's slim hands disappeared within the folds of her saya, to reappear after a moment with a necklace of gold. "Here," she whispered, "take it!"

Bianca stared at the necklace, which was made of gold wire drawn to the fineness almost of a human hair, and soldered together in a pattern so intricate as to defy the skill of the makers of the finest European lace. At its apex swung the figure of a woman, cast in heavy gold. The figure was nude, and all the attributes of femininity were vastly overemphasized, but for all its primitive heaviness of form, it was beautiful. Bianca's black brows rose questioningly.

"It is a *tunja*," Quita explained. "I do not know her name, I am vastly ignorant of the lore of my people. But this I do know—she will aid you in finding your love."

Bianca looked at the tiny Chibcha Astarte, grossly sexual almost to the point of obscenity, then looked up at the state of the Virgin, standing serenely in her niche. With quick revulsion she started to put the little figurine away from her, but midway in the action she wavered, halted. There was a curious fascination about the little pagan goddess; there was something fresh and free about her—a hint of open fields and blue skies and mountains veiled in rainbow mists like those encircling the Cauca Valley near Cali. And suddenly Bianca understood that whatever evil there was in the little goddess she herself had read into it with her European-trained mind, with its habitual deification of the asceticism it finds so hard to practice. The little Indian figurine would henceforth represent to her the fertility of the earth, the fruitfulness of fields, and a clean and joyous love, free of shame and dark doubts and questionings, wholly good.

"Thank you, Quita," she said. "I shall treasure it always. But is it not of great value? It is gold, isn't it?"

Quita laughed. "I am no Spaniard," she said. "Gold is nothing to me. We get it from the Panches, who grub it up from the earth and sell it to us for blankets, pottery, and salt. And who knows but what they get the better bargain, since they obtain useful things for this yellow dirt?"

Bianca looked at the girl, dawning respect in her gaze. "You are wise, Quita," she said, "very wise."

Quita opened her mouth to say something, but outside in the street they both heard the clatter of hoofs. Quita bent and picked up the silver bowl and fled silently to her own quarters.

Bianca heard her husband's heavy tread in the hallway. Swiftly she dropped the figurine down the front of her dress and, picking up a goose quill, dipped it into a bottle of ink that stood on a table at her side. She put out her hand and drew paper toward her. So it was that when Don Luis entered the enclosed patio he found her busily engaged in writing. He stopped short, his dark face twisted into a scowl.

"You can write?" he asked. "I do not like that. And can you also read?"

"Yes," Bianca said firmly. "Though this is but a poor greeting from a husband away so long."

Don Luis strode to her and took her gently into his arms.

"Forgive me, Bianca," he said. "Seeing you writing shocked me. A woman's mind is too delicate to be troubled with such things, and there are many things set down in print not fit for feminine eyes to see."

"I read only my catechism and my prayer book," Bianca said tartly. "Besides, I am no longer a girl—marriage, naturally, has robbed me of my innocence."

Don Luis threw back his head and laughed aloud. "A ready tongue," he said with a chuckle. "Well, I have the most accomplished wife in Cartagena. There is not another woman in all this region who can read print or scrawl her name. But, knowing your goodness, I will not let it trouble me. Besides, I have news for you. Letters granting me a patent of nobility, carrying with it the title of Count of the Realm, arrived from Spain today."

Bianca freed herself from his grasp and made him a deep curtsy. But Don Luis, who was not lacking in subtlety, detected in its very graveness a hint of mockery.

"My lord," she murmured.

"You do not seem overjoyed," he remarked dryly.

"No, but I am pleased," Bianca said, "for you. As for myself, what can a title add to my life?"

"Nothing," Don Luis growled, "since you have perversely persisted in gloom since the day we were married. But don't mistake me. I care little for the empty honor or for the lying flattery of all the obsequious lackeys who will presently fawn upon me. It is only that it carries with it a grant of *mayorazgo* that warms my heart."

"That means that the land . . ." Bianca began. "I cannot recall—explain this thing, Luis."

"You know what it means. My holdings can never be sold or divided, but must pass down in unbroken succession from eldest son to eldest son—forever."

"From eldest son . . ." Bianca whispered.

"Yes," Don Luis said quietly. "And in that you have failed me—but no more. Tomorrow we set sail for Lima. There are physicians there who will put an end to your barrenness."

"You took me to Cali," Bianca mused, "because there the air was good. And so it was. I loved the Cauca Valley with all my heart. It was a paradise of light and color, and the air was like wine. I hated to leave Popayán, it was so much cooler there, but what good did it do? Or the valley of the Rio Atrato in Chocó when we stopped there for some weeks on our way back?"

"I didn't want to take you to Atrato," Don Luis growled. "You insisted upon going there."

"Yes," Bianca sighed, "and I wish now I had not. Those Indians standing waist-high in the waters all day panning out your gold, with the hot sun beating down on them and the whips of your overseers continually biting into their flesh . . . How many of them died while we were there, Luis?"

"Enough!" Don Luis spat.

"They were beaten," Bianca went on as though she had not heard his command, "for panning out the green gold. Your men made them throw it back, and whipped them for bringing it out of the water. Why must it be thrown back, Luis? Isn't it lovely metal—much like silver?"[1]

"It is worthless. It is much too hard to be worked. Besides, if left long enough it ripens into true gold. But enough of these silly questions. You have work to do. We sail at full tide tomorrow for Porto Bello."

Bianca bent her head in a gesture that was just a shade too submissive. "As you will, my lord," she murmured, but in the doorway she turned and her black eyes lifted to her husband's face. "What reason does my lord give to the *oidores* and the caballeros for this voyage? It is best that I know, so that I may be in accord with you if I am asked."

Don Luis looked at her keenly, a sardonic smile playing about his bearded mouth. "What would you tell them if I did not instruct you?" he asked.

"That I am barren and my lord would have me cured of it," Bianca answered.

Don Luis frowned. "Say rather that my godson Ricardo Goldames, nephew of the Archbishop of Cartagena, has completed his studies for the doctorate at the University of San Marcos in Lima. Of course I must attend the ceremonies—bear the expense, as is befitting a godfather. And that, my pretty little wife, happens to be true." He sighed. "The expenses will not be light. . . . But off with you, there is much yet to be done."

Again Bianca made her husband a low curtsy, and swept through the doorway to her bedchamber.

The next day when the tide was at the full, the great ship *Garza*, which is by interpretation the *Heron*, moved silently down the Bay of Cartagena, heading southward toward the Boca Chica channel, which led out into the open sea. Bianca

[1] The metal was platinum. The Spanish, who did not know its value, threw it back to "ripen into gold." The San Juan and Atrado rivers in Colombia still produce the world's chief supply.

sat on the high deck under an immense silk canopy that shielded her fair face from the sun, and watched the Getsémani section drop behind. The ship inched over to starboard, rounding the long tongue of land on which stood the fortress of Santa Cruz. Beyond it the land sank suddenly almost to the level of the sea, and lay flat and regular until the rounded hump of the Terra Bomba rose out of the ocean.

It was nearly nightfall when they hailed the fortress of Boca Chica, almost a full day having been spent in passing through the treacherous lower reaches of the Bay of Cartagena. But once in the open sea, the *Garza* spread her wings and moved majestically over the face of the waters. Three days later she dropped anchor in the harbor of Nombre de Dios and rested there for the night. The next day she sailed the short distance to Porto Bello.

Bianco was most anxious to go ashore, for if there is any one thing true of the Caribbean, it is that its waters are never calm. Even upon bright, blue days the *Garza* had rolled and pitched with ponderous deliberation, the very slowness of the motion lending misery to the seasickness that it caused. As the great vessel nosed into the lovely harbor that had inspired Columbus to give the port its name, Don Luis stood on the forecastle and swore softly. Bianca lifted a white face with greenish circles about her eyes toward her husband.

"What ails you, Luis?" she demanded.

"It's fairtime," he growled. "We could not have chosen a worse season in which to arrive."

"Why?" Bianca asked.

"Look," Don Luis said, and pointed.

Even from that distance Bianca could see the throngs on the wharves. In front of the vast customhouse, the streets were black with humanity.

"Did a fleet arrive at Cartagena during my absence?" Don Luis asked. Bianca nodded. *"Diablo!"* he swore. "Every thieving merchant from Lima to Mexico City is in Porto Bello tonight. Once they have news of the convoy's arrival they descend on this place like a flock of vultures."

106

"Why don't they come to Cartagena?" Bianca said. "That is where the fleet first drops anchor."

"Too far," Don Luis grunted. "Besides, the Isthmus has its narrowest neck here, so the merchants from Lima and other cities on the Pacific coast find Porto Bello easiest to reach. If we can find a place to lay our heads tonight, we may thank the Holy Virgin for her kindness."

A few minutes later Don Luis had handed Bianca over the side to the young officer in command of the ship's boat. Then he climbed down beside her. As they came in to the quays, the helmsman had to weave his way through the tightly packed mass of pirogues, hoys, and even rafts that blackened the water, lying so close to one another that it was impossible to glimpse the sea on which they rode.

Ashore it was worse. Though she was flanked fore and aft by her husband and his retinue, Bianca was buffeted and shoved by the howling crowd of merchants. Tents had been set up in the main thoroughfare; open-air stalls were everywhere, piled up with all kinds of cloths, laces, shoes, hardware, wine, machinery, clothing, notions, tools, oils, perfumes. And there were slaves. Before these last, Bianca halted, staring open-mouthed at the slim Dahomey maidens whose glistening naked bodies looked as though they had been carved out of ebony. Nor was she the only one; a crowd of men were clustered about the slave mart, and from their winks, gestures, and bawdy talk, Bianca soon gathered that it was the singing perfection of the black girls' willow-slim bodies, the curve of hip and ebon thigh, the high, conical upthrust of breast, that was evoking the feverish bidding, rather than any work that the Negresses might be able to do. She turned a stricken face toward her husband.

"I should have warned you," Don Luis said grimly. "Come."

At the intersection they had to wait a full hour before there was any break in the parade of mule trains, come from over the Isthmus, laden to the limits of the beasts' endurance with sugar, cacao, cotton, tobacco, hides, indigo, vanilla, pearls, gold, silver, copper, tin, salt, cochineal, and emeralds. Finally they made their way to a smoky hostel, where for a single night's stay Don Luis was forced to pay a thousand pesos.

107

Their meals, Bianca soon discovered, were to cost them twenty times the price of a much better meal in Cartagena, and when the food was brought she found it inedible. After supper Don Luis left her in the care of Quita, guarded by two stout men-at-arms.

Bianca lay talking to Quita, and then began a short prayer for her husband's safe return. He had, she knew, gone to engage mules to transport them and their goods over the Isthmus to the Pacific side, where they would board another ship and sail southward to Lima. But midway through the prayer the face of Kit interposed itself, and all unbidden, her thoughts set sail upon dark voyages. . . . If, she mused, Luis were not to return —Holy gentle Mother, forgive me!—I might return to Cartagena and send him word. . . . But no, this is wickedness. It is evil to think thus. I must not, I must not. . . .

It was at this moment that Don Luis returned. Overcome with contrition for her secret wickedness, Bianca sprang up and flung herself into his arms. A moment later she discovered her mistake. The smoldering fire in his dark eyes blazed fiercely in an instant. His great arms tightened about her until her breath was almost gone.

"Leave us," he growled over his shoulder to Quita. Bianca heard, with a kind of icy terror, the swift rustle of the girl's departure. Then, slowly, with oddly mingled strength and gentleness, Don Luis laid her down on the great bed.

Afterward, as he lay sleeping beside her in the darkness, Bianca sat upright and stared into the lightless void of night. This time it had been different; this time her traitorous body had leaped with unbidden fire; this time her short whimpering cries of passion had been real. It was hot in the close little room, and her naked body was wet with perspiration, but upward from her heart the glacial chill of terror stole slowly until she was shivering in all that dense tropical heat like one half-frozen.

"Good-by, my Kit," she whispered. "Now and forever, good-by." Then: "Holy Mother of God, blessed among women, grant me that it be a son."

9

KIT SAT STIFFLY on the back of the great white stallion. In his early youth in Cádiz he had ridden frequently on the pack mules that formed the backbone of Spanish overland transportation. And not infrequently he had obtained from one hidalgo or another employment that meant his riding the blooded Andalusian horses of the peninsula. But years at sea do not help a man's horsemanship, and Kit found that managing the spirited animal he had bought from a neighboring planter required more attention than it had formerly.

He was aware, too, that Bernardo Díaz was watching him with a curious expression. Bernardo managed his own animal with ease, a fact that Kit found somewhat annoying. Kit tightened his already firm grip on the bridle and touched the white stallion's side with the big Spanish spurs he wore. They were of silver, as were the great stirrups hammered from the soft metal into the shape of the toe of a jackboot. To the horse, however, the rowels of the silver spurs felt the same as those of any baser metal; his rearing almost unseated Kit. Kit brought him down again, loosing about the beautiful animal's head a volley of trilingual oaths.

Bernardo grinned wickedly. "You should never leave the quarter-deck, Kit," he said, chuckling. "With horses you display a most unpracticed hand."

"Enough," Kit growled. "What brings you here? I can see by the look of smug contentment on your homely face that you have news."

"Alas," Bernardo said cheerfully, "I have always had an open countenance. It is my greatest misfortune, Kit. In this world a man has great need of dissembling and guile."

"Never mind the philosophy," Kit said. "Get to the news. It must be important to part you from your gaming and wenching."

"A wench or two might cool the fever of your impatience," Bernardo observed. "You were not cut out for monkhood, Kit."

"The news!" Kit roared.

"I have none, but I do have an invitation from His Excellency the Governor for you to dine with him on Monday next at his house at Léogane."

"The Sieur Ducasse invites me to dine with him? How did that come about, Bernardo?"

"I have often ridden through his cane fields. Three times a week, to be exact. Near Léogane there's a small pigeon who puts up enough resistance to the plucking to make it interesting —and the shortest route to her home lies through the Sieur Ducasse's lands."

"Are you sure you did not waylay him with some tortuous scheme?"

"I am grieved," said Bernardo, grinning, "at your suspicious nature. What scheme could I have?"

"Who knows, my old one?" Kit smiled at him. "You of course chanced to meet Ducasse?"

"Yes. And the Governor, who is of Huguenot parentage, can take a mass or leave it, though I think he likes the leaving better than the taking. Therefore neither the question of my birth nor the fact of my conversion concerned him in the least. We talked of ships and sailing. It was a good talk, Kit—the man knows the sea."

"So? How came this invitation to dine?"

"I dropped, in passing, word that I had served aboard the *Seaflower*. The good Sieur was at once all ears, and asked if I knew you. Your fame has spread abroad, Kit. The Governor very probably would like to employ you in some service."

"I don't like that," Kit growled. "I'm done with such a life."

"Patience, Kit. For miles on end one rides through a sea of cane, tilled by blacks brought from Africa. His Excellency hinted that such a plantation was not beyond your attaining.

Here in the New World great wealth is much easier earned than in the Old. If I were you, I would lend a most attentive ear to what Ducasse has to say."

"This has a pleasant sound," Kit agreed, "still . . ."

"What harm can come of eating the man's food and drinking his wine, since both are reputed to be excellent?"

"I stand persuaded," Kit said. "You will of course also be present?"

"Of course. Now ride with me a bit while I inform you about His Excellency. Nothing is more pleasing to a man's ear than knowledge of his previous doings—especially when they have been noteworthy. And Jean-Baptiste Ducasse is a great man, I assure you. He began his career as a slave trader for the Compagnie de Sénégal, and at once distinguished himself by helping to drive the Dutch out of the island of Gorée. Then he took all the rest of the islands in the Cape Verde group. He made his first voyage to Saint-Domingue in 1680. . . . Are you listening, Kit?"

"Attentively," Kit said. "Go on."

"There he displayed his intelligence by taking heed of what everybody in the Antilles knew, but what no dealer in black ivory had ever bothered to consider: the fact that to continue to bring in Coromantes, Fantis, Ashantis, and Dahomeans was not only foolhardy but suicidal. Those tribes of blacks fear neither a white skin, God, nor the devil, and wait only for the first dark night to begin cutting their masters' throats. He came back loaded with Whydahs, Nagoes, Pawpaws, Congoes, and Angolans—all diligent, tractable slaves. And to prove that the man can think, he brought not one Ebo, the easiest of all blacks to obtain, and the stupidest. From that one voyage, Ducasse made his fortune—never before or since has a shipload of Negroes commanded a higher price."

"You are oddly expert in these matters," Kit mused. "Have you studied the blacks, Bernardo?"

"Yes," Bernardo replied with a smile. "When you get to be a planter, you will need a manager."

"You were speaking," Kit said slowly, "of Jean-Baptiste Ducasse. The selection of my plantation manager can wait."

"So I was. My wits grow addled with age. With the money that he made, Ducasse outfitted himself as a privateer. Soon he had made such a name for himself that Louis XIV commissioned him a lieutenant in the Royal Navy. By this time Pouançay was dead and Paul Tarin de Cussy had become Governor of Saint-Domingue. We were in these waters with Lazarus when the news of De Cussy's elevation reached us, remember?"

Kit nodded patiently.

"Ducasse was exceedingly busy. He attacked the Dutch in Guiana and chased the English completely out of St. Kitts; then he sailed back to France. When he returned he found that he was now governor, for De Cussy had fallen in the sack of Cap Français in 1691. Ducasse chased the British away from Guadeloupe. Then he settled down to rule, with such effectiveness that Saint-Domingue has become a model colony—even the buccaneers obey him. There the matter rests until this day, except for the forays by Daviot and Laurens de Graff against Jamaica—also at His Excellency's orders. All in all, a most excellent leader, in my opinion."

"Yes," Kit mused, "he seems a real man. Have you any idea what he wants of me?"

"Something touching Jamaica. It would do no harm to find out. Out here the world is young, and there are not the old quarrels, old schemes, and old jealousies to contend with. If filibustering were the only way a man could gain sustenance in the Antilles, I would say depart; but the white crystals of the sugar mills and the great hogsheads of rum will make all the gold of El Dorado paltry by comparison. It will not be amiss to gain the Sieur Ducasse's favor."

Kit did not answer. He bent his bronzed face and stared fixedly at the white arch of the great stallion's neck, feeling the rhythm of the horse's motion.

They rode on in deep silence. The sun burned blood-red into the Caribbean and the night crashed down without twilight or dusk between it and the dazzling day gold. The palms and the mountains and the thickets disappeared in the abrupt darkness, and the profligate heavens flung out their treasure of stars.

The horses moved on slow-clopping through a night like man's destiny—filled ·with sound and motion, traveling unceasingly onward toward a goal whose outlines cannot be discerned.

Exter, Jean-Baptiste Ducasse's residence at Léogane, was a pleasant mansion built of great cypress clapboards, and the Governor himself was a tall, heavy man whose immense brown wig, curling over his back and shoulders, gave him the look of a benevolent lion.

He greeted Kit and Bernardo with bluff cordiality, and led them to the great dining salon. Glancing at the silver service, Kit saw at once that the table was laid for only three. This was strange. For what reason had the Governor thought it necessary to maintain such privacy?

His Excellency was not slow in getting to the point. Over the golden mound of the roast fowl, he eyed Kit quizzically, the light of humor dancing in his small blue eyes.

"The captain of the *Seaflower*," he chuckled. "You are young for such a command, Monsieur Gerado."

"What do years matter?" Kit answered. "It is the straightness of the aim and the strength of the arm on the tiller that make the difference."

Ducasse reached out a powerful hand and took up a glass. He raised it to his lips and held it there without tasting the amber wine while his eyes studied Kit above the rim.

"There is," he mused, "in my office at Port de Paix a record of French ships lost to enemy action in these waters. I seem to recall a *Cygne*, a *Gallant*, and a *Gloire* sunk by one brigantine called the *Seaflower*. There were more, but those come most easily to mind at the moment."

Kit put his own glass down with deliberate slowness and his eyes were cool and grave. "Not while I commanded her," he said flatly. "I have never fired on the fleur-de-lis."

"So?" Ducasse said calmly. "If not, it is most strange for one who was born in Cádiz, in the realms of His Most Impotent, Bewitched Majesty, that royal idiot Charles II of Spain!"

Kit looked at Ducasse, and smile wrinkles played about the corners of his eyes. "Would you bait me, your Excellency?" he

113

asked. "If so, you take the wrong track. My mother, it happens, was born in Normandy, and my true name is Giradeaux."

Ducasse bounded to his feet. His arm swept across the table, reaching for Kit's hand.

"There!" he roared. "I knew you were no dog of a Spaniard! I should have known it before—your French is better than mine."

"And if your Excellency's records are complete," Bernardo put in dryly, "they should show that the *Seaflower* has sent twenty-two Spanish ships to the bottom within the past three years."

"They do show that," Ducasse said, and laughed. "That was what puzzled me. But no more of this. Now to business. You know that the town of Port Royal was ruined two years ago by an earthquake."

"Yes," Kit growled, "we were in the harbor when it happened."

"So? You were supremely lucky to have escaped, then."

"We were," Bernardo said, "but pray continue. You were speaking of Port Royal."

"Since that explicit manifestation of Divine displeasure, I, in my small way, have implemented the arm of the Almighty. I have sent Daviot and De Graff to slow the English work of reconstruction, but for all that they rebuild much too fast and too well." He leaned forward confidentially. "Not that I fear their fortifications and batteries, but there is a slower thing that over the years can ruin us here." He glanced past Kit and Bernardo and his eyes took on a dreaming look. "All the world will one day make a track over the waters to Saint-Domingue. The Cul-de-Sac and Cap Français and the harbor at Port de Paix will be black with shipping come from Europe to buy our sugar and our rum. There is where our wealth lies! Let the Spaniards grub gold out of the earth—still it will flow back to us. I do not fear the Englishman's guns, but I do fear their sugar mills and their slaves. They must not compete with us here; in this Saint-Domingue must reign supreme!"

"Therefore," Kit said quietly, "you want me to take the *Seaflower* out and raid them once again?"

"No! I would have you join me in a full-scale expedition

against Jamaica. I shall have more than twenty ships, and from this blow the English will never recover. But I can use your youth, courage, and skill. What do you say, Captain Giradeaux?"

"I don't know," Kit mused. "I have no quarrel with the English. The only Englishman I have known well was a kindly man. Still, this inaction begins to pall on me."

Ducasse crossed to where Kit sat and took his arm. "Come," he said, helping Kit up. They walked to the window, and Kit followed his finger pointing over the immense expanse of cane fields to the very foot of the mountains. "There is," he said softly, "over against Petit Goave, arpent upon arpent of such rich land, as yet untilled. As governor of this colony, it lies within my power to grant that land to whomever I will—in reward, of course, for services justly performed."

"And if I refuse," Kit said, "you might recall to a court the Seaflower's former misdeeds, and leave it up to me to present proof that I had no hand in them."

Ducasse looked at the lad, seeing him young, fair, and very spirited. "No, Christophe," he said quietly. "Your choice is free. Accept or refuse as you will."

Kit frowned. He tugged thoughtfully at the golden spike of his beard. "When do you sail?" he asked.

"Next month."

The next month was June of the year 1694. There were yet nine more months of waiting before Kit's promise to Rouge was to be fulfilled. And there was little hope that she would appear before the time appointed. He had much to gain and nothing to lose.

"The Seaflower will take her place in the line," he said.

10

ON THE MORNING of June 22, 1694, Kit and Bernardo lay in a little copse of woods on the island of Jamaica, looking out on a great cane field. Behind them hid the crew of the *Seaflower*.

"Look, Kit," Bernardo was exulting, "you have no country. By birth you are a Spaniard, but Spain's star is setting and you have killed too many dons to face the reckoning. Likewise, you are not French, for men reckon descent after the father, and no man, not even I, knows with any certainty who your father was. But now you have gained a country! Ducasse loves you like a son. He could not be more joyful over the feat of saving Major Beauregard's troops from that ambush if he had performed it himself. He will not forget how many times you have turned the tide of battle in his favor. As a planter of Saint-Domingue, who knows what greatness you might attain?"

"Who knows indeed?" Kit said dryly. "Still, this attack sits unhappily in my gullet. I have known but two people of English blood in all my life. One of them was a great sea captain and the other the woman I want for my wife."

"She will know nothing of this, and she would care less if she knew. What can it matter, since by this you gain the means to make her the greatest lady of Saint-Domingue?"

"Yes," Kit growled, "as to that you have much logic, though small right. But right and logic were always at variance, is it not so, my old one?"

"Always," Bernardo agreed.

To their left the tall chimney of a sugar mill sent volumes of black smoke into the air. Kit paid scant attention to the mill. He was watching the young Englishman who was directing the

116

Negroes as they fed the stalks of cane into the great stone crushers. A team of mules drew the millstones around. Kit could see that their left eyes had been covered with a length of cloth to keep their endless circling from making them dizzy.

A humane people, the English, he reflected, and turned his attention back to the young man. He was, Kid had to admit, an uncommonly handsome youth. A shade too handsome in fact, Kit thought. The young man was shouting at his blacks and his clear tenor voice came over to Kit. It took Kit a moment to understand the meaning of the English words. Had it not been for Smithers' insistence upon speaking English to him, Kit might have forgotten the tongue that Lazarus had taught him with such painstaking care.

" 'Od's bodikins!" the young man swore. "You black beasts! Get it in there—push it closer or I'll have your bloody hides!"

"Yas, Marsa Reginald," the black who was feeding the crushers groaned. "Doin' best I kin."

Kit saw the young man rise in the saddle and bring his riding crop down, full across the Negro's back. The black man cringed, and gave the stalks of cane a convulsive shove. The next moment Kit heard him scream. It was a terrible sound, like a loon night-maddened or like a parakeet loosing his insane, fiendish laughter. Looking closer, Kit could see that the Negro had caught his hand in the crusher.

"Mother of God!" he whispered. "Why doesn't he stop the mules?"

But the young Englishman—wasn't it "Reginald" the Negro had called him?—sat there like one stupefied. The great mill-stones dragged the black's wrist and forearm and upper arm between them, so that the slave was pulled round and round the outer rim of the crushers and the cane juice came out red with his blood.

"Idiot!" the Englishman shrieked, suddenly completely beside himself with rage. "You've ruined the entire batch! Brutus! Bring the ax!"

Kit and Bernardo watched in cold stupefaction while another Negro hurried off, to return after a moment with a broad-bladed ax.

117

"Set him free!" the young man ordered. Brutus, his black face the color of old ashes, swung the ax skyward. Kit saw it arching against the sky. Then it whistled downward to strike the imprisoned slave's shoulder with a sound like no other sound on earth—except, perhaps, the sound of the poleax in the slaughter pens.

The black man lay on the earth, his arm sheared off at the shoulder, and the great flood of his life pumped out until all the earth beneath him was muddied. No one made the slightest effort to aid him or to stop the bleeding.

Grimly Kit turned to his buccaneers. "All right, men," he said quietly, "burn the field!"

In a trice the flints snapped against the steel, and the buccaneers blew lustily on the smoldering tinder. One of them got a tiny yellow flame and stuck the tarred end of the huge torch into it. Instantly it flared, and all the buccaneers crowded around the man, lighting their torches from his.

It was the misfortune of the English on the southern shore of Jamaica that their land was exceedingly arid. They were able to grow cane only by irrigation, and even so many of the stalks that stood in the fields were brown and dry. To the north, beyond the mountains, torrents of rain fell; but the Blue Mountains—as the Jamaicans so accurately called the range that separated the north from the south of the islands—effectively stopped all rainfall from reaching the southern shore. It was in the south that the flatlands lay, and the industrious English had made them grow.

The cane about the margins of this field was so much tinder. The system of irrigation was crude and misapplied. So it was that when the Englishman looked up from his blood-ruined cane juice and his dead slave, he saw a wall of flame advancing upon him, and through it a horde of buccaneers, shrieking like fiends and firing their great muskets.

He stood there open-mouthed until Bernardo was upon him. The Jew's great arm swept up, and his open palm made a sound like a pistol shot against the young man's face. The next moment the Englishman was rolling in the dust.

The fierce buccaneers pulled him to his feet and began to bind

118

his arms. He jerked his face around and his eyes fell on Kit, beplumed, beribboned, lace at throat and wrist, a slim Spanish sword dangling at his side.

"Your name," Kit demanded.

"Reginald Parish," the young Englishman spat. "And if I were not bound . . ."

Kit's blue eyes searched his face; they were as cold as ice. "Release him," Kit said quietly. The buccaneers hesitated. "I said release him!" Kit growled. The men hurried to obey.

"I have no sword," Parish said.

"Give him your sword, Bernardo," Kit said. "I would not deny even such a dog as this the chance of an honorable death."

"You're a fool, Kit," Bernardo said. "How do you know this fop is not a maître d'armes?"

"I'll chance it," replied Kit, smiling. "On guard!"

Reginald Parish brought his sword up in a practiced flourish. The blades made blue lightning in meeting, the air was loud with the clang of steel even above the crackle of the flames. Parish pressed the attack so that Kit was forced to give ground, parrying the Englishman's thrusts with negligent, deceptive ease.

"Reginald . . ." he mused aloud as he fought. "That name has a familiar ring." He stretched forward suddenly, his right knee bending, his left leg straightening out until the lace at his knee swept the earth, and the Englishman's sword swept upward from his hand. Kit straightened and put the point of his sword against the earth.

"Recover your weapon," he said coldly.

"You're twice a fool," Bernardo muttered. "Run the bastard through!"

Reginald Parish picked up the sword and saluted Kit with it. Then he lunged forward, beginning a furious attack. Kit gave not an inch; he parried in tierce and his blade continued along his opponent's sword, opening a cut above the man's eye.

"Have you had enough?" Kit asked, lowering his weapon.

Instead of answering, Parish lunged forward with all his might, so that Kit was forced to leap aside, parrying in seconde so late that the rounded bell guards of their weapons' hilts clanged together. Kit came up body to body, forcing his opponent's arm upward while the ribbons of sweat and blood bedewed young Parish's face.

"Without honor, ah, Reginald!" he mocked. "Now to make an end to this."

He started forward, his blade a moving blur, so that Reginald was forced to give ground, meeting Kit's blade in quinte, in sixte, now in prime, his hand held up before his face, the blade angling downward across his breast while Kit laughed and beat him back. Then, in sudden riposte, Kit laid the point of his rapier against Parish's heart. Suddenly, abruptly, he halted.

"Reginald!" he whispered. "Now I know! It's the name of the man Rouge was to wed!"

"Rouge?" Parish panted. "I do not know that name."

"A maid," Kit said, "with hair the color of flame and eyes of emerald."

"Jane!" Parish croaked. "Lady Jane Golphin!"

Kit sheathed his sword. "Take back your life. I will not harm anyone once dear to her."

"Then it was you," Parish cried, "who barbadoed her away!" He sprang forward, the point of his rapier aimed straight for Kit's heart, but the crash of Bernardo's pistol echoed above the raging flames. Reginald loosened all over at once, becoming suddenly boneless, Bernardo's rapier spinning from his hand.

Kit stood there watching him fall slowly toward the earth, then he raised his blue eyes to Bernardo's face. "Thank you, my old one," he said quietly.

Reginald Parish lay on the ground coughing blood. "Rosalind," he gurgled. "You will not harm her? . . . Swear it."

"Rosalind?" Kit said. "Who is she?"

"My wife," Reginald gasped, but the word brought a rush of blood to his throat, so that he strangled from it, his face purpling.

"I swear," Kit said.

Something like peace came into Parish's eyes. He opened his mouth to say something, but whatever it was it was never voiced, for at that moment he died.

"An ugly business," Kit said. He looked out at his men,

120

who were busily overturning the vats and prying loose the mill-stones with great staves. "The price of becoming a gentleman of Saint-Domingue runs high," he mused.

"He had scant claim upon Rouge," Bernardo observed. Then: "I wonder where the manor house is?"

As if in answer to his question, the high cry of a woman rang through the woods. A moment later the woman came in sight. She was as naked as the day she was born, except for a few rags of clothing that clung to her arms and shoulders. Behind her as she ran pounded two buccaneers. Hope flared suddenly in the woman's eyes. She sped straight toward Kit, forgetful of her nakedness. When she was close she hurled herself into his arms and lay against his iron-hard body, shivering and whimpering like a whipped child. Kit disengaged her grasp gently, and taking off his greatcoat, wrapped it about her.

The buccaneers gathered about Kit and the woman, mutters running from man to man. Kit faced them, one hand about the woman, the other holding a freshly primed pistol that Bernardo had that moment given him.

"I told you last night," he said flatly, "that I would have no rape! Whoever disobeys me dies! Understand?"

The freebooters fell back, their faces black with scowls. Kit heard the woman gasp.

"Reginald!" she whispered. She was looking at the dead Englishman.

"I am sorry, my lady," Kit said in his slow, accented English. "I would have spared his life, but he forced the issue."

Lady Rosalind Parish turned her heart-shaped face toward Kit, seeing the clean chiseled lines of his jaw, the thin falcon's beak of a nose, the mouth firm beneath the white-gold mustache, and the great mane of his hair spilling down over his shoulders like a golden fleece.

Kit looked at her, seeing her face small, lovely, fierce. There were no tears in her blue eyes, the trembling was gone from the corners of her rose-pink mouth, which was curving upward at the corners in a terrible kind of joy.

"I'm glad! Now I'm free!" she said, her voice calm with a dreadful calmness. "How I hated him!"

121

Kit was puzzled, but said, "Lead me to the manor—if these dogs of mine have not yet burned it."

"No," Lady Rosalind whispered, "they have not—they were far too busy—with me."

Kit turned back toward Bernardo and commanded, "Bury the dead." Then very gently he led Lady Rosalind away from the smoke and cinders of the burning cane field.

She marched ahead of him. Only three buttons of his coat were fastened, so that her white legs gleamed softly in all their slender length each time she took a stride. Once inside the manor house she asked him to sit down while she went to the wine cupboard. She returned with a decanter and two large goblets.

"To my freedom!" she cried, and drained her glass.

Kit sat there with his glass untouched, looking at her in amazement. The three fastened buttons of his greatcoat concealed nothing of her, but she moved before him like a graceful doe, entirely without shame. She downed another glass, then a third, her blue eyes brightening, her gaze moving intently over his face.

"Hadn't you better go and dress?" Kit said slowly.

Rosalind Parish threw back her head and laughed. "No, good Captain," she said, laughing. "I have no shame! Your sea dogs removed all need for it. Besides, it's nice to be naked—so very cool."

"Your husband," Kit said. "Why did you hate him?"

She put down her goblet with a crash. "Because he didn't love me! Because he was always mooning over another woman, Jane Golphin, who was barbadoed during the earthquake! Because he was a weakling and I needed a man!" She leaned forward, her lips dew-petaled, warm and inviting. "Such a man as you—perhaps . . ." She stood up suddenly, her slim fingers toying with the topmost button. "If you had come yourself, instead of sending those evil-smelling rogues, I fear I would not have struggled."

She came slowly up to Kit and put her head against his chest.

"There is no need for haste," she whispered. "You can continue your raid—tomorrow."

Kit put his hands roughly on her shoulders and pushed her away from him.

"This day your husband has been killed. I fear that the dog in the human race is not confined to the male alone."

She looked up at him, her smile sensual and excited. "Yes, I am evil!" She laughed as she said it. "I am glad of it! I have held it pent up too long." She studied Kit's frowning face. "Do not go!" she whispered.

"In my lifetime," Kit growled, "I have sent many a soul to hell. But I have not sunk so low as to kill the husband and take my pleasure with the wife. Good day, madame!" He bowed, and turning, marched through the doorway. And as he strode through the woods, he heard the high, hysterical titter of her laughter.

Four days later, at the head of his ship's company, Kit marched back toward the sea. His men drove a hundred Negroes—all Eboes, selected by Bernardo—before them. The raid, as a raid, had been a success. Two hundred and fifty mills and plantations had been destroyed and more than thirteen hundred Negroes captured. But the attack designed to reduce Jamaica to the status of a French colony was an abysmal failure. The English had been wounded. They had not been defeated.

The long line of buccaneers, their faces lost amid the great dark forests of their beards, filed downward toward the shore in ragged lines, driving the slaves. Behind them, above the royal crests of the palms, Kit could see the huge plumes of black smoke billowing in the still air.

"Fifteen," he counted silently, "sixteen, seventeen, eighteen, nineteen . . ." And every one of them the house a man had loved or the mill he had built or the cane field he had made to grow on the arid soil. How many of the owners lay charred and blackened in the smoking embers of their manors? How many of their women had run shrieking into the thorn thickets and marshes, only to be pulled down by these goats and satyrs he had helped loose among them?

His fingers strayed down to the frayed sash of gold he had made from Don Luis's Heron Banner. Now while he was loosing his fury on the innocent, Luis del Toro was taking his ease in his house at Cartagena. Beside him, no doubt, Bianca was sitting, fair Bianca whose beauty still moved with troublesome brightness through Kit's memory.

If, he mused, it were not for the chance that Rouge might yet join me at Petit Goave, I would scale those walls and strike him down! No, more than that, there is the possibility of a still richer vengeance! What worse could I do, before I send him into hell, than to bind him hand and foot to a pillar, with this banner stuffed in his mouth for a gag, and then take my pleasure with Bianca there before his eyes? Death ends all suffering, but with the sight of her writhing in my arms, even in the grave his sleep would be troubled. . . .

They topped a rise and looked down at the surrounding country. Kit frowned, for there before them lay still another plantation, which somehow had escaped burning. Bernardo looked up at Kit with questioning eyes. Kit's frown deepened, his hand came up and tugged at the golden spike of his beard. Then he looked about at his men.

"Well, lads?" he said.

"God's blood!" Smithers said. "A few more blacks won't hurt none. The more the merrier!"

The others nodded assent. Kit sighed. From the first he had known what they would say.

"Spare the manor," he ordered. "I will drink the owner's wine. And no ravishment—there will be bawds aplenty when we reach Saint-Domingue."

"If we don't bust first," said Smithers, grinning. The men laughed. They were in rare good humor, which increased with the imminence of their homeward voyage.

At Kit's signal they swept down on the cane fields. Kit and Bernardo made straight for the house. Long before they reached it the dry cane fields were a sea of flame, and the crash of the overturning vats and crushers resounded from the mill. They turned down a neat roadway flanked by rows of white-trunked palms, leading to the great white mansion in the center. They had brought with them five or six buccaneers, considering this number sufficient to overcome the scant resistance they expected.

When they were a hundred yards from the manor, a dozen armed Negroes came out. Bernardo peered at them intently, gauging the shape of their heads, their bone structure, and the flare of their nostrils.

"Whydahs," he pronounced. "Have no fear, these blacks are not fighters."

"Fire a volley over their heads," Kit commanded.

The long buccaneering muskets leaped to the freebooters' shoulders. The crash of their fire echoed from the road. As the smoke drifted up through the palms, Kit saw the timid blacks scrambling for safety.

"Life is strange," Bernardo philosophized. "Either a man buys fierce Dahomeans or Coromantes and gets no work, or he buys Eboes, or Whydahs and has no defense from aggression."[1]

Kit did not answer. He was leaning forward, pinpoints of fire in his blue eyes. A woman had come out of the manor and was beating the blacks back to the fray with the flat of her sword. She used the weapon as though she had handled a blade all her life. Kit hung there a moment, staring. Wildly, wordlessly, he began to run toward her. Bernardo looked after him in astonishment. He lifted his eyes toward the woman, then he too broke into a gallop. Even from that distance he could see that her hair was as red as the flames that devoured the cane fields.

Kit came running straight toward the trembling blacks. The muzzles of their muskets came up, pointing at his chest. The woman spoke to them sharply.

"Hold!" she commanded.

Kit came up to her, his blue eyes searching her face. "Rouge," he whispered, "my little Rouge."

"Lady Jane Golphin, you murderous dog!" she said, her green eyes fixed upon his face. "Get away or . . ."

Kit slowed, a smile playing about the corners of his mouth. "Or what, Rouge?" he mocked. "What, my red-haired sea witch turned gentlewoman?"

"You are mistaken," she said evenly, her red mouth moving,

[1] The troops of Toussaint, Dessalines, and Christophe, a century later, were nearly all of Dahomean descent, as were their leaders.

shaping the words, her skin white as the petals of water lilies beneath the amazing brush fire of her hair. "I know no Rouge."

"Then I will instruct you, Lady Jane. You are oddly expert with that sword of yours, and your eyes are as green as sea water, your mouth still hungers to be kissed."

He moved toward her, but the point of the rapier came up and rested on his bare chest.

"Come no farther," she spat, "or I'll kill you!"

Kit glanced down at the rapier making a small dent in his bronzed skin. Then slowly, deliberately, he moved forward. A drop of blood showed around the point. Then, as he lifted his foot to move forward again, she drew the sword back, and the next instant Kit held her in his arms. Tears spilled over her dark-gold lashes and penciled her fair cheeks.

"I am weak," she wept, "weak! You should die!"

"Why, my little Rouge?" Kit whispered.

Her pale face lifted, and her eyes blazed with emerald fire.

"For taking away all I had left of belief in the goodness of men! For proving that you too are a murderer, when I was learning in my heart to care for you deeply!" She stared at him, the tears in her eyes like diamonds. "You came here to a land that had never harmed you. You burned and ravished and destroyed. And when you found Reginald Parish, you killed him because I had once loved him! You fool, he was married, and I had long ago become merely his friend and neighbor!"

Kit tried to interpose, but he could not stem the rush of Rouge's words.

"You killed poor, spineless Reginald," Rouge continued, her voice rising, "and then you lay with his wife! Forced her, she says, though I doubt that, for Rosalind has scant need of forcing!"

Kit stared at her, light dawning in his eyes. "She lied," he said gravely. "On all counts, she lied. I did not slay Parish. I left Rosalind untouched."

"I will not listen to you!" Rouge cried. "All men are dogs, and worse! Go away, Christopher—get out of my sight, for my forbearance wears thin."

Kit did not move back. Instead, his arms swept up and drew her to him, and his lips found her mouth. He could feel her body trembling through the rich fabric of her clothing, sense the terrible warfare within her: the fierce demanding surge of desire, the great swift, sweet lassitude of assent struggling with her rage, her hurt, her hate. His mouth moved on hers, feeling her lips slackening into surrender, the beat of her heart beneath the soft-cushioning globes of her breasts becoming a drum roll, swift-pounding against his own. He bent down and swept her into his arms, oblivious of the stares of the buccaneers. With one booted foot he kicked open the door and entered the cool gloom of the great mansion.

"Which way?" he said, his voice hoarse. Mutely, she motioned with her head. He shouldered open the second door, and paused for a moment before the large bed, canopied with netting against the mosquitoes. Then, very gently, he laid her down upon it.

"No," she whispered, "not yet, Kit. Talk to me—say that you love me, that I not another Rosalind whom you take because you can."

Kit murmured: "No, never that! You are my love, my heart, my bride."

Her white hands came up and lay along the bronzed curve of his cheek. "I am through with fighting against you," she whispered. "I came here to Jamaica to learn again to be a woman, that I might not be ill of grace when I came to you. The lesson went hard. Teach me, my Kit—teach me to be whole again. Kiss me—hold me—never let me go!"

Kit bent down and kissed her mouth. Her pale fingers stole upward and caressed the bright blaze of his hair.

"Now," she sighed, "I am ready. Do what you will. Perhaps this time I shall find true joy in it."

Kit's lean, iron-hard fingers trembled on the fastenings of the gown. Then suddenly her hands caught at his wrists and she sat up, staring out of the window.

"My fields!" she said. Then she turned the great blaze of her slanted eyes on him. "You," she whispered, her voice edged and harsh, "you did this too! You ordered the burning!"

Kit swung about, seeing the great wall of flame riding before the wind, roaring down upon the manor. The house, he saw in an instant, was doomed. He half-turned back toward her, but the motion came too late. He saw the flash of the silver candelabra as she swung it with all her force. He jerked aside, but not fast enough or far enough. The blow that might have stoved in his skull merely glanced along the side of his head, leaving him swaying dizzily on his feet and shaking his head to clear his reeling sight.

He heard the swift rustle of her garments as she fled from the room, and staggered after her. She fled down a long hallway toward the rear of the house. Kit ran unsteadily after her, and came out into the courtyard in time to see her mount and ride away. He was still there, supporting himself by an arm about a pillar, when the others joined him. Bernardo looked at him with anxiety, but Smithers and the men, seeing the thick ooze of scarlet spreading down his face, roared with unconcealed joy.

"No ravishment, eh, Captain! A good rule, sir! You should practice it sometime!"

Kit looked at them, and a wry grin spread under the blond mustache. "I am bested," he admitted. "But for this, that red-haired sea witch shall pay!"

Then he turned and took Bernardo's proffered arm. An hour later they started their final march to the sea.

11

KIT STOOD MOROSELY on the foredeck, watching the *Seaflower* thread her way delicately between the whitecaps, pushing her prow into the deep-curving troughs of the sea. For three days they had been running due west, almost at right angles to their true course, but now the gale whose fury had driven them some three hundred leagues out of their way was blowing itself out. In another hour, perhaps they would be able to set a new course for Saint-Domingue.

His fingers stole up and touched the swath of bandages that encircled his aching head. *I almost had you won that time, my little Rouge, but for a wind and flame and obedience to the orders governing an expedition I joined against my better judgment—which, in fact, I joined only to gain for you the station befitting you. Now I have gained these things only to lose you. . . .*

Lose her? Lose Rouge? Never while she lived! Twice now she had lain trembling and lost within his arms, soft with the lassitude of surrender. And the second time would have been the first repeated, made more glorious, but for the hellish mischance of that burning field. That first time on shipboard when she had come to him unwillingly only to surrender at the last, to brand him hip and thigh with her beauty that was both snow and flame—with how bright a glow did the memory flare in his mind still! To the end of his days that thought would warm him, no matter how cool his blood would grow with age.

But what had been could be again—and this time for as long as they both should live. He had burned her house. Very well, he would build her another, and such a house as she could not now imagine in her wildest dreams. He had burned her fields. Now he would fling down at her feet fields bathed in sea mists, fragrant with rains, in which in the space of days the cane would spring up taller than a mounted horseman—fitting recompense for those dry, brown Jamaican fields that had to be watered at the cost of so much labor.

He stopped short. He would do these things, but what then? How was he to find one small corvette on the trackless bosom of the sea? Two years had passed between the time he first saw Rouge standing drenched and trembling on the *Seaflower*'s deck and the time when by purest chance he had stumbled upon her attacking the great plate ships. How many weary years would pass again before he found her? She would not go back to Jamaica, that he knew; she would hurl her renewed fury down upon the heads of men—and he, God help him, must find a tiny craft that might be anywhere within three thousand wind-whipped leagues.

He was interrupted in his reverie by the lookout's shout, floating down through the diminishing shriek of the wind.

"Vessel astern!" he called. "Three points to sta'board!"

Kit and his officers crowded aft, staring at the apparition, their minds refusing to credit the evidence of their eyes. For there, on the crest of the still wildly racing waves, a ship rode with every sail bent to the wind, heeling over at so great an angle that her lee rails were actually awash, boiling after them at a speed no sailing vessel was ever intended to make.

The vessel alternately appeared and disappeared as she drove through the walls of spray, and each time they saw her she was nearer. Now she was upon them, and Kit could see that she was a corvette with lines as clean and trim as the *Seaflower*'s own. Then as she drew abeam a great roar burst from her single line of guns, and she disappeared momentarily behind the cloud of gun smoke. Instinctively, Kit hit the deck, and the balls sang over him by inches, smashing the gunwales into matchwood, and overturning four of the *Seaflower*'s guns.

"Gunners to station!" Kit howled, and the *Seaflower* became an anthill of frenzied activity. The passers and the powder monkeys skidded over the wet decks, their deadly burdens cradled in their desperate arms. The gunners had trouble with their matches, but after several agony-laden minutes they got them burning despite the storm. The touchholes had to be cleared and filled with dry powder, and by the time they were ready, the *Seaflower* had taken another broadside that killed three of the men.

Bernardo swung at Kit's sleeve, pointing. Kit looked down at the glowing object that hissed on the wet deck.

"Mother of God!" he breathed. "They're serving red-hot shot!" Then he turned back to his gunners. "Hold your fire!" he called. "Helmsman, run her in until we can't miss!"

Again the corvette loosed her murderous hail, but the men were better sheltered now. The *Seaflower* veered in toward the attacking vessel, riding in so close that Kit could see the name on her prow.

"*Seawitch*," he spelled out, his brow knitted with frowning. He lifted his sword high, holding it there while the gunners crouched beside their silent pieces, waiting for his signal. The *Seaflower* fell off a bit, running exactly parallel to the corvette, her guns at point-blank range aimed at the slim and deadly vessel scant yards away. Then, slowly, Kit's sword arm started downward. Halfway down he halted the movement abruptly, his breath a tangled burning within his lungs, for there on the high deck of the corvette the woman stood, her long red hair streaming to leeward like a banner of blood.

"Hold!" he got out, but the word was a mere croak. The wind snatched it from his lips, and before he could reshape it the titanic thunder of the *Seaflower*'s guns rocked sea and sky with their belly-deep roar. The walls of smoke rose before his eyes, and he heard his own voice shrieking like a man gone mad: "Hold! Hold your fire for the love of God!"

Then the smoke cleared, and he saw the light corvette, never designed to match guns with so stout a vessel as the *Seaflower*, heeling over as though mortally wounded. Even as he watched, he saw the fire break out amidships, and as he swayed there, his face gray as death, Bernardo chortled.

"We hit the furnace for the hot shot!" Bernardo yelled. "Knocked it over, hand bellows and all, and the bastard's burning! Give him another, Kit! Finish him off! God's blood, didn't he know enough not to attack the *Seaflower*?"

"Ride her in," Kit called. "Cease fire. Grappling irons ready! Stand by to board her!"

Bernardo turned an incredulous face toward his captain. "You're mad, Kit? You can't board her in such a sea!"

Kit turned his face, gray-pale and haggard, to Bernardo. "It's *her* ship," he whispered. "And board her we must, though we drown in the attempt."

The *Seaflower* drew closer, her own crew watching the mountainous seas with fear-stricken eyes. From where they stood, Kit and Bernardo saw Rouge walking up and down the deck, swinging the long Spanish whip, the crack of the lash sounding even above the storm. Somehow she got five gunners back to their stations, and the guns roared out one after another. At such a distance, it was impossible to miss. Kit kept his gaze fastened on the dying *Seawitch*, but as he watched, the *Seaflower* veered suddenly, the distance between the two vessels widening.

Kit turned to growl at the helmsman, then his jaw dropped blankly. Where the *Seaflower's dos d'âne* had been there was only a smoking mass of timbers, the whipstaff itself was a thousand ragged splinters, and the brigantine was entirely out of control. He stood watching the blackening seas growing broader between the two vessels. The tarred stays, shrouds, halyards, and clews of the corvette were burning rapidly, the sails catching, too, despite their wetness. A great weakness stole up through his limbs. He sat down abruptly on the deck, watching the boiling masses of mist and cloud blotting out the *Seawitch's* outline. For a long time he could mark her by the bloody glow that she cast upward on the enveloping cloud, then all was mist and grayness and silence and death.

He sat very still on the *Seaflower's* deck, without moving, until Bernardo touched his arm and led him away. Bernardo knew it was not well for the *Seaflower's* crew to see her captain weep.

In the morning the sun broke through the high, fleecy mare's-tails and all the sea to the east was a rosy pink, breaking in gentle swells so mild that the brigantine scarcely rolled at all. On the deck the ship's carpenter and a crew of hands sweated and swore as they fitted a new whipstaff into place.

Kit trod the deck forward and aft, his blue eyes blank and unseeing, his thin mouth held in a tight line, his fingers clenching and unclenching. He stopped before the laboring group.

"How long now?" he demanded.

The ship's carpenter looked up and wiped the sweat away from his brow with a grimy hand. "God knows, Cap'n," he said. "Another four-five hours."

"Mother of God!" Kit whispered. Bernardo, who kept constantly at his side, put out a restraining hand.

"It's no use, Kit," he said kindly. "By now that corvette has gone down with all hands. It was vile luck, but you must not blame yourself."

"Not blame myself!" Kit exploded. "Whose fault was it, then? Had I not seen that vessel before? Had I not set foot on her deck? And the name—how often have we both applied it to Rouge herself? That little sea witch—that little red-haired sea witch! If I were not a prince of asses, she might be here now—alive and with me. Holy Mother of God! What have I done to deserve this?"

"Gently, Kit, gently. In this life there is much that a man can never understand. You are young, and all of life is before you. Time heals all wounds, and . . ."

"Enough of your ancient saws! There is nothing left in life for me. Rouge is dead, and her blood is on my hands."

"She tried to kill you often enough," Bernardo remarked.

"Would to God she had succeeded! Better that than this!"

Bernardo shrugged and turned away. Then, after three long strides, he stopped short, perched on one leg like a grotesque waterfowl.

"Kit," he whispered.

"Be quiet!"

"No, Kit, this you must see!" He pointed, and Kit, raising his head, saw what it was that had stopped Bernardo. There on the horizon lay four bright sails. Kit stared at them fixedly, watching them grow larger.

133

"Ducasse's squadron?" Bernardo ventured.

Kit shook his head. "No," he said. "I fear they are English, from their cut. Order more men to help the carpenter."

For two hours more a beehive of men sweated and fumbled and swore, trying to complete the repairs, while the sails of the four vessels grew ever larger. Finally, they were upon the *Seaflower,* four fast English frigates, bristling with guns. While the stubborn timber resisted all efforts to fit it into the badly bent socket of the former whipstaff, the first of the English vessels drew close enough to open fire with her chase guns.

"Gunners to their stations," Kit ordered quietly. His voice was a husky whisper, flat and calm, drained of all feeling. The men scurried to their places, but at the moment only the guns beneath the stern castle could be brought to bear. Kit watched the Englishmen's roundshot tearing through his rigging with an expressionless face. If, his whole bearing seemed to say, this be doom, then I am ready. . . .

But Bernardo turned a face dark with fury upon him. "You have no right to do this," he said coldly. "We cannot maneuver, while they can. They outgun us four to one. They can beat in and pound us to pieces!" Kit shrugged eloquently. "If you are tired of life," Bernardo pleaded, "at least consider the men!"

Kit studied the face of his friend, his own eyes cool and grave. "I think they would prefer to die as seamen should," he said, "rather than to hang on the end of a yardarm."

"Stop, Kit," Bernardo said, "the English are not wanting in honor. Do we not bear letters of marque from both His Excellency and the King? As the crew of a commissioned privateer, all they can do is hold us prisoners of war until this conflict ends."

"But will they honor these letters?" Kit asked mildly. "The *Seaflower* is well known in all these waters."

"We have never taken an English prize," Bernardo reminded him. "We have preyed chiefly upon the Spanish, with some minor forays among the Dutch. I think they will treat us well."

Kit gazed toward the fat mushroom of smoke that ballooned out of the mouth of one of the English chase guns, and heard the whine of the ball as it passed overhead.

"Very well, Bernardo," he said quietly, "you may order

Smithers to strike our colors." Then, turning on his heel, he marched below.

The English vessels moved alongside and slung over their grappling hooks. Then their boarding parties came over the side, to find the *Seaflower*'s crew drawn up ready to receive them. Kit had returned to the deck.

"So," the young English captain said, smiling, "this is the celebrated *Seaflower!* I had expected a hotter reception, Captain Gerado."

Kit made a slight bow. "We were disabled," he said shortly, "in a chance encounter with one of your vessels yesterday. I wished to spare my crew needless bloodshed."

"So," a cold, sneering voice spoke up from the English captain's elbow, "you deliver them up to be hanged!"

Kit turned and looked at the Spanish officer who stood there in breastplate and helmet, his black beard curling fiercely.

"Who said anything of hanging, Don Enrique?" the English captain demanded.

"Is it not the fate commonly dealt out to pirates?" the Spaniard countered.

"The court at Port Royal will have that to decide," the Englishman said coldly.

Kit smiled. "I trust that the good Captain . . ."

"Neilson."

"That Captain Neilson will be so good as to remind the court that the *Seaflower* has never taken an English prize."

"But what of Spanish vessels?" Don Enrique demanded. "What of England's ally and true friend?"

"I have had the pleasure," Kit mocked, "to send to hell above a hundred of the vessels of that monarchy which lacks both wit and honor. I think that Their Majesties of England will one day thank me for a signal service, once their eyes have been opened to the tragedy of this mésalliance."

Don Enrique sprang forward and struck Kit full across the mouth with his open palm.

Kit smiled softly. "With Captain Neilson's permission, I will rid England of one more false friend," he said quietly.

"No," Neilson growled. "Enough of this farce. Captain

Gerado, you will be good enough to accompany me to my vessel, the *Glorious*. You may bring with you such of your officers as you designate."

Kit nodded to Bernardo and Smithers. An hour later, they sat with Captain Neilson in his own cabin drinking his good wine.

"I will do what I can," Neilson said. "I like this alliance as little as you do. The letters will be presented in evidence. I think they will do some good."

Four days later the crew of the *Seaflower* stood before the King's magistrate at Port Royal, listening to a fierce denunciation by the royal prosecutor.

"These men have shed English blood!" he roared. "They have burned plantations and ravished Englishwomen! If your lordship is so disposed, I would call in evidence Lady Parish who suffered dishonor at the hands of this man and his crew."

The barrister assigned to their defense made a perfunctory gesture of protest. It was quickly overruled. There was a rustle of skirts and the whole court rose as Rosalind Parish was led to the witness box. She raised her hand and took the oath in a quavering, tear-laden voice. The court was hushed and silent.

"And now, my fair lady," the Crown prosecutor began, his voice sinking to a low rumble that he evidently intended to sound benign, "the court wishes to spare you as much embarrassment as possible. If you will answer my questions as simply as you can, I think we can word the matter so as not to offend your—ahem—delicate sensibilities."

"Object!" the defense squeaked.

"Overruled," the magistrate boomed.

"Do you, my dear lady," the prosecutor began, "recognize this man?"

Rosalind's blue eyes lifted and met Kit's cool stare. "I—I do," she whispered.

"Is he not the man you saw shoot down your husband!" the prosecutor thundered.

Again that quick nod. Kit smiled grimly.

"And—ahem—afterward did he not force his way into your

136

bedchamber—and hah—ahem—force you to submit to—ah—certain indignities—at—ahem—pistol point?"

Kit looked at Rosalind and threw back his head and laughed aloud. A furious buzz ran through the courtroom. The magistrate thundered with his gavel. Rosalind's face was scarlet, her blue eyes alight with anger.

"He did!" she said in a high, clear voice. "And afterward he turned me over to his crew!"

The whole court became bedlam. The magistrate pounded his gavel in vain. It was long minutes before order was restored.

"Captain Gerado," the magistrate boomed, "what have you to say to these charges?"

Kit stood up with almost insolent deliberation. "I am not so ungallant," he smiled, "as to contradict a—lady." The pause was deliberately, insultingly prolonged. "But I might say that my crew and I were here in open warfare, at the orders of the King of France. The letters of marque submitted bear that out. I say that this court has not established our guilt upon the charge for which we were brought to trial, that of piracy against the Crown. Since we have not been charged with violation of the articles of warfare, it seems strange that we should be tried for it. As for our having violated the honor of Madame Parish, I dare say that half the young blades of Port Royal have personal knowledge that such a feat is beyond possibility—since one cannot destroy what does not exist."

Again the thunderous uproar. The head of the gavel broke away from the shaft under the magistrate's furious pounding. As the room quieted, Kit could seen Don Enrique standing with his right leg forward, his head bent in a half-bow in the magistrate's direction. At once the magistrate recognized him.

"Don Enrique!"

"I beg to suggest that His Spanish Majesty's Government could but regard it as an unfriendly act if these men receive less than the extreme penalty," the Spaniard said smoothly.

The magistrate waved a hand airily, as though to dismiss all thought of that remote possibility. Kit watched Rosalind's face as the magistrate rose. It was chalk-white and her eyes were seeking his. He gazed at her coolly, ignoring the agonized pleading in their depths.

"The prisoners will rise and face the bar," the bailiff intoned. The *Seaflower*'s crew rose in a ragged semicircle.

"In view of your high crimes and misdemeanors against Their Majesties' Government and against that of our royal ally, Charles II of Spain, I hereby sentence you to be taken from the gaol at dawn tomorrow, paraded through the streets for the edification of the populace, and finally hanged by your necks until you are dead. And may God have mercy on your souls!"

The silence had thickness and texture. It could be felt. Every man in that court drew in his breath and held it, none daring to be the first to let it out. So it was that Rosalind's explosive gurgle had all the carrying power of a musket shot. Every eye in the court swung in her direction. She stood up, swaying a moment, before she crumpled in a dead faint at the foot of the bar.

Silence then—heavy as death. Then the uproar, complete and terrible.

12

AFTERWARD BIANCA preferred not to think of that journey across the Isthmus by mule train. Here was country the like of which she had never seen before—steaming jungle through which a path had to be hacked with brush hook and machete; fetid swamplands alive with mosquitoes, filling her delicate nostrils with their ugly marsh stench; monkeys and harsh-voiced parrots howling overhead; fer-de-lance and venomous bushwhacker slithering their deadly, twisting bodies through the undergrowth.

To make matters worse, her miserable morning sickness brought her daily proof that she was indeed with child, and the jolting of the mule did nothing to add to her comfort. She said nothing of her condition to Don Luis, and bore his chafing with silent dignity. Finally, however, her condition had become so bad that Don Luis was forced to use a litter for her, which was suspended between two mules. After that the journey was easier.

They came down to the Pacific side, passing the blackened ruins of the old city of Panamá, which stood in silent rebuke to Henry Morgan's infamy. Bianca turned away, and the weary mules clopped the last league of their journey into the small but bustling hamlet that was growing into the new Panamá. When Bianca sat up in her litter and saw the great ship that was awaiting them on the blue waters of the Gulf of Panamá, she wept from sheer joy.

Once aboard ship, she recovered her health with the boundless elasticity of youth. By now, her morning sickness had passed, and she felt so well that she was a little ashamed of her high spirits, having been taught that delicacy, especially during pregnancy, was the hallmark of the patrician.

The galleon crawled southward over sunlit seas balmy with eternal spring. Here, off the northwestern coast of the vast Viceroyalty of Peru lying along the rugged Pacific shores, the sea was of a blueness that stunned the imagination, rolling majestically inland in waves like long folds of lapis lazuli until it reached the shoal waters. There, as clearly and as sharply as though the line of demarcation had been drawn by the hand of a giant, it blazed pale-green, as bright as emerald.

On the shore, in the declivities between the mountains, thick forests of palms and thickets of bamboo tossed their bluish-jade crowns against the azure sky. Birds like feathered jewels, crimson and maize-yellow and topaz, exploded their rainbow brilliance against the somber trees. They sang and screeched and arched their bright trajectories between sun wash and tree shadow until, watching them, Bianca wept.

Don Luis laid his arm gently across her shoulders and drew her to him. He looked down at the small face from which all color had drained, leaving it like Andean snow except for the almost savage scarlet of her trembling mouth. His big hand came up and stroked the hair—black almost to the extent of suggesting blueness, so that in its sheen no hint of brown or red showed—that fell like starless night shadow about her shoulders. He felt again the momentary start of surprise that this foaming cascade of blue midnight was so warm to the touch; his eyes registered for the thousandth time the startling juxtaposition of ebony and spring snow, so that when he spoke the boom of his great bass had an underlying hint of pain in it.

"Are you thinking of another bird of fine plumage, Bianca?" he said.

The quick black eyes lifted to his suddenly and their gaze rested cool and grave upon his face.

"All that—is past," Bianca said, her voice utterly wanting in expression.

Don Luis frowned. The little nagging whisper that had lain buried since the day he had retrieved his captive bride from the cove of Cul-de-Sac probed its ugly way to the surface of his consciousness.

"Is it?" he growled. "Are you sure of that, Bianca?"

The dark eyes darkened even more, becoming night-black. Bianca searched her husband's face, and the corners of her mouth stole upward in the merest ghost of a smile, but she did not answer. She stared at him coolly, gravely, quietly, until the great veins of his temples stood out and beat with his blood.

"Answer me!" he thundered. "Have you forgotten him, Bianca; forgotten this nameless bastard of a worthless Frenchwoman?"

"At any event," Bianca said quietly, "you have not, my lord."

Don Luis glared down at her, his face dark with anger above the jutting night cloud of his beard.

"I am not sure," he said evenly, slowly, spacing his words with the menacing deliberation of a man accustomed to control all things, even his rages, "that I have heard a convincing account of what happened in Hispaniola while you were—detained."

"Didn't you?" Bianca answered tartly, and turned her gaze toward the tangled jungleland of the shore.

Don Luis stared at her, lovely and defiant, the green bile of tortured jealousy boiling inches below the level of his throat. His hands shot out and spun her around, none too gently.

"Speak!" he roared. "What happened there?"

"Your voice is overloud," Bianca said with exasperating sweetness. "Would you share our tête-à-tête with the crew?"

"Enough of your raillery!" Don Luis said, but his voice was lower. "I think an answer on that score is due me."

"Why?" Bianca asked innocently.

"Because . . ." Don Luis began. Then he realized the trap into which he had fallen. It was impossible to maintain dignity and at the same time admit his jealousy. "It is enough that I await an answer and command that you give it," he said.

"And if I refuse?"

"To refuse," Don Luis said heavily, "is to lend weight to the supposition that I—perhaps—took a dishonored woman for my wife."

Bianca paled, her eyes black fire coals in the whiteness of her face. "Has it ever occurred to you," she whispered, "that such a supposition is a most vile insult?"

"That I do not know," Don Luis blustered. "I know only that he is young and fair to look upon, and that you are young and

141

susceptible." He paused, searching her pale face, and the rage died within him, leaving only the sickness and the hurt. "Say again that nothing happened there," he whispered, "and I will believe you."

Bianca studied this great, strange man who had become her husband, who would sire whatever children she would have, and the intimacy of both these reflections did not detract from his strangeness. He might have been a graven image for all the warmth that kindled in her eyes. She could answer him, she knew. She could say in all honor and all truth that nothing had happened between her and Kit—nothing, save only a kiss. So her thoughts ran. But Bianca was not lacking in that strange quirk of utterly feminine cruelty which is so much a part of every woman.

"Think what you will, my lord," she said at last. "I will not deny you the solace of your thoughts."

Then, very deliberately, she turned away from him. Don Luis took a half-step toward her, but his dark eyes fell on a little group of harquebusiers who had stood staring curiously at him and Bianca. He stopped short and turned his furious countenance toward the slowly backward-slipping land.

The ship butted her way southward across the equator, and suddenly all the warmth was drained from the air. Bianca stood on the deck with a shawl about her shoulders and watched the steaming tropical forest disappear to the northward while directly abeam of the vessel lay scrub trees, dwarfed by the chill. She was conscious of her husband's dark, tormented gaze as she stood there, but she would not turn.

Under the prow of the ship the water was icy-green, and the bleak, forbidding, bone-dry land stretched southward in austere beauty as far as Bianca's eye could see. She gazed at the gray skies lowering above land that might have been the Sahara for all the moisture it contained. Then she turned puzzled eyes upon her husband.

"So many clouds," she mused, "and yet there is nothing here but sand and rock. Why is that, Luis?"

Don Luis spoke up quickly, almost jovially, delighted that

142

Bianca had at last broken the strained silence between them.

"It has not rained in Peru," he said, "for seven years. Often, it is said, babies have grown to manhood in these parts without seeing rain. Yet in this season the clouds are always there. God and Virgin alone know why no rain falls from them."

"Then," Bianca queried, "how do the people live?"

Don Luis put out his hand and pointed.

"See those mountains beyond the lower foothills of the coast? In the season of clouds, a mist but little heavier than a fog descends upon them. It is called in this country the *garua*. Where it sits on the mountains, the soil is drenched with moisture, and overnight, almost, plants and grasses spring up. Men call these grasses the *loma*. They make excellent feed for the cattle, the sheep, and the llamas."

"Llamas?" Bianca echoed.

"A beast not unlike a camel, but without a humped back. Truly there are many wonders in Peru."

Within the first hours of the next morning, Bianca was given proof of the truth of her husband's words. She was awakened by the cries of sea birds, and the beat of uncounted wings. She dressed hastily and mounted the deck. Looking up, she could no longer see the sky, except as momentarily revealed patches of light between the wings of the birds. The whole heaven was blackened by them. From horizon to horizon they brushed each other with their wing tips and made the air hideous with their screeching. Over the port bow a line of pelicans passed, their ugly sacked beaks thrust out and their small heads resting on their curved necks in the recess between their wings. Bianca watched them pass with a growing sense of amazement. Idly, she began to count them, but she wearied when she reached five hundred, and she missed count frequently because of the sameness of the birds. So she stood quietly and watched the pouch-beaked sea birds fly past until her knees ached with the standing. She shifted position and hung on, unable to tear her gaze away from the spectacle. At last she gave way to her weariness and sat down on a coil of rope. She was still sitting there watching the pelicans when she heard the clang of the watch bell, and realized with a sudden disbelief in the evidence of her senses that she had been watching a line of pelicans fly across the ship for two full hours and that the last bird was not yet in sight.

She turned her astonished eyes toward the other side of the ship and saw that the water ahead was boiling ceaselessly. She watched this for another half-hour until the ship nosed into this white-whipped whirlpool. Then she saw that the wild white foam was the continuous splash being made as one gannet after another dived into the sea after fish. She stared at them until she realized that this too was not going to end, and turned her eyes to a stop just abaft of the starboard beam where a black cloud hovered over the water. She heard a step at her side, and Don Luis was pressing a telescope into her hand.

"Cormorants," he said. "Look!"

Through the glass the black cloud became broken up into a mass of individual birds, whirling across the lens so fast that they made Bianca dizzy. And above them all soared albatrosses, frigate birds, man-of-war birds, terns, plovers, and the omnipresent gulls. There was nowhere she could look without seeing the flash of wings. Even the surface of the ocean, for a full twenty miles, bore the floating shapes of the sea birds, resting quietly on the dancing wavelets with folded wings. Bianca turned an awed face toward Don Luis.

"How many are there?" she said.

"God alone knows,"[1] Don Luis replied. "A man standing in one spot might wear out ten lifetimes counting them—and yet would not have begun. . . . Come, it is time you went below. We should reach Callao before nightfall."

But the galleon made even better speed than he had hoped. It was still bright afternoon when the cold, greenish Peruvian current flattened out into still, almost waveless waters. On their starboard the great island of San Lorenzo lay, with its low foothills breaking the force of the waters. Off to the port side Bianca could see the promontory aimed like a dagger straight at the heart of San Lorenzo, and beyond it the low, thatched huts of Callao. The galleon beat in against the wind, which on this

[1] A twentieth-century naturalist has counted 5,600,000 birds on one small island near Lima. This flock alone consumes a thousand tons of fish a day.

stretch of coast blows forever from the southwest, and came gracefully up alongside the wharf without having to drop anchor at all.

On the wharf there was a great bustling, but a bustling in slow, dance tempo. The Indian roustabouts took the hawsers of the galleon and belayed them about the piles in a manner that stated plainly that tomorrow or the day after would have served as well.

Standing beside her husband, Bianca let her dark eyes stray over the nondescript crowd. Then, abruptly, her gaze halted. For there on the wharf a young man had swept off his great plumed hat and made her a sweeping bow. As he straightened, she could see that he was uncommonly handsome, with brown hair so light that it was almost the color of honey and eyes as blue as Kit's own. I shall always, Bianca thought miserably, have a most uncomfortable weakness for eyes of that particular shade. . . . Then she turned toward her husband in time to see that he was smiling and returning the young man's salute with rare good humor.

"My godson," Don Luis said.

Bianca took Don Luis's hand and came down the gangplank. At its foot, Ricardo Goldames waited, his blue eyes widening with every step she took toward him.

"My esteemed godfather," he whispered. "I am overwhelmed!"

"With your joy at my coming, no doubt," said Don Luis, chuckling, his deep voice filled with irony.

"Of course!" Ricardo was smiling. "But also at the sight of my new godmother. I trust that the closeness of our relationship will permit me to kiss her hand." Thereupon he did so though with a great deal more ardor than any religious dutifulness could have inspired.

"Señora," he said cheerfully, "I am desolate!"

Bianca looked at his young, handsome face on which not the slightest trace of sadness showed. "Why, señor?" she said gently.

"Because this old he goat of a godfather of mine has snatched the fairest flower of all earth's beauties, and hereafter I must mourn my loss in vain."

This quite outrageous statement was made so calmly and with

145

such a pleasant expression that Bianca took a half-step backward, glancing fearfully at Don Luis. But her husband merely threw back his head and roared with laughter.

"You are not changed, Ricardo!" Again he chuckled. "You are still a scoundrel. I warrant that the proctors at San Marcos grew so weary of your deviltry that they closed one eye at your lack of knowledge. But come, you have transportation to Lima for us, haven't you?"

"The best," Ricardo said. "I have prevailed upon the Viceroy himself to lend me his own coach. And His Excellency hopes that you will honor him with your presence in his house during the festivities."

Bianca glanced up at her husband. This was high honor indeed. In his own right, the Viceroy of Peru was an actual monarch—many times more powerful, in fact, than many a princeling of the worn-out houses of Europe. Don Luis took the invitation calmly, as no more than his due.

"We accept, of course," he said. "Lead on."

The Viceroy's coach was a splendid conveyance, carved of quebracho wood and much ornamented with giltwork and metal fittings of pure silver. It was drawn by four of the finest horses Bianca had ever seen. The coachman and the footman were Negroes of a blackness defying description, but the sable hue of their skins set off their splendid livery all the more vividly.

The whip cracked over the backs of the horses, and the coach moved off toward Lima. Despite the dust and the jolting of the heavy vehicle—which was entirely wanting in springs or any reasonable substitute—Bianca found the eight-mile journey from the seaport of Callao to the mighty capital of Lima most interesting. Ricardo talked incessantly, but Bianca heard scarcely a word. She was far too busy gazing out the window at the strange new world into which she had come. So far she had not seen another white face. All about her were Indians talking quietly in their liquid Quechuan tongue, moving slowly over the dusty highroad driving their herds of llamas or alpacas before them.

She noticed that one of the strange camellike beasts was lying down and, despite a shower of blows from his driver, was refusing to get up.

146

"This," Ricardo said, grinning, "is worth seeing." Putting his head out the window, he called to the driver to halt. As the coach ground to a stop, the incensed Indian made a grievous mistake. He moved around to the beast's head and began to tug furiously at the bridle. At once the llama lifted its slim head and spat a mouthful of foul green liquid into the Indian's face. The Indian sprang back, wiping his blinded eyes. Then he whipped out a knife and sprang at the animal's throat.

"Stop!" Ricardo cried. "You know better than that! Ease him and he will stand."

The Indian turned a sullen face toward the young Spaniard. Slowly he sheathed his knife, and walked around to the side of the squatting beast. He opened the great bag it carried and handful by handful began to throw out the dried maize it contained. He had thrown out no more than ten small handfuls when the llama gave a low, contented grunt and got awkwardly to its feet.

"You see," Ricardo said triumphantly. "A llama has far more brains than an Indian. He knows how much he can carry. There are times," he added ruefully, "when I myself have been less wise." Then he put his head out the window again and ordered the coachman to go on.

They followed the curves of the Rimac River past the thatched adobe huts of the Indians. The stench of the cooking fires smote them in the nostrils. Bianca lifted a perfume-drenched handkerchief to her nose and glanced inquiringly at Ricardo.

"*Taquia*," he said. "Dried llama dung. This land is starved for wood. Were it not for the beasts, they would have no fuel. Everything here depends upon nature. You have seen the birds? Well, we send ships out to their nesting places, which return loaded with their offal. We call it *guano*—and with it we enrich the land."

"I think," Don Luis growled, "that this is hardly a subject to talk about to your godmother, Ricardo."

"A thousand pardons, señora," Ricardo said. "Here in our barbaric land it is easy to forget our manners."

"Not that you ever had any," Don Luis observed. "Isn't that Lima ahead?"

Bianca put her head out the window and took her first look at the capital of the great viceroyalty. Lima, she saw at once, was a great city—a great Spanish city. The spires of the cathedral, the cabildo, the Casa Real, rose in the faintly misty air.

As they moved into the city, the first impression—that of the Spanish nature of Lima—was altered but not dispelled. Through the streets shuffled hundreds of Indians, the descendants of the proud Incas, now broken and dispirited. They moved with bent heads, their colorful serapes and rebozos picking up the light, gleaming dully brown and blue and white and green over their bent shoulders. Before them moved the herds of mules, sheep, cattle, llamas, and alpacas. These latter, unlike the hardier llamas, were bearing no burdens, being driven in merely for the shearing.

Here in this quarter the filthy huts of plastered mud, shared alike by Indians, goats, pigs, and chickens, assailed Bianca's gaze. The naked children stared back at her with great wondering eyes. Then the earthen streets of the Indian quarter gave way to the paved avenues of the Spaniards, and the barred-and-shuttered houses of the mighty stared forbiddingly down upon them. Through the middle of the street the stinking gutters ran, and now and again a window of an upper story opened, to reveal some Indian or Negro serving-woman with a bucket of garbage. Then, with a mumbled cry of *"Agua va!"* she would unceremoniously dump the foul-smelling contents into the street, and woe betide the passer-by who failed to dodge!

Bianca shuddered, seeing all this. However, Lima was alive with pageantry, too: the caballeros on their fine steeds, dressed in velvets stiffened with embroidery and sitting tall in their splendid gold-inlaid saddles; the dark eyes of the *limeñas* peering coquettishly through the curtains of their coaches at the magnificent *charros* in their broad-brimmed hats edged with silver and gold lace, fur-trimmed and embroidered jackets, silver-buttoned pantaloons, leather leggings and immense silver stirrups and spurs, raising their ivory-inlaid whips in gallant salute to the señoritas. Lines of goldsmith shops vied with the even more numerous ones of workers in silver. Portuguese Jews, whose wealth and business acumen had won them a measure of security

148

from the grasping fingers of the Inquisition, hurried through the streets intent upon their drafts and papers. Nuns and bearded friars lent a note of sobriety to the otherwise brilliant throng.

And everywhere were the beggars, sticking their filthy and diseased paws even into the windows of the coach, so that Don Luis was forced to strike them with his cane. Here too were the Negroes, permitted by law to wear the cast-off garments of their masters, so that it was easy to tell a mulatto from a mestizo, though in coloring and features they might be identical. Here were the women of the town, gay, abandoned, noisy, of every race and hue and combination thereof.

Jewels sparkled on hatbands; mere merchants adorned themselves with almost priceless pearls. Even the half-breed women, the lovely mestizas, wore sandals and belts of silk and gold, with pearls and rubies—presents, no doubt, from doting hidalgos, as were their ornamented skirts and jackets of fine cloth. On the walls of the public buildings the rude scrawls prohibiting public nuisance testified to the want of even the rudiments of delicacy or restraint among the people, but half a glance sufficed to show that these warnings had no effect. Bianca turned her scarlet face aside and gazed out no more until an uproar smote her ears.

Looking out, she saw a crowd of Negro retainers engaged in a furious brawl. One group, dressed in bright liveries of green and gold, was having much the better of it. They were armed with short swords, pikes, and daggers, while the others, whose much more splendid livery was of gold and royal purple, had only staves. Don Luis turned questioning eyes on his godson.

"The blacks in green," Ricardo explained, his tone full of good-humored enjoyment of the bloody riot, "are the retainers of the rector of the university. Of all the slaves in Lima, they alone are permitted to wear sidearms. The others are the servants of the Viceroy, who hold it ill that they are not so honored. They fight every time they meet. All the blacks—those of the Archbishop, the *oidores,* and the regents of the Audencia—hate the Negroes of the rector worse than poison. They always attack them, which is most stupid, since the rector's Negroes always win. Ah, here come the officers of the guard!"

The officers of the guard, heavily armed and wearing coats of mail, swept down on the brawling Negroes. For a moment the uproar increased, then abruptly it ended. The guards had brought the shafts of their heavy pikes down over the heads of half a dozen blacks, leaving them sprawling in the street. The rest stared down the gaping muzzles of the muskets of the guards and discretion took precedence over valor. The driver of the coach cracked his whip, and the heavy vehicle moved on toward its destination.

That night Bianca sat at the fiesta table and tried to follow the light chitchat of the conversation. At the head of the table the Viceroy himself was suffering from mild social confusion. The recent elevation of Don Luis to the rank of count had upset protocol. The Count of Monclovia knew how to talk to his inferiors. If Don Luis had been a mere grandee, he could have dealt with him with graceful condescension, but with the Count del Toro, his newly made equal, he was at a loss. Don Luis's dry, half-ironic remarks did nothing to help the situation. Little by little he was letting Monclovia know that in wealth, in extent of holdings, in everything except the office of viceroy, he exceeded his superior officer. The silences between the two men lengthened.

Bianca too found the evening difficult, but for a different reason. Across the table from her, Ricardo Goldames's glances dwelt more and more on her face. And his eyes were naked with adoration. She wanted to warn him, to tell him to turn aside his gaze, but the women prattled on. Bianca was sure that they had noticed, that every señora in the great salon was aware of this wild and secret indiscretion. The evening dragged on, every moment crawling with leaden feet over her tortured nerves. When at last it was over Bianca found that she was to be alone except for Quita, for Don Luis had been summoned to discuss urgent matters of state.

Sitting in her nightdress, with Quita brushing out her long night-black hair, Bianca was not even surprised when small stones thudded against her window. Quita smiled slowly and prepared to depart.

150

"No!" Bianca said, her voice high, breathless, filled with terror. "Stay—I need you."

Then step by slow step she crossed to the barred window and stared down at Ricardo Goldames.

13

Sometime during the night of July 1, 1694, the great clock of time stopped for Cristóbal Gerado. He was made aware of it by the stars. On many a night before, while the *Seaflower* swung at her creaking hawsers, anchored in some quiet cove, he had seen them wheel in great white circles above the masthead. Sometimes under full press of canvas, the sails tugging at the sheets, he had watched them reel and dip with the cadenced rise and fall of the leeward rail. There had been a slow and awesome majesty about their dance, as though if a man listened hard enough, he might be able to attune his hearing to the mighty music of the spheres.

Tonight, however, they were still. It was, Kit knew, simply because he saw them from the land—more exactly, through the stout iron bars of the Port Royal gaol. Strange, he mused, that never since my youth have I watched the stars from land. . . . The stars were the seaman's friends, guideposts in the great inverted bowl of heaven, but now they were still, for time had stopped . . . and his life, too, would presently stop with it.

Sighing, he looked at the humped silhouettes of his crew, black and motionless in the fetid darkness. The gaol was scarce a year old, but already it had taken on the noisome stench common to dungeons everywhere, reeking with human smells and more—the indefinable gaol odor, the sweet-sick putrefaction scent of liberty dead and hope lying rotting.

He shook his head to clear it of such thoughts. Oddest of all, it seemed to him, was the fact that he did not want to die. Why this strange, instinctive clinging to life? Rouge was dead, and by his own hand. Bianca was perhaps worse than dead—living in the loveless thralldom of his ancient enemy. In either case, he was powerless to remedy the situation. On the morrow it would be remedied for him. The choking embrace of hemp would assuage his griefs forever.

He heard the swift-scurrying passage of rats in the darkness, then the low intonation of Patricio Velasco's prayers: "Hail Mary, full of Grace, the Lord is with thee. Blessed art thou among women. Blessed is the fruit of thy womb, Jesus. Holy Mary, Mother of God, pray for us now, and at the hour of our death. . . . Amen."

He found his own lips repeating the solemn words, murmuring, *"Sancta Maria, Mater Dei, ora pro nobis peccatoribus, nunc et in hora mortis nostrae!"* He crossed himself reverently at the end, and saw from the movement of Bernardo's great shoulders that the Jew was doing likewise. In this hour the differences of faiths had melted: Bernardo could pray in two religions with no sense of conflict. The heretic Smithers knelt alongside the Catholic Velasco, and the sins of them all were heavy burdens of scarlet on the nakedness of their souls.

Kit heard the rustle of motion as Bernardo rose and approached him. The great hands groped through the darkness and found his shoulders.

"Kit, my son," Bernardo whispered, "forgive me. I brought you to this."

"We could not have fought," Kit reminded him. "They would have sunk us with ease."

"Yes, but better that death than this. Better a clean death at sea than this filthy, dishonored dying."

"Fret no more about it, my old one," Kit said gently. "It is good that we end the voyage as we began it—together."

"Kit," Bernardo began, but the sound of footsteps halted him. Every man in the dank common cell was on his feet as the fat bulk of the turnkey loomed before them.

"Avast, ye rogues!" he bellowed. "Stand back! I have a visitor to see Christopher Gerado—and mark ye that ye show her every courtesy! It would please me to add a taste o' the cat to what awaits ye tomorrow."

The key turned in the massive lock, and the door creaked

open a little, just wide enough to admit the slender figure of Rosalind Parish. She held a lantern in her hand, and by its light Kit could see that her blue eyes were filled with tears. The moment she saw him she passed the lantern to Bernardo and sank on her knees before Kit, her whole body shaken with sobs. Kit stretched out his hand to her.

"Get up," he growled. "This is not fitting."

Instead of rising, she caught at his hand and covered it, back and palm, with kisses. Kit bent and raised her gently to her feet. Then he glanced around at the others.

"Leave them!" Bernardo said, hope glowing in his eyes. "The wench might save us yet!" The men drew apart hastily.

Rosalind's white arms stole up and encircled Kit's neck. "I am sorry," she said, weeping. "God and His Angels witness that I love you!"

"So much," Kit remarked dryly, "that you send me to the gibbet with your lies."

"I—I know," she said at last, her voice scarcely a breath. "I have been to see the magistrate to tell him the truth. He refuses to believe it. Oh, Kit, can you forgive me? Say that you can. . . . Please—for the love of God."

Kit looked down at her, his blue eyes luminous in the semi-darkness. "My life is nothing to me," he said gravely. "And for it, I forgive you freely. But why did you do it when a word from you would have freed us?"

"Because you didn't want me," she said. "Consider, Kit, I was never really in love before. I married Reginald thinking I could learn to love him, but I could not. I have taken lovers—out of bitterness, out of hatred for the fop that he was—but I am a decent woman at heart, that you must believe. . . . Say that you believe me, Kit."

Kit smiled above the bright crown of her head. This he could grant her; this small comfort he could give her before he died.

"I believe you," he said gently. "Go on."

Rosalind raised her head and searched his face. It was grave and calm. With a glad cry she went up on tiptoe and kissed him.

"When you came, when you saved me, everything stood still for me."

154

"And then?"

"And then you scorned me. I know it was my fault. I was lacking in subtlety. I should not have flung myself so hungrily at you, but I had felt your arms and I was on fire. Kiss me, Kit—kiss me."

She was oblivious to the mockery in his deft embrace. At last she sighed, slowly and with deep content. She drew back a little, and her hand disappeared in the bodice of her gown. It came out holding a razor.

"Here," she whispered, "take it and shave off your beard! Your hair and mine are much alike in color. I will strip off these garments and you shall change with me. Before morning you should be far away."

Kit threw back his head and laughed. "You have read far too many romances, Rosalind!" he said. "Look—I am over six feet in height. Your gown would swirl about my knees. That bodice of yours would rip into pieces if I forced it over my shoulders. No, Rosalind, I fear that I must accept my fate."

"Try it!" she wept. "If you wrapped yourself in my cloak and bent your head . . . The skirt contains much cloth. I could let it down so that . . ."

"No," Kit said gently. "Even if I could, I would not leave my men. I hope that you will enjoy the spectacle tomorrow."

Again she hurled herself upon him, convulsed with such a titanic upheaval of grief that her wild sobbing brought the turnkey hurrying to the gate. He put his head through the bars to see the better and opened his mouth to bellow at them, but no sound came out—no sound at all. For Bernardo's enormous hands were encircling his neck. Kit saw the man's eyes bulge from their sockets, saw the sweat rise and glisten on his forehead in the dim light of the lantern, then the man's ugly face turned blue and his tongue came out of his gaping mouth. Bernardo hung on long after he was dead. Then, holding the turnkey effortlessly with one hand, he sought and found the bunch of keys.

"You and your taste of the cat-o'-nine-tails," Bernardo said contemptuously. "Sleep well, you obscenity, until Satan wakes you up in hell!"

"The streets are alive with soldiers," Kit observed. "Let us decide on a plan."

"No," Rosalind said, "there will be no soldiers. Captain Neilson assured me of that. They are all at the tavern, being entertained at his expense."

"And the guards at the doors? . . ." Smithers growled.

"They have drunk by now at least a gallon of sack I brought them with the good Captain's compliments."

"Uncommonly thoughtful of him," Kit mused. "Why should he be so kind to me, Rosalind?"

"Because I asked him to. Also because the verdict angered him. He said that he would be pleased to meet you at the cannon's mouth on the open seas, but that he'd be damned before he'd serve at the hanging of a brave and honorable foe."

"He's a real man!" Bernardo grunted.

Kit stared at Rosalind a moment, then turned to his crew. "Away, lads!" he said softly. "Make no sound. We will seize the *Seaflower*. We can rig two gun tackles at each side of the whipstaff socket and station a man at each. A tug at the ropes and she will heel right handily. And God knows there's no vessel afloat can catch her. Come!"

With the ease born of long practice they went down on their bellies and worked their way through the corridor. The gates opened one by one to the keys on the iron ring that Bernardo had taken from the turnkey. At the gates, the guards fell an easy prey, one to the butt of the turnkey's pistol, the other to Bernardo's encircling fingers."

"Scatter!" Kit commanded. "And make for the harbor. We will reassemble there."

By the time they had all reached the place where the *Seaflower* lay, five more of the men were armed with muskets, pistols, and cutlasses they had taken from the drunken soldiers they had met reeling through the streets.

At the end of the wharf they slipped into the water and swam out to the *Seaflower*. Coming up on her decks, they swarmed over the sleepy Britishers who guarded her. They used belaying pins, musket butts, pistol barrels, and the flat of their cutlass blades, for out of respect to Captain Neilson, Kit had ordered

156

that there was to be no killing. Then they loaded their unconscious victims into a longboat and set it adrift.

Bernardo and a picked group worked feverishly at the jury tackle. In twenty minutes they had it rigged. Soon the square sails bellied out on the foremast, the spritsail ballooned, the white triangles of the flying jibs caught the fresh night wind, the great spanker on the main heeled hard over, its boom almost at right angles, and the *Seaflower* moved out of the harbor, running free before the wind like a spirited thoroughbred that had taken the bit in its teeth.

They made Saint-Domingue in less than two days, steering southward toward the lower peninsula, for at the command of Ducasse their old haunt at Tortuga had been deserted, the entire town of Basse-Terre having been moved to Port de Paix.

When they finally reached the harbor of Petit Goave, the men turned gleeful eyes toward the white town sliding in toward them over the port bow. True, the English had taken back the Negroes with which the crew had hoped to gain a fortune. However, they had not bothered to search for the loot the men had taken from the manor houses, thinking, no doubt, that they would have time and to spare to search the *Seaflower*'s hold after the hangings. There was enough left, the men knew, for one brave rout.

Watching Kit's face, Bernardo was aware that he did not share the mood of his crew. One would think, Bernardo mused, that he was going toward the gibbet rather than away from it.

When the *Seaflower* lay at last at anchor, Kit paid off the men, adding liberally to their loot from his own share. Then, after having told them to hold themselves in readiness if he should require their services again, he and Bernardo went down the ladder into the last of the boats.

That night every bawd in Petit Goave and above half of those from the near-by town of Léogane descended on the tavern in which the *Seaflower*'s crew celebrated their return. These were reinforced by many of the young matrons and maids of the town who so far had escaped the professional status. Kit, however, was not present. Bernardo sighed as he contemplated the plump little maid who was turning a most attentive ear to his flattery. Time enough tomorrow to console his captain, tonight there were more attractive prospects in view.

He was not to go uninterrupted. An hour later he looked up from the lips of his companion into the smiling face of a richly attired courtier. The man was obviously a gentleman. Even to Bernardo's rum-bemused eyes he had a look of authority about him. Bernardo scrambled hastily to his feet.

"A thousand pardons, Monsieur Díaz," the man murmured. "It pains me deeply to interrupt your most pleasant occupation, but I am here in behalf of His Excellency"—Bernardo stiffened in anticipation—"who urgently wants to see Captain Giradeaux. The Sieur Ducasse asked me to congratulate the entire company on their miraculous escape, and to present every man with a purse as a token of his gratitude and esteem. I trust you will see to the distribution of the money?"

Bernardo grinned. "That I will! But as for Captain Giradeaux, I do not know his present whereabouts."

"A pity. Still, there is no great haste. His Excellency is much taken with the young captain. He desires to reward him suitably for the great part he played in the late expedition."

"I will have him at Exter," Bernardo promised solemnly, "the day after tomorrow at the very latest."

"My thanks, Monsieur Díaz. And now, if you will be so good . . ." He held out a huge leather sack, crammed to the bursting with gold pieces. Bernardo saw at once that here were at least a hundred gold louis for every man. Catching the courtier's arm to prevent his escaping, he sprang to a table and bellowed in a forecastle voice:

"Look, my lads! Gold! From the land of His Excellency the Sieur Ducasse! Give a cheer to his messenger!"

The men shook the rafters with their lusty hurrahs. The bewildered gentleman found himself hoisted to the shoulders of two sweating, evil-smelling seamen and paraded about the hall, half the trulls in the place smearing his hands with winy kisses. The courtier took these attentions with good grace, and made them all a flowery speech in beautiful Parisian, which the bearded buccaneers and their blowsy women only vaguely understood. But if he thought he was going to be permitted

158

to escape, he soon discovered his mistake. He found himself seated at a table with a lithe quadroon wench on his lap and a tankard of rum in his manicured hands. After three pulls at the tankard, he began to relax; after five he found, to his amazement, that he was actually enjoying himself. Besides, the quadroon was lovely. When the dawn light poured into the windows, the fine Parisian gentleman, his rich attire in disarray, was roaring a lusty sea chantey with as much fervor as any sea wolf in the tavern.

When Bernardo recovered himself enough to recollect his promise, it was afternoon. He was, he realized, no longer in the tavern, but in a room belonging, in all probability, to the plump maid. By a mighty effort he raised his head, now of ten tons' burden, and surveyed his surroundings. His surmise had been correct. The girl slept, in all her voluptuous innocence, by his side. Bernardo lowered his great head and groaned. Of what worth were pleasures taken in the dark that a man could not remember in the morning?

But such thoughts must be put away. He had a task to do. Groaning again, he heaved himself erect and began to dress. When he had finished and started for the door, he glanced down. The plump maid, her skin dewed all over with a faint film of perspiration, had not even stirred. Bernardo made the doorway in one great lurch, and stood outside blinking blindly at the brilliant light.

He knew where to find Kit. Half an hour later he came to the door of a small hostel that was vastly unpopular in Petit Goave because the angular Huguenot widow who kept it insisted upon at least the appearance of respectability. He had no excuse to enter, because Kit was standing there beside his white stallion, holding the lead rope of a pack mule in his hand. Bernardo's brows made pothooks of questioning.

"It is no concern of yours," Kit said almost cheerfully, "but if you must know, I am bound to Notre Dame de Léogane to pay a call on Father Dumaine."

Bernardo surveyed the heavily laden pack mule. "With all your spoils from the expedition?"

"All," Kit said quietly.

"Why?" Bernardo demanded, his own quest momentarily forgotten.

"It is not too much to ensure perpetual masses for her soul. And certainly not enough to lift the burden of sin from my own."

Bernardo ran the tip of a dry tongue over drier lips. "How long will you stay?" he demanded.

Kit's blue eyes were cloudy with pain. "Until tomorrow. Why?"

"Good!" Bernardo said, relief audible in his voice. "His Excellency sent a special emissary to ask you to call on him. I think he plans to reward you for saving Beauregard's troops from destruction."

Kit shrugged. "What need have I now for rewards?" he said quietly. "The lands that the Sieur Ducasse promised me, what good are they now that she is dead?" He looked out over the blue waters, seeing the white sails of the hoys and sloops creeping over it under the blinding sun. "Here I had planned to build her a great house of gray stone . . ." He looked at his friend and the anguish in his eyes was like smoldering flame.

Bernardo put an arm about Kit's shoulders and gave him an affectionate squeeze. "Easy, Kit," he said. "There are limits to all things, even grief. This was an accident—God in His mercy knows you never would have harmed her willingly. Still"—Bernardo paused a moment and a look of shrewdness crept into his dark eyes—"I would like to see you build that house."

Kit looked at him. "Why, Bernardo?" he asked.

"Life has not been kind to me," Bernardo answered with a sigh, "yet I have not been entirely cheated of a son since chance threw us together. Would you deprive me then of grandsons—for they'll be mine, Kit, because of the great love that I'll bear them. Grieve for a space, that is only natural, but afterward build this house of yours, and spare a room for me."

Kit smiled at him slowly. "So I must provide you with grandsons, you old villain? Why does it fall on me to remedy your neglect in not siring a son?"

Bernardo grinned and waved a deprecating hand. "A son of

mine would not have been so fair as you, Kit," he said. "Listen to me, Kit. There are other maids as fair as she."

"Name one!" Kit snapped.

Bernardo rubbed his long clean-shaven chin. When he pronounced the name, he flung it out like a challenge.

"The Señora Bianca del Toro," he said. Kit stiffened, but said nothing. "I think that she will someday become a widow," Bernardo continued, "for Don Luis has many enemies."

Kit's hand strayed down to the sash of gold that he always wore, and his blue eyes hardened.

"Yes," he said, "she will be widowed—and soon!" He turned again to Bernardo, the fury leaving his eyes. "Bianca," he mused. "It has been so long that my memory nearly fails me and I mistrust it. Could there have been such a maid as my mind recalls? Or do I create the image out of my loneliness and my pain?"

"And what sort of maid do you recall, Kit?" Bernardo asked.

"A small maid," Kit said slowly, "scarcely reaching to my shoulders, with a face like an angel's, yet with a spice of mischief in her eyes. And what of those eyes, Bernardo, for here my memory fails me? Black, I think, and so deep and sure. Thus does my mind recall her. Tell me, Bernardo, is this an illusion?"

"No," Bernardo growled. "So indeed she was. I had hoped that when I left the two of you together at Cul-de-Sac she would turn your mind from Rouge, but you were always stubborn, Kit. So, now . . ." He shrugged eloquently.

"So now I shall complete my errand," Kit said calmly.

"His Excellency expects you on Wednesday," Bernardo said quickly.

"Very well," and Kit sighed, "I will be there."

Early Wednesday morning, before the coolness had yet left the land, Kit and Bernardo rode with Governor Ducasse up the steep mountain trail. They rode very slowly, each of them occupied with his own thoughts. Ducasse was thinking that the menace of commercial competition from Jamaica still existed and that all his letters to the court of France asking for aid with which to drive the Spaniards from the southern half of

Hispaniola had gone for nothing. If he controlled the whole island, what greatness might he not attain? Shaking his head, he urged his mount upward through the cool morning air.

Bernardo, for his part, was savoring the thought of settling down at last in a land where men did not consider the question of religion, where no one paid any attention at all to the Semitic cast of his countenance. Here he might even take a wife, for he was still in his early forties, though he looked older. Kit's taunt that he had failed to provide himself with a son had struck home. But what chance has a man to take a wife, or beget sons, Bernardo reflected bitterly, when he is being hunted like an animal from land to land? . . . Now all that might at last be changed! For the prospect of such peace he was willing even to forget Del Toro, who had set the Inquisitorial machinery in action against him.

Kit's thoughts were on a different plane. There is, he mused, a devilish irony in the workings of fate. Here at my finger tips I have the chance to gain all that I wanted, but now that the chance has come it is meaningless to me. How lovingly had I planned this house for Rouge, so that once it had been built, I could go from room to room with no feeling of strangeness or newness. In Spain I was a nameless bastard kept hidden in the house, but here I might have been a lord over men and acres. . . . Might have been? I might be still—life goes on and I must live out my destiny, though God knows I shall find scant joy in it. Without her it will be an empty triumph, entirely without meaning. Yet in this world nothing stands still, so I must achieve what I can before the path of Luis del Toro again crosses mine. . . .

On their right hand now the bayonet-shaped leaves of the agave plant stood in neat, orderly rows. Between the plants the Negroes moved, gathering the leaves for their fiber. Beyond the field, on long lines stretched from pole to pole, the golden fiber dried, for this was a sisal plantation. The horses moved upward, sure-footed as goats, through the thatched villages occupied by the blacks, who had entirely replaced the Arawak Indians. On every hand were the slow, sweet-moving signs of husbandry— the pounding of a black man's stick as he hulled the rice in a mortar hollowed from a cypress log, beside him his wife winnowing the chaff from the grains by throwing them up from a flat pannier woven of reeds. Kit saw the golden chaff blowing away downwind, and the deft black fingers picking the brownish rice grains from the pannier and placing them in a box of carved teak.

At a distance another black ground the yamlike manioc root against a rough barked pole, and caught the wet, dustlike cassave flour in an earthen urn. His small son was squeezing out the poisonous juice from the flour through a coarse cloth, and on the flat, hot rocks placed in the embers of the fire a young woman baked the thin cakes for their evening meal.

Slowly, like poison being drawn from a deep wound, Kit could feel something of his bitterness leaving him, something of his grief. They paused now and drank ice-cold water from a calabash gourd offered them by a slim Dahomey maid.

The village dropped below them. Above them the hills were amethyst, while from brush and tree the tropical flowers flaunted their vivid hues. The whole world seemed like a sea of nodding flowers: hibiscus, poinsettia, bougainvillea, frangipani, and others whose names Kit did not know but whose beauty was a healing song in the hurt darkness of his heart.

They came out at last upon a plateau as flat and level as a table, as though someone had cut off the mountaintops with an incredibly sharp knife, leaving what had been jagged peaks as even and green as a lowland valley. Here was a sweep of pleasant fields, bathed in the rainbowed mists of the mountains through which a little silver stream ran, making a noise like joyous laughter.

"This," Ducasse said gently, "is yours, Christophe—if you still want it."

"Want it?" Kit breathed. He plunged down from his white stallion and walked through the uncut grasses that came up to his waist, toward the stream. On the journey up through the foothills, he had been of half a mind to refuse the Governor's bounty, but how can a man refuse a slice of paradise that he has earned? He came back to the Governor.

"My thanks, your Excellency," he said. "It far exceeds my greatest desire."

"Then it's yours," Ducasse said gruffly—"at a price."

"A price?" Kit echoed, wonderingly.

"That your door will always be open to a tired old man who might want to escape now and then from the duties and cares of officialdom. Is it too much?"

"No." Kit laughed. "Come and welcome to you, but it will be long before my house is built. My coffers run low of gold for the building."

"The Spaniards," Ducasse remarked, "still have as much as they ever did."

That, Kit reflected, was true. He could take to sea again and exact his tribute from his foes. In two years at the most he should be able to recoup the fortune that his generosity to his crews and his long series of misfortunes had so badly depleted.

"Here is where we should erect the house," Bernardo said, gleefully surveying the land with his eye.

"You're mad—as usual," Kit growled. "It should be here." They quarreled good-naturedly over the location of the manor. After a time the shadows lengthened deep-blue on the trail, and they turned to go.

Kit sat on his mount, looking back at the fair fields. When Del Toro lies dead, he mused, I will bring Bianca here. These halls as yet unbuilt shall someday know the noise and scamper of my sons at play. His blue eyes darkened suddenly, somber with pain.

"Yet she shall be," he whispered, "only a tenant in a house I built for you, my Rouge."

Turning, he rode down the trail after the others.

14

BIANCA GAZED thoughtfully at the dark profile of her husband outlined against the light that came through the window of the great coach. It was the day Ricardo Goldames was to receive his doctorate. A tiny frown appeared between her brows and drew them together. Why is it, she mused, that though I do not love him, though time stopped for me that day in Cul-de-Sac, there is something about his face that moves me deeply? . . . She turned away and her glance fell on the pale face of Ricardo, who sat opposite them in the coach.

His blue eyes were like those of a wounded dog, wretched and imploring. Since that night almost a week ago that he had scaled the walls and stood "eating the iron" (as the Spanish called the fruitless braying of a young lover) outside her window, Bianca had not spoken to him. She had dismissed him coldly that night, reading the naked, animal desire in his eyes, the absence of tenderness despite all the stilted poetry he had mouthed. To Bianca, this had been inexpressibly shocking. Convent-bred, she instinctively believed that the demands of a husband were one of the crosses a woman had to bear. A lover, on the other hand, was a kind of cavalier servante who supplied poetry and romance—and demanded nothing in return.

Ricardo had demanded something. Were all men, then, alike? She shook her head, trying in vain to clear it of the confusing burden of thinking. Nothing in this life seemed to fit the patterns of her preconceived notions. For instance, she did not love Don Luis. Therefore his love-making should have been utterly repugnant to her. But was it really? Truthfully, Bianca had to admit that she felt no real distaste toward her husband's passionate embraces—that indeed on more than one occasion she had responded to him with ardor. Was she then depraved? she asked herself. The answer, when it came, was in itself a kind of mystery. There was in him, her subconscious mind told her, something that moved her, something not of himself—something of another.

What other? To that there was no answer. Bianca's mind drifted off, as it always did, to Kit. She had vowed that she would never forget him, but at the moment certain features of his appearance escaped her. She loved him still, that she knew. But what kind of love was it that after two years could not recall the exact shade of his eyes? Blue? Ricardo's eyes were blue, for he was a Galician. Half the inhabitants of that province, the descendants of the Teutonic Visigoths who had ravaged the north of Spain centuries before, had blue eyes, and not a few of them were blond. But to say "blue" meant nothing—what exactly was the shade of Kit's? It is of no importance, she told herself, but her forgetfulness rankled. What was important, her conscience told her, was the fact that if it had been Kit who stood beneath her window she would have sent down Quita to open it for him.

Bianca lay back against the cushions of the coach and closed her eyes. Like the tumultuous throbbing of her own blood, the sound of the kettledrums that headed the parade in which they rode came back to her, and through them the moaning of flutes and oboes. Without opening her eyes, she knew that behind the richly arrayed band that led the procession came the faculty of the University of San Marcos, dressed grandly in their caps and gowns to honor Ricardo. Behind them strode the *bedeles*, the monitors, also decked out in their finery, carrying the maces of the university.

Her eyes came open and she stared at Don Luis. Then, suddenly, they widened and a kind of terror flamed within their depths. For now, beyond all remote possibility of doubt, she knew—she *knew!* She sat there, studying her husband's face and wondering how all this time the recognition had escaped her. Then that too explained itself—it was all a trick of coloring. A person sitting between someone and a strong light is robbed of

166

color, his profile becoming, in effect, a silhouette. So it was that at last the superficial differences were canceled out for Bianca—Kit's blond fairness and Don Luis's almost Moorish swarthiness were as nothing, and the two faces were one face—the same. True, Don Luis's profile was older and a trifle heavier, but the likeness, now that the coloring no longer stood in the way, was almost agonizingly exact.

At once her mind was off, racing down forbidden avenues. On the day that he had abducted her Kit had acknowledged that he knew Don Luis. He had known Don Luis's Black Heron coat of arms. He had secretly nurtured a terrible hatred for Don Luis that she had sensed. The evidence mounted to the skies, exact and damning.

What was it her husband had said? "This bastard son of a worthless Frenchwoman." How did you know that, Luis? How else but that you yourself sired this fair and princely bastard? How had Kit come by his manners, his grace, his courtliness? And why did you spare him when you had him at your mercy? Why else but that you knew he was your son!

She bent her head and the great tears stung and tugged at her eyelids. It all fitted, and it explained so many things. And I am with child now, the bitterness in her heart mocked, because this unrecognized resemblance with Kit melted me into submission—even more, into passionate response to you, Luis. . . . She felt the bitter pain of frustration, but she had to look up now, for Ricardo had reached out and touched her hand.

"We are here," he said.

The footman opened the door and Don Luis climbed down and put up his hand to help her. He could feel her trembling, and a little questioning frown wrinkled his brows, but Bianca turned her face away.

Then the three of them followed the procession into the cathedral. When the ceremony was over, Ricardo, now a Doctor of Letters, was surrounded by an admiring throng who pressed their congratulations upon him in a shower of costly gifts. Finally Don Luis announced that after the banquet to which they were all invited there would be a bullfight. The crowd broke into cheers.

At the bullfight Bianca sat with Ricardo because Don Luis, as a sign of his courage, had entered the lists against the bull. There had been talk at the banquet of the cowardly patron who a few years ago had hired a beggarly fellow to fight his bull for him. The men had cried shame at such lack of manliness.

Ricardo, who was an extremely rational young man, had excused himself from the bullring on the score of fatigue due to the arduous preparation he had made for the ceremony. He had better ideas of how to spend an evening than by risking his fine figure as an offering to the sharp horns of an angry bull. Half the young hidalgos of Lima were in the ring, mounted on their fine chargers, their lances ready in their hands. The bull, Bianca saw, didn't have a chance.

"Afraid, Señor Doctor?" she asked Ricardo.

"I am giving a demonstration of a higher form of courage," Ricardo said sadly, "for I run the risk of being transfixed by the displeasure in your eyes. Believe me, señora, that is a crueler stab than any bull could deal."

Bianca looked at him quietly. "Give me your promise that you will never again behave so disgracefully," she said, "and I will forgive you."

"Alas, how can I promise? Ask me not to breathe. Say to me, 'Die, Ricardo!' and I will kill myself at your feet. But do not ask me not to love you, because such a thing is beyond my power."

Bianca could not help laughing at his extravagant speech. "You are a wicked lad, Ricardo," she said. "Love me if you will, only do not expect me to love you in return. That I cannot do."

"No, you can't, can you?" Ricardo said softly. "Nor my revered godfather and patron either—not while this blond devil of a pirate still lives!"

All the color drained from Bianca's face, leaving it ghost-white. Her lips moved once or twice before they succeeded in shaping the words.

"Who—who told you of that?" she whispered.

Ricardo looked at her. He saw her face white, her lips pale, her eyes widening into great pools of darkness into which all his happiness was sinking.

168

"Who told you, Ricardo?" The tone was edged like a blue-steel blade glinting in the sunlight.

"I have an informant who served on the *Garza*," he said finally. "But say it isn't true," he whispered, his voice unrecognizably hoarse. "Say that he lied—that you do not love this buccaneer."

The blue-midnight cloud of matchless hair moved slowly sidewise.

"No, Ricardo," she said gently, sensing his grief and shame, "your miserable informant did not lie."

Ricardo fell back against the seat, hearing the thunderous roar of the cheering far off and faint, like the surf-pounding of a distant sea. Below them Don Luis was standing in his stirrups goading the maddened bull with his lance. Bianca looked down, and the black, rebellious thoughts crowded resistlessly into her mind. If that horse should stumble, or that magnificent animal should raise his mighty head . . .

"Holy Mother of God," she whispered to herself, "forgive me! Do not permit me to will his death."

Ricardo sat up, and his voice was filled with savage mockery.

"So," he said, "you too pray for the bull!" Bianca lowered her head and the great tears ran like strings of diamonds down her pale cheeks. "Forgive me," Ricardo said. "I have been beastly to you. My whole life is not worth one of your tears."

Gently Bianca patted his hand. "No," she said. "I wept for my own wickedness."

"Tell me about him," Ricardo said, "this English sea dog who has stolen your heart."

"Do you really wish to hear, Ricardo?" she said sadly.

"Yes. Perhaps then I can understand."

"Well," Bianca began, "he is not truly English, though he commanded a vessel sailing under that flag. His mother was French. His father—he does not know. He was born in Cádiz, and speaks Castilian that is like music. He is fair like you, though much burnt by the sun. His eyes are like sea water, his hair like the sun's own gold."

"But a sea robber—a pirate! A man of rude manners and coarse speech!"

169

Bianca shook her head.

"No, you wrong him. He was well reared. He has the manners and the grace of a prince."

"Then why does he follow so vile a trade?"

"Because his father, who is a very great nobleman, cast him off. If this grandee were to acknowledge him, he would rank among the great names of . . ." She stopped short, realizing that she had said too much.

"Of Spain," Ricardo finished for her. "Already you have said his father was a grandee. And yet you say he does not know who his father is."

"He doesn't," Bianca whispered.

"But you do?" Bianca nodded mutely. "Who is it, Bianca? This interests me strangely. Tell me!"

"I cannot do that," Bianca said firmly. "It is my secret, and it will die with me."

"But . . ." Ricardo began.

He was interrupted by a tremendous roar from the crowd. Don Luis had killed his bull. He stood in the center of the ring, holding his horse by the bridle, and bowed right and left to the crowd. He came forward now and bowed low to Bianca. The cheers redoubled as she loosened the blossom behind her ear and threw it down to him.

It was then that the stranger, clad in the rough garb of a seaman, approached Ricardo. With a word of apology to Bianca, Ricardo drew the man apart. They stood there for a moment in whispered conversation. The crowd began to drift away. Then Ricardo led her down to the gates, where Don Luis awaited them.

"A brave fight, my lord," Bianca told him. "You were magnificent."

Don Luis glowed visibly at her words of praise. He bent over her hand. He straightened, and was opening his mouth to thank her when a hand plucked diffidently at his sleeve. Raising her eyes, Bianca saw the same man who had engaged Ricardo in conversation.

"What is it?" Don Luis growled.

"It is of great importance, my lord," the stranger said calmly. "And it is for your ears only. If my lord would step a bit apart . . ."

170

Something in the man's bearing caused Don Luis to heed him. His assurance, perhaps, the calm surety in his eyes. Bianca saw her husband walk away a little distance. The seaman began to talk swiftly, earnestly. Don Luis's face was a study. It was frozen with intentness. His great dark eyes leaped suddenly with tremendous fire. Bianca saw his hand go into his pockets and come out with a purse, which he tossed to the man. Then he rejoined them. But it was to Ricardo that he spoke.

"You will see Bianca home," he commanded. "This man has brought news that must be looked into—and at once!" Bianca gazed at him, her eyes filled with questioning. "I go to Callao, my love," Don Luis said gently.

"And when will you return?"

"I don't know, but I will send you word." Then he swung himself into the saddle and thundered away. He had reached the first corner and was half around it before it occurred to Bianca to question the nature of the news that could cause Don Luis to ride away without even pausing to kiss her good-by.

"It will be a dreary time," she said, half to herself. "A woman without a husband might as well be imprisoned in a dungeon."

A crafty gleam appeared in the corners of Ricardo's eyes. He looked at Bianca and the gleam kindled, became fire. But when she turned toward him he hid his gaze with a quick toss of his head.

"A woman," he observed softly, "need not have a dreary time."

Bianca's voice was tart. "Not if she is without shame and would abuse her husband's faith in her!"

"You misunderstand," Ricardo said slowly. "A woman should have some pleasure in life. All pleasures are not sinful. What harm would there be if you veiled yourself and allowed me to show you the town?"

"None—except that would encourage you to make other requests. And those gained, you would proceed to still others, Ricardo, until . . ."

"Until the time came when the decisions would lie between you and your heart, Bianca. Would you have me believe that the lovely Countess del Toro fears—herself?"

"And have I nothing else to fear?"

Ricardo smiled wickedly. "No," he said. "Nothing."

"Still, it is necessary to avoid even the appearance of evil," Bianca persisted. "I would not set matronly tongues wagging because of some harmless escapade. You know how easily evil can be read into even the most blameless action."

"To be talk, there must be some knowledge of what happens," Ricardo said. "If they don't know, what can they say?"

"And you, of course," Bianca said scornfully, "can arrange it so they know nothing?"

Ricardo studied her pale, lovely face. Time now to change tactics, he thought. This line of procedure was getting him nowhere.

"I can arrange it," he said soberly. "But there is yet another side to this matter, Bianca. In a little while, you will go away—out of my life. And when you go something of my life will be gone. The better part, the fairest, richest part. I ask so little—a smile, a word, the joy of your nearness, nothing else."

Seeing the small smile trembling about the corners of her mouth, Ricardo knew before she spoke that he had won—the first engagement, at least. As for the future, if he were prudent, might not he gain all he hoped for, one small step at a time?

"I will go," she said at last, "but see that you are careful. I want no scandal attached to my name."

"Have no fear of that," Ricardo told her gravely.

"And see, too," she added, "that you do not forget yourself. It would pain me to have to end our friendship altogether, Ricardo, but end it I will if I must."

"With you," Ricardo said, "I am honor's soul and body."

That night, with the aid of Quita, Bianca slipped into the darkened street. She was heavily veiled, and wrapped in her thickest cloak, for the nights of Lima are bitterly cold. Outside in the icy darkness Ricardo sat impatiently on his horse, holding the bridle of another mount. Seeing Bianca, he smothered a glad cry and helped her up into the saddle.

Savage joy sang along the network of his veins. His mind went racing ahead filled with pictures that had him reeling in the saddle. If her face is so white, he thought, what of her body? He almost fell from the saddle, thinking of it.

172

Bianca put out a warning hand. "Are you ill, Ricardo?" she whispered.

"No. I am only overjoyed at your coming."

"Where are we going?" she asked.

"To a little place where the wine is good and the food excellent. A gypsy of Cádiz is there who makes music that tears apart one's heart." He felt very sure of himself.

If at that moment Ricardo could have listened to Don Luis as he addressed another sailor in Callao, he would have been somewhat less sure of himself. He would have discovered, as most of the Don Luis's enemies had at one time or another, that it was a fatal error to underestimate him.

"I was told," Don Luis was saying to the sailor, who had been pointed out to him by the man who had brought him the message in Lima, "that you encountered a pirate vessel in these waters two days ago."

"Yes, my lord," the man said confidently.

"This vessel bore the name *Seaflower*?"

"That she did, and a bitter fight she gave us. We were off Chimbote when she bore down on us and . . ."

"The *Seaflower*," Don Luis mused. "I think I know that vessel. A great ship of the line, is she not, mounting, say, sixty guns?"

"Right you are, my lord, and sixty-four-pounders they be. Why, I tell you . . ."

But Don Luis's great hand shot forward and caught the seaman by the throat.

"You miserable, lying dog!" he spat. "Who paid you to tell this monstrous lie?"

"My lord," the man gasped, "I speak truth—this great ship . . ."

"Whoreson!" Don Luis snorted, shaking the man until his eyes bulged from their sockets. "Don't you know that the *Seaflower* is a small brigantine, mounting no gun above thirty-two pounds, and that you and your master are the first of fools to think that you could trick me? Who paid you? Tell me, or you'll die!"

"I—I don't know him, my lord," the sailor gasped. "It was a young hidalgo of Lima. I don't know his name."

Still holding the man, Don Luis looked around for the man

173

who had brought him here, but the second conspirator had vanished into the shadows of the water front.

"A young hidalgo," Don Luis said. "Hmmmm. . . . If that forked tongue of yours can manage a syllable of truth, tell me the color of his eyes."

"Blue, my lord," the wretch said hastily. "I noticed them, because they were most uncommon."

"And his hair?"

"As fair almost as that of a Dutchman or an Englishman."

Don Luis drew the wretch back and sent him sprawling with a tremendous shove. Then as the man attempted to rise he kicked him savagely in the face.

As he swung aboard his weary horse, he thought grimly: You are a fool, Ricardo—so young and already tired of life? . . .

Then he thundered away in the darkness, back toward Lima.

Bianca stood with Ricardo in the darkened entrance of a den of almost unbelievable foulness. They had eaten supper at a quiet inn, but Ricardo had insisted on showing her the seamier side of Lima. This place was dark and filled with the reek of stale pipe smoke, the stench of unwashed bodies, the mingled smells of wine and chicha—maize beer—and the nose-stinging scent of the vile perfume the women wore. Above the variously offensive odors, the noises blended into a nerve-shattering din. Some of these sounds, Bianca perceived, were intended to be music. Native performers blew into panpipes of reeds of various lengths tied together with fiber; the quena flute lifted its weird wailing above the other anguished cries, while whistling pots shrilled, gourds filled with seeds or pebbles rattled, and trumpets of cattle horn blared. In a corner an Inca lad played an imported instrument, the *charango* of Bolivia—a kind of mandolin made of the shell of an armadillo—with a rapt and haunted expression on his dark face. Bianca had half-turned to flee from this place of terror when the music caught her. She hung there, one foot still raised to take the first step of flight, listening.

The music throbbed, wailed, rose and fell in the thick, smoky gloom. She could feel it possessing her, crawling insidiously along the network of her nerves. It had no harmony as such; it was direct, repetitive, hypnotic. Centuries of civilization, ages of restraint, slipped away from her like cast-off garments. She felt a wild impulse to leap into the center of the room, where the greasy flambeaux flared, and pound the earthen floor in a mad and savage dance. Ricardo bent down to her.

"Do you want to leave, Bianca?" he whispered.

"No!" she exulted. "No—this is magic, Ricardo!"

A lean figure out of an Inca carving approached them, pride of race showing in every line of his emaciated figure.

"A table, Titicaca," Ricardo said. "Wine—your best, man."

"Food?" the Indian grunted. Ricardo looked at Bianca.

"Yes, yes!" she said gleefully. "I'm starved again."

"Quinoa soup with peppers," the Inca suggested. "Cakes of *chunu*—maize?"

"Indian dishes?" Bianca guessed.

"Yes. They're delicious."

"All," Bianca said. "Bring them all."

Seated there in the throbbing darkness while the savage music entered her and beat along her blood, Bianca looked about. As her eyes grew accustomed to the darkness, she saw that there were other women present. Most of them were prostitutes, mestizas and mulattoes; but at a near-by table sat a woman as white as Bianca, and obviously of high station. The woman's eyes were feverish, darting through the smoke-laden gloom. Now and again she dipped her aristocratic fingers into a bowl and ate what seemed to Bianca to be a mess of red clay. Bianca turned her startled, questioning eyes upon Ricardo.

"Coca," he explained. "It produces a kind of sweet madness when its leaves are mixed with clay and chewed. The Indians use it as a specific against mountain sickness. Unfortunately, it is habit-forming, for it is the source of cocaine. That grand señora is doomed—she will die in shrieking horror before long."

"How horrible!" Bianca whispered.

The rattle of the gourds quickened, the *charango* achieved a wilder strain. There was a deep blare from the cattle-horn trumpets and a girl leaped into the circle of the flambeaux. She was entirely naked, and her supple young body had been anointed all over with oil. She planted her young feet firmly

on the red earthen floor, and every muscle of her trunk undulated, beating savagely in tune with the music.

Bianca found, to her vast astonishment, that she was neither
shocked nor offended. The Inca maid was indescribably beautiful, her pagan dance a votive offering to powerful mountain
gods. It went on and on, the flutes and reed pipes silent, the
charango still, only the pebble-filled gourds sounding now, and
the llama-skin drums filling the dark air with savage frenzy.
Bianca could hear the rasping of Ricardo's breath above the
low thumping of the drums; she knew, without turning, that he
was leaning forward, rapt, lost.

But at that moment a shrill shriek tore the close air in the
little den and Bianca saw that the grand señora was swaying
on her feet, tearing with clawing fingers at her garments. She
wore very few, for a moment later she had joined the Inca
maiden in the flickering light of the flambeaux, naked. This was
indeed shocking. The Inca dancer was a bronze statue, oiled
and glistening, so that her sex was submerged in the primitive
surroundings, becoming unreal, so much a part of the mood and
the music that seeing her one forgot that she was human and
she became a work of perfect, savage art—a statue moving, a
wild poem fleshed in life. But the whiteness of the other's skin
was like a cry, her slender body demandingly, oppressively
voluptuous. Against the primitive purity of the Inca, she was
the decadence of civilization, the epitome of naked lust. Bianca
got to her feet, but it was then that the señora's younger escort
hurled himself upon her and wrapped her shameful nudity in
the enveloping folds of his great cloak. She fought him fiercely,
so that it was only after two other men rose to help him that
she was finally subdued.

Bianca picked up her own cloak and was taking a step or two
in the direction of the door when Ricardo touched her arm. In
some curious way she felt unclean, as though the other's shame
had been her shame, as though she herself had engaged in that
sickeningly disgraceful performance.

"Wait," Ricardo pleaded. "Caviedes is coming!"

"Caviedes?" Bianca echoed.

176

"Juan Valle y Caviedes," Ricardo said. "See, he is entering now."

Bianca looked at the small man who stood dramatically in the doorway. His face was hideously marked with syphilis, his figure thin and bent, so that only his eyes seemed alive. But they were wonderful eyes, Bianca saw, strangely godlike eyes that soared above the dying wreck of his body as though they had a life of their own. The music crashed at once into silence. Every eye turned toward the doorway.

"Caviedes!" The name went up in a shout, a roar of welcome, bursting from the lips of every man and woman in the place. The Inca dancer crossed the room in one great bound, like the *grand jeté* of the classic ballet, and hurled herself into his arms. Caviedes stared down at her with contempt, then he opened his arms and let her drop unceremoniously to the floor. Men left the sides of their paramours to reach for his bony hands. He received their homage as his due. So a pagan god would receive mortals, Bianca thought, upon a rare descent from Olympus.

"Who is he?" she began, but Ricardo lifted a warning finger.

"Lima's greatest poet," he whispered, "though those fools who surround Monclovia don't know it. He can toss a gongoraism[1] with the best, though for the most part he scorns such folly."

"A verse!" a woman cried. "Come, Juan, give us a verse!"

Caviedes fixed her with an icy stare. *"Before* wine?" he drawled.

Instantly a dozen young hidalgos leaped forward, bottles and glasses in their hands. Caviedes tossed back the heavy cloak he wore to protect his thin body, seated himself at a table, and began to drink. He emptied glass after glass, tossing them down as though his very life depended on it.

"He is slowly dying," Ricardo murmured.

"Oh!" Bianca whispered.

"I think he wants to die. He holds himself guilty for his wife's death. You see how eaten up he is with French sickness? Well, he was contaminated by a woman of the town and passed the

[1] At that time Spain's best loved poet, Góngora, was widely imitated. He was noted for the intricate, involved, and tortuous nature of his verse.

177

disease on to his wife. She died of it! He has never forgotten that. Monclovia's circle will not receive him because of the licentiousness of his life, but I think he lives this way to still the pain within his heart. And what a mocker the man is! He has set up a wooden beggar's stall in front of the Viceroy's palace. The soldiers tear it down, but he sets it up again. He is so loved among the people that Monclovia dare not touch him."

"Bless you, my children," Caviedes mocked. "Now—a verse." He launched into a devastating attack on the medical profession, his favorite target. Before he was done, Bianca found herself laughing so hard that the tears tugged and stung at her eyelids. Then, almost without pausing for breath, Caviedes began another, describing the monumental stupidity and the trusting nature of a cuckolded husband. The laughter rose in waves and beat against the ceiling. Juan Caviedes looked about him, a sly grin on his ugly face.

"I now give you a piece in appreciation of those true benefactors of mankind," he announced, "the whores of Lima!" The poem held Bianca rigid in her seat. Caviedes left nothing to the imagination; his language was fluid, pungent, and exact. He described lovingly portions of the feminine anatomy that Bianca had not known had names—at least not such names as Caviedes gave them. This time the applause shook the room.

Bianca raised her white hands to cover her scarlet cheeks. Something in the gesture caught Caviedes' attention. When Bianca looked up, he was standing before her, peering down at her with rapt attention. A great fear entered her heart. She wanted to run wildly from the place, out of this fetid hole, out into the icy night, but for the life of her she could not move. Then Caviedes began to speak.

She realized at once that he was improvising. Others recognized this too, and one of his more ardent admirers seized a burnt-out torch and began to scribble the words hastily on a tablecloth.

This time, Juan Caviedes' voice was different: it was low, chaste, reverent. He began describing Bianca, comparing her face to dawn sunlight on the snows of the Andes, her hair to a starless night. Her eyes, he said, were limpid pools of pure

178

darkness in which all man's ardent hopes sank down and drowned, never more to rise. . . . There was nothing in the poem of disrespect; here was another man speaking. Here, perhaps, was the Caviedes that might have been. The finished poem was an exquisite thing, a masterpiece of pure, exact statement, so that Bianca sat there with the unashamed tears streaking her pale face, feeling more humble and more honored than she had ever felt before.

She was conscious of the great and echoing silence. Everyone in the room sat as though stunned, caught up in the blinding recognition of genius. Her lips moved, and the corners of her mouth, smiling, diverted the track of her tears.

"Thank you, Señor Caviedes," she whispered. "I thank you with all my heart!"

This time the applause was a frightening thing. After the long, intense silence it echoed and reverberated, filling the room so that its pounding could almost be felt. As Caviedes made Bianca a low and reverent bow, no one in that room had eyes to notice the tall grandee who had entered; his footfalls were swallowed up in the stupendous outburst of sound.

Bianca became aware suddenly that something was wrong with Ricardo. He was on his feet, his blue eyes goggling. She reached up and took his arm to draw him down beside her, but he threw off her grasp so roughly that at long last, in deep puzzlement, she turned to look into the coldly murderous eyes of her husband.

Again the silence in the place crashed down, layers deep. Men stood up one by one and began to edge away. Alone of all those present Don Luis del Toro looked as though he were enjoying himself.

Ricardo's hand flew to the hilt of his sword.

"How now, godson?" Don Luis said, almost genially. "I have no wish to fight with you. There is no honor to be gained by spitting a sniveling whelp. Besides, I see no marks of rope burn on my lady's arms, or any other sign that she was abducted."

"Sir," Ricardo began, his voice high and breathless.

"A man fights, Ricardo," Don Luis continued gravely, "for the honor of his lady. Since it is all too apparent that mine has none, I see no cause to exert myself. I have never bothered to defend the honor of a whore, no matter how unprofessional her status."

Glancing down at the sheet-white horror in Bianca's face, Ricardo did the only thing possible under the circumstances. Drawing back his hand, he smote Don Luis a stinging blow full in the face. The Count smiled.

"I'm sorry that you did that, Ricardo," he whispered, "for now I must kill you. Come, my Bianca—or should I say *our* Bianca, lad? Yours and mine, and God knows how many others'—a pleasant thought, is it not?"

He took Bianca's arm in a grasp that for all its seeming gentleness had a grip like steel.

"Come, Bianca," he said almost gently. "It is time you were in bed. I hope it will not grieve you to sleep alone for just this once."

Bianca's gasp was a blade of fire entering Ricardo's heart.

"Now, see here, Luis!" he got out. "You wrong Bianca! Why, she is as pure . . ."

"As Caviedes," Don Luis finished for him. "Don't be impatient, Ricardo. I will meet you within the hour."

The time of waiting within the barred and shuttered confines of her room Bianca found agonizingly long. Actually, it was scarcely half an hour before Don Luis returned from his encounter with Ricardo. He strode into his wife's room with one arm hanging limp at his side, drops of blood dripping from his fingers. For an instant hope leaped in Bianca's heart, but Don Luis stilled it.

"The whelp fought well," he growled. "Too well—I had hoped to spare him."

"Then he is . . ." Bianca whispered.

"Yes, he is dead," Don Luis said slowly. "I shall order masses said for the repose of his soul. I loved him well."

"And yet," Bianca whispered, her voice freighted with horror, "you killed him!"

"Let us say," Don Luis growled, "that *we* killed him. Where is Quita? Order her to pack. We must leave Lima tomorrow."

180

"This—this murder of yours does not please the Viceroy?" Bianca asked. "Good! You should be hanged for it!"

Don Luis eyed his wife sternly, the pain from his wound visible in his face. "Let us not speak of hanging," he said quietly. "I might be tempted to use the whip you so richly deserve on your own fair back. If it is of interest to you, the Count of Monclovia has already absolved me of this. It is only that I do not want to flaunt your shame in the face of decent women that we are leaving so hastily."

Bianca looked at him, a smile showing on her ghost-pale mouth. "But flaunt it you must, Luis," she mocked, "for I fear that I cannot travel."

Don Luis straightened up, grasping his wounded shoulder. It pained him frightfully, but his impassive face gave no sign. "Why?" he demanded.

"Because," Bianca began, then the words came out in a rush, "because I am with child!"

Seeing the joy leaping and flaming in his great dark eyes, Bianca felt that at some other time, under other circumstances, she could have forgiven him; but now the corners of her mouth lifted into a tighter curl, and her black eyes were as cold and cruel as death.

"I am disappointed in you, my lord," she said.

"And how have I disappointed you now?" Don Luis asked wearily.

"You have not yet asked who sired it," Bianca said ever so gently, "this child who kicks beneath my heart."

Don Luis lay back against the bedpost, naked anguish in his eyes. "And if I were to ask?" he whispered. "What answer would you give?" Bianca looked at him, her eyes cool and grave, the scarlet returning to her mouth, two bright spots of color burning in her cheeks. "Answer me!" Don Luis thundered. "Who fathered this bastard?"

"You, of course, my lord," Bianca said demurely, "who are so wonderously good at it. Though I doubt that this one will be as fair as your eldest, since I have not that worthless French-woman's gold upon my head." Then she turned very quietly and went out of the room.

181

And Don Luis, hanging there against the bedpost, wondered as his blood-wet fingers loosed their hold and the roaring tide of blackness rose to engulf him which wound it was that bore him down—the one made by cold steel through his shoulder or this invisible dagger left twisted in his heart.

15

THE FRIGATE *Santa Elena,* Don Francisco Alvarez commanding, beat her way southward along the coast of Panamá. She had left Port Royal in Jamaica some days before, and after touching briefly at Porto Bello, was on her way southward to Nombre de Dios. Today, however, both the wind and the current were adverse, so that the frigate made very poor speed.

Nightfall caught Don Francisco and his crew some leagues from Nombre de Dios. Under ordinary circumstances, any of the Spanish commanders familiar with this coast would have proceeded without hesitation into the harbor and dropped anchor there, where they could await the coming of morning in perfect safety. However, the circumstances on this night early in July 1694 were far from ordinary. Don Francisco had been ordered from Spanish waters upon an official mission; neither he nor any member of his crew had ever sailed in the waters of the Caribbean before.

Being a man of sound practical sense, Don Francisco proceeded to do the worst thing he could have done under the circumstances: he pointed his prow toward the shore line, clearly visible off his starboard beam, and inched the *Santa Elena* in, taking careful soundings with a weighted line every few yards. When the depth seemed to him to be right, he ordered his crew to drop anchor and, lighting his pipe, settled down to take his ease.

The night was deep and soft. From the mainland a breeze brought the scent of dense, steaming vegetation, and the cry of the gulls circling like the ghosts of drowned seamen in the moonlight sounded mournfully through the still air. The stars were very big and close, like a Midas profusion of diamonds pinned in an endless black-velvet curtain, and the frigate creaked peacefully on her anchor line as she rose and fell in the easy swells. Don Francisco's head fell forward on his broad chest and he slept. So did his entire crew, including the single lookout he had posted.

When he awoke it was to the scream of a man in the death agony. He stumbled clumsily to his feet and, seizing his sword, climbed out on deck, where his dazed eyes beheld his half-armed and totally unprepared crew being cut down by a legion of bearded fiends. With an oath, he sprang forward into the fray, only to be confronted by an apparition that quite unmanned him.

He had raised his slim Spanish sword only to have it met in the darkness by a blade of Toledo steel as fine as his own. Sparks flew from the impact, and Don Francisco realized at once that he was engaging a swordsman of no mean caliber. He found himself being beaten back, step by step, to where the light flooded out from the opened hatch of his cabin. He stepped back once more, furiously parrying that dancing blade which seemed everywhere at once. And at that moment someone came up behind him and laid a belaying pin over his head.

But just before the light went out inside his skull, Don Francisco had seen his apparition. The slim and graceful swordsman who had fought him with such deft and mocking skill was no swordsman at all, but a woman—a woman in boy's pantaloons and a tattered shirt, neither of which were sufficient to conceal the lissom quality of her beauty.

On the deck of the frigate the battle was over. Even in daylight, this crew, inexperienced in the ways of fighting buccaneers, would have been doomed; at night, bemused by sleepiness, they were like so many sheep. Rouge stood on the foredeck, her long red hair streaming over her shoulders, and addressed her buccaneers.

"Step lively now," she said. "Have you any further cause for grumbling? I got you off the *Seawitch,* though she flamed to her topgallant yards, and endured your goatish bleating across the rest of the sea. Now, look alive and pull hearty, lest what remains of my patience desert me. To your stations!"

184

The men swarmed upward amid the rigging, loosing a cheer that floated deep and lusty across the soft night air. Leaning over the bow, Rouge once more read the name of the frigate.

"The *Santa Elena*," she mused. "I doubt there is any saint-hood here. I christen her the *Gull*, for her broad wings will sweep the seas free of anyone who opposes me." She called the ship's carpenter to her side, ordering him to reletter the name in the morning.

She remembered the sufferings of those four days in the longboats after she had seen that every man had left the *Sea-witch* before she herself left a deck that quite literally burned beneath her feet. Then the hunger and the snakes and the mos-quitoes of the Panamá coast, where they had hidden themselves in the very heart of Spanish territory. Later she could think some more. Now there were things to be done.

"Bring the don aft," she said crisply to a seaman, and re-turned to her cabin.

The man saluted and went forward. After a few minutes he returned with Don Francisco. When the Spaniard was shoved unceremoniously into Rouge's cabin by the two villainous rogues who guarded him, he found her seated, her long legs propped gracefully on the carved oak table. That Don Francisco found this disconcerting was apparent. His hot little black eyes trav-eled over the long, sweet-curving length of thigh down to where her slim ankles disappeared into the gaping tops of her low jackboots. Rouge smiled at him, her green eyes brimming with mockery.

"Be seated, señor. I would like to ask you some questions."

The hidalgo made her a stiff bow and remained standing. Rouge nodded wearily to the guards, and the Spaniard found himself slammed vigorously into a chair.

"Will you have a tankard?" Rouge inquired. Don Francisco shook his head angrily. At once one of the guards was ready with a heavy pewter tankard. Rouge watched with quiet amuse-ment as they forced the Spaniard to drink it down, sloshing it freely into his eyes, his mouth, and his beard.

"Now that we are done with the civilities," Rouge said, "we can attend to business. Where did you come from, señor?"

Don Francisco clamped his jaws grimly shut. Rouge lifted a weary eye toward the guards. Slowly they brought out their sheath knives. After a moment one of them leaned forward and plucked a hair from the Spaniard's heavy beard. A quick motion of the knife and the hair fell to the floor in two clean-cut halves. The Spaniard stared at it, a trace of sweat bedewing his forehead.

"I asked you a question, señor," Rouge said softly.

The Spaniard stared at the blue gleam of the knife blade and discretion won out over valor. "From Port Royal," he growled. "Your countrymen are more civil than you, señorita."

Rouge frowned. This traffic between Englishmen and Spaniards was not to her liking. Most Englishmen shared her feeling in this, she knew. Since the beginning of the long war of the Palatinate in 1688, all English sea dogs had had to swallow the bitter pill of finding themselves allies of the nation they hated above all others. Indeed, during every one of the joint forays against the French the English commanders had found it difficult to restrain their seamen from polishing off the Spanish long before their joint objectives were reached. Among the leaders, a frozen politeness was carefully practiced, but no power on earth could restrain the descendants of the sea hawks of Drake, Raleigh, Frobisher, and Hawkins from shouting "Papist dogs!" every time they sighted a Spaniard, or could prevent the crews of His Bewitched Majesty's galleons from replying "Filthy heretics!" with equal fervor.

"Then I am a truer Englishman than they," Rouge answered, "for I would have greeted you with roundshot the moment you hove to in the harbor."

"For which act," Don Francisco replied testily, "the authorities would have hanged you as they hanged that blond fiend your Captain Neilson captured."

Rouge's booted feet dropped smartly to the deck. She stood up and faced the Spaniard, the emerald blaze leaping in her eyes.

"'Blond fiend,' did you say?" she demanded. "More of this, Captain! A tall lad with a sunburst of hair about his shoulders, and a face like a sea god come down to earth?"

"The señorita exaggerates," the hildalgo observed, "but otherwise the description fits."

"Did you hear his name? Was it Christopher? Or Cristóbal or Kit?"

The Spaniard looked at her, seeing the stark emotion written in her eyes. Then, with evident pleasure, he nodded.

"Yes," he said, "such indeed was his name."

Rouge felt the stiffness leaving her knees. They were quite boneless suddenly, watery and weak. She sat down abruptly.

"You—you saw him hanged?" she whispered.

"No," the Spaniard said regretfully. "He was being brought to trial the day we sailed. It was said that an Englishwoman was to give evidence against him, of mistreatment and dishonor suffered at his hands. The outcome was scarcely in doubt."

Rouge was on her feet again, her face crimson with rage.

"Rosalind!" she spat. "The lying, fork-legged wench! Rosalind Parish!"

"Again you are right," Don Francisco said. "Señora Parish was indeed the name mentioned. You are well acquainted with the gentry of Port Royal, señorita."

Rouge signaled the guards with a wave of her hand.

"Take him away!" she commanded.

After the Spaniard had been escorted from the cabin, Rouge sat before the great table staring blankly into space. She could feel the great scalding tears gathering just back of her eyelids, and blink as she would, she could not hold them back. She shook her head angrily, dashing the tears away from her eyes in a bright shower.

When last we met, she mused, I opened fire on him with intent to kill. Why is it that now I weep for him? . . . She must think, she must. This whole matter must be made clear. But the stubborn thoughts refused to come. Instead, before her eyes rose the image of Kit mounting the gibbet, his blond head held high, pride in every line of his lean frame, no fear upon his face. She could see the hangman stepping up to him, see the loop of hemp in the man's hands, and . . .

But beyond that she could not go. She ground the knuckles of her hands into her eyes, trying to shut out the hideous picture that presented itself: Kit—tall, handsome Kit—swinging like a grotesque pendulum at the rope's end, his princely head bent sidewise at that terrible angle which has no counterpart in life. Her head went down on the oaken table and racking sobs tore unbidden up from her bosom. Then another thought, more horrible than any of the others, came to her mind.

"I crippled the *Seaflower!*" she whispered. "That was it! That stiff-necked fool, Neilson, could never have beaten Kit in a fair fight! But I—Oh, God, I! . . ." Her green eyes stared toward the bulkheads of the cabins like icy emeralds, hard and free of tears. And there, before her sight, she saw it all again, imprinted mercilessly upon her memory: her own corvette *Seawitch* flaming to its topgallant yards, and the thunderous backward recoiling bellow of her last broadside as her gunners poured their withering fire into the *Seaflower*. A gallant thing, this last gesture of defiance, heroic, magnificent—only it had sealed the doom of Kit Gerado as surely as though her hands had looped the hangman's noose about his neck. If the *Seaflower* had not been crippled by the last blast of her guns, Kit might have outfought Neilson's squadron; certainly he could have outrun them. She had done this. She, Jane Golphin, had murdered the man she loved.

Murdered him! And for what? For a house that he burned, not knowing that it was hers, for fields that he had destroyed in obedience to the orders of his superior officer in open warfare. What was a house that Kit should die for it? What was a cane field, ten thousand cane fields, the whole green earth to be compared to the lightest kiss from his firm mouth?

"For these paltry things," she whispered, "for these unbelievably petty things, I pursued him half across the sea and pulled him down to a death unworthy of a dog! Oh, Kit, my Kit. . . ." Her voice trailed off down a bright glissando of sobs, and her clenched fist beat a fierce tattoo upon the table.

She wept a long time until she had no tears left. When she at last attempted to stand up, she found to her surprise that she had not the strength to move her limbs, she who had prided herself on her lack of feminine weakness. Then a new realization came over her: she was whole again. She was a woman once more, wholly and entirely feminine, and she could admit clearly and simply something that in darkness and secret she had always known—that she loved Kit Gerado with all her heart.

188

She sat quite still in the darkness and stared at the dim bulkheads of her cabin, her mind moving along curious paths.

"I will return to Port Royal," she said aloud, "I will find Rosalind Parish and kill her with my own hands."

She stood up at last and went up on deck. "Put about," she said to the helmsman.

The man stared at her, his jaw dropping open. "Put about?" he demanded.

"Yes," she said quietly, "put about—back to Port Royal."

The man stared at her a moment longer, then shrugged. Lifting a hairy hand to his mouth, he bellowed: "Ready about!"

The crew scurried to their stations. The helmsman pushed the tiller down toward the leeward side and lifted his head again.

"Hard alee!" the helmsman roared, and brought the frigate around smartly. They were now sailing a broad reach with the wind abaft the beam. The wind held. Three days later they dropped anchor in a secret cove not far from Port Royal. Rouge told them to wait until she returned, or in the event she did not return, to remain there for four days and then sail without her.

Late that same afternoon, the Lady Jane Golphin, clad in a trim green riding habit that pointed up marvelously the color of her eyes, rode into Port Royal. She was greeted on every side by astonished people curious to know the reason for her recent disappearance and her activities during the past fortnight.

Rouge passed off their questions lightly. Of one, Gilbert Williamson, whom she knew better than the rest, she asked lightly: "Do you know the whereabouts of Rosalind Parish?"

Williamson smiled at her. "I know there is little love lost between you," he said. "Still, if you want to see her, she lives at the house of Captain Neilson, having lately—and in some haste—married that gentleman."

Rouge laughed. "She wastes no time," she said.

She saluted him with her crop and drew in on the reins. Gilbert Williamson lifted a protesting hand.

"Stay awhile," he pleaded, but Rouge was gone, thundering off down the narrow street.

At the house of Captain Neilson, Rosalind herself opened the door, her single serving-woman being busy at other tasks. Rouge's hand vanished into her bag and her slim fingers closed about the butt of the slim silver-mounted pistol that she had hidden.

"May I come in?" she asked quietly. Rosalind stood aside and allowed her to enter. She pushed forward a chair. Rouge sank down into it.

"You know why I came?" she said.

Rosalind shook her head. "No," she whispered.

"Then will I inform you," Rouge said, speaking slowly, carefully, spacing her words so they came soft and clear and deadly calm. "Upon the commons a fortnight ago, a man was hanged." She paused, watching Rosalind's face. There was in it nothing but wonder and questioning. "I—I loved that man. He was a tall man, with a sea hawk's face and God's own sunlight on his head."

"Kit!" Rosalind breathed.

"Yes, Kit," Rouge said, and her hand came out of the bag holding the tiny pistol. "Before you die, explain to me why you sent him to his doom with your lies."

Rosalind was fighting for breath. "You're wrong!" she got out at last. "He wasn't hanged! He escaped. I aided him in his flight!"

The black owl's eye of the pistol wavered for a moment, then came steady again.

"You lie," Rouge said flatly.

"No, no!" Rosalind wept. "God help me if I lie! It's true I betrayed him, but only because he scorned me. Afterward I was overcome by shame and remorse. I slipped by night into the gaol and provided the means for his liberation—his and all his crew's. Believe me, Jane, he is not dead!"

Again the pistol wavered. "If that whorish tongue of yours is not speaking the truth . . ."

Rosalind strode abruptly to the door. She flung it open and called out to the old street vender who was crying his wares outside.

"Come here a moment. I have a question for you."

The old man shuffled forward, scratching his mangy head.

"There!" Rosalind said. "Ask him!"

Rouge looked at the old man and put the question to him.

"No, ma'am," the old man quavered. "That un got away

clean. Stole his ship back and sailed her out past the harbor guards slick as a whistle! They couldn'ta come near to him—not that un!"

Rosalind went to a drawer and came back with a gold sovereign. She pressed it silently into the old man's hand. When she turned Rouge was standing beside her, her green eyes glistening with tears.

"I have never liked you," she said to Rosalind. "Yet from this hour we are friends. God bless you, Rosalind, for you have saved both his life and your own."

Rosalind put out her arms and swept Rouge into them. "Go to him," she whispered fiercely. "Give him all the love he should have, all the tenderness, and—and bear him many tall sons!" Then she fled sobbing into the other room.

Rouge stood staring after her for a moment. Then with swift, decisive steps she crossed the room and went out into the street to her waiting horse. The cobblestones echoed to the swift dancing clatter of the horse as she mounted. In a moment she was gone, thundering down the street in the direction of the hidden cove where the *Gull* lay. She would scour the Caribbean in search of Kit, and when she found him she would never again leave his side. "Pray God," she muttered, "that I find him soon."

She leaned forward over her mount's neck, urging him on with crop and spur and prayerful words.

16

AFTER HE HAD COLLAPSED in her bedroom, struck down as much by Bianca's words as by the wound that Ricardo Goldames had given him, Don Luis had lain near death for many hours. Bianca had pulled the bell cord and summoned his manservants. These, with the aid of the women, had put the heavy bulk of the grandee into bed and undressed him.

While they attended to him, Bianca knelt at an altar set into a small niche in her bedroom. It was not for Don Luis that she prayed, but for herself. Kneeling there before the image of the Virgin, with the flickering candlelight bejeweling the tears upon her face, Bianca fought her battle in silence and in tears. It was a grim struggle for all its saintly stillness, for Bianca was being assaulted by temptations as great as those hurled against Saint Anthony.

It would all be so easy, she thought as she prayed for guidance. She needed only to withdraw herself and Don Luis would die. Not one of the Indian servants was capable of nursing the Count, and the doctors of Lima were all Caviedes had said they were— and worse. Yes, she had only to let matters take their course and her husband would die. Then she could take ship to Jamaica and stay there awhile, waiting her chance to slip across the short stretch of sea in a coasting hoy into one of the blue harbors of Saint-Domingue. And once there . . . Her mind reeled, thinking of it.

However, Bianca was cursed—or blessed—with an extraordinarily lucid mind. A woman who withheld herself when she could save her husband's life was bloodguilty. To will his death, deliberately to let him die—how fine a line divided such an act from murder? To have Kit's strong arms around her, to feel his mouth upon her own—would she accept eternal damnation and hellfire for that? For a moment the hot rebellion in her blood shouted Yes! But then the training of the good Sisters of the convent and years of dutiful attendance at mass were too strong.

As she rose from her knees and approached the inert figure of her husband lying on the bed, a softer emotion awoke in her than even the mighty voice of her faith could inspire. She was moved by real pity for the big man who lay before her, his life visibly draining from his great body. As she knelt beside him, her deft fingers busy with the bandages and hot water and poultices that the servants brought her, she remembered that here indeed was her husband and her lord, the father of her unborn child. She remembered, too, that the outward harshness of his nature had never been directed at her, that Don Luis was, in fact, no better and no worse than any other grandee of his day. And, at the last, it came to her that her husband had spared Kit's life when he held him helpless. Could she, in honor, do anything else than help him now?

For three days and nights she did not leave his side. She got food into him, water, broth, and wine. When on the fourth morning she dozed off from sheer exhaustion, she dreamed that Kit stood beside her with grave approval in his eyes, but when she woke it was to find Don Luis's dark eyes upon her, clear and free of delirium and soft with tenderness.

"I have wronged you," he whispered. "Had you been what I thought, you would have let me die. Bless you, my little dove—and know that your small folly is forgotten."

Bianca put out her hand and took his. "I am glad, Luis," she said softly. "I would not have our son come into a house filled with strife. From this day on there must be no dissension between us. You must trust me, I will never betray you."

Don Luis's recovery was rapid, but because of Bianca's pregnancy they could not leave Lima for Cartagena. Soon, in fact, their positions were reversed. As Bianca grew heavy with child, the Count began to minister to her. By December of 1694,

Bianca, in her seventh month, was rendered nearly helpless by her condition.

She awoke one morning during the Christmas week with the feeling that her head had been smothered all night in a blanket. Lima, cold Lima, where the temperature rarely rises above sixty degrees, was held suddenly in the midst of a dense and steaming tropical heat more reminiscent of Panamá than of Peru. Outside her window she could hear the thud of running feet and the shouting of many voices.

At her puzzled nod, Quita opened the shutters and the voices came clear.

"*El niño!*" they shouted. "*El niño!*"

"*El niño?*" Bianca puzzled aloud. The words meant simply "the little boy" or, more likely at this season of the year, "the Christ Child." Yet why should they shout the name of the Christ Child with so much fear in their tones? She looked at Quita, but she was as mystified as her mistress. Bianca threw back her covers and put out her legs. Quita knelt and placed her soft slippers on her feet, and at that moment Don Luis strode into the room.

"What is it, Luis?" Bianca demanded. "Why do they shout?"

"They fear disaster," Don Luis growled, "and rightly, I am afraid. Don't you feel the heat?"

"Yes," Bianca said, "very much. What does it mean?"

Don Luis dropped heavily into a chair, his dark face troubled.

"Every year at this time," he said, "the winds blow from the north, from the hot regions about the equator. And with them they bring a back eddy of warm water that spreads over the cold offshore current. Once in every thirty years or so that north wind is much stronger than normal and the hot-water current increases a thousandfold. Men call the current *el niño*, because it comes most often at Christmas time."

"But why do they fear it?" Bianca demanded.

"Because it upsets all that is usual in Callao and Lima. Wait and you will see. You know it never rains here? Well—listen."

Bianca bent forward listening. Far off and faint there came the distant rumble of thunder, and on the roof sounded the first widely spaced spatter of the rain. The raindrops increased, became a downpour slanting straight down past the window in hard, exact lines. In five minutes the downpour had become a thunderous torrent so heavy that it was impossible to see even across the narrow street. The rain went on and on, hour after hour, with no apparent intention of slackening.

Bianca sat huddled in a chair while Don Luis, wrapped in his greatcoat, walked through the streets with other officials inspecting the damage caused by this unaccustomed torrent. On the coastal region of Peru, only fifty-two streams descend from the western slopes of the Andes to the ocean, and most of these dry up in summer. By November they have grown to thin brooklets, and by December they are usually in flood. But in December of 1694 they were raging cascades of boiling white water, inundating the surrounding territory for miles.

From where she sat, Bianca could hear the low crashes as the adobe buildings collapsed into muddy ruins. Lima was not built for heavy rains; even some of its stone structures gave way before the torrents. In the Indian section not one of the plastered mud huts survived. The crazed Incas ran howling through the streets, and women and children drowned by the hundreds in the flash floods. From the window of her great stone house Bianca saw the bodies of pigs and chickens drift by in the flooded street, and now and again the small brown corpse of an Indian child. By nightfall her nerves had been reduced to a quivering mass of terror, and she wept aloud in Quita's arms.

All night the rains continued, but in the morning they ended as abruptly as they had begun. Still the heat did not abate. In the coastal waters off Callao, the cold, greenish Peruvian current disappeared, to be replaced by a brownish, slow-moving southward current that was hot to the touch. The uncounted millions of microscopic sea life upon which the birds fed died and sank to the bottom, and the fish swam toward the open sea in search of cooler water. On the islands and promontories the myriad colonies of birds were abruptly deprived of food. Because of the tremendous demands of their great wing muscles, the sea birds spend every waking hour feeding, so in a matter of hours they began to die of starvation. Hundreds of thousands of them died, their feathered bodies making small mountains on their island nesting places. When the wind shifted and blew up the Rimac River toward Lima, the stench was past all belief or bearing. *"El niño!"* the people wailed, *"el niño!"*

In the cathedral the Archbishop called on the people to pray and said this catastrophe was a punishment from God for Lima's many sins. The rains fell in torrents and disappeared as abruptly, leaving the streets filled with stinking yellow water and sticky black mud. Afterward, most maddening of all, came the insects. Because of its dry, cool air, Lima is usually free of flying pests, but now they descended on the city in clouds.

None of the fumigants that Quita burned in Bianca's bedroom seemed to do any good; the people of Don Luis's household were being devoured alive. The mosquitoes buzzed from dusk till dawn, and afterward the flies, the *colorojes,* took over, bringing sickness in their wake. Before a week was out the city was in the grip of an epidemic of smallpox. The Indians died like flies, and more slowly the Spaniards began to die too. It was this fact, more than Bianca's bitter pleas, that caused Don Luis to consider seriously leaving Lima at any cost. When at last the plague appeared in their very street and the death carts, piled up with cordwood stacks of bodies, began to groan through the mud before their very eyes, Don Luis could hesitate no longer.

In Bianca's delicate condition, it was a serious risk to move her at all, he knew. But if they remained in Lima, Don Luis ran the much greater risk of losing her altogether. So it was that early one morning he wrapped her tenderly in her velvet coat and lifted her into his waiting coach. They crawled over the eight long miles to Callao, but no matter how slowly they drove, Bianca was ghost-white and weak from repeated vomiting when she was lifted aboard ship.

Once clear of the harbor, it was better. Farther out to sea they found the cool currents again, and Bianca was more comfortable than she had been in months. But as they approached the equator the heat became an agony to her. It had been Don Luis's intention to remain in the new city of Panamá until the birth of the child, but Bianca would not hear of it. She stormed and pleaded until at last Don Luis gave in, and ordered the construction of a litter to bear her across the Isthmus to Porto

Bello, where they could take ship for the cooler climate of Cartagena.

Bianca lay staring alternately at the leaf-fringed sky and the great vines that looked like serpents. Now and again she glanced downward at her swollen body and the rebellious tears came to her eyes. If, she reflected, it were Kit's child who kicked beneath my heart, I would be out of my mind with joy. As it is, I cannot even find comfort in the fact that the same blood will flow through its veins. . . .

The journey went on. On the morning of the fourteenth day Bianca was in the grip of a raging fever. Bending over her, Don Luis could see her parched lips drawn tightly away from her teeth and her fine head like that of a skull covered with white parchment. Opening his stone flagon, he forced the remainder of the carefully saved water between her teeth. Much of it ran out of the corners of her mouth, but she did not even stir. Don Luis turned on his drivers, roaring.

"Bestir yourselves!" he cried. "We must reach Porto Bello before dawn tomorrow!"

The men lashed the weary animals onward. By the time they stumbled, drunken with weariness, into Porto Bello, they had lost half the remaining mules. Even then Don Luis did not pause. He went on, carrying Bianca in his great arms when the second of the two mules that bore her litter died on its feet in the plaza of the city. Grimy, sweat-covered, he made his way to the house of Porto Bello's best physician, a Jew of Portugal, a man far in advance of his times.

"She has an even chance, I think," the doctor said after examining Bianca, "because of her youth."

"But what of the child?" Don Luis demanded impatiently.

The Jew shrugged eloquently. "That," he declared, "is in the lap of the gods."

Throughout the months of January and February 1695 Bianca lay in a comalike state in the house of the physician. The doctor himself was openly astonished that she did not die. Early in March her dark eyelids fluttered open for the first time, and Don Luis knelt beside her bed, the unashamed tears clouding his eyes. Gratefully, she put out a pale hand and stroked his head. After that her recovery was rapid.

Still, it was the first of April before she was strong enough to travel. They resumed the journey by easy stages, sojourning for many days at Nombre de Dios before proceeding southward to Cartagena. Never had Bianca dreamed that she would be glad to see the grim-walled city of Cartagena, but as the *Garza* slipped through the narrow opening at the Boca Chica and began to inch its way up the twisting channel, a feeling of peace descended upon her. Kit was gone, perhaps lost to her forever, but if that thought troubled her it also stilled the doubts and confusions that had so long racked her brain. She looked at her husband gently, almost tenderly. In all things have I failed him, she mused—and, so thinking, put out her hand.

"Home, Luis," she whispered. "It's good to be home."

Don Luis took the much-too-thin hand that she offered him and stood gazing at the pale, ethereal beauty of his wife. Like an angel come back from the grave, he thought, holding the slim hand hard in his grip, and wondering, with a quiet kind of terror, why she did not ask what had become of the child—the long-hoped-for son of his bosom, a babe as pale and lovely as the mother who bore him, who had come into this world on the second day of February 1695, and quitted it the same instant—without ever drawing the first faint breath of life. . . .

"Yes," he said at last, "it is good, my Bianca—wonderfully good. Come, the carriage awaits us."

17

EARLIER ON THE same morning that Bianca and Don Luis del Toro returned to Cartagena, Bernardo Díaz stood on the deck of the *Seaflower*. It was still dark, and he was checking the ship's position at sea. Now he lowered the cross-staff he had been sighting at a star and glanced wonderingly at the astrolabe. He looked at the needle, touched curiously with loadstone imbedded in a float of cork that floated in its bath of oil and water. Then, picking up a parchment chart, he traced the distance to the nearest shore with a pair of dividers. Again he lifted the astrolabe, hanging it on his thumb. Even with this most inaccurate instrument, affected as it was by the roll of the ship so that its usual error was as much as fifteen degrees, the results checked. He hurried forward to Kit's cabin.

"Do you know our position?" he growled. Kit nodded, a slow smile on his lean face. "When I said yesterday that there was scurvy among the crew, you said that you would make land and replenish our supplies, but why of all spots on this broad and miserable earth must you land at Cartagena?"

"I think you know," Kit said slowly. "When we embarked on this voyage my purpose was to gain the gold with which to establish myself forever on the lands the Sieur Ducasse granted me. I have obtained the gold and I am going back to Saint-Domingue, but first I intend to stop off at Cartagena."

"And your intention there is to deprive Don Luis del Toro of his wife?"

Kit studied Bernardo, small fires leaping in his eyes. "Let us say to deprive him of all his sorrows and all his joys forever," he growled. "Bianca is of but secondary importance."

199

"You will not leave her behind, will you?" Bernardo persisted.

"No, Bernardo," Kit said evenly, "but Don Luis comes first in my plans. After that, his wife."

"I think," Bernardo said with a grin, "that she will come willingly."

"I do not agree. This blood and slaying is likely to awaken within her so great a horror that she will refuse to touch my hand."

"Then why kill him?" Bernardo asked. "Think how much keener your vengeance will be if he lives knowing that each night she lies warm and panting in your arms! To a man of his tremendous pride wouldn't such a fate be worse than death? Take her away and leave him to spend his life in sorrow and shame!"

Slowly Kit shook his head. "Even if I wanted it so, she would not come. Night and morning at Cul-de-Sac I saw her kneel and pray. God is very close and very real to her. She never would break the vows she has taken." He stopped, a grimace of pain on his face. "Yet not even for her would I forbear. In Cádiz I swore that I never would rest until I had taken vengeance."

"So now?" Bernardo demanded.

"So now," Kit finished for him, "we will run the *Seaflower* in near the Santo Domingo section just past the Tenaza and lie at anchor there until nightfall. Then you will drop the longboat over and put me ashore. If I do not return by dawn, there will be little need of waiting. You will then deliver the *Seaflower* and her crew safely back in Saint-Domingue, and ask Father Dumaine to have masses said for my soul."

"*Smithers* will then deliver the *Seaflower* to her berth at Petit Goave," Bernardo corrected softly, "and Father Dumaine can include me in his prayers."

Kit was touched by Bernardo's unfailing generosity. He put out his arm and let his hand rest upon his friend's great shoulder.

"Your loyalty will one day be your doom," he said, "but it is true—I have need of you."

Bernardo stared eastward, toward the pearl-gray flush on the edge of the sky. "There is," he said, "one other thing that troubles me. You know, Kit, how many ships put in and out of Cartagena in the course of a day. What if the *Seaflower* is sighted?"

Kit frowned. "After we are put ashore," he said slowly, "the *Seaflower* must stand out to sea for some little distance—not far, but far enough to keep her out of sight of the walls. Most of the vessels lay a course broadside of the walls; otherwise it would be difficult to find the Boca Chica channel. By this means, she should escape all harm."

"Yes," Bernardo growled, "if these famished seahounds of ours can resist the temptation to drop a roundshot across some plate ship's bows while we are not there to restrain them."

"It's a risk we'll have to take," Kit said quietly. "Call Smithers aft."

The *Seaflower* held her course, angling sharply in toward the rugged shore. Off her port beam the sun broke water suddenly, a red-hot ball with blood across its face.

Later, above the mastheads the sky was blue and clear, utterly cloudless, with a fresh quartering breeze that sent them along at a merry clip. Now the mighty hill of the Popa grew out of the sea, blue, dim, and misty, discernible long before the closer-lying land at its feet could be seen. A low white edge, half imaginary, half real, broke the water before it and grew into a gray pile of rock—the mighty walls that had stopped Drake and Morgan and that had caused every other freebooter in the Caribbean to take a second thought before attempting the richest prize of them all. Here was the small outcropping fortress called the Tenaza, aimed like a pistol straight at their hearts. Below it they could see clearly the great dome of the Templo de Santo Domingo rising above the walls. Once it was in sight, Kit ordered the *Seaflower* to heave to.

By this time it was late afternoon and they could do nothing more than wait. Smithers put the *Seaflower* on a new tack so that they swept along the coast almost as far as the Boca Chica entrance. As they passed the Boca Grande, filled now with a mound of earth and rock, they could see the white sails of the native schooners flying like gulls over the surface of the Bay of Cartagena, though their slim hulls were hidden by the intervening land.

Then the helmsman put the whipstaff about so that they swung around and sailed back in the direction from which they had come. By the time the *Seaflower* had won her way back to the Santo Domingo section of Cartagena, it was dusk.

Kit looked at Bernardo, seeing his powerful hands clasping and unclasping. Across his broad chest he wore the crisscrossed leather belts from which his twelve great pistols were suspended. Kit had armed himself with two long pistols, stuck into his sash. In addition, both he and Bernardo carried daggers and cutlasses.

The tropic night crashed down and the palms that peeped above the gray walls were crowned with silver mist, the walls themselves becoming silver-gray, magically transformed by the moon's touch into things of beauty. Looking at the fair night, Kit sighed. It would have been far more to his advantage had it been clouded, the stars hidden and no moon showing. Once before such a night had almost cost him his life, but now there was no time for such reflections.

The longboat splashed into the indigo sea, and like grim shadows the oarsmen sat at their benches, their gnarled hands gripping the broad sweeps. The blades of the oars had been muffled with rags. Still, this was a perilous attempt, for one cry from a sentry would bring down upon them such a hail of shot that not even a ship of the line could survive. They moved out now from the lee of the brigantine, the men bending and straightening slowly, their motions stiff and hampered by their desire to avoid all sound. Quietly the longboat crept forward, making scarcely a ripple on the night-blue sea. Kit lifted his eyes toward the stars. They burned bright in the dark-blue vault of heaven. Who knew when, if ever, he would again see the stars? He lowered his head again toward where the moon track burned bright across the face of the waters. It was necessary for them to cross this, and there lay their chief danger. Here in the blue shadows of the night, the longboat was all but invisible, but there in the liquid silver of the moonlight they would stand out gigantic and black, a target for every eye that chanced to glance in that direction. Kit leaned forward.

202

"Double beat!" he growled. "In this moonlight, only speed can save us."

The men bent forward, grunting deep in their lungs, their belly muscles knotting with the pull of the oars. Then they hauled back and the longboat shot ahead, pushing its prow into the moon track like the point of a hard-driven knife. They raced full into the glow, running over the surface of the moon-silvered water like a gigantic water beetle. Then at last, utterly spent, they gained the protective shadow of the great walls.

"Skirt the edges on your return voyage and meet me here at dawn," Kit whispered to the boatmen. He and Bernardo went over the side, wading through the surf, their jackboots slung over their shoulders, their bags of powder and shot tied about their necks. Behind them now they could hear the low splashing as the longboat moved out, and though they would not have admitted it, a feeling of awful loneliness came over them.

The rough stones of the wall rose forbiddingly before their eyes. Exploring them with his fingers, Kit discovered that their very roughness was a help. Here were toeholds in God's plenty; an agile man could scale these walls with ease. Kit started upward first, with Bernardo close behind him.

Twenty minutes later they lay on their bellies on the broad top of the wall, gulping the air into their famished lungs. Lying there, the first thing to strike their ears was the ring of heavy boots against the cobblestones. Bernardo loosened his dagger in its sheath. Kit put out a restraining hand.

"No," he whispered. "Let him alone. His death would only set off the alarm. Follow me."

Kit crawled swiftly to the edge of the wall and let himself down, hanging by the tips of his fingers. Bernardo did the same, and the two of them hung there, listening as the sentry's foot-falls went by with agonizing slowness, hammering through the red haze in their ears, beating against the white torture in the sockets of their shoulders. The sentry paused just above their heads to gaze seaward. Then, with a gusty yawn, he moved onward until his footsteps died out in the direction of the Tenaza.

Slowly they drew themselves up and, scuttling across the

bright expanse of the top of the wall—broad enough to let two coaches pass abreast—they let themselves down into the welcome shadow of the other side. Now they had reached the streets and, passing in front of the great church of Santo Domingo, they headed toward the square. Here, the first thing that Bernardo saw was the building bearing the arms of the Inquisition. He shuddered as the two of them moved onward past the church of San Pedro Claver, named for that most saintly of men who had given his life to aid the black slaves. In the square crowned by Cartagena's great cathedral not a soul moved, for it was past the hour of the curfew.

Kit paused, frowning. How on earth was he to find the house of Don Luis? Without someone to give them directions they were hopelessly lost. As he pondered, the echoing footfalls of a guardia civil sounded in the street. Here indeed was a dilemma. If they asked directions of the guard, how could they prevent his arresting them for breaking the curfew? If they attacked him, he would almost surely cause an outcry.

Then, to Kit's vast amazement, Bernardo began to sing. As Kit's jaw dropped open, Bernardo winked broadly at him and shoved him back into the shadows. Then he meandered toward the approaching guard, the perfect picture of a man much the worse for drink. The guard stopped short, angry amazement on his dark face.

"Cap'n," Bernardo wheezed, "Good Cap'n—a favor, *por Dios!*"

"What is it?" the guard growled. "And what keeps you on the streets at such an hour?"

"Drink," Bernardo babbled sorrowfully. "I wasch at Rosita's house. You know Rosita, Cap'n?"

The guard's face relaxed a bit. Evidently he did know Rosita. This, Kit reflected with amusement, was a tribute to Bernardo's sagacity. Among all the whores in the great city of Cartagena there must be at least one Rosita.

"She did it, Cap'n," Bernardo went on. "Befuddled me wif drink, that she did—until I fell 'sleep, so help me. Then she tossed me out, wifout a taste of what I'd really paid for! Ever heard o' worse luck, Cap'n?"

The guard was grinning now. That this drunken fool had

been cheated of Rosita's favors seemed to him infinitely amusing.

"You old he goat! Do you think that Rosita needs such as you? Now get on before I remember my duty and lock you up for being abroad at such an hour!"

"Cap'n," Bernardo quavered, "I'm stranger here—came from Santa Marta yesterday—but have a friend, coachman of Don Luis—Don Luis del Toro. He'll put me up—let me sleep in the stable. Will you direct me, please?"

"All right," the guard said. "It's not far, only three streets beyond the square. Now, here is how you can reach the house."

Bernardo listened attentively. Even Kit could overhear most of the words. He waited until after Bernardo had finished his profuse thanks and the guard had gone his way. Then he joined Bernardo and the two of them raced through the darkened streets toward the house. Upon reaching it they circled it three times, unable to decide which window opened into Bianca's room. Finally, in desperation, Kit loosed a handful of small pebbles against an upper window.

There was the quick flicker of candlelight, the window opened, and a woman stood peering down at them. Her dress, Kit saw with dismay, was the saya of an Indian serving-woman. He held his breath, expecting every moment to hear her voice lifted in a screech of alarm. But the woman stood there very calmly and studied them without haste. Kit realized that they were standing in a moon-washed street that revealed them as clearly almost as daylight.

"What do you want?" the woman demanded.

"A word with your mistress," Kit whispered.

Still the woman did not move. She stood like a statue of bronze and looked down on them with complete impassivity. The seconds ticked off on the clock of doom while she looked at them. Their breaths tightened in their throats, became a long-deep burning. Suddenly the Indian woman made a gesture, a little motion not unlike a start of surprise—or, more curiously, of recognition. She leaned forward, pressing her bronzed face against the bars.

"If the tall cacique will remove his hat . . ." she whispered.

Wonderingly, Kit put up his hand. The ostrich plumes

blazed silver as he swept off his broad-brimmed hat. Then the moonlight was spilling down over the heavy, lionlike mane that fell in great curls about his broad shoulders, so that it was white-gold suddenly, shimmering in the sweep of light.

"You," the woman said clearly, exultation in her tones, "are the great cacique Kit, are you not? I've often heard my mistress speak of you!"

"Yes," Kit said, "I am he. And if you will conduct me to your mistress, I will reward you."

"My mistress's joy at the sight of you will be reward enough," the Indian woman said. "Go toward the stables and I will meet you there." There was the scurried rustle of her slippered feet and the candle glow disappeared from the window.

"You're in luck, Kit," Bernardo said with a grin. "This cuckolding of Don Luis seems to go easily."

"Don't speak of cuckolding," Kit growled. "I didn't come for that purpose. I came to kill him!"

Beyond the house, the night drifted black in the narrow alley, the smells of hay and animal dung stinging their nostrils. They scrambled over a low wall into the courtyard, and there by the gate the Indian maid awaited them.

"Come," she whispered.

Bernardo bent forward, seeing her youth, her proud and pagan beauty, and a low whistle escaped his lips. "You," he said, "what are you called?"

"Quita," the girl said. "Now if my lords will come."

"Wait," Bernardo said. "What of Don Luis?"

"He went this noon to the hacienda," the girl said, smiling. "He will return tomorrow."

"Then," Kit said, cold determination in his tones, "I will wait for him!"

"Kit," Bernardo implored, "don't be a fool! Take the girl and be off! That's revenge enough."

"I will be the judge of that," Kit said evenly. Then to Quita, "Lead on."

Quita led them to the enclosed patio and there she turned.

"Wait here," she whispered. When she had gone Bernardo turned to Kit.

206

"I'm going now," he said. "You need privacy and a guard, both of which I can provide, but please, Kit, don't wait for Don Luis!"

"Enough!" Kit muttered. Bernardo shrugged and walked out of the patio, looking for all the world like a benevolent gargoyle.

Kit strode about the patio listening to the hammering of his heart. All time seemed to have stopped, the flux of the universe frozen, and every breath had to be forced out of his lungs with great labor. The patio was a wilderness of tropical blossoms, but Kit did not see them. He moved back and forth like a caged animal, listening with his heart for footsteps long before his ears could catch their sound. Then he halted abruptly, for now unmistakably there came the sibilant whisper of slippered feet. Kit stopped his feet cautiously on the tiles and stood there, waiting. A moment later Quita appeared, leading her mistress.

Bianca stopped some distance from him. Quita smiled happily on them both and hurried away into the darkness. Still neither of them moved. Bianca's face paled, grew ghost-white, the color draining even from her lips. Her hand came up slowly in a curiously abrupt motion and rested at the base of her throat.

Kit could see her mouth moving, shaping the single word "You," but it was a shape without substance, for no sound came from her lips, no sound at all. He stepped toward her, for the moment forgetting Don Luis and his revenge, forgetting even Rouge. Three feet from her he stopped, seeing her face paler, thinner than he had remembered it, her body wasted beneath her robe to a slimness that escaped emaciation by only a narrow margin, her small, exquisite head almost burdened by the foaming blue-night cloud of her hair.

She faced him wordlessly, without moving, until at last she put up her hand and touched his cheek, letting her fingers stray lightly over his face in sheer wonder at the evidence of her eyes. Then a sob escaped her throat, a high, hysterical sound like the wail of a violin, and she fell forward into his arms.

Kit held her close, stroking her soft hair while she stained his shirt front with her tears, her body quivering against his like that of a small doe on the hills who hears the horns and the hounds of the hunter. When her weeping had passed Kit lifted her face with his hand, and bent down to kiss her mouth.

"No!" she whispered. "You must not! I could not stand that. Dear Kit, have mercy on my weakness."

Frowning, Kit drew back a little. She rose on tiptoe without willing it, and her lips found his face, covering it with kisses —light as moth wings, brushing his eyes, his mouth, his throat.

"Oh, Kit, Kit," she moaned, "why did you come? I was winning, I was gaining peace—but now, now . . ."

Then ever so slowly she drew her face away, her eyelids coming open by almost imperceptible stages until her eyes looked up at him, tear-wet and glowing. She put her small hands against his chest and pressed so gently that it was a hint merely, a suggestion rather than an actual gesture of protest. Kit released her at once and stood back, her hands cradled in his great golden ones.

"You must not kiss me, Kit," she said quietly. "When I knew you at Cul-de-Sac I was a girl, with a girl's folly, but now I am a woman and a wife."

Kit smiled. "I see only that you are lovely—and dear to me."

"Please, Kit, be generous to me! I need your mercy. Do you know what your kiss does to me? It stops my heart and makes all my blood run molten in my veins. Would you make me turn away from God and damn my soul for love of you?"

"I know little of God," Kit said slowly.

"That may well be," Bianca whispered, "but only He in His infinite mercy can release me. I love you and I cannot help that. But now I want you also—and that is a great sin. I took my vows in good faith, always meaning to keep them. Don't, Kit—dear Kit, don't make me sin now!"

"I came," Kit said, his voice harsh and pained, "to take you with me out of this prison. I beg you to come with me. Don't deny me all chance of happiness."

Bianca gazed at him, her eyes soft with adoration. "It lies beyond my power to grant you that, Kit," she whispered, "even though to refuse you is a kind of death. I made my pledge in the cathedral in the sight of God, and while Don Luis lives I cannot do otherwise."

208

Kit's hand closed around the hilt of his dagger and gripped it until his knuckles whitened from the strain. "Then he dies!" he spat. "Nothing shall stand between us!"

Bianca's arms flew upward about his neck. "No, Cristóbal. Promise me you will not kill him. Swear by what you hold most dear that you will not lift a hand against him!"

Kit's thin nostrils flared. "You—you love him!" he said slowly. "*Madre de Dios!*"

"No, Kit," Bianca said softly. "It's you and you only that I love. Because I love you, I would not have you harm him—especially not him, for that is a sin greater than you know."

"Why so, Bianca?"

Bianca shook her head so that her hair shifted about her shoulders.

"You must not ask me. One day you will know the reason. But know only this—it does not concern me and lies only between him and you. Don't be troubled. Stay here with me while you can."

Slowly Kit sank down upon the stone steps of the patio and Bianca lay beside him, her head pillowed in his lap.

"Tell me about yourself," she said. "Tell me all that has happened to you since last I saw you. It would be a consolation for me, Kit—it would give me something to dream of and remember when you are gone."

Looking down into the angelic sweetness of her face, Kit made the attempt, but the words came out labored and slow, with scarcely any meaning or connection between them. A little frown knotted Bianca's brows.

"What of your Rouge?" she said. "You have said nothing of her."

"She is dead," Kit said flatly, his voice drained of expression.

Bianca's mouth formed a soft, rounded "Oh! . . . How did she die?" she asked. "You said she was very young."

"I killed her," Kit whispered. "Mother of God, must we talk of this?"

Bianca looked at him, her dark eyes widening. "Yes," she said quietly, "we must. Why did you kill her, Kit? Had she wronged you?"

Kit whirled upon her and for the moment his temper leaped out of his eyes.

"Never!" he said. "She was sweet and pure and . . . Forgive me, Bianca. Forgive me. It's a wound that will take a long time to heal. I fired upon a vessel not knowing it was hers. When I last saw her, her whole ship was in flames and my own craft was so crippled that I was powerless to help her."

"I see," Bianca said very quietly.

"You do not see!" Kit burst out. "How could you?"

"Perhaps I cannot see in the precise sense that you mean, but I do see why you stayed away from me so long and sent no word to me. I see clearly now that you have come at last to your second choice, having lost the one you loved most."

"I thought of you," Kit said contritely, "much and often."

"Do not lie!" Bianca whispered. "I hated her! I thought I would be glad if she were dead . . ."

"And you are not?"

"No. If ever I had been free to come to you, I might have won you from her fairly, but now what chance have I? What chance against the ghost that haunts you? What chance against a bright memory?"

Kit looked at her, and his eyes were very clear. "No chance at all," he said softly, "nor should it concern you. You cannot replace her—I do not want you to. I want you not as a substitute for Rouge, but for yourself. You are most unlike her, and though night can never take the place of day, a man needs both. I want you in my life to make a new life of it, a life entirely different from the one I would have had with her. And you should never try to seduce me from my memories. I shall be a better man because of them—kinder, gentler, I think, and more loving."

Bianca hid her face suddenly and her whole form was shaken with weeping. "Still," she said, "still you are free, and I am bound—and one day I shall lose you. Oh, Kit, Kit, promise me . . ."

"Gently, Bianca," Kit whispered. "Do not cry. What promise do you want?"

"What I have no right to ask," Bianca said through her sobs, "that you take no other wife, lest you redouble the barriers between us. I know I have no right to ask this, Kit. How can I doom you to loneliness? If you find another, go to her, find joy and—and happiness."

Kit drew her to him, smothering her sobs against his chest.

"Don't cry," he said gently, "for now upon my mother's grave I swear never to wed another while you live."

Bianca lay back contentedly, her head on his knees, cushioned in the soft cloud of her hair. She lay there a long time, studying him, and as he watched he could see her face change. Her lips softened, became more deeply scarlet, parting just a little until he could see a thin thread of pearl between them, and her breath came out slowly, deep-sighing, with a rustle in it. Her eyelids drooped over her eyes, and the pulse at the base of her throat was a visible thing, beating wildly.

"Go!" she whispered, her voice low and intense. "Go!"

Gently Kit lifted her to her feet. Then he touched her mouth, his kiss as light as a spring wind. He released her and took a stride away from her, one stride only, for then he heard her cry.

"Kit!" she cried, agony in her voice. "Kit—oh, Kit!"

He turned back to her then, and her arms were about his neck, brands of cool white fire, tightening more and more. Her mouth flamed upon his, soft lips parted, and her body through the flimsy stuff of her robe was one long caress, moving into his, working slowly. She drew away her mouth, but tightened her arms about him, and the small sweet-curving hollow of her waist undulated in a motion as slow and fierce as the pulse of life itself, so that through the velvet of his heavy, broidered clothing his body felt scalded.

He could feel the sweet fire running molten through his veins, and his hands tightened about her until her white flesh purpled under the grip of his fingers. But as she tilted back her head to receive his kiss he halted suddenly.

From the sea wall a sound rode in upon them—the slow-rolling, belly-deep boom of cannon fire. He hung there like one frozen, unwilling to let her go, but the sound came again, a mighty roar as the cannon on the walls smote the sea and the sky with their bass thunder. Her hands fell away from him, and the look on her face was one of stark terror.

"What—what is it, Kit?" she whispered.

"I can only guess," he growled. "But I think they have caught the *Seaflower* in their sights. I must go at once."

He released her suddenly, not even pausing to snatch one last kiss, and raced away through the dark corridors. Bianca stood very still after he had gone, knowing with a curious sense of certainty that her congealed breath would loosen after a time, that feeling would come flooding back, that these daggers of pain, being pushed slowly upward along her veins would, in another moment, drive through her fast-beating heart.

18

By THE TIME that Kit and Bernardo reached the walls opposite the Tenaza, half the city of Cartagena was gathered there. They moved through the crowds with casual confidence, for no one had eyes for anything except the sea. In one quick glance Kit and Bernardo saw what had happened. There in the graying light of morning a great plate ship lay, listing far over to starboard, mortally wounded by the *Seaflower's* guns.

His crew had been unable to resist temptation after all. Months at sea under Kit's stern driving, weeks of passing one rich prize after another with linstocks unlit and bronze cannon muzzles cold, had at last proved too much for them. Even the trusted Smithers must have succumbed.

Kit realized that they had signed their own death warrants, because in pursuing the treasure ship they had run recklessly inshore and the wind was from seaward. A little farther out, the great ship *Garza* lay. With any kind of wind the *Seaflower* could have shown so clumsy a vessel a clean white wake, but lying as she did to leeward, she had to claw off the lee shore, sailing close-hauled, working her zigzag tacks to within four points of the wind's eye. The difference in speed of a vessel working to windward and one sailing free before the wind is immense. Even the *Garza's* great size and poorly designed hull did not slow her to the crawl to which the *Seaflower* was reduced.

Smithers undoubtedly was handling the trim brigantine with skill, but it was too late. The *Seaflower* was doomed. She lay between the great guns of the fortress and the mighty cannon of the *Garza*. Even as Kit watched, the great sixty-four-pounders in the fortress opened up, and the wall of smoke blotted out the ocean. As it cleared, Kit saw the geyser plumes of spray rising all around the *Seaflower* while her helmsman moved the whip-staff back and forth, trying desperately to escape. But there, beyond, the *Garza* waited. The guns in the Tenaza opened up again, their round balls rising black against the sky, seeming to hang there for one awful moment before they whistled down-ward to crash upon the brigantine. When the smoke cleared the *Seaflower* lay hull down on the water, totally demasted, wallow-ing helplessly in the choppy sea.

Now the *Garza* was bearing down for the kill. Kit watched her move in, only half hearing Bernardo's whispered, mon-strously obscene Castilian curses; but when the great ship was close, to their astonished joy the whole side of the *Seaflower* exploded into smoke and flame. Smithers, gallant to the last, had let loose a broadside. They saw the *Garza* reel under the impact of the *Seaflower's* fire, but she continued to come on, only slightly hurt by the *Seaflower's* thirty-two-pounders.

When she was too close to miss, she squared off, sailing parallel to the *Seaflower*. Then her entire hull disappeared behind a wall of smoke and flame that reached as high as the yardarms of her topsails. The hoarse bass thunder of her guns, slow-rolling over the face of the waters, echoed hollowly in the sickened emptiness of Kit's heart. He saw the roundshot strike home, saw the masses of splinters leap from the brigantine's deck. At last, knowing it was inevitable, he saw the red and yellow tongues of fire leap up from her powder magazine—and the *Seaflower* was gone, only a white splotch on the sea's bosom marking her passing.

Kit leaned forward. Something in the *Garza's* behavior had caught his attention. She was reefing sail, as though preparing to heave to. Kit turned a wondering face toward Bernardo only to be met by a look of complete incredulity on that worthy's own face. Still, there was no mistaking the *Garza's* intent, for already they could see her longboat descending seaward on the lines of its davits. In spite of that tremendous explosion, some of the *Seaflower's* crew must have survived.

"They would not let them drown," Kit muttered. "That would

be far too kind a death. No, Bernardo, it is the gibbet for my brave lads, and all because of me."

"Nonsense," Bernardo declared. "They agreed to the risks when they signed on. The loss of the *Seaflower* is due entirely to disobedience of your orders. Lying to, out of sight of the walls, they would have been safe enough."

"That's true, but how much safer would they have been if I had not ventured into these waters! No, Bernardo, the fault is mine."

"Milk!" Bernardo spat. "Buccaneers don't die in bed. If it's not the blue sea's mouth, then it's the rope's end. Why concern yourself? If you had returned them safely to Petit Goave, they would have put to sea again until someday the gibbet got them. Besides, speculation is useless. We have ourselves to think of unless we want to end by being hanged too. Let's hurry to get out of this city."

Kit looked out to where the *Garza*'s longboat was moving back and forth. He counted silently each time she paused to drag an object from the sea. Five, he counted, five—but which five? Slowly he shook his aching head.

"Leave if you want to," he growled. "I'm staying."

"Fifty times we've had this out," Bernardo said flatly. "The answer is still the same. If you stay, I stay with you. My stars and yours have been linked too long for us to be separated. Come, Kit, let's hide until tomorrow. Then we will see what we can do."

They moved quietly through the milling crowds away from the sea wall, but they had gone only four squares when Bernardo, who was ahead, flattened himself against the wall of a building and signaled for Kit to do the same. As they stood there, hardly daring to breathe, a party of horsemen thundered through the street in the direction of the wall. At their head, towering in the saddle, rode Don Luis del Toro, Count of the Realm.

Kit looked at that burly, black-bearded man who time upon time had brought anguish and despair into his life, and his hand tightened on the butt of his pistol. But Bernardo's fingers were tempered steel on his wrists, holding him hard in a grip of incalculable strength.

"Not now," he whispered.

Slowly Kit's fingers relaxed their grip on the hilt of the pistol and the tight-knit muscles of his arm loosened.

"You are right," he muttered, "but one day it will be different."

"Perhaps," Bernardo said mildly. "But come, we must find the bridge that leads to the San Lázaro section. We can hide in the Cienaga, the marshes west of the city."

They hurried off, strain and anxiety apparent in their faces. By the time they reached the bridge it was night. They crossed boldly, knowing only too well that any furtive gesture would have instantly betrayed them. On the other side, they angled off from the road, wading through the sticky mud and marsh water until they came to one of the thousands of low islands of saw-grass that stood in the swamp. They lay down there, completely hidden by the man-tall grass; and despite the clouds of mosquitoes, so great was their weariness that they slept like men turned to stone.

During that same night Don Luis was busy. He strode slowly up and down before the five dripping buccaneers who had been dragged from the sea. As president of the Audencia, it was within his powers to question them, but thus far he had not uttered a word. His dark eyes glowed in his swarthy face as he continued his leonine pacing. Suddenly he halted before the tall figure of Smithers. His big hand shot out and yanked Smithers' shirt front open. Smithers chest was bare of ornament.

"No crucifix," Don Luis said quietly. "No Saint Christopher, Saint Anthony, Saint Cecilia! Nothing! Observe this carefully, caballeros, for we have here, I believe, a case for the good Fathers of the Inquisition." He looked into Smithers' face, a mocking light in his eyes. Then, quite suddenly, he lapsed into English. "Whoreson," he said softly, almost expressionlessly, his words moving out through the fixed, almost peaceful smile on his lips, "what do you now think of your Captain Gerado who has betrayed you?"

"You lie!" Smithers roared. The instant the words left his lips he realized his mistake, for Don Luis turned to the *oidores* with easy grace and spread his hands.

"An Englishman, hidalgos," he said, smiling, "and hence a

216

heretic. The good Fathers will no doubt be pleased." He made a gesture to the captain of the guard, and Smithers was dragged off in the direction of the courts of the Inquisition.

The same test applied to the other four produced a different result, because each of them had a golden crucifix hanging about his neck. However, one of them was a Negro, and to Don Luis this meant that he must be a runaway slave.

"This one," the Count drawled, "is obviously an escaped black. We will make an example of him as an example to our own slaves. To the rack with him!" He glanced at the others, his eyes filled with icy contempt. "We might as well hang these forthwith, unless you gentlemen insist upon a trial—which I think is plainly a waste of time."

The *oidores,* the lawyers who made up the Viceroy's privy council, the Audencia, shrugged their shoulders. The people plainly wanted a spectacle. Far be it from them either to interfere or to delay.

As the men were being dragged away toward the dungeon, another thought crossed Don Luis's mind. What of Cristóbal? What of that fine young lion cub, that fair and princely bastard he had himself made? Had he gone down with his ship? The Count felt something like pain at the thought. He wondered why he had not legitimated him long ago. What an heir he would have made! . . . But in the middle of these regretful thoughts a sudden suspicion stirred in his brain. His own captain of the *Garza* had declared that the black-bearded Englishman, Smithers, had been in command. The Spanish sea captain knew, for he had watched the *Seaflower*'s movements with contemptuous leisure through his glass. What, then, of Kit? Was he dead, killed in some previous encounter? Or was he very much alive—here in Cartagena?

The *Seaflower* had been cruising slowly off the coast. Why? Was she perhaps waiting for someone? Someone who, bone of his bone, blood of his blood, had the same lusts as himself? The cub—for so Don Luis always thought of his bastard son—had snatched the red-haired English girl from the sea. And certainly since that time at Cul-de-Sac, Bianca had never been the same. Had she not looked with favor upon Ricardo, who in his northern fairness resembled this Cristóbal Gerado who should have been a Del Toro? Could it be that now, even at this moment . . .

Don Luis turned a thundercloud face toward the struggling prisoners. Son or not, if Kit had touched his most precious treasure, he must die! He pointed a strong finger at the smallest of the pirates, a former Parisian sewer rat, who doubtless could be persuaded to talk quite easily.

"Take this one to the Tenaza," he growled, "I would like to talk to him."

Three hours later, Don Luis emerged from the dungeons beneath the fortress. The little Parisian had proved stubborn. It was not until they had applied the boot, that cunning device which left a man's foot a purpled, bloody, boneless mass, that he had spoken. Afterward, Don Luis himself had supervised the removal of the man's tongue. It would not do to have him babble before he faced the hangman.

As he thundered homeward, his dark face lined and troubled, Don Luis wondered how he would put the question to Bianca. She would, of course, deny it if it was true. How would he get the truth out of her? Threats meant little to his wife, he knew. Too often she had seemed quite willing to die. . . . When he strode into her bedroom he found her kneeling before the altar, her young face white and shattered with overwhelming grief.

"Was he here?" he roared, not even thinking to call the name.

Bianca turned her face with painful slowness. Her dark eyes rested gravely on her husband's face.

"Yes," she said very simply, no evasion or fear in her tone. "He was here."

Don Luis stood over her, towering into the shadows, his powerful hands clenching and unclenching, his dark face filled with a torment greater than the agony on the Parisian's when they had applied the boot. What now? If he opened the floodgates and let the green and sickening bile of jealousy flood out, what answer would she give? Knowing Bianca, he realized that she might lift her head and say quite simply:

"Yes, my lord, I have betrayed you. Now do with me what you will!"

And if she said that, what then? Punish her? How? What punishment could he devise that she would not welcome—yes, even death? Looking into his face, Bianca read his thought.

"No, my lord," she said quietly. "I have not dishonored you, but only because your son is more of a man than you, and did not take advantage of my weakness. If he had wanted me to bed with him, I would have betrayed you, but he was honorable. He, not I."

Don Luis stood gazing down at the slim figure of his wife and wondered if he could trust himself to speak.

"He was a fool, then," he said heavily, "for he has lost his chance. He, at least, will never have you."

"Is he—is he taken?" she whispered hoarsely.

"No," he admitted, "but he will be. And when he is he will hang."

Bianca looked at her husband, her eyes night-black, fierce.

"And when he is taken," she whispered, "I will see that you do not harm him. You will do as I say."

Don Luis stood staring at her for a moment longer before he whirled and started for the door. "For this alone," he threw back at her, "for these words of yours, his doom is sealed!" Then he strode away out into the coming dawn.

In the morning, after the age-long night of waiting, Kit and Bernardo stole out into the street, hearing the distant throbbing of the great drums that called the people of Cartagena to the city square. Now it would begin. Now these men who had followed him so long, charged with him through gun smoke, would die—ignominiously, ingloriously, terribly. And all because of him, because of the green lovesickness of his youth.

Kit and Bernardo reached the square, already closely packed, and saw at once that all preparations had been completed. The executioner took his time. At the foot of the gibbet, the kettle-drums never ceased their rolling beat. Now they quickened as the first of the men was led to the scaffold. Step by step the man mounted upward, accompanied by a black-robed priest and two stout guards, and at every step the drums cried out in gloating triumph.

Kit tried to turn away his eyes, but he could not. There was the blare of horns, the roar of gunfire, and a mighty roll on the drums. Then silence. And black between them and the sun, the awful pendulum swung, amid a stillness so great that its very creaking could be heard.

The crowd was roaring now, hoarse-voiced, bestial. The second buccaneer followed the first, walking proudly to the scaffold. Kit was sure he heard the bone snap, even above the shouts of the crowd. In the echoing quiet after the beast bellows of the mob was stilled, two figures creaked gently at the rope's ends, their necks bent far over in that terrible angle which has no counterpart in life.

The little Parisian died badly. He had to be carried to his death, making hideous noises from the bloody, tongueless socket of his mouth. Now, at last, Kit found the strength to turn away. When he looked again, it was not yet done. The little Parisian's weight was insufficient to break his neck on the drop, and he hung there kicking, his thin face purpling slowly, until two soldiers, moved by some strange compassion, caught both his legs and swung downward with all their force.

Then they brought out the black. The Negro had been stripped naked, and his body was a magnificent thing, rippling with superb muscle, bull-throated, deep-chested, great of limb and thew, like a statue carved from ebony. Four helmeted Spanish soldiers hurled him flat on his back on a rack, and the cords were tightened about his wrists and ankles. Kit saw the executioners place their poles into the sockets of the winch and turn it slowly until the sweat stood out on the black body as the Negro was slowly stretched until every major bone had been dislocated. Then the chief executioner stepped forward. In his hand he held a long, limber rod of iron, no thicker than a man's thumb. Now, slowly, lightly, with apparent grace, he began to strike the Negro, and with every blow a bone was broken.

Kit could hear the black man's low, deep-throated grunting become louder, change into a heavy moaning, until at last the man's heavy lips tore apart and he loosed his last, piteous dying screech. When they cut the cords, he was a spongelike thing, lacking entirely in rigidity, so that when the soldiers picked him up he folded over in their grip like a dummy stuffed with cloth.

The hot tears stung and tore at Kit's eyelids, his face was ghost-white beneath his tan. So that was how his mother died. Suddenly, weakly, he bent down his head and retched on the earth. Bernardo put a great arm across his shoulder.

"Courage, Kit," he whispered.

The drums picked up their rolling again. This time it was different—a slow and solemn beat. Lifting his head, Kit saw a procession of friars of the Inquisition, and among them, stumbling blindly, so beaten, burned, lashed, and tortured that his bruised and branded face was almost unrecognizable—Smithers. He was not led to the gibbet; instead the friars drew him on to another structure, which up to now Kit had not noticed. It was a pole of iron girded with chains, and at its foot was a heaping pile of fagots. Kit had to grip Bernardo's shoulder hard to keep from falling. This, then, was the ultimate cruelty.

The executioner made short work of the business of binding Smithers to the upright rod. The torch was applied. The pitch-smeared fagots caught at once. The tongues of flame leaped up, caressing Smithers' bare feet. He seemed too numbed to care, but at last he stirred when the flames leaped upward to his knees. His mouth came open, and clear above the angry cackle of the fire Kit could hear the inrush of his breath as he gulped air into his lungs. His head went back, pressing against the iron pole, and the red maw of his mouth showed plainly, his lips drawn back from his yellowed teeth. But the scream never came out, for clearly, cleanly, across the square the crash of Kit's pistol sounded. The shot awakened echoes endlessly reverberating, and Smithers hung limply against the pole, a dark, spreading stain blossoming on his ragged shirt front exactly above his heart.

"Well done, Kit," Bernardo said.

There was no time for more. The outraged mob, thus cheated of its spectacle, was howling down upon them. With sword and cutlass Kit and Bernardo fought back, but there were too many. Except for the intervention of Don Luis at the head of a company of harquebusiers, they would undoubtedly have been torn limb from limb. Instead, bloody and bruised, they faced each other in the dank dungeons beneath the Tenaza, gazing up at the tiny square of light that filtered through the bars of the high window. That it was the last light they would ever see they had not the remotest doubt.

19

WHEN DON LUIS RETURNED to his house that afternoon, there was no triumph in his stride. He walked slowly, almost dejectedly, his bearded chin sunk against his mailed chest. The executions had left him exhausted, the constant furor of the crowds had played more havoc with his nerves than he cared to admit even to himself. Luis del Toro was no longer a young man, and tomorrow's business was exceedingly distasteful to him.

Beyond the fact that the peace and serenity of his household would probably be wrecked forever after Kit's hanging, Don Luis found that he was loath to pass sentence on the young man for quite another reason. That reason seemed a curiously shameful one to him. It was simply that, try as he would, the Count could not help feeling a warm surge of love for his unlawful son.

He had fought Kit, true enough, but as one fences with a master, for the joy of the combat, watching with detachment even in the heat of battle the courage and the skill that nearly equaled his own. He had never hated as Kit had; rather his son's seamanship and courage in battle had filled him with pride. Kit's blond fairness, except for the golden tan the sun had given him, was so like that of Jeanne Giradeaux that Don Luis, looking at him, felt again a nostalgic sadness, remembering his youth. He had wronged the mother; must he now kill the son?

No, it would not be easy to hang Kit, yet what else could he do? The boy was indisputably a pirate, with many sinkings and pillagings charged against him. Perhaps he should be glad that Kit's simple dignity would assure his dying well.

As he entered his wife's room, he was a little surprised to

223

find that she was fully dressed and calmly awaiting him. He had expected to find her prostrate, far gone in hysteria. She came forward to meet him, her face still and composed, with something regal in her stride.

"Is it true that he is taken?" she asked quietly.

"Yes," Don Luis growled, "and truer still that tomorrow he hangs."

Bianca studied his face, an expression in her eyes like that of one who gazes through bars at a caged and loathsome beast.

"Then he has already stood trial?" she said.

"No. Not until tonight, but the result is inevitable—he will be sentenced to be hanged."

Again that curiously cold stare.

"And you, as president of the Audencia, will of course preside?"

"Yes," Don Luis said. "Why?"

"Because you will take steps to see that he is not hanged," Bianca said calmly.

"And if I do not?"

"You want a son, my lord. If Kit dies, you will never again so much as touch me!"

Don Luis stared at her, his dark face heavy with frowning. "I believe," he said evenly, "that I have some control over that."

"You are mistaken, Luis. If you think you can force me, be warned. The instant Kit strangles on the gibbet, I will take my own life!"

"You wouldn't dare!" Don Luis thundered.

"Would I not?" Bianca whispered. "Since you are so determined to take his life, I will even precede him—now!"

Don Luis sprang forward in one great feline bound, his fingers closing on her wrist. He twisted cruelly so that the small vial that she had raised to her lips was turned upside down and the pale-green liquid spilled out, a drop or two falling on one of the roses that stood in a vase on the table. Before the Count's astonished eyes the flower began to wither, to droop—in half a minute more it was brown and sere.

"That is how I will die," Bianca whispered. "And you can't prevent me. I have twenty of these vials hidden about the house, and you'll never find them. So, my lord, if I am anything to you, you will spare him. If you say the fatal words you are condemning two—not one."

Don Luis studied the pale face of his wife, his own expressionless, but thoughts moved swiftly through his mind. He knew already that he was defeated; it remained for him only to retreat as gracefully as possible, and to extract what concessions he could from the situation.

"What if I do spare him?" he suggested dryly.

Bianca's dark eyes leaped. "You will find me from now on a good and dutiful wife," she whispered, "in all things."

Don Luis's mouth curved into a slow smile brimming with self-mockery. "My humblest thanks," he said, bowing his head in a burlesque of servility, "for your graciousness, my lady Countess. Now, if you will excuse me, I must return to the Casa Real."

With fear-constricted heart, Bianca watched him stride away. Kit's fate was in the hands of this man of tremendous pride, and only God and the Virgin knew what the outcome might be. Slowly Bianca turned back to her private altar and sank down on her knees.

Don Luis wasted little time on self-pity as he rode through the streets of Cartagena. He had reached an age and a degree of wisdom when such thoughts become superfluities. The business at hand occupied his whole mind. How, indeed, was his son to be saved? It was only because Kit had admitted that he was captain of the *Seaflower* that the *oidores* bothered to go through the formality of a trial. As he toyed with the question, Don Luis came upon the only answer. The gaolkeeper and the torturer of the Tenaza must be brought in to testify. It had been more than a year since the *Seaflower* had engaged in piracy. Don Luis was almost certain that there was no one in Cartagena except himself who had suffered looting at Kit's hands. The *Seaflower* had never, so far as he knew, ventured into these waters before. Therefore the whole defense must turn upon the fact that Kit was not aboard the *Seaflower* when she had attacked the plate ship, that the attack had been contrary to his orders. The little Parisian pirate had testified under duress that Kit's sole purpose in Cartagena was to visit a former sweetheart.

Don Luis made a wry face at the thought. Fortunately, the Parisian had either not known or had failed to reveal the name of the woman involved. That secret might yet be kept. Even the stiff-necked *oidores,* being Spaniards, were inclined to be charitable toward young love. Yes, such indeed would be the defense of his bastard son.

What troubled him was the fact that the same defense was also applicable to the Jew. Don Luis would have been delighted to torture Bernardo to death, but try as he would his logical mind kept reminding him that to condemn Bernardo Díaz was to tear holes in the argument that he was preparing for Kit's defense. Besides, here in the New World, the question of Judaism was rarely raised, the Jews being so few in number that no one could convincingly make a menace of them. There were even grandees so long away from Spain and young hidalgos born in the New World who had no anti-Jewish bias at all. Don Luis knew that while in Madrid or Seville it would have been possible to put Bernardo to death on the ground that his conversion was false, these Peruvian *oidores* would accept it at its face value.[1] No, regrettable as it seemed to him, Bernardo too must be permitted to live.

When Bernardo and Kit were led into the Casa Real, manacled at wrist and ankle and flanked fore and aft by helmeted and cuirassed soldiers, they presented a sorry spectacle. Ragged, begrimed, their faces marred with the dried smears of their own blood and the greenish purple of their many bruises, they contrasted strangely with the dignified *oidores* and their president.

Lifting his head, Kit stared coolly, almost insolently, into the face of Don Luis, holding his eyes so long that the Count flushed under the heavy weight of his judicial wig. Don Luis was seated on a dais, high above the rest of the court. From it he had upon one occasion defied the Viceroy himself and had won. Now, looking down into the icy-blue eyes of his natural son, even his lofty position was of no aid to him. He felt that he himself was

[1] In the seventeenth century the Viceroyalty of Peru included all of Spanish South America. The Viceroyalty of New Spain (Mexico) included all of Mexico and Central America. Later, about 1718, the region we now call Colombia became a viceroyalty under the name of New Granada, but in Don Luis's time the citizens of Cartagena and Bogotá were considered Peruvians.

on trial, that this tall, blond lion cub and the ragged Jew were weighing his fate rather than he theirs.

With a nod, he signaled to the clerk of the court to begin. Slowly the man began to read out the charges. To Don Luis's relief, they were few. Cristóbal Gerado and his mate, Bernardo Díaz, were accused of having unlawfully and willfully entered the waters of Cartagena in search of loot; of having committed the high crime of piracy; of having taken Spanish gold; and of having killed an Englishman who was being burned at the stake.

No reference, Don Luis noted, was made to Kit's former career. Indeed, he was little known in this part of the New World. In common with most pirates, he had allowed his prey to sail almost to his own doorstep before attacking them. Whatever was known of Kit's exploits was merely hearsay and rumor in Cartagena. Don Luis stared down at Kit, and in spite of himself a warm feeling of pride came over him. The erect boldness of Kit's carriage, the look of defiance on his face, his princely grace—all these had their effect. Perhaps he was growing senile, Don Luis told himself, but the emotion persisted.

Kit was, Don Luis mused, after all of good blood. The best of France and Spain flowed in his veins. This was not a peon or a slave, his very arrogance was lordly. . . . Suddenly Don Luis shook himself. He realized that the court was waiting for him to speak. He sighed.

"You have heard the charges," he said to Kit and Bernardo. "What is your plea?"

"Not guilty!" Kit snapped at him, and Bernardo repeated the words.

"You will tell the court," Don Luis instructed him, "why you entered Spanish waters."

Kit looked up into Don Luis's dark face. His lips curled in a mocking smile under the begrimed blond mustache. It would give me joy to tell you, he thought, but it's no concern to these others. No, I will not mention her name if it costs me my life. . . .

"My reasons," he said at last, speaking coolly, "are my own affair."

The viceregal prosecutor was on his feet now, his face dark with fury.

"How dare you lie to this court?" he roared. "You came here to pillage and murder."

"Such was not my intent," Kit said quietly.

"You lie!" the prosecutor thundered. "As evidence there is your ship, sunk outside this harbor."

Don Luis looked at the young *oidor* appointed to defend Kit. As was usual in such cases, the man was distinguished only by his ineptitude. He sighed again and rapped with his mace.

"If the learned doctors and you, Prosecutor Godoy, will forgive me this irregularity," he said mildly, "I should like to point out that Captain Gerado speaks the truth."

The silence that followed this announcement was as profound as death. Bernard turned to Kit, his dark eyes goggling.

Don Luis was continuing. "His Royal Majesty has often declared that these courts would temper their justice with mercy. In this matter there is little need even for that, for though I have hanged many a rogue, it is beyond my province to condemn a man for the folly of falling in love."

"If His Excellency pleases . . ." Prosecutor Godoy blustered.

Don Luis lifted a calm hand.

"Hear me out, caballeros," he said. "As many of you know, I have my own private sources of information. In this case they corroborate the Captain's statement."

"If His Excellency would be so good as to elaborate," the prosecutor sneered.

"Gladly," Don Luis said. "Guards, summon the turnkey and the torturer of the Tenaza."

The court settled back to wait. The delay was short, for Don Luis had summoned the men before the trial, and they awaited their call in an anteroom. Under his skillful prodding, they told their story briefly, but well. At its conclusion the prosecutor was in a fury.

"Would you have us believe," he demanded, "that these villains were not aboard the ship, that they were on a peaceful errand, and that the crew mutinied in their absence?"

Don Luis bowed his head. "Such is indeed the case," he said simply.

Godoy controlled himself with an effort. "Might I be permitted to inquire," he rasped, his voice filled with biting sarcasm, "what interest my lord has in the case?"

"To see justice done," Don Luis said serenely.

"Justice!" Godoy shrieked. "He brings his lying hirelings and calls it justice! Why are you shielding this man, my lord Count?"

Don Luis stood up, towering on the dais. "I think," he said, his voice cold and deadly, his words glinting like steel being slowly withdrawn from a scabbard, "that the learned prosecutor exceeds his intent. Surely he does not intend to question *my* integrity?"

Godoy's knees turned to water suddenly. He was staring at that moment into the naked face of death.

"No, no," he protested, "it is only that the strangeness of it all . . ."

Don Luis waved his words aside. "In order to see justice done," he said slowly, "I shall forget your impertinence. I see here in this court the captain of the *Garza*. He is, I believe, an appointee of yours, my good Señor Godoy, sent by you to me not two weeks ago, when my own captain was sick with the fever. You believe him to be a truthful man?"

"Yes," Godoy said stoutly. "He is a man of honor!"

"Many of the *oidores* present heard his report to me," Don Luis said calmly, "but for the sake of the record I will have him repeat it. Captain Hernando, take the oath."

After the ceremony was over, the stout hidalgo stood at his ease before the court.

"Who was in command of that brigantine," Don Luis asked him, "when you fired on her?"

"The black-bearded Englishman," Hernando answered calmly. "I watched the whole thing through my glass. Of these two I saw no sign."

"Might they not have been below?" Godoy demanded.

"During a battle?" Hernando growled. "Any captain that did that would have his gullet slit by his crew within an hour. In my opinion they were not aboard."

"I don't care for your opinion," Godoy snapped. "Facts are what I want."

As if in answer to this testy remark, there was a sudden confusion at the door. Two of the guards raced outside. A moment later one of them returned. Bowing low to Don Luis, he craved the court's pardon.

"My lord, there is a woman outside who claims knowledge bearing on this case," he added nervously. Don Luis's dark face grayed. He was sure, beyond reasonable chance of doubt, who the woman was—Bianca. Bianca, the anguished murmur ran through his heart. What manner of man was this bastard of his that he could make her fling down her shame like a gauge before all the world? His concern at the moment was not for himself but entirely for his wife, who was prepared to brand herself an adulteress publicly if she could save Kit's life.

"I do not see," he began weakly, but Godoy had seen the naked pain in his eyes.

"Bring her in!" the prosecutor squealed triumphantly.

The guards disappeared through the door. When they returned Don Luis, who had been standing, sank weakly into his high-backed chair. The woman who was being led in by the guards was an ancient crone of a fishwife whom he had never seen before in his life.

"If you will be so kind as to take the oath, my good woman," he said with relief.

"That I will, my lord!" the woman squeaked. "Truth will out! I just want to say . . ."

"The oath!" Godoy barked.

The old crone raised her right hand and swore with calm conviction.

"Now," Don Luis asked gently, "what is it?"

"This pretty _niño_ is innocent! Wasn't even on that boat. Stood alongside me while the fighting was going on, and when the little ship was sunk he cried."

"You are sure, grandmother?" Godoy demanded.

"Find me another such! Find me another _muchacho_ with God's own gold on his head! Wasn't sure it was real. I didn't know hair could be that color. Why, yesterday when I saw him again, just afore he shot the Englishman, I was trying to feel it."

Don Luis bowed his head. How like a woman to mingle evil with good! True, she had saved Kit's life, but she had also

230

reminded the court of the one remaining charge on which they could hold him. He felt very tired suddenly, and totally unprepared for the ordeal that awaited him.

As for Kit, he scarcely heard the remainder of his trial. His mind was a seething tumult of confusion as he tried to fathom the reason for Don Luis's having come so valiantly to his defense. Twice now this had happened, twice now this proud and violent grandee had spared his life. Why? In the name of God and the Virgin, why?

The trial lasted for hours. Godoy argued that Kit had killed a man in cold blood, for which the penalty was death. Don Luis replied that the man was a member of Kit's crew and that his death might be regarded as a fitting punishment for mutiny. Besides, rightfully, it was a matter that concerned only the English courts, as Kit had harmed no subject of the Viceroyalty of Peru.

He had balked the Inquisition in the rightful performance of its duty, the prosecutor insisted. This was indeed blasphemy.

All right, Don Luis said mockingly, to the lesser charge of blasphemy he would agree, but not to murder, for if the slaying of heretics was murder, he himself would have been hanged a hundred times.

This shot was a telling one. The *oidores* roared with laughter. The nonplused prosecutor had to swallow his pride and sit idly by while Don Luis sentenced Kit to six years at hard labor on the walls of the still uncompleted fortress of San Lázaro. Bernardo drew four years for aiding and abetting Kit.

As the court was dismissed and the prisoners were being led away, the sound of hoofbeats rang through the dark street. As the horse thundered around the corner, kicking up a small shower of mud, Don Luis recognized the rider. The premonition that had tortured him just before the guards had admitted the old lady had indeed proved to be true. Bianca sat on the racing animal.

At the risk of his limbs, Don Luis charged to the middle of the street and caught hold of the bridle. The beast reared, almost unseating Bianca, but Don Luis's tremendous arms fought

231

him down again until he stood glistening with sweat and trembling all over in the light of the torches.

"Wait!" Bianca cried. "He must not be hanged! He is innocent! I can testify . . ."

Don Luis caught her cruelly by the arm and jerked her from the sidesaddle, catching her as she fell. One great hand closed like a vise over her small mouth. Out of the corner of his eye he could see the exultant gleam leaping in Godoy's eyes. The man's thoughts could almost be read aloud: So, you cuckold! Of course you were sure of his innocence! You had your wife's confession to prove it. . . .

Don Luis sighed heavily. A hired assassin would cost him dearly, but he could not fan the flame of gossip by openly challenging the prosecutor. Of them all, he was sure, only Godoy had got the point. The rest stood there staring with open mouths, unable to conjecture the reasons for his actions.

"You are late, my Bianca," he whispered. "The lad is already saved. There is no need for your testimony." Then, very gently, he released her.

Bianca stood there, the red ridges of the grip of his fingers showing clearly on her white face.

"My wife has been very ill, gentlemen," Don Luis said quietly. "I hope that none of you will misinterpret this outburst. It is, I assure you, due entirely to overwrought nerves. Come, Bianca. . . . Come, *mi carissima*."

He had spoken softly, but the underlying menace of his tone was unmistakable. He saw Godoy's face pale beneath the torch he held in his hand. A slow smile stole over Don Luis's dark countenance. Good! he mused, it would perhaps not be necessary to go to the trouble of hiring an assassin after all.

He helped Bianca to mount and swung himself into the saddle of his own horse. As they rode away, he could not resist watching her face. He knew that she would turn and look back at Kit, but he had thought that he himself would maintain his pride. But the look on Bianca's face unmanned him; slowly he swung in the saddle and followed her tender, anguished gaze.

Afterward he was sorry. Kit had stood there in his chains like a young god. For all the dried blood on his face, the tattered

232

rags of his clothing, the mud and dirt matted into his blond hair and beard, he was still as slim and graceful as Mercury, as broad of shoulder and great of thew as a young Hercules. This one, Don Luis knew, would never bow. This one could never be defeated.

Perhaps, he thought bitterly, I should have had him hanged, after all. Then, touching his spurs to the horse's side, he thundered away in the darkness. After a moment, Bianca followed him.

20

Lady Jane Golphin sat in her garden under the shade of a
wine palm. A ray of afternoon sunlight stole through the over-
hanging palm fronds and fell on her hair so that it blazed as
bright as a brush fire. She sat very still with her slim white
hands folded in her lap, though now and again she unclasped
her fingers and toyed with the rich stuff of her dress, cunningly
chosen to point up the matchless sea-green of her oddly slanted
eyes.

At the moment, her face was pensive and sad, for her eyes
rested on the rank weeds and sawgrass that had grown up in
the burnt-out area where the manor of her plantation had stood.
A new manor stood behind the garden in which she sat now,
one larger and lovelier than the old. But the gaunt blackened
rafters standing among the skyward-reaching bamboo shoots
still remained to taunt her. She could have had them torn down;
even now she did not understand the curiously elegiac mood
that had caused her to leave them standing.

So has my life been, she mused. These charred timbers shall
be its monument. . . .

After a moment, she turned and gazed at the white-painted
exterior of her new home. It contained every comfort and luxury
that money could buy, and yet, oddly, she hated it. There had
been some question in Port Royal about the source of the money
that had enabled her to rebuild so quickly and lavishly after the
disastrous French attack from which most of the planters had
not even now fully recovered. But there was always some question about Lady Jane Golphin. That a lady of her great beauty,

culture, and many accomplishments had not yet married was a perennial topic of discussion at tea parties. Not even the most feline gossip of them all could deny the fact that she had suitors aplenty. That she had not yet wed was plainly through her own choice. Earlier, the most furious of speculations revolved about the matter of her frequent disappearances. On this score, the rumors had been as conflicting as they had been wild. One of the most popular had it simply and comprehensively that the lady was a witch, and disappeared to consort with her master, the Devil.

The more sophisticated gentry rejected this, of course. Yet even they were not able to come up with a more enlightening theory. But during the last year this peculiar habit of vanishing had apparently palled upon her, for since the early spring of 1695 Lady Jane had remained very quietly at home, supervising the reconstruction of her plantation.

Now, July fifth of that same year, all the work was done. The tall cane grew up in her rich fields, nodding all together with every passing wind. Her slaves were fat and glossy black and very well treated. Unlike the sullen demeanor so often noted among the workers on neighboring plantations, the servitors of Lady Jane Golphin often sang as they worked. Whatever the source of her mysterious wealth, it was apparent that she was growing richer by the season. This fact spurred on her suitors to redoubled activity, though it was not to be denied that many among them who were as wealthy as she sought her for herself alone.

She turned her head from the house and stared down the drive that led for two arrow-straight miles up to the manor. She leaned forward in her chair. Would God, she thought, that as little distance separated me from him I love. . . .

She straightened, frowning. On the sea in unclear weather, a distance less than that would be enough to make her miss Kit forever. Finding a needle in a haystack was child's play to finding a vessel whose course she did not know—course, or whereabouts, or base of supply.

Base of supply! She sprang up suddenly, her fingers gripping the flesh of her fair throat. Fool and daughter of fools! Why had she not thought of that before? Kit had sailed with Ducasse from Saint-Domingue! And among the other things disclosed at the trial from which he had barely escaped with his life was the fact that he bore allegiance to the King of France! Where else then would he base if not at Saint-Domingue? Martinique? Guadeloupe? Saint-Christophe? These were possibilities, but Kit had been with Ducasse, and Ducasse was Governor of Saint-Domingue.

Already she was running hard toward the house. Now, finally, she would have her answer. Saint-Domingue lay across the channel, scarce a hundred leagues away. No more would she sit and brood in an empty garden, no more would she beat the trackless sea. Now, if God were willing, and French gallantry toward women—even women of their enemies—were unchanged, she could wait very quietly in the very port of call to which Kit Gerado must sometime return! The very thought made her almost sick with joy.

Inside her bedroom, she pulled off her garments in such savage haste that they tore in several places. Then, entirely naked and shivering from anticipation, she raced to a locked chest. Her fingers were clumsy with the key, and it was several seconds before she got it open. With true feminine lack of logic she took from it first a pair of barbaric earrings, great heavy circles of gold. Then, removing the dainty rosettes of pearl that so demurely adorned her ear lobes, she fastened the heavy hoops in her ears, standing slim and flower-petal white before her mirror, lithe-limbed, slender, soft-curving, like a sea nymph rising from the foam.

About the bright blaze of her red hair she wound a blood-red kerchief, and then only did she slip into the tattered shirt that clung about her bosom like a second skin, and the abbreviated trousers that, thin as she was, required an effort to draw on.

She was still barefooted when the trusted slave whom she had had summoned by her maidservant knocked on her door. He was admitted. Three minutes later, he scampered down the stairs, raced to the stables, and saddled two of the finest, swiftest horses. As Lady Jane drew on her jackboots and hung her cutlass about her handspan of a waist, the slave was already thundering away in the direction of Port Royal. There he would move among the lowest dives of the water front. He would bend and whisper into a hairy ear and a strolling wench would be unseated suddenly as a bearded seaman rose to his feet and dumped her unceremoniously from his lap. He would murmur a few low words and a card game would end instantly with no question of stakes or winnings. He would raise a beckoning finger and half the tables of a grog-seller's inn would be suddenly deserted. Then he would steal out into the night, and a motley crew of the most villainous ruffians who ever cut a purse, or a throat, would materialize like shadows from Hades and creep silently after him. Knowing these things, Jane Golphin smiled.

"Ah, Kit, my Kit," she breathed. "You were with this Ducasse once. Pray God you are with him now."

She raced down the stairs to where the saddled horse waited, and pounded away toward that hidden cove where the *Gull* lay, tugging impatiently at her hawsers.

It took His Excellency Jean-Baptiste, the Sieur Ducasse, some little time to fathom the cause of the uproar that burst so suddenly on his peaceful realm some five days later.

"A woman, you say?" he growled. "What's that? An *English*-woman! Then she's a spy. Take her out and hang her directly!"

The captain of the guard smiled quietly. "I fear," he said suavely, "that if I were to hang so beautiful a woman, His Excellency himself might later call me to task for my impetuosity."

Ducasse looked up, a merry twinkle creeping into his little blue eyes. "Beautiful, eh?" he mused. "The English are not fools. Do you think they'd send an old crow to peck at us? No, *mon capitaine*, a swan would serve their purpose much better, knowing our well-deserved reputation in such matters."

The captain bowed. "A swan, your Excellency?" he said. "I assure you they have sent a bird of paradise!"

Ducasse allowed a bass chuckle to escape his lips. "That being the case, *mon capitaine*," he said, "perhaps it would not be beneath my dignity to examine the culprit myself."

"Your Excellency knows your duty," the Captain said, smiling.

"But if I may be so bold, I might suggest that not even your Excellency has many such opportunities to wed duty with pleasure."

"You turn a nice phrase," Ducasse grunted. "Where is she?"

"Outside in the anteroom, awaiting your Excellency's pleasure."

"Then show her in, man! Show her in at once!"

The Sieur Ducasse had time for one quick pat at a stray curl of his enormous wig before Rouge entered his office. She was clad in a dress of green velvet, and a hat of the same material ornamented with peacock feathers. At once she swept down in a curtsy that would have been noteworthy even at the court of St. James. Courtier that he was, man of the world, Ducasse was for the moment completely nonplused. Then he recovered.

"We are honored, madame," he said in English. "That your masters had such respect for our taste as to send one of your beauty is indeed flattering."

Rouge smiled. "No one sent me, my lord," she said quietly. "I came of my own free will upon a most private errand."

Ducasse shook his head with heavy gravity. "I am, madame," he said, "as bemused by your loveliness as you could well expect— but not so bemused as to believe so transparent a fabrication."

Rouge stiffened. Her small head lifted on the snowy column of her neck, and her green eyes gazed fearlessly into the face of the Governor.

"If you will hear me out . . ." she said clearly.

Ducasse inclined his massive head with all the civility in the world. "To listen to your voice is a pleasure," he said. "It is as lovely as your fair person. Please continue."

"You have, do you not, among your subjects a young captain called Christopher Gerado?"

"Christophe!" Ducasse exclaimed. "But certainly! How do you know of him? Tell me." He stopped suddenly, awed by the great joy leaping and blazing in Rouge's eyes.

"Where is he?" she whispered. "Tell me, my lord! Lead me to him and you will give me back my life!"

"He is not here," Ducasse said, "but Petit Goave is his home port, and to it he often returns."

238

"Then I will wait," Rouge exulted. "Even if it is a hundred years, I will wait his return!"

Ducasse studied the small, lovely face with great care. "And what," he demanded, "makes you think that I shall permit you, an enemy subject, to remain in my territory?"

Rouge swept out an imploring hand. "Please, my lord," she said, with tears in her eyes, "do not send me away. If you think I have come to do you harm, imprison me—gladly will I submit to it. But do not send me away. . . . I love him so. Without him I shall die or go mad. . . . Have you never been in love?"

Slowly, softly, Ducasse smiled. "No, child," he said, "I shall not send you back, for already you have seen too much, and your masters would profit by the knowledge. Nor will I imprison you. I shall assign you a house in the town, and there you may stay until Christophe returns. He is a good lad, and much do I love him. I think, if you speak the truth, you may bring him happiness."

"You—you think I lie about this?"

Ducasse shook his head. "Either," he said crossly, "you are the world's finest actress, or you speak the truth. I cannot decide. Nor can I take chances. Our countries, unfortunately, are still at war. Therefore I must quarter guards with you, and keep this crew of yours under close watch."

Rouge bowed her head submissively.

"These guards," added Ducasse, chuckling, "will be men above seventy, for none younger would I trust to keep their hands off you. I must ask you to respect their old bones and not elude them. Have I your promise?"

"You have more, my lord," said Rouge, laughing, "you have my heartfelt thanks!" Then suddenly she went up on tiptoe and kissed him lightly on the mouth.

His Excellency's naturally florid complexion turned beet-red. "Captain!" he roared. The captain of the guard appeared and saluted. "Take this woman," Ducasse spluttered, "to the house that lies vacant in the Fifth Square—and be quick about it, for I fear I am bewitched!"

He stood there a long time after Rouge had gone, and gradually his face resumed its natural hue. Then the corners of his mouth crept upward into a low smile.

"Jean-Baptiste," he told himself, "you're a sentimental old fool—praised be all the saints!"

21

THE FORTRESS OF San Lázaro was designed to be the most imposing military structure in the entire Viceroyalty of Peru.[1] However, in July of 1695, when Kit and Bernardo were thrown into its prison camp, it was less than half completed. In one week, whatever feeling of gratitude they may have felt toward Don Luis for sparing their lives had vanished. The Count, they now believed, had merely considered hanging too kind a fate.

From so early in the morning that the stars still hung in the sky until so late in the evening that the moon had reappeared Kit and Bernardo worked on the walls of the fortress. During the day the sun shone above their heads and smote them, its glare so bright that all the sea and the land swam in a white-gold haze that took the edges off everything, so that sky and cove and slow-moving white sails on the bay had a curious indistinctness of outline, as though they were not quite real.

To view them with heat-stricken, bloodshot eyes did not help their clarity. Often, they danced crazily before the sight as the oxhide whips of the Spanish guards came down on their bare backs, the long, loaded lashes curling around their trunks so that even their bellies were striped. Their backs and shoulders were a mass of crisscrossed sores above which the *colorojes* buzzed endlessly. Even Kit soon learned to groan when he was struck, for if the soldiers did not hear a cry, they considered the blow too light and repeated it. It was hard to tell which part of the

[1] Now called the fortress of San Felipe de Barájas, it still stands in perfect preservation between the hill of the Popa and the old city. Completed in 1752, after nearly a hundred years of work, it cost 11,000,000 pesos and uncounted human lives.

241

day was the worst. In the morning, in the soft-slumbering tropic dark, they worked in the quarry, bending and lifting the jagged stones until their hands were bloody masses that somehow healed and somehow managed to keep on moving. During the day the blinding heat was added to their other burdens.

They put the quarried stones in the oxcarts, groaning as their biceps and belly muscles knotted and protested, bending, lifting, the whole world a shifting haze of sweat-blurred agony, their bodies one long ache from sole to crown. They lifted stones that no one man should have been able to lift, the sinews of their loins threatening to tear loose, backs bowed, shoulders ridged, thigh and calf thrusting upward against the inert mass, the thick hot stench of sweat and filth and fresh blood unnoticed in their nostrils, their momentarily superhuman strength begotten by the whistling, white-hot agony of the oxhide whips and foaled by the fury of their own impotent rage.

Then they would make their way to the fortress, totter on bare feet over the cobblestones and up into the hills, pushing against the clumsy wheels of the carts when they were stuck in the black mud—an event which happened with monotonous regularity—while the whips of the Spaniards sang through the air and curled about their bare backs, bringing blood. By now the cool darkness was gone, to be replaced by the merciless furnace heat of the sun.

They spread mortar and lifted the roughhewn stones into place. With hammer and chisel they chipped them into some semblance of squareness. For the most part, they worked without any gear or tackle. The helmeted soldiers, sweating under their heavy breastplates, were not disposed to be kind. The human cattle they drove were far cheaper than mules and oxen, and far easier to replace. The Chibchas, brought down from the cool blue reaches of their native mountains, felt it worst. They would have died even without the added burden of their labors. Week by week, it was necessary to replace the entire group of Indian slaves, who perished to a man under the blows of the sun and the whistling crack of the Spanish lashes.

Finally, the captain general in charge of the engineers gave it up. After all, his primary purpose was to build a fortress to

242

protect the landward approaches, not to slaughter Indians. It was efficiency, not mercy, that moved him. He requested the governor of the province to give him a working force of Negroes. His request was promptly granted, for the fear of attack was a phobia in Cartagena. After that the work went better.

To the blacks, the mere eighty degrees of heat was as nothing. So well did they work that the captain general was inspired to grant them the same consideration that he extended toward his blooded Andalusian stallion—they, after all, were valuable animals, far more useful than the political prisoners and the Chibcha scum. He ordered his guards to use the whips sparingly, and doubled the Negroes' rations. It was this fact that saved Kit's and Bernardo's lives in the early days of their imprisonment.

Bernardo, being a man of immense goodwill, did not draw apart from the Negroes as did the other political prisoners. He moved among the blacks, talked with them in pidgin Spanish, laughed with them, attended to their illnesses, and gradually broke down their suspicions. In an unbelievably short time, he had won their trust—even more, their love. The affection they felt toward the little padre—for so they had come to call him—manifested itself in sharing their rations with him. Bernardo in turn shared with Kit. As a result, they lived. The other political prisoners died. By April of 1696, Kit and Bernardo were the only white prisoners left in the fortress. Even the guards had come to regard them as fixtures, and beat them almost as seldom as they did the Negroes.

The blacks trusted Kit too, but they never learned to love him. Kit was taciturn, not given to wordiness and display of emotion. At night he sat with Bernardo among the blacks in the prison camp inside the uncompleted walls of the fortress, but he said little, for his thoughts were far away. Neither he nor Bernardo was healthy; even with the gifts of the Negroes they lingered on the verge of starvation. Though in many places Kit's bones were outlined through his flesh, his muscular development approached that of Bernardo's, and where Bernardo's great strength was confined to his upper trunk, Kit had become a young Hercules, although a sadly starved one.

The problem of escape occupied his every waking thought.

The tales of the buccaneers ran through his mind, a thousand stories of escape stirred in his memory. Kit tried. With a stolen chisel, he and Bernardo worked for four months to loosen the stones through a six-foot section of wall. They were discovered within two feet of freedom, and beaten almost to death. It was three weeks before they could even stand. Upon another occasion they made a break from the quarry, but a harquebusier put a ball through Bernardo's thigh.

Bernardo, Kit realized, would now be lame for life. To escape, Kit would have to leave his old friend, and that was unthinkable. As a result, he settled deeper into gloom and hopelessness. To make it worse, the dungeons beneath the fortress were now completed. As dangerous prisoners, Kit and Bernardo were locked in one of the new cells, and manacled to the walls with long chains. True, the Negroes now and again managed to slip food to them, but they were rapidly losing their last reserves of strength. Bearded, filthy, infested with vermin, they resembled nothing human, and the light in Kit's eyes was close to madness.

So it was that when the captain of the guard approached their cell one night in 1696 and announced a visitor, Kit refused to credit the man's words. Five minutes later he hung against the iron bars, looking like a blond ape, his face half-hidden in the golden sweaty tangle of his great beard, his matted, filthy mane covering his bare shoulders. Outside in the corridor Bianca stood, wrapped in her cloak, unable to speak because of the gasping flood of her sobs.

She had brought with her a basket of food. She passed the fine bread and wine and cheese and fruit through the bars, unable to force her shocked tongue to utter a syllable. As she stood there watching Kit wolfing down the food like a great beast, the stench from the cell beat sickeningly about her head. To this had her lover come—more animal than man, his grace and courtliness gone, his tongue so thickened by thirst and silence that when he spoke his formerly liquid Castilian was a guttural growl that sounded scarcely human.

"Bianca," he muttered.

"Kit," she wept, "Kit! Oh my God, what have they done to you?"

244

A slow smile moved amid the matted tangle of mustache and beard. "They have not broken me," Kit said slowly. "I am happy to see you. Nothing else matters."

Bianca's white hands reached between the bars and grasped his. She clung to him, going up on tiptoe so that her small mouth could reach through the bars, and kissed his bearded face. Bernardo, seated in order to favor his newly lamed leg, got up painfully and turned his back as he ate. At last Kit pushed her away.

"Don't add to my torment, Bianca," he said softly.

Bianca stood shuddering against the bars and the tips of her slim fingers traced the lines of half-healed stripes with a tenderness that was almost pain.

"You must escape," she whispered. "You must be freed!"

Kit shrugged hopelessly. "We've already made a dozen attempts," he said. "They have come to nothing. This place is too new and far too well guarded. If we were at the Boca Chica, we might have fled to the jungle that lies so near, and the sea is even closer. Old Don Sancho Jimeno and his garrison of ancient harquebusiers could not stop us." He sighed heavily. "But we are here. And here, I fear, we will one day die."

Bianca's pale face was radiant suddenly. "You will be transferred there!" she said. "So small a thing I can accomplish easily."

Kit's face darkened. Bianca saw the stricken look of jealousy flare suddenly in his eyes.

"No, Kit," she said gently. "Don't trouble yourself with such thoughts. I will have to make no new sacrifices."

Kit gazed at her, his face bleak and frowning. "Bernardo goes with me," he warned, "or I don't go."

"Very well," said Bianca with a smile. "You can have your precious friend—of whom I am sometimes jealous."

Bernardo turned around to grin wickedly at her. "I fear," he croaked, "that I am a little less pretty than you."

Bianca blew him a kiss. "God bless you, Señor Bernardo," she said gently, "for the many times you have saved Kit's life."

"And you, my lady," Bernardo replied, "for your graciousness."

Bianca stretched out her arms to Kit again. "I must go now, Kit," she whispered, "but before the end of this month you will have a chance at freedom. God and the Virgin grant that you win! I could not endure life if you were dead."

"Bianca!" Kit croaked, his voice failing him.

Bianca smiled up at him, blinking back her tears.

"You must escape," she whispered. "Now kiss me, Kit. I have to go."

Kit and Bernardo listened to her footsteps dying out on the stones of the corridor. Bernardo threw an arm across Kit's shoulder.

"You're a lucky man, Kit," he said, "to have a woman like that one."

That the task she had undertaken was no light one Bianca understood as soon as she looked into the frowning face of her husband.

"You want him transferred to the Boca Chica," he mused, "and the Jew likewise. Why, Bianca?"

"Because he is dying!" she stormed. "You promised to spare him. What does it matter that he escaped the gallows if they beat him to death at San Lázaro?"

"Would he be better off at the Boca Chica, or would he merely better his chances to escape?"

"He would get better treatment. The fortress there is completed. They would not drive him like a starved and naked animal."

"So? But why the Jew?"

"Because Kit will not leave him. Consider, Luis, Kit is your son."

Don Luis smiled at her, a dark and mocking smile. "My son—and your lover. An interesting situation, eh, Bianca?"

"I love him, I don't deny that, but that anything will ever come of my love is quite another matter."

"Then nothing has yet come of it?" Don Luis mocked.

"If you mistrust me in this, it reflects only the evil of your own heart," Bianca said tartly.

Don Luis frowned. "And if he were to escape?"

"It would be the best of all solutions. He would leave this land, and you would have no further need to trouble yourself."

246

This, Don Luis reflected, was true—if his fair wife did not fly away with Kit. His dark face relaxed suddenly.

"Very well," he said, "it shall be arranged—on one condition."

Bianca looked at him. When she spoke, her voice was high and breathless.

"And that condition is . . . ?"

"It is this," he said, smiling. "The day that Kit reaches the Boca Chica you will go with me to Santa Marta and there consult Mendoza, who, Jew dog that he is, is still the greatest physician in all Peru. If any man can cure you of your barrenness, he can. I ordered him to come here, but he makes excuses. And the captain general, a liberal-minded fool, sustains him in this effrontery. But no matter. What do you say to that, my Bianca?"

Bianca stood there facing him, unable to hide the pain in her eyes. At last she bowed her head. "Agreed," she whispered. Then she turned very slowly and walked away.

Don Luis took his time about writing out the order for the transfer of Kit and Bernardo. It would, he knew, cause much whispered criticism and, what was worse, speculation. Don Luis cared little about criticism, but speculation was another matter. He wanted no one to question his motives. So far Godoy, the viceregal prosecutor, had held his tongue; but in the general babble of public gossip he might feel safe to let slip a few veiled innuendoes, and once loosed, the scandal would spread like wildfire. Luis del Toro was prepared to appear a scoundrel, a petty tyrant, an oppressor of the innocent, but a cuckold—never!

His dark face creased with frowns as he laboriously wrote out the message in his own bold hand. Ordinarily, he would have employed a secretary, but this was too confidential a matter to trust to outside eyes. He finished the parchment, sanded it, dripped a blob of candle wax on it, and affixed his seal. Still the matter troubled him.

As he went into the street to deliver the order—for this, too, he would not trust to anyone else—his eyes fell on the rotund figure of Don Felipe Gálvez. Don Felipe was a great trencherman, with an extravagant fondness for wine and talk. In his youth, the story ran, the list had also included women, but as his girth and senility had increased Don Felipe had had to curtail his activities in that particular. In self-defense, he attempted to make up for his failings with his waspish tongue.

As Don Luis greeted him, the ghost of an idea began to dawn. Here was one of the greatest gossips and scandalmongers in Cartagena. Why not cap the prosecutor's tale before it had even been issued? It would drown the present scandal in a much greater one, one which, oddly enough, would reflect only credit on Don Luis's own virility. He took the fat arm of Don Felipe and steered him toward the nearest inn. Don Felipe came gladly, for something about Don Luis's expression intrigued him. The Count was plainly troubled with some momentous matter and needed a sympathetic listener.

Later, over the mounds of steaming viands, the talk was slow and hesitant. Don Luis allowed himself to be drawn out, inch by inch. Yes, it was true that he was greatly troubled. There was a matter in which duty conflicted with the dictates of his heart. Here he paused to sip his wine with maddening deliberation, a far-off look in his eyes.

A woman? No. At least no woman now living. This was an old tale, and a sorry one, which he hesitated to inflict upon his friend's kindly ears. (That those ears were agog and titillating he could plainly see, but he preferred to carry the pretense even farther.) Ah well then, he would speak out, for Don Felipe was a man of discretion and the tale would go no farther. Don Felipe assured him with a fine excess of oaths that such was indeed the case.

The matter, Don Luis sighed, concerned a prisoner now held at San Lázaro, a blond lad who had been captured as a result of the *Seaflower* incident. Don Felipe was leaning forward now, his fat lips slack, his little pig's eyes filled with curiosity.

That lad, Don Luis said, his voice dropping into a conspiratorial whisper, was related to him by blood. He was in fact a— a nephew, although an unhallowed one. The pause before the word "nephew" was deliberately prolonged. Don Felipe, the Count knew, was nobody's fool. He would make the proper substitution for that transparent "nephew." How correct he was in his judgment of Don Felipe was proved a moment later. The fat grandee fell back in his chair, slapping his thigh and roaring with laughter.

"Oh come now, Luis," and he guffawed. "Your nephew! Now, really, who do you think will believe that?"

Don Luis's face assumed an injured expression. "I know," Don Luis said slowly, "that it's hard to credit that one so fair could spring from the swart house of Del Toro. But then, you have not seen his mother." He sighed heavily.

"But you have?" Don Felipe was grinning. "Nephew—pah!"

"Your skepticism is unworthy of you," Don Luis said with a slow smile that in itself was almost an admission of Don Felipe's surmise. "The point is that I cannot permit the boy to die at San Lázaro, nor can I order him released. So I thought of your friend and mine, Don Sancho Jimeno out at the Boca Chica. Out there Cristóbal might survive, as the tasks are less arduous. Later, who knows?"

"When the matter blows over, you might procure his release, eh, Luis? And even acknowledge him—as your nephew, of course," Don Felipe added hastily.

"Yes. What do you think of it, Felipe?"

"It does you credit. I'm sure that if it came to anyone's attention—not through me, Luis, of course—it would be well understood." He stood up, a pleased smile on his oily-fat face. "Yes, I'm certain it would be understood."

So it was that Luis del Toro went on his errand with a complacent look on his face. Let the prosecutor talk. His words would not be believed after Don Felipe had begun to gossip.

Two days later Kit and Bernardo were kicked awake by their guard much earlier than usual.

"Come," the guard growled. He made no attempt at explanation, nor did they ask for any.

As they reached the prison yard, a stir of excitement began to move sluggishly through their veins, for there they were flanked by a platoon, and a kettledrum sounded. They moved through the gate and down the hill into the dense jungle, stumbling wearily. Now and then a soldier prodded them with the butt end of his pike. At last they came to the shore of the bay. A narrow bridge connected it with the city of Cartagena, but they did not go up the ramp. Instead, they were ordered into a great pirogue waiting quietly on the water.

Late in the afternoon they came to the fortress on the tip of the peninsula, the celebrated Castillo de Boca Chica, against whose stout walls Drake and Morgan had hurled their furious assaults in vain.

The prow of the pirogue bumped softly against the quay, and a helmeted soldier made it fast. Then the guards scrambled ashore, dragging Kit and Bernardo after them. On the stones beneath their feet a vast replica of the royal arms was carved. They heard the slow, rattling clank of the great chains and the creaking of oak timbers as the drawbridge was let down. It came level and they crossed over, passing under the archway into the vast stone-paved courtyard of the fortress. There Don Sancho himself was waiting for them.

Kit was surprised that Don Sancho had come to meet them, but he did not know that the grandee had spent the last week vacationing in Cartagena, where Don Luis's carefully planted story was making the rounds. The Count could have done no better if he had employed the town crier, for Don Felipe Gálvez was constitutionally incapable of keeping a secret.

Don Sancho, of course, had heard the story. Despite his seventy-odd years, he retained a lively curiosity as to human affairs. Therefore he waited under the blinding glare of the sun to greet his new prisoners. The soldiers marched Kit and Bernardo up to him. The old man, still as fierce and strong as a sea eagle, studied Kit with intensity.

"Del Toro's bastard, eh?" he growled. "It could be. You have the build and the set of the Del Toro line. Well, Cristóbal, Del Toro or not, you can expect no favors from me!"

Kit took a staggering step backward, and the walls of the fortress, broader across the top than any street in Cartagena, reeled suddenly before his eyes. Del Toro's bastard! At last the mystery of his birth was explained. This man who had taken his mother's life, who had forced himself on Rouge, who had killed his entire crew, was also his father! It could not be—the whole idea was too fantastically cruel. Yet, completely, utterly, damnably, it fitted. Why else had his mother run down those stairs to check the grandee's horse that day in Cádiz? Why else had Don Luis on two occasions spared his life? Why else had Bianca whispered, "I would not have you harm him—especially not him"? He turned a stricken face toward Bernardo, but Don Sancho was speaking again, some of the sternness gone from his tone.

"Are you ill, lad? Yes, I can see you are." Then, turning to the soldiers: "Take him to his cell and see that he is well fed. It's not my responsibility to relieve Del Toro's conscience."

Afterward, in the cool darkness of their subterranean cell, Kit faced Bernardo.

"It's true, isn't it, Bernardo?" he asked. "Why didn't you tell me before?"

"I had no proof," Bernardo said, "although I suspected it. What now, Cristóbal?"

Kit studied the dim light filtering in between the heavy iron bars. "When we're free, I'll pay him a visit. It will be the last he ever receives," Kit said evenly. "Even though he is my father, I'll not spare him!"

Bernardo picked up the earthen vessels filled with coarse wholesome food.

"Eat," he said. "You will need your strength."

22

To his own surprise, Kit found that he had no immediate desire to escape from the fortress of Boca Chica. Almost a year of semistarvation, brutality, exposure, and exhaustion had had a more serious effect upon him than he realized. Not only had his body been depleted, but also his mind, his spirit and his will.

Bernardo, on the other hand, had actually toughened under the ordeal. He had seen men die before. He knew that the bravest man on earth can be reduced to a gibbering idiot by long-protracted torture skillfully applied. He realized that there is a limit beyond which no man can be expected to go, and upon entering prison late in his forties, still bearing the scars of earlier tortures and imprisonments, he had wondered whether he would be able to endure. That he had endured, that he was yet alive and in possession of his faculties, was a source of pride to him. Moreover, he was glad that Kit did not urge an immediate attempt at escape. Every day that they waited increased their chances for success.

Don Sancho saw that they were well fed; and at the Boca Chica, manned as it was by a skeleton garrison, there was little or no work to be done. Kit and Bernardo drew water from the well, tended fires, and cleaned the barracks. Those tasks done, they had many hours of leisure in which to recover their strength and explore the situation.

Because of the location of the fortress, they were confined to their cell only during the night. In the daytime they could wander about the vast, rambling fortification as they pleased. This situation was due in part to Don Sancho's knowledge of

252

Kit's origin. Kit found this galling, but Bernardo accepted it calmly as a valuable asset. In their spare moments they made their plans. Bernardo drew a map of the Bay of Cartagena on a scrap of parchment, indicating their own position. Looking at the map, they realized that the land about Cartagena formed a hollow circle around the bay. Behind the fortress of Boca Chica extended the arm of the Terra Bomba peninsula, a dense jungle that led only northward to the city itself.

The plan Kit devised had nothing to recommend it but its audacity. Again and again Bernardo pointed out that its chances of success were so slight as to be almost negligible. But Kit was not to be deterred.

"In a mad world," he growled, "only greater madness succeeds!"

In the end, Bernardo was forced to give in. Kit proposed to scale the walls somehow and beat northward through the Terra Bomba to the city. Once there, a knife would flash in the darkness and Don Luis would render up his account before the throne of God. Then, with gold stolen from the grandee's coffers, the girl Quita would be dispatched to buy new garments and Indian dyes, which would darken the dangerous blondness of Kit's hair and beard.

He anticipated no difficulties from Bianca. She would journey with them to the great port of Santa Marta. There the three of them could buy passage to Santo Domingo. And as that city lay on the other side of the great island of Hispaniola, whose western half was occupied by the French colony of Saint-Domingue, it would be comparatively easy to bribe a coasting hoy to set them down in French territory. A splendid plan—except that there was not one chance in a million of reaching Don Luis's house in Cartagena without being cut down by the guardia civil.

To make it worse, how were they to escape from the Boca Chica in the first place? They might dive from the walls into the sea, but in the daytime either the shots of the harquebusiers would cut them down or the swift pirogues manned by the Negroes would catch them. Their only hope lay in avoiding being returned to their cell at night. In the darkness they might be able to climb silently down the walls, slip into the black waters, and gain the shores of Terra Bomba.

Their opportunity, when it occurred, came about through the purest chance. One afternoon while Kit and Bernardo were carrying their skins of drinking water to the sentries in the little rounded towers that marked the junction points of the corners of the inward-sloping walls, one of the soldiers drew Kit aside.

He had, he told Kit, spent his two-day leave in Cartagena. While there, a beautiful Indian girl had approached him. Apparently she had questioned him most deftly, for he had casually told her all about himself. Upon learning that he was attached to the garrison of the Boca Chica, she had begged him to deliver a note to Cristóbal Gerado. What she had given him in return, Kit could guess.

Kit listened with impatience to this wordy narrative. When the soldier finally passed him the note, he tore it open and read:

My Own:

When this reaches you, I shall be far away on a journey to the city of Santa Marta with my husband, there to consult the great physician Mendoza. I do not know when I shall return—if ever.

My anguished heart cries out to you—farewell, my Cristóbal. The vows I swore when I became Luis's bride are too weighty to be set aside even for a cause as great as my love for you.

Yet if God is just, He will grant you deliverance. As for the rest, I can only wait and hope.

Ever your
Bianca

Bernardo could see Kit's expression changing as he read the note, the pallor spreading under his tan, the fire of madness leaping in his blue eyes. But even Bernardo was not prepared for what happened. In two swift strides Kit reached the wall and split the blue waters in a dive as clean as any knife. Bernardo had no choice but to follow him.

That they did not die in the first two minutes of their swim was due entirely to Don Sancho's stern orders that Kit was not to be harmed. Before they were halfway across the channel,

254

the first of the pirogues overtook them. After staring into the gaping muzzle of a musket, Bernardo allowed himself to be pulled aboard without a struggle, but it was not until the butt end of a pike had rendered him unconscious that they dragged Kit into the boat.

When they had been returned to the fortress, they faced the captain of the guard, for Don Sancho was enjoying himself with a new Chibcha concubine in Cartagena.

"So," the captain growled. "You love water, eh, Cristóbal? Well, you shall have your fill of it! Give them the Indian treatment, my lads!"

The soldiers of the guard roared with laughter. Kit and Bernardo were marched through the stone-paved courtyard and across the drawbridge spanning the moat that surrounded the inner walls of the fort. In the middle of the bridge they were suddenly halted. They waited there in the dense heat while the captain surveyed the scene. Apparently satisfied, he ordered the march resumed. They crossed over the moat and came to the gates of the outer walls on the landward side. Through these they also passed, coming out on the sandy beach of the channel.

They marched through the wet sand until they reached a spot where the palm trees came down to the edge of the sea. The guards pushed them through the low thickets of bamboo and reed without slackening their pace. Kit saw Bernardo bend down quickly and break off some lengths of reed, receiving a blow across his buttocks for even so short a delay. They emerged from the jungle at last and Kit saw that they had made a great semicircle, for the fortress of Boca Chica lay again before them.

As they approached it, another matter came to his attention. On this side of the outer wall was no wall at all, but a natural precipice, the inner face of which had been smoothed and lined with stones so that it formed the far side of the moat. One of the guards was paying out a great coil of rope so that it went down into the moat itself. The black-bearded captain bowed to them mockingly.

"If Señor Cristóbal will be so kind as to go down . . ." he said, a pleased smile on his dark face.

Kit had no choice. Very quietly he let himself down over

the edge of the artificial cliff and went down the rope hand over hand. When his feet were almost touching the green-slimed, fetid surface of the water, he realized that it was not the Spaniards' intention to drown him immediately, because there in the side of the artificial precipice a low, stone-lined tunnel opened before his gaze. He swung himself into it and released the rope. Inside it was cool and dark. There were six inches of black mud on the floor.

The significance of the mud escaped Kit at the moment. He was too busy leaning from the tunnel's mouth, craning his neck to watch Bernardo's progress down the rope. He saw at once that he had little need for worry. The curious disproportion of Bernardo's build, with its immense arms and slight lower body, made the descent even easier for him than it had been for Kit. As he came down, blocking off the light from the opening, Kit saw that he still held the slim reeds. When Bernardo had swung himself safely inside, he tossed them aside.

"Thought they were going to drown us in the moat," he growled. "A man can stay under water a long time if he has a reed to breathe through. But I think these dons have other ideas."

Before Kit had the opportunity to reply, the rope came down again. At its end a wooden bucket had been tied.

"Take it!" the captain roared down at them. "You'll need it!"

Bernardo put out his long arms and took the vessel. He studied it in some puzzlement, then his eyes fell on the oozy slime of black mud in which they sat.

"Their mothers!" he spat. "The water of the moat rises with the tide!"

He stood up as far as the low roof of the tunnel would allow and examined the sides. From the watermark, he could see that the tide rose to within eight inches of the top of the tunnel. They would have to stand in a hunched-over position all night to keep their nostrils above the level of the surface. If they bailed with the bucket, they might be able to keep the water level a little lower. This, then, was the Indian treatment.

Without a word, Kit began to crawl toward the interior of the tunnel. About ten yards farther on it sloped downward a little, and here even at low tide there was a pool about eight feet deep. It was far too dark at this point to locate the watermarks, but Kit guessed that the tide came up here to within three or four inches of the roof. He swam across the pool and climbed out on the other side, but after twenty yards his journey ended abruptly, for the tunnel was closed off by a wall of stones.

Kit sat down weakly in the mud, feeling tears of frustration rising behind his eyelids. After a moment the fierce resolve that had possessed him since he had received Bianca's note came back. He turned and began the swim across the pool.

"It has no opening," he said calmly, "so we must think of another method."

Slowly, painfully, they returned to the mouth of the tunnel. Kit sat very still, his mind busy. At last his blue eyes cleared.

"If," he said to Bernardo, "the waters of the moat rise with the tide, there must be some connection between them and the sea!"

Bernardo looked at him. Then he nodded slowly. "There must be," he said, "but we must wait for night to look for it."

As night approached, the water began to rise in the tunnel until they sat in it up to their waists. Patiently, they waited until the edges of the tunnel's mouth were no longer discernible, till all was blackness without and within.

Silently, Kit waded through breast-high water and let himself down into the green-slimed moat. He began his slow, silent swim.

Bernardo followed, going in the opposite direction. Every few minutes they sank down and groped with their fingers along the outer walls. With half-hour intervals of rest, forced upon them by pure exhaustion, they kept this up all night. At the first flush of dawn, they were forced to admit defeat. If a passageway through the walls existed, they had not been able to find it.

They made their way back to the tunnel and entered it. The tide was receding now, so that once again they were able to sit. They had been there no longer than an hour when they heard the soldiers calling down to them:

"Had enough bathing, caballeros?"

Bernardo started forward, but Kit caught his arm. "Don't answer!"

257

"Say something, you stubborn swine!" the captain roared. "Don't force us to come down for you."

Bernardo watched in some mystification as Kit groped about in the water with his hand. A moment later, Kit gave a low grunt of triumph, for his fingers had come up holding the reeds.

"Come," he whispered and began to move away from the mouth of the tunnel. They reached the edge of the subterranean pool and waited there, holding their breaths in the stillness. When they heard the Spaniards splashing the waters, they slipped silently into the pool and sank to the bottom. Lying on the floor, they pushed the reeds upward until they protruded an inch or two above the surface.

It was not a pleasant feeling to lie as still as death with eight feet of slimy water above their heads and wait while the Spaniards moved nearer and nearer. Suddenly there was a great commotion almost directly over their heads, and the water was churned into foam by a man's wild thrashing: one of the soldiers had fallen into the pool. Fortunately, he wore no armor, or he would have been doomed. He bounded to the surface like a cork, and was drawn ashore by the shafts of his comrades' lances.

On the bottom of the pool, Kit and Bernardo could not hear his words, but if they had, they would have been comforted, for as he was drawn into shallow water, he cried: "If they're in that pool, they're drowned. By the Virgin, it has no bottom!"

Kit and Bernardo lay on the floor of the pool for another hour, drawing in their breaths through the tubes of the reeds. Then slowly, quietly, Kit swam upward. He put up his head, ducked under again, and waited. No sound came. He swam over to Bernardo's reed and gave it a triumphant shake. A moment later Bernardo's dark head broke the surface.

"So," he spluttered, "we've gained another night, but we're still inside these walls!"

"In that cell," Kit answered slowly, "no chance at all existed. Here, there's at least a possibility."

They settled down to wait for the coming of night. As the day wore on, they were conscious of their hunger and thirst. Their tongues thickened in their parched mouths until they could scarcely speak, and the growling of their empty bellies increased. The night, when it came, came with a difference. Whereas the previous night had been clouded, tonight the sky was clear and star-studded. The danger of swimming the moat was tripled, but it was also easier to discover their bearings.

Telling Bernardo to wait, Kit slipped into the black water. He swam below the surface until his chest felt as though it would burst, then eased his head up so cautiously that he made scarcely a ripple. When he had reached the far end of the moat, he was astonished by what he saw there. Here the wall slanted down. It was so low at one point opposite the second drawbridge that a man could easily scale it. He swam back to the tunnel and told Bernardo of his discovery.

After Kit had rested they moved out, swimming close to the inner wall so that they were in shadow, their hands pushing back the water so gently that they made hardly a ripple. At last they came to the place opposite the drawbridge. There they halted, prayerfully treading water, for black on the face of the moon-silvered moat they could see the shadow of the sentry on the inner wall. Going down, they sought bottom, and stayed there until the need to breathe became overwhelming. They popped up again, close to the slimy rocks. The sentry had not moved.

Nine times they went down and up before the shadow vanished. Kit struck out at once, underwater. When his groping hand touched the stones of the opposite side, he stole upward, scarcely daring to breathe. The inner wall lay blank and bare in the moonlight. The sentry had moved on about his rounds.

Kit waved frantically to Bernardo, who was clinging to the stones on the inner wall. Three powerful strokes brought Bernardo across the moat, and the two of them climbed out on the narrow ledge of rock beside the wall. Kit knelt down, signaling Bernardo to mount his shoulders. When he forced himself upright again, Bernardo's powerful hands easily reached the top of the wall. He drew himself up and, without pausing for breath, stretched a hand down to Kit. He pulled Kit up and then the two of them dropped down onto the silent sand of the beach.

Keeping just under the wall, they ran for the protective screen of the palm trees. Only when they had buried themselves in the overwhelming gloom did they stop to recover their spent breath.

"Now what?" Bernardo panted.

"We start for Santa Marta," Kit growled.

"No, Kit," Bernardo said. "Let us consider the matter with some care. We need weapons, clothing, food—maybe even gold —before we can start for Santa Marta."

Kit grinned suddenly, a light of mischief leaping in his eyes. "Thoughtful of Don Luis, wasn't it," he said, "to transport Bianca for us to the place of our departure. And one thing more, good Bernardo. In yet another way he can serve us."

Bernardo's dark face was filled with questioning. "How, Kit? In what way can Don Luis help us?"

"Simple. We return to our original plan. Cartagena is the last place on earth where the guards would expect to find us. And with Don Luis absent from his house, what's to prevent us from helping ourselves to all the things we need?"

A slow, crafty grin spread over Bernardo's dark face. "Excellent!" he exclaimed. "What a happy thought—to make Don Luis supply us with the sinews for our journey!"

"Let's start," Kit said, and got to his feet.

They moved through the tangled forest of the Terra Bomba at a rapid pace. It was soon apparent that it would be full daylight before they reached the walls of the city, so they decided to lie in the tangled bamboo thickets and wait for night. Their hunger was unabated, but they managed to find fresh water. After drinking all they wanted, they let themselves down into the little stream and washed away their filth. Refreshed, they lay on their backs and stared at the sky through the rents in the canopy of leaves. When it was dusk they resumed their journey, coming to the walls of the city just after nightfall. The gates were about to be closed; groups of stragglers were rushing to get inside so they would not be locked out for the night.

Boldly, Bernardo joined the throng, and a second later Kit followed him. So it was that they re-entered the city, and they went directly toward Don Luis's house. Since the incident of the sinking of the *Seaflower*, there had been no further hostilities near Cartagena. The citizens had sunk back willingly into comfortable apathy. Even the enforcement of the curfew had become lax. As a result, Kit and Bernardo were able to reach Don Luis's house without being stopped by a single guardia civil.

While Kit waited, hiding his blond hair and beard in the deepest shadows, Bernardo went to the stables. Here at last he was stopped, by a sleepy old caretaker. But Bernardo was ready for him. In a flash, the Jew's powerful hands shot out, and a moment later the caretaker was incapable of uttering a sound. Bernardo let him slip limply to the cobblestones, and relieved him of his ring of great keys.

He rejoined Kit, and the two of them studied the watchman. Finally, deciding not to take any further chances, they left him in the stable, trussed up with rope and gagged. Inside the house, they found cold meats and wines that were no doubt intended for the caretaker, for their quality was not of the best. Kit and Bernardo sat down and gorged themselves. Then, taking candles, they proceeded to ransack the house for valuables.

When they departed they were both decently dressed, with stout jackboots on their feet. They even took the additional precaution of trimming their hair and beards. Weapons they had found aplenty: two pistols apiece, daggers, cutlasses, and a long-barreled musket. In their duffle bags were flagons of wine, black bread, cheese, and dried fruits. That this supply was far too little they knew well, but they depended on the musket to supply them with game.

In the full light of morning they proceeded out of the city, walking leisurely through the crowds. Kit had his golden mane tied back in a great kerchief, and his beard and mustache were stained black with soot. They went down to the quay and hired a Negro boatman, who with the help of another black rowed them down the bay. Toward evening, they passed through the Boca Chica channel and were pleased to observe that there was no visible stir within the fortress from which they had so lately escaped. The belief that they were dead, then, had taken root.

When they reached the sea, the blacks continued rowing, bearing southward toward the Dique canal, which connected the Cartagena area with the Magdalena River, the arterial high-road to the interior of New Granada.

As soon as they came to the Dique, they ran into trouble. The Negroes refused to go farther and demanded their pay. Kit glanced at Bernardo, a slow smile lighting his eyes. A moment later the blacks found themselves staring into the muzzles of two great pistols. At Kit's command, the pirogue was edged into shallow waters; then, without more ado, Kit forced the Negroes over the side, and Bernardo took up the oars.

Looking back at the shivering Negroes, Kit was moved with pity. Reaching into the purse he had stolen from Don Luis's house, he brought out a gold piece and tossed it to them. The old Negro who owned the pirogue looked at it and his face lighted up; he had received twenty times his fare and the price of his homemade boat put together.

23

As Bianca stood before the cathedral in the plaza of Santa Marta, she shivered a little. In no way was her trembling caused by any chill in the air, for Santa Marta lies in a smiling horseshoe-shaped valley at the base of the towering Sierra Nevada de Santa Marta and is blessed with eternal spring. It was, she well knew, the doubt and confusion in her mind that made her limbs quiver so.

With slow, hesitant steps, she and Quita crossed the plaza, moving toward the fine old cathedral with its twin belfries. Slowly they mounted the steps. In the doorway Bianca paused before entering. The light was dim, and the air seemed cooler than outside in the square. Dipping her hand into the holy-water font, Bianca crossed herself and genuflected in the direction of the altar. Then, very quietly, she knelt before a lesser niche and tried to pray.

Her confused mind refused to shape either the words or the mental images of prayer. She was overcome by loneliness and fear. She had no way of knowing whether Kit had succeeded in escaping from the grim gray pile of the fortress of Boca Chica. Even now he might be lying dead of wounds suffered in the attempt. Or, God willing, he might be free and on his way to her. It was this last thought that sowed the blowing seeds of confusion in her mind. If Kit were free, if he were to come to her—what then?

Don Luis would never release her from her vow. Of this she was certain. She knew, moreover, that having sworn to remain faithful to her husband, to bear him a child if she could, she

would not go back on her oath. Don Luis had kept his share of
the bargain and she would keep hers. Though she loved Kit
enough to give her life for him, though she shivered with ecstatic
pain even at the thought of his arms around her, she was trapped
by her vow. While Don Luis lived, she must remain his. Only
Providence—or Kit—could find a solution.

There was, curiously, another side to the matter. Long ago
she had discovered how much there was to admire about Luis
del Toro. In truth he was a great man, considered against the
background of his times. That his benevolence did not extend
beyond the narrow limits of his own particular race, religion, and
social position was in his own eyes only natural and right. If
it had been suggested to him that the kindness with which he
habitually treated Bianca, his friends, and even his blooded
stallion, should be shown to heretics, Jews, and slaves, he would
have dismissed the idea as insane. He might, for the moment,
seriously consider better treatment for his mules, for they were
valuable animals; but to feel humanitarian sentiments toward
heretics and such seemed to him insulting to his Iberian pride,
for, by inference, it would include this scum within the orbit of
the human race. If such a belief were ever established, the status
of all humanity would be lowered.

Bianca understood these feelings of his even better than he
did himself, and she knew how futile it was to try to change his
mind, so she left him in peace. But she knew also that to her
he was kindness itself, gentle and tender. Whenever he lashed
out at her with bitter words it was only because he was tormented
by jealousy. Moreover, she was almost sure that Don Luis loved
his natural son, and might, but for certain scruples and a very
touchy pride, have owned him. Certainly he had once spared
Kit's life of his own free will; and that second time when his
eloquence had stirred the halls of the Casa Real in Kit's behalf
—was it really only her pleas that had inspired him?

Groaning, she shook her small, lovely head. There was more
to all this, much more. If Luis were to die, either by accident
or by Kit's enraged hand, could she then go to her lover with
unmixed feelings? After having been married to the father,
after having more than a little *loved* the father, could she then

264

turn to the son without having a secret feeling of guilt in the whole matter—as though the new relationship were a little beyond the pale? And it would be even worse if Kit killed Luis, for in that she, being the cause, would be bloodguilty also—and with the blood of parricide.

Her poor head ached so. As the stained-glass windows shifted with the light, their outlines growing blurred and confused, the outlines of her thoughts blurred, her mind blurred, so that the angels from the niches seemed to come down and waver vaguely at her right hand, their illumined smiles alive and inviting. She was tired, deathly tired. If Kit came, had she the strength to turn to his impetuous arms? How much easier to forswear love and lovers, forswear all men, and go to the beckoning angels, where she might forever rest.

Rest! That was it, rest! More than even love she needed rest—more than joy, more than the panting, pounding fury of passion, she needed peace. No longer could she stand as a death challenge between two strong men. She would go with the angels, and as a bride of Christ escape from doubt, confusion, and terror forever. . . .

She stood up suddenly, and so great was the joy on her face that her small countenance seemed to glow with unearthly light. Seeing it, Quita was frightened.

"Señora!" she gasped.

Bianca raised her hand.

"Hush!" she whispered. "They are calling me, Quita—the angels are calling. . . . Don't you hear them?"

"I hear nothing," Quita quavered. "Oh, Doña Bianca, come!" Then, taking her mistress by the arm, she drew her from the dim recesses of the cathedral.

That same afternoon, Don Luis finally obtained an audience with Dr. Mendoza. By the time he faced the great physician he was in a cold and towering rage, for he had been forced to wait in an anteroom while the doctor attended to the sufferings of beggars, stolid Chibchas, and Negroes afflicted with running sores. As much as he needed the great Jewish physician's help, he could not resist pointing out his monstrous discourtesy.

"They are all God's children, are they not, my lord?" Mendoza said gently. "I have great sympathy for the poor. My father, you see, was a swineherd."

Don Luis ground his teeth to stifle the furious burst of words that threatened to escape his lips. The advantage was all with the physician. Don Luis needed Francisco Mendoza, while Francisco Mendoza needed no man. There was perhaps a pride beyond pride in this flinging of his humble origin into the Count's face, as though he were saying: I came from nothing, yet you, with generations of wealth and power behind you, must come to me. . . .

Mendoza stood very quietly, eying the Count with something curiously akin to compassion. He understood how great a struggle Luis del Toro was having with his pride; but pride to him was nothing, so he waited very quietly for the nobleman to speak.

"I would like you to come to Don Avila's, whose guest I am," Don Luis growled, "to determine what causes my lady's barrenness."

Mendoza bent his head with courtesy.

"I am at your service," he said. Then he hesitated, a slow and secret smile lighting his eyes.

"What now?" Don Luis barked.

"If you will not take it amiss, I might suggest that unfruitfulness in a union is not always the fault of the woman. Sometimes the excesses of youth prove damaging to the fulfillment of later and more serious desires."

Don Luis snorted. "You need have no fear," he said. "My wife has already conceived, but the child was stillborn. Since that time, there has been nothing."

"I see," Mendoza said gravely. "I will see her tonight. And if you will permit, I should like to bring with me a young colleague, Dr. José Pérez, who is very wise in these matters."

"Bring the whole of Santa Marta, if it will do any good," Don Luis answered, and left the house.

To a woman of Bianca's modesty the very thought of being examined by a physician was an ordeal, but under Mendoza's grave and gentle manner she relaxed greatly. Pérez, however, she distrusted on sight. The man had a look of slyness and deceit about him; his gaze darted from object to object without ever coming to rest upon any of them. Bianca suspected that he was a charlatan, but in this she was wrong. José Pérez was as good a physician as existed in Santa Marta—which is to say that he was monstrously, criminally ignorant of many of the most rudimentary facts of human life and health. However, this ignorance was shared more or less completely by every other doctor in New Spain, even by the great Mendoza himself. What distinguished Mendoza from the rest was an instinctive sympathy and understanding that probed deep into human nature. Coupled with this, he had a healthy skepticism that made him realize his own ignorance and walk carefully in the face of it.

Mendoza examined Bianca under a huge sheet, without looking at her body at all. Pérez clearly found this disappointing, for Bianca's beauty had instantly inflamed him. But he was too wise to protest, the more so when he noticed that Mendoza's tactics had won Don Luis's unqualified approval.

The examination took a long time and was most thorough. Afterward, the men went out of the room leaving Bianca feeling sick with humiliation from the mauling and probing to which her body had been subjected. She was filled with curiosity to overhear the talk that was going on in the great hall, but she would have had to rise and dress herself, with Quita's help. Suddenly an idea struck her. With a quick gesture she pointed to the door, bidding Quita listen.

Quita smiled and hastened to obey. In common with most servants, there was nothing that she enjoyed more than eavesdropping, and to be told to do so made her pleasure complete. In the salon, Don Luis was listening attentively, his face heavy with concern.

"So far as I can find," Mendoza said slowly, "there is nothing the matter with the señora. She is young and capable of conceiving, although she is a trifle delicate."

"Then why have I no son?" Don Luis thundered.

"Frankly," Mendoza said calmly, "I do not know. There is an explanation I strongly suspect to be valid in this case, but

I hesitate to give it, because it could only prove offensive to you, my lord."

"Give it," Don Luis said dryly. "This is no time to consider delicacy."

"Your wife does not want a child. At least, not your child. Forgive me, my lord, but you asked me to tell you."

Don Luis, who had half-risen, sank down again.

"There are many different degrees of fertility in women. Your wife, I suspect, in all her life would bear no more than two children in any event. Now her fear of childbirth—or could it be some other confusion of her emotions?—acts as a powerful barrier to conception. If you will accept my advice, you will woo her once more as a tender lover. If this does not succeed, you should adopt an heir, for Doña Bianca will never conceive unless . . ."

"Damnation!" Don Luis spat. "This is old wives' babble!"

"Perhaps," Mendoza said calmly, gathering up his instruments, "but that is my diagnosis."

Don Luis looked at José Pérez. "And what," he demanded, "is your opinion?"

"It is different from that of my colleague," Pérez said without hesitation. "I should prefer to voice it only to my lord himself."

Mendoza looked at the younger doctor in some surprise. It had not occurred to him that the young man was an opportunist, seeking his own gain above all else. That this was so came to him now as a cruel shock. Being far too wise to expect human beings to be anything else but human, he bowed ironically and prepared to leave. Without moving from his chair, Don Luis tossed him a fat purse of gold, exactly as one tosses a bone to a hungry dog. Mendoza caught it deftly, and stood there looking at it a moment.

Then, very quietly and with immense dignity, he said: "Since I have accomplished nothing, I can take no fee. If you wish, you can give this to charity." He crossed the room and laid the purse noiselessly on a low table. Then he was gone, leaving Don Luis feeling fatuous, enraged, and ashamed, all at the same time.

Quita swung her lithe form deftly behind the door as Mendoza came out, then she returned to her post.

"And now that we are alone," Don Luis said, looking at Dr. Pérez, "speak your piece."

"It is not my intention to flatter my lord with untruths or half-truths," Pérez said. "Doña Bianca is indeed barren. Totally, completely barren. I wish to offer my lord two most useful suggestions."

"Go on," Don Luis said, his voice deceptively soft.

"My lord should petition the Archbishop for a decree of annulment. In cases of this sort, where there is no issue, the good Father is most amenable to suggestion."

"I don't like that," Don Luis said, with the same appearance of mildness. "You have another suggestion?"

Emboldened, Pérez plunged in. "In my work among the Chibchas," he said, "I have encountered rare and curious substances—poisons, if my lord does not dislike the ugly word—that bring death quickly and painlessly, with every appearance of natural causes. So freed, my lord might, after a short period of mourning, turn to a young and lusty lady who would assure him of many sons."

"Interesting," Don Luis said as he rose. "Very, very interesting."

Pérez, seeing the cold ferocity in his eyes, could only gurgle wordlessly as he backed away from the Count's powerful grasp. But Quita, on the other side of the door, could see none of this. Nor did she wait to hear more. Overcome with fear for the life of her mistress, she ran from her hiding place and told Bianca what she had heard.

"If," Bianca said sadly, "my husband wants to kill me, what can I do?"

"No!" Quita was weeping. "No, my lady! Only I will cook your food and serve your wine. You must touch nothing but what I bring. I will stop him! Oh, why didn't you go with the young cacique with the golden hair?"

"Hush," Bianca said gently. "Hush, Quita. The Blessed Virgin will protect me, for I am innocent of sin."

If Quita had lingered a moment longer, she would have heard the crash of overturning furniture as José Pérez scurried to escape. Don Luis caught him about the throat with one tremendous hand and lifted him clear of the floor, shaking him all the while as a terrier shakes a rat. When finally he released Pérez, the young physician collapsed into a gasping, sobbing heap at his feet. Don Luis kicked him contemptuously.

"Get up!" he snarled. "And thank all the saints that you still have your miserable life!"

Pérez scrambled to his feet and fled with such haste that he left both his instruments and his books behind.

The three weeks that followed were a period of slow starvation for Bianca. Quita was able to obtain but little food for her, and the succulent meals that were set before her went untasted. She made many excuses to avoid eating with her husband. Don Luis watched with gathering astonishment as his wife grew paler and weaker, failing before his eyes.

Finally he announced that they would go back to Cartagena, for the hot climate of Santa Marta was obviously making her ill. Bianca, who at last had been unable to find an excuse to stay away from the table, looked at him with horror. How could he be so callous? Then she rose from the table and, overcome with sudden weakness, fainted at his feet.

Don Luis knelt anxiously beside her. Grasping a goblet of wine, he started to force a little between her colorless lips. Instantly Quita was upon him. She struck the goblet from his hand so that it crashed into a thousand fragments, the wine making a bloodlike stain on the floor.

"Murderer!" Quita shrieked. "I will not have her killed!"

Don Luis stared at the lovely Chibcha girl, blank amazement in his eyes.

"What is this madness, Quita?" he growled. "Who said anything about slaying Doña Bianca?"

"You!" Quita whispered, her voice filled with horror. "I heard you—the day you plotted with that wicked doctor! He said he would bring poisons, and you could . . ."

Don Luis threw back his head and his laughter boomed against the ceiling.

"Bless you, Quita," he roared. "I should have you lashed for your impudence, but I forgive you. You make things clear."

He looked down at Bianca, whose eyelids had fluttered open and who was staring at him curiously. "And you, my dove, also thought that I meant to poison you?"

Bianca struggled faintly in his great arms.

"Quiet, my love," he whispered. Then to Quita he said sternly, "Fill another goblet from the same flagon!"

Quita hesitated.

"Do as I say!" he thundered.

With trembling fingers the Indian girl obeyed. Then, taking the goblet, Don Luis raised it to his lips and drank half of it.

"Now you," he whispered to Bianca, placing the rim of the glass against her pale lips.

Slowly Bianca drank. It was cool and sweet, with no trace of bitterness in it at all.

"My heart is filled with grief," Don Luis whispered, his voice sinking to a bass rumble, "that you could think this of me. Did you know that Pérez barely escaped with his life? All these viands which all these days you have not tasted were both untainted and rich."

He stood up and lifted her tenderly in his arms. He looked back over his shoulder at Quita.

"And you, you untamed savage, go and prepare food for your mistress." Then he carried Bianca into her bedroom and put her down on the great bed. Bianca looked up at him, her dark eyes bright with tears.

"Forgive me, Luis," she whispered. "It is only that I knew how much you want a son."

"Trouble yourself no longer, Bianca," Don Luis said. "When we return to Cartagena, I will petition the good Fathers for a fair lad from the orphanage, and we will lavish our care upon him. Now eat and rest, so that you may be strong enough for the journey."

Lightly he kissed her, and getting up, beckoned to Quita, who was bringing steaming viands on a tray. The Indian maid knelt beside her mistress and Don Luis took his leave. But long before the hot broth was half gone from the bowl, Quita hesitated, the spoon of hammered silver poised in midair, for Bianca had turned

271

aside her face. Quita leaned forward, listening to the quiet rustle of her breath. Then, very quietly, the maidservant got up and closed the curtains and tiptoed from the room, and on the great bed Bianca at last slept the sleep of deep peace.

24

On reaching the Magdalena, Kit and Bernardo started downstream with scarcely a pause for rest. Bernardo groaned at the killing pace Kit set at the paddles, but Kit dug in grimly and said nothing. And as they were rowing with the current, they made good speed.

They had assumed from the beginning that it would be necessary to travel overland from the shores of the river to Santa Marta, once they had reached the Caribbean coast, and to that end they had brought a large supply of gold, filched from Don Luis's strongbox. This gold was intended for the purchase of mules and other supplies. For this purpose it was more than sufficient, but to their pleased surprise they discovered that in a boat that drew as little water as their pirogue, it was possible to sail through the green Cienaga up to the very doors of Santa Marta itself.

So it was that on the second day of February 1697, after two long years of imprisonment, they set foot on the streets of their gateway to freedom. Here all things might be brought to a fitting conclusion—escape, vengeance, love.

Love? Kit mused. No, for my love is buried at sea in the *Seawitch*'s smoke and flame. Companionship and affection—many a man has accepted baser and less reasonable counterfeits for love, and these will serve me. These and the fulfillment of the solemn vow I made to Bianca when we last met that I would marry none other while she lives. And if I miss the sweet spring madness of my love for Rouge, this that remains, being less fierce, may prove more durable. . . .

They had come by this time to the house of Francisco

Mendoza, for in Santa Marta they needed only to ask and a dozen leaped to direct them to his house, so greatly was Mendoza loved by the poor and humble he had so often befriended. His manservant, after studying Kit and Bernardo with some care, admitted them without question. Years in Mendoza's service had given him a keen insight into what sort of men the great doctor was willing to receive. These two, with the look of far horizons in their eyes, were the kind he most enjoyed, for he loved to hear the tales of seafaring men.

When they were ushered into his presence, he rose with courtly grace to receive them. His gaze flickered briefly over Bernardo's face and read there the signs of kindred suffering and brotherhood. But when he looked at Kit, a keen professional interest lighted his eyes. This one, he saw at a glance, was deeply troubled.

"Bring wine," he said, turning to his manservant, but Kit refused with a gesture.

"I'm afraid there is scarcely time for civilities. I beg your pardon, honored sir, but the information I seek of you is of great importance. Do you know the whereabouts of the Count del Toro and his lady?"

A little frown creased Mendoza's forehead. Then suddenly it vanished. "Has anyone ever told you," he countered, "that you resemble the Count to an astonishing degree?"

"I asked you a question, sir!" Kit spat.

The physician shrugged. "They are beyond your reach," he said dryly. Then softly, in the tone of a man talking wholly to himself, he added, "Doña Bianca is perhaps beyond any man's reach."

Kit took a step forward, deep concern in his eyes. "What do you mean by that?" he demanded. "She is not dead?"

"No, not dead, nor even dying. But I have no right to tell you these things. To a true physician, a patient's secrets are sacred. Why do you ask? Are you in love with her?"

"Why do you ask me questions," Kit growled, "when you have answered none of mine?"

Mendoza smiled. "Gently, my boy," he said. "You're distraught. I parried your queries only because if harm came to

274

Del Toro or any other grandee through information given by me, my life would not be worth a piaster. I care little for my life, but many lives depend upon it. Sit and have wine, and I will tell you what I can."

Bernardo looked at Kit and nodded emphatically. Kit sighed.

"It seems," he said dryly, "that I have no choice."

Mendoza sipped the red wine the servant had brought and studied the two of them across the table. "Your coming," he said to Kit, "has been most opportune. It enables me to complete a diagnosis. I'm sorry. I can understand your impatience."

"Then for the love of heaven tell me where they are!"

"They have returned to Cartagena. I fear I proved a disappointment to the Count del Toro, for I could do nothing for his lady."

"Is she so ill?" Bernardo asked.

"She is not ill at all," Mendoza said. "Not in any ordinary sense. That's why I tell you this, for it violates no confidence. It isn't a physician she needs—a priest, perhaps. I don't know."

Kit, who at the mention of Cartagena had already got to his feet, stood still, listening.

"There is a confusion in her," Mendoza continued. "In her mind, I could say, but it's not wholly there. It's more of the spirit. What she wants to do she cannot, not because of her husband but because it runs counter to all the teachings of her lifetime. Now she no longer knows what she wants to do—most of all now, I think, she wants to escape, to be troubled no more. While I examined her she spoke once of angels. I fear that the tendency exists in her to take refuge in illusion."

Kit leaned forward, putting both hands on the table. "Are you," he asked, "suggesting that Bianca's mad?"

Mendoza shook his head. "No. Only that she could go mad, if her problem is not solved. There's nothing more hellish than warfare within the soul. But that, I think, is up to you. For as certainly as I sit here, you, young sir, are the root and branch of her trouble! Am I right?"

Slowly Kit nodded. "You are right," he admitted. "And even more right in the thought that I will be the solution of it. My thanks, good physician."

Mendoza took his offered hand. "One thing more," he said gravely. "In your solution, be not hasty or rash, or you'll force her into the very state we wish to avoid."

Kit and Bernardo bowed and took their leave. But Mendoza's final warning weighed heavy on Kit's mind. So troubled was he that he allowed Bernardo to persuade him to delay their departure until the next day. What Bernardo had in mind he did not voice. He hoped that given a whole night in which to ply the oil of persuasion, he might show Kit the wisdom of abandoning the whole thing and returning to Saint-Domingue. That Kit was determined to go back to Cartagena he knew without even having to ask.

Kit sat at a table in the inn, his viands and wine untasted before him. Bernardo looked at him, trying to find an opening to begin his campaign. But Kit did not even look up. Finally, in desperation, Bernardo put out his hand to pluck at Kit's sleeve. It was then that the uproar burst on their ears.

Turning, Kit saw a thin, small individual who might have been the twin of the late Parisian sewer rat hanged at Cartagena by Del Toro, struggling in the grip of the burly innkeeper.

"But of course I have no money!" the little man screeched. "Tomorrow I shall have it—thousands! Name of a name! When I tell the captain general that the French are coming, he will reward me. Just you wait!"

Bernardo leaned forward, excitement moving in his dark eyes. "That accent!" he whispered. "Did you hear it?"

Kit nodded and stood up. Only a Frenchman would speak Spanish with that nasal tone. This would bear investigation.

"The French!" the innkeeper spat. "Pah! Beribboned jackanapes! Let 'em come! That doesn't pay for the good wine you've swilled . . ."

He stopped short, for Kit had touched his arm.

"If you'll permit me," Kit said, "this gentleman is a friend of mine. What's the extent of his bill?"

"Twenty reales," the innkeeper growled.

Smilingly, Kit passed over the money, adding a piece of eight for good measure. The innkeeper's bow after he released the seedy individual was magnificent. Kit took the small man's arm.

276

"Come," he said gently, "my friend and I would like to talk to you."

Flanked by Kit and Bernardo, the little man stumbled out into the night.

"You said," Kit suggested mildly, "something of the French. That interests us greatly. Please go on."

A look of greedy cunning stole into the man's little black eyes. "What's it worth to you?" he whispered.

"Another twenty reales," Kit declared.

The little Frenchman hiccoughed loudly, and the wine-perfumed cloud of his breath made Kit turn aside. "Make it twenty-five, señor," he whined. "I've gone to great trouble."

"All right," Kit growled, "but not one centavo more. Speak your speech!"

Still the little man hesitated. Then with sly, drunken cunning, he extended his hand. Kit dug into his pockets and came out with the gold.

"Well, señor," the man began, "it's like this. I worked for Governor Ducasse—gardener, I was. And last month I got wind of something. Great ship came in from France, and what her captain told the Governor fair set him wild. They're planning an expedition"—his voice dropped into a conspiratorial stage whisper—"against Cartagena, no less! The minute I got wind of it I thought to myself, I did, here's your chance, Pierre! They hadn't treated me fair in Saint-Domingue, señor, that they hadn't."

"Get to the point, man!" Kit snapped. "What proof have you of this?"

"Name of the frigate from France is the *Marin*. Her captain is the Sieur de Saint-Vandrille. And here, señor, is the copy of the orders that Ducasse sent throughout the colony, calling every able-bodied man to arms."

Kit took the printed poster and read it. He passed it to Bernardo without a word.

"That," Pierre whined, "you must give back to me. The captain general will pay me thousands for that, señor, thousands!"

Bernardo, his dark face creased with frowns, passed the notice back to Kit. Kit's hands moved swiftly, contemptuously, and the paper was ripped from top to bottom.

"Señor!" Pierre shrieked.

Kit paid him no heed. Slowly, carefully, he tore the notice into tiny bits and scattered them in the gutter.

"You witless, treacherous, foul little dog!" he said quietly. So softly did he speak that long moments passed before Pierre realized that he had shifted into pure, accentless French, the tongue he had learned at his mother's knee. When the recognition at last struck Pierre, he collapsed into a shivering hulk of abject terror.

"French!" he whispered. "You're French! Oh, holy, blessed Mother of God!"

"A pity," Bernardo growled, shaking his head sternly, "but we'll have to kill him, Kit. He can't run around loose with that knowledge."

Kit nodded grimly and slipped his dagger out of its sheath. The blade glinted blue in the dim light of the lanterns, and the breath caught in Pierre's throat in a wordless gurgle. Then, as though touched by a bolt of lightning, the informer sprang backward and began to run swiftly through the dark streets. Without a word, Kit and Bernardo pounded after him. But fear lent wings to their quarry's feet. Kit and Bernardo were both much larger and heavier men than he, and he was drawing ahead of them with every jump. But as he rounded a corner, he burst almost into the arms of two soldiers of the guardia civil. He sidetracked beautifully and scampered away.

"Stop him!" Kit roared. "Stop that thief!"

At once the soldiers joined the pursuit. In three minutes they realized that they would never catch the swiftly running little man. They halted there in the street and leveled their muskets. The shots echoed through the narrow way, the echoes reverberating back and forth between the close walls of the houses. And little Pierre went over on his face and rolled, kicking up a small cloud of dust. He was dead when the four of them reached him. The men of the guardia civil looked at Kit inquiringly.

"If you will search his pockets," Kit said smoothly, "you will find twenty reales that he picked from my pouch in a tavern."

The soldier knelt and went over the body. After a moment he straightened. In his hand he held the money and some papers. He looked at the papers, holding them high to catch the glow of the lantern, and his face frowned with puzzlement.

"It's not Spanish," he growled.

Instantly Kit crossed to his side. Looking over the soldier's shoulder, he read swiftly.

"It's French," he said slowly. "A permit to leave the colony of Saint-Domingue. You've done well, Captain—apparently our small friend was also a spy."

A glow of triumph showed in the guards' eyes. Such things could mean a promotion. Seeing the look, Kit at once took further advantage of the situation.

"As to the twenty reales," he said, "I think it no more than fair that you and your brave companion keep ten of them as a reward for your trouble."

Wide, white-toothed smiles flashed in the guards' dark faces. They passed the money over to Kit, who counted out ten reales and gave the money to them.

"Adiós, caballeros!" He smiled and saluted them gravely.

"What now, Kit?" Bernardo asked as they walked away.

Kit grinned. "On to Cartagena!" he said.

"To Cartagena!" Bernardo gasped.

"Yes," Kit said, laughing, "with a slight detour by way of Saint-Domingue!"

They returned to their inn, which was much frequented by seamen, and listened carefully for talk of ships and sailing. But they had to linger in Santa Marta for over a week before they learned anything that would be of use to them. Then they heard that a large plate ship had left Cartagena, and would pause briefly at Santa Marta before proceeding to Santo Domingo and from there to Spain.

Santo Domingo, Kit reflected sadly, was on the opposite side of the island from Saint-Domingue, which meant more weary leagues of traveling. Still, so be it; in this he had no choice.

By dint of dropping a coin here and there in the right quarters, they obtained permission to see the captain of the *Santa Isabella,* as the great vessel was called. The captain told them bluntly that he had no right to take aboard paying passengers, but as they seemed likely lads, he would sign them on as seamen, but for the entire voyage—not merely to Santo Domingo.

"Look alive," he growled. "No French leave when we reach the island. I'm damned short of hands. If you must reach Santo Domingo, I'll bring you back from Spain on my next voyage—a little delay, that's all."

A delay, Kit reckoned, that might stretch into a full year or more. But what choice had they? Time was the vital issue. If he and Bernardo could not outwit this thick-skulled don, on their own heads be it. He picked up the pen.

"Agreed," he said with a sigh. "You drive a hard bargain, señor."

But by the time the *Santa Isabella* reached Santo Domingo the captain was occupied with other matters. Kit and Bernardo went about their tasks with seamanlike skill as the great vessel hove to in the harbor, waiting only for the dense tropical night to fall. Unlike the other seamen, they had not even asked for shore leave, which the captain had brusquely denied the others, fearful as he was of having to cross the broad Atlantic with too small a crew to handle the clumsy giant he commanded.

But late in the night watch, Kit and Bernardo went over the side, their pistols, powder, and shot in canvas bags they had tied on top of their heads, and the rest of the gold they had brought from Cartagena in leather sacks fastened to their belts. They swam through the warm water to the shore. Then they hid in the woods during the whole day that the captain searched the city for them.

Don Luis's gold solved everything. It brought them new garments, hats, and boots, and hired them the services of a coasting hoy that took them around the island almost to the borders of the French colony. There they hired a sloop, and beat their way into the harbor of Petit Goave through the greatest assembly of ships of the line their astonished eyes had ever seen in Saint-Domingue.

"Ah, Cartagena!" Kit whispered. "I slipped like a rat into

your streets once. Now shall I loose thunder upon your head, and bury Luis del Toro under a mountain of smoking rubble!"

But Bernardo, who remembered the walls of Cartagena, said nothing. He had seen too many battles. He knew well that the outcome of this venture, like all others, lay in the lap of chance.

25

His Excellency Jean-Baptiste Ducasse, Governor of the colony of Saint-Domingue, was in a thoroughly vile humor. Usually a most temperate man little given to displays of emotion, on this seventeenth day of March 1697 he was having great difficulty controlling himself.

"Name of a dog!" he muttered as he strode up and down. "How much longer do I have to deal with this madman?"

The madman to whom he referred was His Lordship Jean Bernard Louis Desjeans, Baron de Pointis, whose formidable flotilla Ducasse could see from the window of his drawing room. He had first met him thirteen days ago on the Baron's arrival in Saint-Domingue, and every day had only added to his detestation of the man.

In the first place, De Pointis was cursedly secretive. Second, he was amenable neither to suggestion nor to reason. Third, he regarded his authority as being greater than and superseding that of Ducasse himself. Fourth, he was a martinet whose fantastic ideas of discipline had the whole water front in an uproar. The buccaneers loved Ducasse like a father. He jollied them, bullied them, and forgave them most of their minor transgressions, with the result that they had on several occasions, notably at Jamaica in 1694, waded through rivers of blood at his command.

But what had this noble of France, this Baron of the Realm, this stiff, ice-water-blooded aristocrat, done on his arrival? Almost on the first day, his officers, all as aristocratic as he, had arrested one of the bravest of Ducasse's buccaneers on the charges of being drunk and molesting a woman. Name of a name! When were the buccaneers not drunk? And as for the ladies of the water front, what honor did any of them have that needed protecting? Still, the thing had had grave repercussions, for a throng of bearded sea rovers had at once stormed the fort, intent upon releasing their fellow, and those stiff French fools had fired into that mob of roaring-drunk freebooters, killing three. For a time it had looked as though De Pointis would need the guns of his fleet to save his own hide. But for the diplomacy of Ducasse, the expedition would have ended then and there.

The expedition! Ducasse held his aching head between his hands. Damn his eyes to deep-blue hell, but this was a monumental piece of folly! If it were gold they wanted, with such a fleet as lay in the sunlight beneath his window they could sweep the Caribbean clean of the plate ships of Spain. But stubbornly, coldly, insanely, to insist upon attacking Cartagena itself! Mother of God, but they were mad!

If they were wise, they would forget this madman's dream of taking mountains of treasure all at one time. The obvious thing to do was to drive the Spaniards from Santo Domingo and raise the fleur-de-lis over all Hispaniola. Wealth, true wealth, consisted of trade and produce, not this delirium of gold fever in the blood.

A dry cough interrupted the Governor's unhappy reverie. His secretary stood there, waiting respectfully for his attention.

"Well," Ducasse snapped, "well, Paul, what folly is it now?"

A smile of real pleasure stole across Paul's emaciated face. "Madame Golphin awaits your pleasure, your Excellency," he said.

Slowly the Governor relaxed. "As lovely as ever, eh, Paul?"

"More lovely, your Excellency," Paul whispered, "if such a thing is possible."

The frown returned to Ducasse's brow, but this time it was tinged with a quizzical sort of amusement.

"I verily believe," he remarked, "that every man in the colony is in love with her. Yet she has behaved with the utmost circumspection. Though I've had to prevent four duels over her, it's well known that she herself has put a stop to ten. . . . Ah well, show her in, Paul."

A moment later, he was bowing grandly over Rouge's small hand. "You do me too much honor, madame," he murmured.

"Nonsense!" Rouge laughed. "If you were not so everlastingly busy, I'd visit you every day. Everyone knows that you are the most charming man in the colony."

Ducasse groaned. "For such overwhelming flattery," he said dryly, "I shall have to pay a high price. What do you want now, madame?"

Rouge's silvery laughter pealed against the ceiling. "Only to do you a favor," she said gaily. "Let me lead my sea hawks against Cartagena!"

Ducasse took a backward step. "Surely you are jesting," he said at last.

"No. I mean it. You would never believe that it was I who commanded the *Gull*. I want the chance to show you. Besides"—her voice dropped into an icy gravity that made the Governor shiver suddenly—"there is one particular grandee in Cartagena with whom I have an ancient score to settle—aside from the fact that I have no love for Spaniards at any place or at any time."

Ducasse looked down into the small, finely chiseled face with its oddly prominent bone structure over which the snowy skin was stretched tight in most intriguing planes and angles, so that it lacked the usual soft curves of femininity, but made up for this lack with a singular beauty all its own.

"I could use the *Gull*," he mused. "Still, consider what you're saying. If I permit this, you become guilty of treason against your own country. It is in alliance with Spain."

"If," Rouge said softly, "Kit ever returns, I shall become a citizen of Saint-Domingue by marriage, your Excellency. What does it matter if I do so prematurely—by my own hand?"

"What if he returns to the colony during your absence?"

"I'll risk it. Besides, I can easily leave word for him to wait for me here. Come, your Excellency, what do you say?"

Slowly Ducasse shook his massive head. "The answer is still no," he growled. "You're a brave girl, Jane. But I am a man, and though you plainly think me old, I can still value your beauty. I've seen small shot smash a man to bloody pulp. The thought of your being torn by grape or canister, or those lovely limbs of

284

yours being mutilated by chain shot, is an utter horror to me. No, no, I cannot. Do not ask this of me!"

Rouge made him a short, mocking curtsy. "Yet I shall ask it again, your Excellency," she said. "I shall plague you until you give in. Farewell for now. But," she added with a smile, "you may expect me again tomorrow!"

Ducasse took her arm and escorted her through the outer offices to her horse. He stood there a long time watching her ride away before he turned back to his tasks.

"Damn my eyes," he muttered, "haven't I troubles enough?"

He had scarcely taken his seat before his desk and picked up the first of the mountain of letters that awaited his attention when Paul appeared again.

"Blessed blue-eyed pig!" Ducasse groaned. "What is it now?"

"Two gentlemen of the colony beg an audience with your Excellency. At least, they claim that they formerly lived here. But as to that I have my doubts."

Ducasse's mind was far away. Only the last phrase stuck in his thoughts like a burr. "Doubts?" he barked. "Why so, Paul?"

Paul leaned forward, speaking in an intense conspiratorial whisper. "One of them speaks French with a marked Spanish accent!" he said. "I think that these m'sieurs are spies!"

"Then send them in, by all means!" the Governor barked. "Spies, eh?" In his present mood the thought of being able to hang someone filled him with the keenest kind of pleasure. Paul returned, leading the two men.

"Monsieur Giradeaux!" Ducasse boomed. "And Monsieur Díaz! Name of an ancient camel, where have you two been?"

Kit smiled, a slow, quiet smile.

"In the bastion of your enemies, your Excellency," he said, "Cartagena of the Indies."

Ducasse lifted a thick red hand. "You too would mock me, Christophe?" he growled. "Enough and to spare have I had that accursed stone pile dinned into my ears! But I myself have sailed close by its walls. It could not be taken by the combined navies of the world. And you have entered it? Pah!"

"With your permission," Kit murmured, taking off his brocaded coat of somber blue, "I'll give you proof."

285

Ducasse sat there frowning as Kit's slim fingers loosed the buttons of his waistcoat, his silk-and-lace shirt, and his lace cravat. These garments had remained untouched at the inn of the Huguenot woman, jealousy guarded by her throughout his absence. A moment later he stood before the Governor, stripped to the waist. His lean, sun-bronzed upper body rippled all over with long, graceful muscle, but when he turned his back, Ducasse drew in his breath sharply.

"Compliments," Kit said dryly, "of the captain general of the fortress San Lázaro of Cartagena, with an afterthought or two from the guards at the Castillo de Boca Chica itself."

"*Mon Dieu,*" Ducasse whispered, "how you must have suffered!"

"Enough," Bernardo said dryly, "to make us hasten to offer our services to your Excellency the moment we learned of the proposed expedition."

A crafty little gleam stole into Ducasse's small blue eyes. He turned on Paul suddenly. "Please close all doors," he ordered, "and see that we are not disturbed!"

He led them over to a small table by the window and rang for his manservant. When the servant had come, he directed him to bring food and wine. Then he sat down, breathing heavily.

"This affair of the stripes is true, isn't it?" he demanded. "You did get them in Cartagena?"

"Your Excellency knows Cartagena?" Bernardo countered.

"Unfortunately, no," Ducasse growled. "I have passed its walls from the seaward side, that's all. And in this you two can serve me, if you speak the truth. Describe the inside of the bay to me."

"That," Kit said, "is easy. The fortress of Tenaza and the hill of the Popa you can see from the sea itself, and these you probably already know." Ducasse nodded. "But once inside the Boca Chica channel, past the fortress of Boca Chica—or more properly, San Luis de Boca Chica—one comes up the bay past the Terra Bomba, on the port side. A little farther north, to starboard one can see the Isla de Manzanillo, and directly opposite it on the left, the fortress of Santa Cruz. A little south of Santa Cruz lies the artificially blocked entrance to the Boca Grande."

"Enough!" Ducasse exulted. "You've been there! Can you make me a chart of these waters?"

"You have no chart?" Kit said incredulously.

Ducasse frowned heavily.

"There have been many changes since your departure," he said. "Today I have little authority. The Baron de Pointis has a chart—whose accuracy I question—but I am permitted not even one peek at it. I, Jean-Baptiste Ducasse, who know the Caribbean like the palm of my hand, am offered a captaincy in the French Navy! A captaincy merely! While he, the ancient fool, delegates to himself the title of General of the Armies of France by Sea and by Land! Insufferable!"

"You accepted this insult?" Kit growled.

"No. Since then the old fop has learned that nobody can control my buccaneers but me. Now, belatedly, he makes me cocommander in charge of the colonial forces."

"Ah," Bernardo breathed, "that's much better."

Ducasse looked at him. "Can you make me that chart?"

"Yes," Bernardo said. "And I'll warrant that it will be better than any other now existing."

"Good. You'll both stay here tonight, and I'll provide the instruments, inks, and parchments. Deliver the chart to me personally, and to none other."

He picked up a glass of the sack that the servant had brought during the conversation and drank it quickly. Then he looked at Kit, a merry twinkle in his small blue eyes.

"It lies in my power," he said, "to reward you at this moment—and such a reward as you could not dream of. But I talk too much. If I were to tell you of this, seven devils out of hell could not keep you here tonight. So—deliver my chart to me tomorrow and claim your reward."

Kit frowned. "I want no reward now," he said. "Just give me a commission. If my chart is of real value and my services are great enough during the expedition against Cartagena, I'll claim a reward. I mean to settle here, your Excellency. I'll need land on which to build."

"*Diablo!*" Ducasse snorted. "You shall have your commission, and if all goes well, your position here on Saint-Domingue is

287

made. I have a brigantine that needs a captain of your ability, the *Providence*. It's a fast vessel, and you're familiar with brigantines."

"Agreed," Kit said, "if I can make Bernardo first mate."

"Of course," Ducasse said. "Where would you find a better?"

They both stood up and made a leg respectfully in the direction of the Governor, but he stopped them with a wave of his hand.

"In confidence now, lads, tell me," he whispered, "do you think that Cartagena can be taken?"

"Yes," Kit said. "If you don't try to batter your way through the walls. San Luis de Boca Chica is staffed only by a skeleton garrison, and old Don Sancho Jimeno, who commands that fortress, can easily be surprised. Once inside the bay, there are manifold avenues by which the city may be taken."

"Good," Ducasse grunted. "To your tasks, then!"

Early the next morning, Kit and Bernardo again waited on the Governor, and presented him with the completed chart. One glance at it told him that it was excellent. He launched into a profuse speech of thanks, but Kit interrupted him.

"I should like," he said, "to see my new craft. Where does she lie?"

Ducasse stopped short and clapped a broad hand to his forehead. "*Miséricorde!*" he gasped. "To think I had forgotten! Look you, Christophe, there is another matter more pressing than the brigantine that wants your attention. I suggest that you ride up to the old De Ville plantation this very morning. There is something there you must see!"

"Can't it wait?" Kit asked. "I'd prefer to see the *Providence*."

"Damn your eyes!" Ducasse roared. "You ride to De Ville's, Capitaine Giradeaux! And that is an order!"

Kit bowed stiffly.

"As your Excellency commands," he said quietly. Then to Bernardo, "You'll ride with me?"

"Yes," Bernardo said. "This mystery intrigues me."

The De Ville plantation, Kit remembered, had long been deserted. Therefore as he came to the gate, he drew up his horse

288

with some astonishment. For the tangle of wild brush had disappeared, the road had been cleared and surfaced, and the twin lines of palms ran neatly up to the door of the manor, from which all the creeping vines had been cut away. Even from here they could see that the manor gleamed with a new coat of white paint and that the rotting timbers had been replaced. New panes shown in the window frames, and the lawns rolled fresh and green all about it. Not even in its heyday could the De Ville place have been more inviting.

Wonderingly, they passed through the gate and moved at a walk toward the house. The sound of the horses' hoofs must have carried, for just before they reached the door it opened, and a woman came out on the gallery.

Bernardo heard the agonized explosion of Kit's breath leaving his lungs and turning toward his young face, saw that all the color had drained from beneath the tan. Then he too looked toward the veranda. The woman who stood there was dressed all in white. She was swaying like a white orchid on a slim stalk, her hand pressed tight against her throat, and it was only when she began to run wildly toward them that Bernardo realized that her hair was like poinsettia petals, like hibiscus, like flame. Kit half leaped, half fell from the saddle, and took long strides forward.

"Kit!" Rouge called, her voice high, breathless; and the next instant she had hurled herself into his arms. Kit hung there, holding her, staring above the flame-red crown of her small head, feeling on his tongue and his lips like wormwood and gall the words he had uttered to Bianca: "Upon my mother's grave I swear never to wed another while you live."

Quietly he released Rouge and stood back, seeing that her beauty had in no way diminished, that indeed it had matured into a mind-stunning loveliness, and a sound caught in his throat that was halfway between a curse and a sob.

"I was a fool," Rouge whispered. "It was you—always and forever it was you I loved, though in my heart I denied it. But now I have found you and I will never leave you again—never as long as I live!"

Kit stared down at her, feeling his tongue curling and thickening in his mouth as it shaped the words he must say, the words he hated to say more than any others he had spoken in all his life.

"I—I found you too late, Rouge," he whispered. "I thought you were dead and I have promised another."

All the color drained out of Rouge's face suddenly, leaving it ghost-white. Then the glow of crimson flowed back suddenly, in small tidal waves of rage.

"Where is she?" she demanded, her voice high and breathless.

"In Cartagena," Kit said sadly, "and I have given my most solemn oath to come back to her."

"I see," Rouge whispered. Her eyes were star emeralds suddenly, jewel-bright with tears. "But there is nothing in this vow of yours, is there, Kit, which forbids you to kiss me—now?"

Kit bent down and found her mouth. It was warm and salt with the taste of tears. She drew back softly and stood there looking at him. So, Bernardo thought with bitter clarity, does a dying man look at the food and drink that could save his life. But Rouge was speaking again.

"Come up to the house," she said, "and tell me of this thing. I'm trying to understand, but I cannot. Yet I must! I must!"

Her slim white arm stole out and encircled his waist, and the three of them mounted the steps to the house. Kit told his tale, omitting nothing. He began with the kidnapping of Bianca at Cul-de-Sac, and admitted freely that she had made him waver in his devotion to Rouge. As the sorry story unfolded, Bernardo thought he could discern a gathering paleness on Rouge's face. At the end she rose and stood looking at Kit.

"You will stay," she said, "both of you, for dinner. I must go and change now. Afterward perhaps we can straighten out this hellish confusion."

When she had gone, neither Kit nor Bernardo said a word. Bernardo drew out two long clay pipes, and after filling them passed one to Kit. They sat very still in the darkness, sending up fragrant smoke.

Afterward, neither of them knew who first heard that sound in the darkness, because they both looked up at the same instant. Rouge stood there in a gown that was like dawn mist and moonlight. It fell in clouds of misty whiteness, curling out in a great bell shape below her tiny waist, and her bare shoulders above the tight-laced bodice glowed pink-white and soft.

Kit sat like one frozen, holding the pipe in his hand; then he stood up, and the same instant her mouth was upon his, burning away his senses like all the fevers of the world. He did not know at what point Bernardo left them, but when at last, breathless, he drew away his mouth, they were alone. Rouge looked up at him, her emerald eyes dancing in her white face beneath the high-piled, smoothly coiled coiffure of her bright-red hair.

"You would leave me for another woman?" she whispered. "Can you, even if you would?"

Kit looked at her, and his eyes were naked with pain. "No," he admitted harshly. "I cannot, even though I break my most sacred oath, and become a man without honor, entirely damned!"

The sea-green blaze softened and darkened, and a look of tenderness spread over her small, strangely Oriental face.

"Which you gave unwittingly, not knowing that I lived," she said. "Let me go to her, Kit. Let me explain how it is with us. If she is a woman of honor, she will release you."

Kit searched her face with grave eyes. "And if she doesn't?"

"Then I'll set you free of her," Rouge said fiercely. "And she'll trouble you no more—you or any other man! The *Gull* is anchored in this harbor and I have men to sail her."

"Rogue!"

"I'll follow you to Cartagena, if I must. I'm still a ship captain, though I am a woman more." Suddenly, tenderly, Rouge stretched out her arms to him. "Forgive me, Kit," she whispered. "I am still more sea hawk than woman. Take me in your arms, and teach me to be gentle."

But Kit's fingers, inside the pocket of his greatcoat, fastened themselves around the single shred of gold cloth that was all that remained of the Heron Banner. Bianca, poor lost Bianca, haunted perhaps with dreams and visions of illusion, must be attended to; and also, finally, the matter of Luis del Toro. Only then would he be free.

"No," he growled, "there will be years of time for such lessons, and now there are matters that cannot wait."

Rouge moved toward him. The moonlight touched her bare shoulders. The air was heavy with the perfume of tropical flowers, barbaric scents, rich with an opium-drugged compulsion. She took another step and her lips, soft-sighing, parting, blurring out of focus from too much nearness, drew out the last particle of clarity from his senses even before they touched his own. When she spoke her voice was husky, the words moving quietly through the scented rustle of her breathing.

"Will not tomorrow do?" she whispered. "Will not the matter wait?"

26

DURING THE MORNING of March 20, 1697, while the great French fleet slipped out of the harbor of Petit Goave and headed westward toward Cartagena, Rouge was striding up and down the confines of her bedroom. Here of late more and more she found herself giving way to the hateful feminine weakness of tears. Never before in all her life had she been more troubled. She who had always taken matters in her own hands must wait here in this silent house, like Penelope spinning dreams of a lover who might never come back to her.

This would never do! If anything were true under the face of heaven it was that happiness belonged to those who grasped it with both hands. She could not wait here and hope that Kit would not be killed. She could not pace this floor and wish that Bianca would free him of his vow. Would she, if the situation reversed itself, release him? Would any woman who could have Kit Gerado give him up?

To Rouge there was only one answer. Already she was slipping the filmy nightdress over her head and racing for her sea chest. Before she reached it, she passed a full-length mirror illuminated by two candles. She stood still and gazed at herself, passing her hands down over her body, so slim and soft-curving that in the flickering glow of the candles it seemed the suggestion rather than the statement of womanhood. The terrifying thought struck her that perhaps Bianca was prettier than she, heavier, more voluptuously curved. And this, perhaps, Kit had already discovered for himself.

Whirling from the mirror, she tore open the sea chest and drew on her pantaloons and shirt. Whatever the comparison between her and her unknown rival, the matter must be put to the test immediately. She raced down the stairs, calling to her buccaneers as she ran. Here in Saint-Domingue she had kept them near her as house servants and bodyguards. And as they could freely consort with the women of the town, they had been docile.

Two hours later, the *Gull* stood out to sea on the freshening tide.

Kit stood on the poop of the *Providence* as the flotilla moved westward across the Caribbean. Bernardo was at his place on the quarter-deck. Knowing Bernardo's skill and seamanship, Kit trusted him to take command most of the time. From where he stood, Kit could see the great, beautiful ships of the line curving seaward before a freshening breeze: the *Sceptre*, the *Saint-Louis*, the *Vermandois*, the *Apollyon*, the *Furieux*, the *Saint-Michel*, great winged men-of-war these, none of them bearing less than sixty guns, or having a complement of fewer than three hundred and fifty men.

Behind them, with reef points taken to avoid outrunning the slower capital ships, moved the frigates *Mutine*, *Avenant*, *Marin*, and *Christ*. The *Christ* had been taken as a prize from the Spaniards, who had named this great forty-four-gun frigate, bearing two hundred and twenty sailors and men-at-arms, for the gentle Nazarene with no thought of either incongruity or irreverence. Among the other frigates, only the *Mutine* exceeded her in size, number of cannon, and complement.

After these straggled a motley flotilla of smaller craft, led by the bomb ketch *Eclatant*, which looked for all the world like a ship that had accidentally lost her foremast in a storm, for her towering square-rigged mainmast and her low lateen-rigged mizzen were set so far back that more than half the vessel did not lie beneath any sail at all. There was a reason for this, Kit knew. The tremendous mortar that was her sole armament was bedded in the great timbers of her foredeck. And as its great bombshell was hurled almost straight upward to crash down upon the walls and towers of a besieged city, a foremast would have been in the way. Still, the bomb ketch was a very ugly vessel, and awkward to handle. Kit had to keep the trim little brigantine *Providence,* which had less than half the displacement of his beloved *Seaflower,* under all reefs to stay in place behind the *Eclatant.*

The rest of the rear-guard flotilla was made up of two smaller flyboats, four traversiers (the small boats used in communication between the larger vessels of a fleet), and the fat-hulled *Drépoise,* the bearer of munitions and supplies.

The fact that he was taking part in one of the greatest naval expeditions of all time troubled Kit not at all. His mind was occupied by other and, to him, not less momentous matters. He was going back to Cartagena. Back to carry the city by fire and sword, level its fortresses, sack its houses. Earlier his thoughts would have been troubled by the visions of bloodshed, wholesale looting, murder, and ravishment that he was helping to let loose upon a peaceful people.

But any tendency toward mercy was checked by his memories of Cartagena itself: the people bellowing with joy in the streets as the dark silhouettes of his crew swung black against the sun from the towering gallows; the gleeful cries that had greeted every blow that landed on the helpless black gunner; and most of all the fiendish near-ecstasy of the populace at the sight of Smithers standing at the stake amid the devouring flames.

Beside him, Bernardo still limped. For this, thank Cartagena. Upon his own broad back not one inch of flesh was unscarred by the biting oxhide lashes. Yes, Cartagena! In Cartagena were lost years of his life. In Cartagena was the tender father who had begotten Kit in drunken lust and had then cast off the sweet, high-minded girl who had surrendered to him because she loved him too much to deny him anything. This was the father who had spurned the child of her love like a homeless cur, striped her across the face with a riding whip, and surrendered her to the torturers! In Cartagena was the man who had taken a gentle woman whom Kit had once loved—the man who with a brave show of kindness had spared him from the noose only to turn him over to the stone quarries, the walls of San Lázaro, and the never-resting whips of the Spanish guards.

In Cartagena. Yes, in Cartagena! Bernardo, who could read Kit's expression, held out his hand.

"Easy, Kit," he said. "Too much thinking beforehand addles the pate. When the time has come, all things will be made right. Who knows? In the battle itself Don Luis may be killed, and so . . ."

He halted suddenly, staring at Kit. The great golden mane was thrown far back, and the hard young face was lifted skyward. Kit bent both arms at the elbow and clenched both fists with almost voluptuous slowness. His head rolled on the column of his neck, and his voice came out low and flat and calm, so that its very lack of emphasis made Bernardo feel cold all over, as though he had been plunged into a bath of brine and ice.

"With these two hands, Bernardo!" Kit said. "With these two hands!"

"No, Kit," Bernardo said sorrowfully. "Don't hold murder in your heart. It will destroy you. I would not have your hands stained with the blood of parricide. I love you too well to have your soul damned in hell."

"He has injured you greatly, too," Kit snarled. "Do you forgive him?"

Bernardo looked away, his dark eyes calm and grave as they swept the surface of the sea. "I have forgiven him," he said. "Now in my old age I have forsworn greed, envy, and revenge." He smiled wryly. "All my former luxuries, for which I once lived."

The fleet swept majestically onward across the blue Caribbean. No enemy vessel opposed them. If any ship of Holland, England, or Spain sighted them, she at once cracked on all canvas and bore away at her best speed. On April 13 they sighted the mainland some four leagues eastward of Cartagena, between that city and Point Hicacos. Then the squadron reassembled at Sambee.

Kit knew it was foolish to try to batter down the thick walls opposite the Tenaza or the Santo Domingo section, but he suspected that such a man as De Pointis might attempt even this madness. What actually happened surprised even him, for the mighty eighty-four guns of the *Sceptre* roared out a challenge, and almost before the echoes of the broadside had died away, her longboats were over the side, racing for the walls.

Beneath the walls, the surf boiled white, and the first of the boats capsized at once. The others were lingering long enough to draw the half-drowned soldiers from the shallow surf when a signal gun from the *Sceptre* recalled them. Even so, it was a miracle that all six of the longboats reached the side of the great ship without being overturned. The *Sceptre* drew them aboard and stood southward toward the Boca Chica channel.

She veered seaward, firing as she passed, but her shots fell short, raising white geysers in the shallow water. Now the frigates *Saint-Louis* and *Fort* tacked in, and opened with all their port guns. Kit could see the clouds of dust rising from the walls where the thirty-eight-pounders smashed, but after they had passed there was no apparent damage. Momentarily, the *Fort* was aground, but by setting even her stuns'les she drew off. The *Saint-Louis* herself scraped bottom.

But the shallow-draft *Providence* could navigate in a heavy dew, so Kit rode her in and hurled his heavy mortar shells over the walls and into the city itself. It was only this last attack that forced the guns in the Tenaza fortress to bellow out their brazen answer; then the peremptory signal flags on the *Sceptre*'s masthead ordered Kit out again.

They had lain overnight at Sambee, and the whole day of the fourteenth of April was spent in desultory bombardment of the walls; but at high noon of the fifteenth all the ships dropped anchor in a vast semicircle ranging two miles out to sea and lying across the entrance of the Boca Chica channel. The frigate *Marin* pushed her prow into the channel itself, and lay there at anchor at its narrowest point, so that any Spanish vessel which attempted to escape would have had the instant attention of all her guns, which in turn would have brought down upon the Spaniards the whole French armada.

Toward nightfall, Kit saw through the glass a row of chaloupes, landing boats, putting out from the *Furieux*. Of these, only one was occupied by officers of the fleet, the rest being manned by Negro sappers. Kit saw Ducasse's imposing figure among the officers, and behind him Pally, who commanded the Negroes. Among the other officers was Beaumont, who commanded the Saint-Domingue brigade. Kit put down his glass with an oath. De Pointis, then, was only too willing to sacrifice the most gallant men of Saint-Domingue to make the first breach, keeping his perfumed fops from the court of Versailles entirely safe.

But when he lifted the glass again he saw among the officers the young Chevalier de Pointis, the nephew of the commander. This young aristocrat, Kit had suspected from the one or two occasions he had seen him before the fleet left Petit Goave, was a real man. Kit laid down the spyglass and called Bernardo to his side.

"You're in command now," he said. "I'm joining the attack."

"Kit," Bernardo began, but Kit lifted a warning hand.

"That is a command, Bernardo," he said quietly, "not a matter for discussion."

Bernardo saluted the young captain gravely, bleak misery in his eyes. Watching Kit go ashore without him was a chilling experience. How many years had he fought and suffered at the side of this great golden sea hawk? He shook his head sadly. Such thoughts had best not be dwelt upon.

As he slipped over the side into the longboat, Kit thought suddenly and with painful clarity of Rouge. The attack was going to be dangerous, almost suicidally so. For all the hideous confusion of his life, Kit did not want to die. Not with Rouge to come back to. . . . Bianca would release him. She must release him. And with his mother's death finally avenged and Ducasse's promised reward, all might be joy and peace.

During the night before the landing, eighty Negroes had hacked their way entirely across the narrow neck of the peninsula, so that Ducasse was able to station sentries at intervals a few yards apart from the shores of the ocean to the shores of the bay, thus effectively cutting off San Luis de Boca Chica from any aid that might reach it. Kit accompanied young De Pointis across the freshly hacked trail until the two of them reached the camp the Negroes were making on the other side, around a bend just above the fort.

Walking up to a soldier, Kit requested the loan of a musket. Somewhat nonplused, the soldier passed it over. Kit was richly dressed, and the soldiers were accustomed to the whims of these gentlemen of France. Then very quietly Kit moved out of the camp. In all his finery, he went down on his belly in the mud and crept to within firing distance of the walls. He heard a slight rustle behind him and whirled, his dagger already out. The Chevalier de Pointis lay there behind him, his rich dress as mud-befouled as Kit's own, a grin on his handsome young face. However much of a stiff-necked old fool his uncle, the commander, may be, Kit decided, young de Pointis is indeed a man. . . .

Kit smiled back at him and the two of them looked up at the towering walls, coming clear in the breaking dawn. They could see the soldiers scurrying about, but Kit waited until the heavy, pompous figure of the captain of the guard, the same man who had given him the Indian treatment, appeared. Then the musket leaped to his shoulder and fired all at the same instant, without his even seeming to have taken aim. The captain of the guard reeled, and collapsed into the arms of one of the soldiers.

The whole wall exploded into fire, all of it aimed badly, showing plainly that the guards had not the slightest idea of the direction from which the shot had come. Then, almost as in answer, from the sea the hoarse booming of great guns rolled in. The *Saint-Louis* had opened up on the fortress, followed by the *Fort*. Half a minute later, the whole world reeled with bass thunder. The *Sceptre,* they both knew, had loosed a broadside.

They lay there in the mud and laughed aloud, their voices hidden by the thunder of the guns. They pounded each other on the back with muddy paws and roared.

Now it had begun. Now it had really begun.

27

By April 28, everyone in Cartagena realized that the city was doomed. San Luis de Boca Chica, the channel fortress that they had depended upon to keep the French out of the landlocked bay, had fallen with ludicrous ease. It had withstood only one day of pounding from the great ships of the line, then a wild attack from the landward side had overwhelmed it. It was scant comfort to them to learn that old Sancho Jimeno had fought like ten demons, so much so that De Pointis had given him back his sword and released him with honor and ceremony.

Even the early hope that had sustained them, of differences between the French regulars and the buccaneers, had proved of little account. True, De Pointis had driven the pirates back into the attack on the fortress with the flat of his sword when they had fled the battle. True, he had tied one filibuster to the stake and brought up the firing squad before the freebooters could be whipped into line. But somehow, somewhere, they had regained their courage, and crossing the bay, had swarmed over the lightly held hill Popa like a legion of fiends.

San Lázaro had fallen to a joint attack of buccaneers and regulars, and in this battle a wounded Spaniard had told of seeing in the forefront of the attack the blond young devil who had been held a prisoner at San Lázaro while he himself was a guard there. Everyone knew that this man, who was in some strange way linked to the Count del Toro, president of the Audencia, had perished during a later imprisonment out at the Boca Chica.

But had he? As the battle wore on, reports of his having been seen, always in the forefront of the fight, grew in frequency

300

until at last they could no longer be denied. And now, with the great guns of La Motte Michel, commander of the Royal Battery, in plain sight across the narrow channel from the Getsémani suburb, thousands of the citizens could make out the tawny gold of his hair among the darker heads of his comrades. Of course several other of the Frenchmen were blond, but once a glass was leveled, there was no mistaking that face. He had been seen by too many of the crowd as he was being led away from that spectacular trial.

Now Coetlogon too had set up his lighter battery of twelve- and eighteen-pounders, for so close to the city had the Frenchmen come that even these light pieces were in range. Between the two batteries, the nine great mortars of De la Motte d'Hérans were rumbling, and Gombaud played his smaller high-trajectory pieces with exquisite precision. In the bay the bomb ketch spoke now and again with its brazen throat, and all the ships of the line stood behind it and hammered the walled city to pieces.

Much of the city was afire, making an evilly beautiful sight in the darkness, the gigantic flames blotting out the stars. From the walls the defending cannon split the night with their thunder. All the air was loud with the shrieks of the dying. That the city did not burn entirely to ashes was due to the circumstance that blew a blinding rainstorm up from the sea on the night of the twenty-ninth. During this, in the howling winds many of the citizens managed to escape the city in the darkness. While the French sentries huddled miserably under improvised shelters, their campfires drowned out by the rain, hundreds of Spaniards stole by them in the inky, rain-whipped night. Past the lines, they wound upward into the hills, and here most of the refugees drowned in the flash floods that turned mountain freshets into roaring cataracts.

On the morning of the thirtieth of April, several things happened. First of all, the brigantine *Providence* had ranged too close to the walls at Getsémani, and had been sunk by the guns of the city. As was not uncommon among sailors of that day, indeed of almost any day, most of her crew could not swim and perished with their vessel. Bernardo made a brave effort to keep the captain of the marines above water, but a sharp-shooter put a ball through the old captain's head as they struggled in the water. Bernardo prudently dived, and swimming a long distance underwater, managed to gain the shore near the San Lázaro hospital.

Even as he drew himself ashore, wet and shivering, he saw Kit run out, fully exposed to the fire from the city, to hurl a hand bomb into a pirogue laden with explosives that the Spaniards were attempting to push under the bridge that connected the San Lázaro section with Getsémani. It blew up with a sound like the end of the world, and Bernardo was hurled several yards through the air to land almost at Kit's feet. Kit caught him by his long silver-threaded black hair, dragged him unceremoniously up the beach with musket balls kicking up the sand all around them, and tumbled with him into a sheltering trench.

Kit grinned at him, and took his place among a group of wild young chevaliers who were grouping to lead the attack. In these aristocratic young Frenchmen Kit had found a reckless courage that passed well over the border line of foolhardiness. And they, in turn, had adopted him as one of themselves. After the battle, they promised him gleefully, he should have a château near Versailles, all the money in the world, a title, and the prettiest woman in France for a wife, if their word with the King meant anything. Kit, who had his doubts, merely grinned at them, and took his place in line.

And now with Lévy, the bravest of all their commanders, at their head, they raced over the bridge toward the gates the heavy guns had pounded to pieces. But at the gates the Spaniards waited and loosed upon them the most withering musket fire they had yet encountered. Kit saw Marolles and Du Roullon go down, shot almost to pieces. Fouilleuse lay with splinters of bone protruding through his broken leg, and Montosier and Vanjoux had so many gunshot wounds that it was a wonder they lived.

Kit knew that without help in another moment they would all lie dead at the mouth of these broken gates, but in that instant Lévy had rallied the remainder of his forces and surged back to the fray. The Spanish fought back fiercely. Lévy got a

302

musket ball through his neck, Frankin, his aide-de-camp, had his right arm broken, but they both continued to charge until they were carried off fainting from their wounds.

It was at this juncture that Kit saw Bernardo storming to his aid in a company of buccaneers, led by no less than Ducasse himself. Ducasse had been wounded in the attack on the Boca Chica, but he limped along firing his pistols and swinging his saber with fierce energy.

Still the Spaniards held, giving ground inch by bloody inch. Kit and young De Pointis fought side by side, for during the battle they had become as brothers. But above the noise of battle there rose a war cry that sounded like the shrieking of tortured souls in hell, and looking up, Kit and De Pointis saw Pally charging across the bridge at the head of his Negroes.

The blacks charged full into the musket fire, went down in rows, yet continued to charge over the bodies of their dead, so that the Spaniards had no chance to reload. At last the weary, heroic men broke, and the shrieking blacks pursued them through the narrow streets. Now the buccaneers of Ducasse joined the chase and Kit and young De Pointis were swept along with them, until they all piled up in wild confusion before the place where the Governor of the new Granada section had closed the doors between Cartagena and Getsémani in the face of his soldiers.

There was nothing for the Spaniards to do but to charge and die or to stand and be butchered. The Spaniards, being men of pride, charged. For eight terrible minutes they hurled back an attacking force of twenty times their numbers. Then they were overwhelmed and massacred.

Looking up at the white flags that at long last fluttered from the walls of the city, Kit could scarcely discern them through the scalding rain of his tears. For in his arms lay the body of the fair young Chevalier de Pointis, who had been shot through the heart at the last instant before the surrender.

28

THE GREAT GATES remained closed, however. When Kit saw
two emissaries marching out under flags of truce to negotiate
with the Baron de Pointis, who lay wounded on his litter, he
decided not to wait any longer. The old general had not been
advised of the death of his beloved nephew, and Kit felt moved
with sympathy for him. Despot he might be, martinet and
extreme disciplinarian, but after the first day of the attack there
was no longer any question of his courage.

So, stumbling with weariness, sooted all over with gun smoke,
through which his tears had left white streaks, Kit started toward
Cartagena. It was here that Bernardo joined him. It was rapidly
growing dark, and inside the city the renewed fires bloodied the
skies with their glow. Slowly the two men circled the near-by
walls looking for an opening. They had little difficulty in finding
one, for there were places in the walls now where the great
mortars had tumbled the stones down in avalanches of rubble,
and over one of these Kit and Bernardo found it possible to
climb with the easy motion of men mounting a low hill. Inside,
the weary, blood-streaked, begrimed guards stared at them in
astonishment, but made no move to impede their progress. Some
of the soldiers, realizing the extent of their city's defeat, even
saluted them.

It was easier still to find the house of Del Toro in the darkness, for almost the entire street on which it stood was aflame.
Kit noted quickly that neither of the two houses that flanked it
was yet burning, but if the wind held, it was only a matter of
time before that entire section would lie in ashes.

They crept close to the house, their footfalls drowned in the

304

crackling roar of the fires and the crash of falling timbers. Where the barred window had been was now only a great jagged hole, and inside much of the splendid furniture had been smashed to kindling by the shot that had torn through.

But when they rose from their crouching positions, their quarry lay before them, for there on the one unbroken chair in the room they looked into sat Luis del Toro, his proud head sunk on his great chest, his whole aspect so eloquent of defeat and despair that even Kit felt a momentary surge of pity move within his heart. Though I have sworn to kill him, he thought, if there is any way—any honorable way—to spare his life, I will spare him. . . . He leaned forward, peering intently at the suddenly aged man who sat amid the ruins of his former grandeur at his banquet table—alone.

Don Luis sprang up at once, pistol in hand, and started toward the window; but he halted suddenly, for Kit had swung himself through it, his own hands resting on his undrawn-pistol butts.

"So we meet again, my esteemed father," he said quietly, "and for the last time."

Don Luis stood there, his own pistol lowered, a look of sad weariness on his dark face.

"So you know," he said at last.

"Yes," Kit whispered, "I know. Do you expect me to make a show of devotion? Raise your pistol, my father!"

Don Luis's shoulders stiffened, a slow, mocking smile curling the corners of his mouth.

"Is not this earth big enough for you and me, my son?" he said. "Go your way, for I do not want to kill you."

"Raise your gun, O begetter of bastards! Though I don't like to kill you in cold blood, I will if I have to."

"You are chivalrous," Don Luis said coldly. "And since it is forced upon me, I will take back the life I gave. But not with gunfire—that's no weapon for gentlemen. Besides, I have no skill with a pistol. You would have our encounter fair, would you not?"

Bernardo, who had crawled through the window, stood beside Kit, rubbing his numbed arm.

"Have done with the frippery," he growled.

305

"A moment," Kit said lightly. He took the two great pistols from his belt and laid them upon the table. Slowly, while Bernardo watched him narrowly, Don Luis did likewise.

"Take your choice, then," Kit smiled. "What say you, my lord? Sabers? Cutlasses? Rapiers?"

"Rapiers," Don Luis said softly, a slow, exultant smile on his face.

"No!" Bernardo roared. "By my masculinity, no! You are a good swordsman, Kit—but he is a past master."

Don Luis bowed with mocking civility.

"I will entertain any suggestion," he said quietly.

Kit's brow creased with frowning. Then suddenly light leaped and flamed in his blue eyes.

"My lord has lived in Seville and Cádiz, has he not?"

"Yes," said Don Luis. "What has that to do with this quarrel?"

"Then my lord has seen the gypsies fight. So will I fight with you, Luis del Toro—gitano-fashion!"

Bernardo could see Don Luis paling beneath his tan. With a lightninglike motion, Bernardo's hand swept down and came out with his dagger. He flipped it end over end so that it stood and quivered in the polished wood of the table. Kit did likewise with his own. The two were mates: Bernardo had purchased them at the same time, sheaths and all, in a bazaar of Algiers.

"Take your choice, my lord," Kit said softly.

Without even looking at the weapons, Don Luis stretched out his hand and picked up one of them. Its fourteen inches of glittering steel glinted evilly in the light of the candle. Kit walked calmly to the table and took the other.

"There remains yet a formality," he said. "Or have you forgotten?"

"No," Don Luis growled, "I have not forgotten."

Kit leaped up on the table, snatching two tapestries from the walls. One of these he wound about his left forearm, so that it made a protective bulge. The other he passed to his father. Slowly Don Luis followed his son's example.

Kit's eyes darted about the room until they fell on the great rope that pulled the bell which summoned the servants. One slash with the dagger and it fell. Kit knotted one end of it tightly about his left wrist. He played out a scant yard of the rope, and cut it off there. Then he held out the other end to Del Toro.

"This is madness!" Don Luis growled.

"Are you afraid, my father?" Kit said.

Angrily Don Luis picked up the rope and bound his own left wrist. Thus linked, they stood and faced each other.

"Now," Kit said, softly, almost peacefully, "now we can begin!"

The daggers flashed through the air and cut great rents in the heavy tapestries as the two men used them to screen their straining bodies. But at a yard's distance, it was impossible not to draw blood. There among the gutting tapers they moved silently except for hoarse grunts, locked in that strange dance of death, their leaps and capers gigantically magnified in grotesquely moving shadows on the walls.

This duel of the long knives was a thing of beauty, all grace and agility, thrust and parry, the furious stab caught harmlessly in the folds of the tapestry, the body hurled back to the limits of the rope's length to avoid the counterthrust, while blood and sweat mingled in glistening rivers on their faces.

A chair crashed over and was kicked aside. Don Luis's knife found the flesh of Kit's shoulder and sank in. Kit wrenched free, his silk shirt dyed crimson with his blood. Don Luis's cheek was gashed open from ear to jaw, and from the point of his Vandyke scarlet drops fell.

But no word escaped them, no cry, no groan. They halted briefly, breathing heavily like wounded beasts at bay, and started in again, each of them cut or gashed or stabbed in a dozen places. How it might have ended Bernardo could not tell, for Kit's lithe agility was made up for by Don Luis's gigantic strength. This one thing Bernardo swore in his heart—in one more minute his own pistol would decide the issue.

He took it out and cocked it, the loud click drowned out by the noise of the ferocious struggle. But it was in that instant that the cry came hanging high and shrill upon the air.

"Stop!" it rang. "Stop it, both of you, for the love of God!"

The two men halted, their fingers gripped on the hilts of the daggers, the great boles of their chests rising and falling with their labored breathing. Slowly their bloody, terrible heads came around, and there on the stairway they saw Bianca swaying, her lovely young face as white as death.

"I will not have it!" she stormed. "Do you think I find honor in being fought over like a scrap of flesh between two savage dogs? Know you, Luis, and you, Kit, that from this hour neither of you has in me an excuse for murder! For, as God lives, and upon the honor of His blessed Mother, I will go this night to the Sisterhood of Nuestra Señora de Cartagena—and over me, at least, there shall be no further bloodshed!"

She drew herself up until even her small figure seemed regal, and her voice came out high, clear, and marvelously controlled.

"Put down those knives!"

Slowly the tight-clasped knuckles loosened and both bloody weapons clattered to the floor. Bianca came down the stairs, step by slow step. But before she reached them she halted suddenly, her dark eyes enormous in her white face, staring past them, past even Bernardo, toward the window. Slowly Bernardo turned to follow her gaze, then his mouth dropped open, for there on the sill Rouge sat, her long, naked legs swinging shamelessly back and forth, her green eyes filled with savage joy, and two great pistols leveled in her hands.

"Your weapon, good Bernardo," she said evenly. "Drop it to the floor."

For all its calmness, there was no mistaking that tone. Bernardo let his pistol slide from his nerveless fingers. Rouge stared at Bianca, seeing her slim, lovely body, little hid by the filmy stuff of her gown, seeing her face, small, soft, heartbreakingly lovely, its whiteness startling in juxtaposition to the matchless, marvelous, vulture-feathered blackness of her long, deep-curling hair.

"I thank you for your vow," Rouge said. "It has saved your life. You're lovely, more lovely than I imagined. . . . But enough of this, for already the entire upper story of this house is afire, and we have little time."

As though to emphasize her words, the crackling roar of the fire sounded clearly above their heads and a tongue of flame leaped down the stairway so that it touched one of the heavy tapestries, which blazed up instantly like a pine torch. The three men surged forward at once, but Rouge's clear voice halted them.

"Not so fast!" she called. "There is still one small matter. I see, Don Luis, that you too recall my face. Good! Then I do not have to waste time in pretty speeches." She leveled the pistols at Don Luis's heart.

It was at that moment that Bernardo sprang at her, catching her wrists so that her arms were thrown upward, the two pistol balls plowing into the ceiling, making two heavy, downward-crashing showers of plaster. Afterward, he was at a loss to account for his action, except to say that there was something in Bianca's face that moved him—something not of this world, a reflection of an inward illumination passing all human understanding. It left no hatred in Bernardo's heart, not for Del Toro or for any other man or anything upon this earth save only of hatred itself.

The room was filled with acrid smoke now, through which they moved like dream figures, their struggles strangely diminished both in intensity and in importance. But Rouge twisted like a tigress in Bernardo's grip, her face contorted with rage. Forgetting the cord that held him bound to his father, Kit sprang forward to help subdue her. The bell cord brought him up short, and he turned. Don Luis was kneeling on the floor, his hand holding the dagger he had again picked up. He came up slowly, his intent masked by the murky smoke that half-hid his dark face. Then his arm moved and the bell cord parted. He stood facing Kit.

"All our lives," he said gently, "we have been so bound together, my son. My error lay in not drawing in upon the cord that bound you to me. Can you not forgive a man grown old and destroyed by his own pride?"

Kit stood there wavering, a fierce battle raging in his heart. He remembered his mother's face, cut open to the bone by this man's lash; he remembered Smithers amid the flames, and the small Parisian's agony as the noose strangled him to death; he remembered the walls of San Lázaro and the oxhide whips of the guards—yet in the end he was half putting out his hand when Bianca interrupted them.

"Farewell, my lords," she said quietly. "I must go now, for

they are calling me." Then she turned and walked toward the flaming stairs.

"They?" Don Luis gasped. "Who on earth are they?"

"No one—on earth, my lord," Bianca said serenely, and turning, dashed up the fire-swept stairway. Don Luis was half a step behind her, and Kit upon his heels, but so great was the smoke and flame in the upper hall that it was impossible to see into which of the rooms she had gone.

"You take the right," Kit choked. "I'll take the left!"

The two men separated and disappeared into the smoke-filled, flame-swept rooms. Below them, Rouge had stopped struggling.

"Let me go, Bernardo," she said, weeping. "Let me go, for the love of God!"

"That you may go after him?" Bernardo growled, his own face ashen. "Never!"

"If he dies," Rouge whispered, "if for her sake he perishes, Bernardo, not one hour will I survive him!"

As if in answer to her words, they saw Kit, sooted all over, coming down the stairs with the still figure of Bianca in his arms.

"Dead?" Bernardo said.

"No," Kit croaked. "Take her, Rouge, and attend to her hurts." He looked about the room. "Don Luis has not come down?"

At Bernardo's quick, negative shake of the head, Kit whirled and started back up the stairs.

"Kit," Rouge shrieked, "do not go! Don't risk your life for *him!*"

Kit half-turned, and his eyes were blue glacier ice.

"You have my love," he said quietly. "Do not make me regret it!" Then he raced into the sea of flame. Bernardo surged up after him, and Rouge followed Bernardo. This time there was no difficulty in finding Don Luis, for his low, hoarse-voiced cries of agony guided them to the spot. Muffling his face with his arm, Kit plunged into the room, but when he was close Don Luis called out to him:

"Go back, my son. Go back, my tall son, for I am finished."

He lay on his back. Across his chest, pressing him down, was a fallen beam of quebracho wood, weighing hundreds of pounds and smoldering sullenly. Every bone in his upper trunk was crushed, and yet he lived. Kit took his arm and tugged fiercely, knowing as he did so that it was useless.

"My son," Don Luis whispered, "my son, go with God!"

Still Kit pulled at him fiercely, oblivious of the creaking as the great beams above his own head, weakened by the fire, bent slowly downward. It was at that moment that Bernardo and Rouge hurled themselves upon him, and drew him, struggling furiously, from the room. Outside in the hall he turned wrathfully toward them, but the words he was about to say remained forever unuttered, drowned unspoken in the avalanche of sound as the room they had left was buried under tons of masonry and charred timber.

They raced down the stairs, and Kit and Bernardo paused long enough to gather up Bianca. Then they all fled from the flaming house. Outside in the street they beat out the fire in their own garments and stood looking at the flames standing straight up in the still-breathing air and throwing great showers of sparks higher still. Then, with majestic deliberation, the outer walls began to buckle, crumbling slowly so that even their fall seemed prolonged, and the slow-rolling thunder of the impact as the house of Del Toro crashed into flaming rubble was almost an afterthought—an echo.

It was then that Rouge opened her lips and let out a cry, wild, high, hysterical wailing. Kit drew her to him, and she lay sobbing against his chest, unmindful of the blood and sweat to which she added her tears.

Bernardo stood looking at Don Luis's smoldering pyre, then, skeptic that he was, freethinker, the eternal alien scourged across the world, he lifted his head and whispered: "Forgive him—and forgive us, too, for the evil and hatred in our own hearts. We are as bloodguilty as he."

Then he and Kit bent and lifted Bianca, and started off through the flame-lighted streets. Rouge walked beside them, wiping the unconscious Bianca's face with a cloth torn from her gown. Softly, slowly, Bianca stirred. Her dark eyes came open and she stared up at them.

"Luis is dead?" she whispered. It was scarcely a question.

Slowly Kit nodded.

"I'm sorry," she murmured. "In his heart he was a good man." Then, seeking Kit's face, she said, "Take me to the good sisters, for there I was always meant to be."

Kit and Bernardo lifted her again and turned in the direction of the nunnery of Nuestra Señora de Cartagena. When they had reached it, Bianca stretched out her hand to Rouge.

"Be good to him," she whispered, "for this too was always meant to be."

Suddenly, impulsively, Rouge bent forward and kissed her. Then she waited while Kit and Bernardo carried Bianca inside the nunnery, standing there in a quiet kind of terror in the empty street, feeling utterly desolate and lost and horribly alone.

When she saw them coming out again, she took a running step forward, then she stopped short, seeing the pain moving in Kit's eyes. They walked through the darkened streets, but it was not until the broken walls were again in sight that any of them spoke. Shyly, softly, Rouge turned to Kit, and lifted her eyes, in which the tears hung glistening.

"Can you," she whispered, "still love me—remembering this?"

Kit turned to her, and in his clear blue eyes was the beginning of a great peace. Slowly, wordlessly, he drew her into his arms.

CARIBBEAN SEA

CUBA

JAMAICA
Port Royal

HISPANIOLA
SANTO
DOMINGO

Santa Marta

Cartagena

Portobello   Nombre
de Dios

·Medellin
·Bogota

VICEROY

LA POPA

Santa Cruz
Fortress

Manzanillo

Boccagrande Channel

Terra
Bomba

Fortress
San Luis de Bocachica

Boccachica Channel

BAY OF CARTAGENA

CARTAGENA of the INDIES 1697

Lima·
Callao·